Plain Jane Makeover

From tomboy to temptress!

These unsuspecting men won't know what hit them, when three Plain Janes unleash their beauty!

Praise for three bestselling authors – Penny Jordan, Miranda Lee, and Barbara McMahon

About MISSION: MAKE-OVER:

'...wonderful character development, a substantial conflict and delightful scenes in this fan-favorite storyline.'

—*Romantic Times*

About AT HER BOSS'S BIDDING:

'...will scorch your fingers with some very hot and sensual scenes with two volatile characters that ignite both love and passion.'

—*Romantic Times*

About THE HUSBAND CAMPAIGN:

'Barbara McMahon pens a delightful tale with charming characters and a witty premise.'

—*Romantic Times*

Plain Jane Makeover

MISSION: MAKE-OVER

by

Penny Jordan

AT HER BOSS'S BIDDING

by

Miranda Lee

THE HUSBAND CAMPAIGN

by

Barabara McMahon

MILLS & BOON®

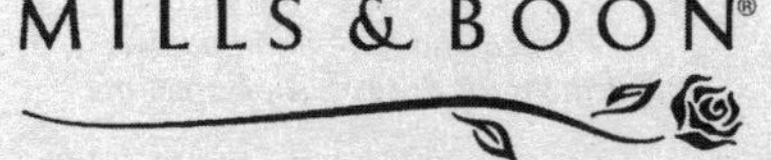

Harlequin Mills & Boon Limited,
Eton House, 18-24 Paradise Road, Richmond, Surrey, TW9 1SR

Mission: Make-Over, At Her Boss's Bidding and *The Husband Campaign* were first published in Great Britain by Harlequin Mills & Boon Limited in separate, single volumes.

ISBN 0 263 84479 X

05-0905

Printed and bound in Spain
by Litografia Rosés S.A., Barcelona

Penny Jordan has been writing for more than twenty years and has an outstanding record, with over 130 novels published, she has hit *The Sunday Times* and *New York Times* bestseller lists. Penny Jordan was born in Preston, Lancashire, and now lives in rural Cheshire.

MISSION: MAKE-OVER

by

Penny Jordan

CHAPTER ONE

'No Lucianna…? Where is she—trying to breathe life into some hopeless wreck of a car?'

Janey Stewart smiled at her husband's best friend as the three of them shared the informal supper Janey had prepared.

'No, not this evening, Jake,' she informed him in response to his wry question about her sister-in-law and the youngest member of the family, the only girl. Lucianna had arrived after her mother had already produced four sons, and, as a consequence of that and, more tragically, of the fact that Susan Stewart had died after contracting a rare and particularly virulent form of viral pneumonia when Lucianna was only eighteen months old, had grown up treated by her brothers and father almost as if she were another boy.

'She's out,' she added in further explanation as he raised a questioning eyebrow. 'Saying goodbye to John.'

'Saying *goodbye*… The big romance is *over*, then, is it?'

'Not exactly. John's going to work in Canada for three months. I suspect Lucianna was rather hoping that he might suggest putting their relationship on a bit of a permanent footing before he left.'

'She hasn't a hope in hell,' said David, her husband and Lucianna's eldest brother, who now ran the farm where he and Lucianna and the rest of the Stewart brothers had been brought up and where in fact Lucianna still lived.

'She's *never* going to get herself a man whilst she goes around dressed in a pair of baggy old dungarees and—'

'It isn't all her fault, David,' Janey interrupted him gently. 'You and the others have hardly encouraged her to be feminine, have you? And you've certainly done your share of helping to frighten away potential men-friends,' she pointed out mildly.

'If you mean I've made it clear that if a man wants Lucianna to share his roof and his bed with him then it has to be with the benefit of a wedding ring, then what's wrong with that?'

'Nothing,' Janey allowed, adding dryly, 'But I seem to remember you worked pretty hard to convince *me* that we ought to move in together before we were married…'

'That was different,' David told her firmly.

'I hope this relationship with John does work out for Lucianna,' Janey continued worriedly. 'After all, she's twenty-two now, not a teenager any more.'

'No relationship is going to work for her until she stops acting like a tomboy…' David told her decisively, adding, 'Perhaps you could give her one or two hints, Janey, point her in the right direction.'

'I've tried, but…' Janey gave a small shrug. 'I think she needs someone to *show* her, *not* to tell her, someone to build up her confidence in herself as a desirable woman and not—' She broke off and smiled teasingly at her husband's best friend. 'Someone like you, Jake,' she told him.

'Jake?' David hooted with laughter. 'Jake would never look at anyone like Lucianna, not after the women *he's* had running after him. Remember that Italian model you went out with, Jake, and that New York banker, and what happened—?'

'Er…you're married to *me*, thank you very much,' Janey reminded her husband firmly. 'Perhaps you aren't the right person, Jake, but she does need help of some kind from someone, otherwise I'm very much afraid she's going to lose John and she'll take it very hard.'

'He really means that much to her?' Jake frowned, his dark eyebrows snapping together over eyes of a particularly clean and sharp blue-grey colour, all the more striking set against the warm olive of the skin tone he had inherited from his Italian grandmother and the thick dark hair that went with it.

His height and breadth of shoulder he had inherited from his paternal relatives; the great-uncle from whom he had inherited the farm and manor house whose lands bordered on the Stewarts' farm had been of a similarly impressive build.

'I rather fear so,' Janey told him quietly. 'She needs help, Jake,' she added, 'even if she herself would be the last person to admit it, especially…'

'Especially to me,' Jake concluded for her.

'Well, you do rather have the knack of making her bristle,' Janey smiled.

As the grandfather clock in the passageway struck the hour, Janey's smile turned to a small frown.

'John's flight will be leaving in half an hour and then Lucianna will be back.'

'Wanting a shoulder to cry on?' Jake asked Janey perceptively.

'Luce never cries,' David informed him. 'She's not that type.'

Really there were times when her husband could be maddeningly dense, Janey reflected as she listened to David. One of the reasons Lucianna was such a tomboy, so uncomfortable about showing her emotions, was that as a child she had been taught by her older brothers not to do so.

It was a pity that Lucianna didn't get on better with Jake because he would certainly have been the ideal person to help her to understand why her relationships with men never developed properly. And it wasn't just that, as an extraordinarily charismatic and sensual man, he had the experience, the know-how, the awareness to help her, he also rather unexpectedly and, in Janey's view, very charmingly for such an intensely male man, had a very compassionate and caring side to his nature as well, even though she knew that Lucianna would have begged to differ with her on that score.

'I really ought to be leaving,' Jake was saying now as he smiled across the table at her and thanked her for the meal. 'I'm expecting a couple of faxes through and—'

'Another multi-million-pound deal,' David interrupted with a grin. 'You'll have to be careful, Jake,' he warned him teasingly, 'otherwise you're going to be a multimillionaire by the time you're forty and then you'll have every fortune-hunter in the district after you…'

'I'm *never* going to be a multimillionaire whilst I've got the estate to finance,' Jake told him truthfully.

'What would you have done if you'd inherited it without the back-up of the money you made during your days in the city trading in shares?' David asked him.

'I don't know; I'd probably have had to sell it. Hopefully one day it will become self-sufficient—the woodlands we've planted will bring in some income when they're mature and with the farming income and subsidies…'

'It would have been a shame if you'd had to sell it,' Janey told him. 'After all, the estate has been in your family for almost two hundred years…'

'Yes, I know…'

'Well, it's high time you were thinking about providing the next generation of little Carlisles if you intend to *keep* it in the family,' David teased him. 'You're not getting any younger, you know; you'll be—what…thirty-four this time…?'

'Thirty-two,' Jake told him dryly. 'I'm a year older than you are…which reminds me, wasn't it Lucianna's birthday last week?'

'Yes,' Janey agreed, adding, 'I rather think she was hoping for an engagement ring from John before he went away to Canada.'

'How's her business doing?' Jake asked Janey, making no response to her comment about Lucianna's disappointed hopes of a birthday proposal.

'Well, she's slowly building up a loyal clientele,' Janey told him cautiously. 'Female drivers in the main, who appreciate having their car serviced by another woman—'

'She's still heavily in debt to the bank,' David broke in forthrightly. 'No man worth his salt would let a woman service his car; we tried to tell her that, but would she listen? No way. It's just as well she's still living here and didn't take on the extra financial burden of renting her own place as she originally wanted to do…'

'You really are a dreadful chauvinist, David,' Janey criticised mildly. 'And whilst we're on the subject Lucianna is, after all, very much what your father and the rest of you have made her. Poor girl, she's never been given much of a chance to develop her femininity, has she?'

CHAPTER TWO

'JOHN got off safely, then?' Janey asked Lucianna cautiously.

They were both in the kitchen, Janey baking and Lucianna poring over her business accounts.

'Only we didn't hear you come in last night,' Janey persisted, waiting until Lucianna had finished adding up the column of figures she was working on before speaking again.

'No... I...I was later than I expected,' Lucianna agreed quietly without looking up, not wanting to admit to her sister-in-law that after John's flight had taken off she had felt so low that instead of driving straight home she had simply wandered aimlessly around the terminal. The brief, almost brotherly kiss John had placed on her forehead before leaving her and the speed with which he had responded eagerly to the very first call for his flight had contrasted painfully with the appreciative and lingering look she had seen him give the attractively dressed woman who had evidently been joining his flight, leaving her painfully aware that despite the fact that they had been dating for several months John seemed more interested in another woman than he was in her.

'Perhaps when John comes home he'll realise how much he's missed you,' Janey began comfortingly, but suddenly Lucianna had had enough. What was the point in pretending to anyone else when she couldn't even pretend to herself any longer? Dolefully, she shook her head, refusing to be comforted.

She and John had originally met six months earlier when John's car had broken down, leaving him stranded a couple of miles from the farm where Lucianna had been brought up and where she now lived with her brother David and his wife Janey.

She had happened to drive past and, recognising John's plight, she had stopped and offered to help, quickly tracking down the problem and cheerfully assuring John that she could soon fix it.

She had first developed her skill with engines as a young girl tinkering with the farm's mechanical equipment—on a farm a piece of equipment that didn't work cost money, and all of the Stewart family had a working knowledge of how to fix a broken-down tractor, but for some reason Lucianna had excelled at almost being able to sense what was wrong even before her older brothers.

This skill had proved to be an asset in her teens when her second eldest brother Lewis had become interested in stock-car racing. Lucianna had happily allowed both Lewis and his friends to make use of her skills in helping them to repair and, in some cases, rebuild their cars.

Because she was the youngest of the family, and had the added handicap of being a girl, she had grown up sensitively aware of the fact that she had to find some way of compensating for the fact that she wasn't a boy and that because of that, in the eyes of her family, she was somehow less worthwhile as a human being.

Unsure of what she wanted to do when she left school, she had continued with her farm chores and increasingly become responsible for not just the maintenance of the farm's machinery but also for the maintenance of several of her brothers' friends' cars, and it had seemed a natural step to move from working with cars as a hobby to working with them as a means of earning a living.

Initially her ambition had been to train and work with some of the top-of-the-range luxury models, but each distributor she had approached with a view to an apprenticeship had laughed at the very idea of a female mechanic and it had been her father who had ultimately suggested she could use one of the empty farm buildings and set up her own business from there.

John had, at first, been shocked and then, she suspected, a little ashamed by the way she earned her living, considering it 'unfeminine'.

Femininity, as she had quickly discovered, was an asset both prized and praised by John and one she did not possess.

Unhappily, she bit her lip. One date with John had led to another and then a regular weekly meeting, but not as yet to the declaration of love and long-term commitment she had been hoping for.

'If he really cared, he'd have…' she began, speaking her painful thoughts out loud before shaking her head, unable to continue. Then she asked Janey tiredly in a low voice. 'What's *wrong* with me, Janey? Why can't I make John see how good we'd be together?'

Lucianna was sitting with her back to the door, and whilst she had been speaking David and Jake had walked across the farmyard and entered the kitchen just in time to hear her low-voiced query.

It was left to Jake to fill the awkward silence left

by her subdued question as he announced, 'Perhaps because he isn't a combustion engine and human relationships need a bit more know-how to make them work than anything you're likely to learn on a basic mechanics course.'

The familiar razor-sharp voice had Lucianna spinning round, hot, angry colour mantling her cheeks, her green eyes flashing with temper, the off-the-face style in which she kept her long, naturally curly hair emphasising her high cheekbones and the stubborn firmness of her chin as she challenged bitterly, 'Who asked you? This is a private conversation and if I'd wanted your opinion, Jake Carlisle…not that I ever would…I'd have asked for it.'

She and Jake had never really got on. Even as a little girl she had disliked and resented his presence in their lives and the influence he seemed to have, not just over her brothers but even over her father as well. Despite the fact that he was only a year older than her eldest brother, there had always been something about Jake that was different, that set him apart from the others—an awareness, a maturity…a certain something which as a child Lucianna had never been able to define but which she only knew made her feel angry…

It had been Jake who had persuaded her aunt to buy her that stupid dress for her thirteenth birthday, the one that had made the boys howl with laughter when they'd seen her in it, the one with the pink frills and sash—the sash which she had later used as binding to tie the wheels of the cart she was making to its chassis. She could still remember the tight-lipped look Jake had given her when he had recognised what it was and the thrill of angry pleasure and defiance it had given her to see that look. Not that he had *said* anything—but then Jake had never needed to say anything to get his message across.

'But you just did,' Jake reminded her, plainly unperturbed by her angry outburst.

'I wasn't talking to *you*, I was talking to Janey,' Lucianna pointed out tersely.

'But perhaps Janey is too kind-hearted to answer you honestly and tell you the truth…'

Lucianna glared at him.

'What truth? What do you mean?'

'You asked what was wrong with you, and why John won't make a commitment to you,' Jake reminded her coolly. 'Well, I'll tell you, shall I? John is a man…not much of one, I'll grant you, but still a man…and, like all heterosexual men, what he wants in his partner…his lover…is a woman. A *woman*, Lucianna—that's spelt W for wantability, O for orgasmic appeal, M for man appeal, A for attraction—sexual attraction, that is—and, of course, finally, N for nuptials. And for your information a woman is someone who knows that the kind of words a man wants to hear whispered in his ear have nothing to do with the latest technical details of a new engine.

'Give me your hand,' he instructed, leaning forward and taking hold of Lucianna's left hand before she could stop him and then studying her ring finger. His long, mobile mouth curled sardonically as he announced, 'Hardly something a man might feel tempted to put his ring on, is it, never mind kiss?'

Mortified, Lucianna snatched her hand away and told him furiously, 'A *woman*…well, I spell it W for wimp, O for obedient, M for moronic, A for artifice and N for nothing…' she told him fiercely.

There was a long silence during which she was uncomfortably conscious of Jake studying her and during which she had to fight to resist the temptation to hide her hands behind her back. Only last weekend she had seen the look of distaste on John's face when he'd complained that her nails weren't long and varnished like those of his friends' girlfriends.

'If that's really how you see yourself, then I feel sorry for you,' Jake declared finally.

It took several seconds for the quiet words to sink in past her turbulent thoughts, but once they had Lucianna blinked and swallowed hard, trying not to cry as the angry, defensive words of denial fought to escape past the hard lump of anguish blocking her throat.

'You aren't a woman, Lucianna,' she heard Jake attack tauntingly into the vulnerability of her silence.

'Yes, I am,' she argued furiously, 'and—'

'No, you're not. Oh, you may look like one, and have all the physical bodily attributes of one—although I must say that given the clothes you choose to shroud yourself in it's hard to know,' he added, with a disparaging glance at the oversized dungarees she was wearing.

'But it isn't looks that make a woman—a real woman—and I'll take a bet that the plainest member of your sex knows more about how to attract than you do… *I* know more…'

'Perhaps you should give Luce a few pointers, then,' David chipped in, laughing. 'Give her a few lessons on how to catch her man…'

'Perhaps I should,' Lucianna heard Jake agreeing thoughtfully, for all the world as though he was seriously considering the matter as some kind of viable, acceptable proposition and not the most ridiculous and insulting thing she had ever heard of in her life!

Lucianna couldn't restrain herself any longer.

'There's nothing you could teach me about being a woman...*nothing*,' she told him defiantly.

'Nothing? Want to bet?' Jake returned smoothly and with dangerous speed. 'You should know better than to challenge *me*, Lucianna. Much better...'

'If I were you I'd take him up on it,' she heard David advising her seriously. 'After all, he *is* a man and—'

'Is he really? Well, thanks for telling me something I didn't know.' Lucianna interrupted her brother with childish sarcasm.

'But you don't know, do you?' Jake slipped in under her defences dulcetly. 'Because you *don't* have very much idea of what a real man actually is, do you, Lucianna?'

'Stop teasing her, both of you,' Janey intervened, adding gently to Lucianna before she could say anything, 'Jake does have a point, though, Luce. And after all with John away for three months it gives you an ideal opportunity to—well, show him when he gets back just exactly what he's been missing,' she concluded lamely, avoiding looking directly at either Lucianna or the two men as she did so.

Lucianna moistened her lips before opening them to tell them in no uncertain terms that they must be mad if they thought she would *ever* entertain such a crazy idea, but no one seemed prepared to listen to her or even to let her speak because Jake was already saying, as though at some point she *had* actually given her verbal agreement to his taunting challenge, 'There'll have to be a few ground rules, of course.'

'Ground rules…' Lucianna glowered at him. 'If by that you mean I'm going to have to take orders from you and…' Then, inexplicably, she had a sudden and very hurtful mental image of that woman she had seen John studying as he'd walked away from her. *Was* it possible? *Could* Jake really show her, teach her…? She swallowed painfully, and to her own disbelief heard herself saying huskily, 'Very well… I agree…'

'My God, you must really want him… Why?'

Underneath the sardonic amusement in Jake's voice ran a fine thread of something else, but Lucianna was too upset to hear it.

'What do you think?' she demanded sharply. 'I love him…'

'I seem to recall you once felt exactly the same about that wreck of a car you insisted on buying—what happened to it by the way?'

'It's still rusting away in the old barn,' David informed him with a grin.

Lucianna gave them both a furious look.

'Right, I want you at the Hall first thing in the morning,' Jake told her. 'Three months may sound a long time but given what we've got to get through… And the first thing you can do—'

'At the Hall? No way. I'm far too busy,' Lucianna told him defiantly.

'Really? That's not what these figures say,' Jake countered, leaning over to study the accounts she had been working on before he'd walked in. 'You're not even breaking even,' he told her.

Lucianna flushed defensively. There was no need for him to point out to her the shortcomings in the financial area of her business; she could see them easily enough for herself, and so too, she imagined, would the bank manager when she next went to see him.

'Of course you're not too busy,' David told her. 'She'll be there, Jake,' he assured his friend. 'Don't you worry.'

Tiredly Lucianna parked her car outside the farmhouse and climbed out. The house itself was in darkness—a sign that David and Janey were already in bed. Their bedroom was at the front of the house, which meant that, hopefully, they wouldn't be disturbed by the security lights springing on at her arrival. She had designed and installed the security system herself, much to David's amusement, and, although the days were gone when she might have expected to find either her father or one of her brothers waiting up to question her late arrival home, farmers and farmers' wives needed their sleep.

She had spent the afternoon with her father. Following his retirement he had moved to a village twenty-odd miles away where he now lived with his widowed elder sister, and Lucianna had promised several days earlier that she would service their ancient Hillman for them. Her mind hadn't really been on the Hillman, though; it had been on Jake Carlisle and his extraordinary challenge, his declaration that he could teach her how to be a woman, the kind of woman men like him—and, according to him, *all* men—really wanted.

Jake, as Lucianna already knew, could be a formidable adversary. It had been Jake, after all, who had persuaded her father to retire when David had given up on ever being allowed to take over and modernise the farm, and Jake who had added the weight of his confidence to her youngest brother Adam's pleas to be allowed to spend time back-packing around the world instead of settling down in a job as her father had wished. Adam was presently working in Australia at a holiday resort on the Barrier Reef.

Dick, the brother between Lewis and Adam in age, was working abroad in China, supervising the building of a new dam, and Lewis was in New York.

What would *they* make of Jake's plan to turn her into a proper woman, the kind of woman John simply couldn't resist? Did she really need to ask herself? First they would roar with laughter and then they would no doubt point out that the task he had taken on was too formidable, too impossible even for his fabled talents.

She wasn't the complete fool her family seemed to think she was, Lucianna assured herself irritably. She knew perfectly well that other young women of her age appeared to have an almost magical ability when it came to attracting the opposite sex that she simply didn't possess, but she refused to believe it was simply a matter of wearing different clothes and adopting the kind of simpering, idiotic manner she suspected that Jake was going to advise her to attempt.

There had been other boys, young men she had dated before she met John, brief friendships which had petered out amicably on both sides, but with John it was different; with John she'd found herself thinking for the first time about a shared future, marriage…children… But, although John always seemed to enjoy her company, so far their relationship had not progressed beyond the odd relatively chaste kiss or affectionate hug.

She had tried to tell herself that John was a gentleman and that he simply didn't want to rush her and she had staunchly held onto that belief until last weekend.

Quietly she let herself into the house and made her way upstairs, pausing on the landing as she heard voices from her brother and sister-in-law's room and then tensing when she realised that she was the subject of their conversation.

She hadn't intended to eavesdrop, she told herself as she recognised that they were discussing the conversation which had taken place in the farmhouse kitchen earlier in the day, but for some reason it was impossible for her to walk away.

'Do you really think Jake's going to be able to teach Lucianna to be more feminine?' she heard Janey asking her husband.

'Not a hope in hell,' she heard David responding cheerfully whilst she held her breath. 'Luce is my sister but, much as I love her, I have to admit that when it comes to sex appeal the poor kid just doesn't have what it takes…'

'Oh, David, that's a bit unkind and unfair,' Janey protested. 'She's got a lovely figure, even if she does hide it behind those dreadful dungarees, and if she paid a little more attention to herself she could be quite stunning. It's not her fault, you know, if all of you treated her like another brother when she was growing up—'

'It doesn't matter what she does,' David interrupted her disparagingly, 'Luce just isn't a man's woman, and not even Jake, despite his experience with the female sex, is going to be able to change that. We might as well face up to the fact that we've got her here on our hands for life…'

Hot tears filled Lucianna's eyes as she crept silently past their bedroom door. Even her own brother thought she was unappealing as a woman. Well, she would show him, she decided angrily. She would show them *all*, and if that meant eating humble pie and taking orders from someone as tirelessly autocratic and bossy as Jake, then despite all the run-ins she had had with him in the past, all the times she had objected to him taking a far too older-brotherly and interfering interest in her life, so be it.

And, loath though she was to admit it, even in the privacy of her own thoughts, she could certainly have no better tutor. She had, after all, had ample opportunity over the years to witness for herself just exactly what effect Jake had on the susceptible and, it had to be admitted, not so susceptible members of her own sex, and, puzzlingly, so far as she could discern, without him apparently having to make any obvious attempts to engage their besotted adoration.

Personally, she couldn't fathom just what it was they saw in him that reduced normally intelligent, witty, independent women to drooling, speechless wrecks; she had never found anything remotely attractive in his black-browed, autocratic and, in her eyes, often censorious maleness. She preferred men like John—fair-haired, kind-eyed men who looked more like cuddly teddy bears than something reminiscent of an adman's image of a truly awesomely male hunk.

She was under no illusions about how unpleasant and unpalatable she was likely to find the entire exercise, nor how much amusement Jake was all too likely to derive from it—at her expense. But enough was enough, and *she* had had enough and more.

Determinedly she brushed away her tears and told herself a second time that it would all be worth it to have John standing lovingly at her side, his ring on her finger.

Five minutes later, in her own room, she paused in the automatic act of getting undressed and walked hesitantly across the room to stand in front of her bedroom mirror.

Only this afternoon her aunt had commented on how like her mother she looked. Her mother had been considered something of a beauty, but wasn't beauty supposed to be in the eyes of the beholder? And she had seen the way John had winced when he had called round unexpectedly earlier in the week, a look of distaste crossing his face as he'd looked at her oil-stained hands and short nails. But John had thought her attractive enough when they had first met and he had been glad enough of her mechanical expertise then too, even proud of it, boasting to his friends about her skill.

It had been later that he had stopped telling others how she earned her living and then, latterly, cautioned her against doing so herself, growing both uncomfortable and irritated with her when she had asked him why.

She knew she was different from the girlfriends and wives of John's friends, and on the thankfully rare occasions when she had been alone with them she had discovered that they very quickly ran out of things to talk about. But what had been even worse, even more humiliating than their silence, had been the laughter she had heard and which had been quickly stifled as she'd walked back into the room after leaving it for a few minutes. She had been in no doubt that they had been talking about her, laughing about her, and that knowledge had hurt even though she had vowed not to let them know it.

At school she had been popular enough and had had plenty of friends, although it was true that once she had reached her teens she had tended to disdain the giggly, boy-focused discussions of her fellow females and spent more time instead with the boys, preferring tomboyish pursuits to long discussions about the latest pop groups or clothes fad.

She had tried, though, with John, really tried. At his suggestion she had bought a new dress for his firm's annual do and she had even gone along with his insistence that she take one of his female colleagues from work along with her to choose it.

And, although she had felt too upset at the time to tell him so, the dress she had so unhappily and unsuccessfully worn had not been her choice but Felicity's. And she still couldn't understand why Felicity had so determinedly and blatantly lied about that fact, insisting in the face of John's disapproval that she, Lucianna, had overridden her advice and chosen her dress herself.

Her eyes filled with fresh tears now—widely spaced, thick-lashed, pretty silvery green eyes which recently had held a far more sombre expression than suited them. It hurt more than she felt able to say to anyone that even her family seemed to think she was somehow lacking in female allure.

Outwardly she might wear jeans and do what appeared to be an unfeminine job, but inwardly... Inwardly, she was every bit as much a woman as the Felicitys of this world, every bit as worthy of being loved and wanted—and she was going to prove it!

CHAPTER THREE

'YOU'RE up early this morning... Not had a change of heart, have you, and planning to do a disappearing act?'

Lucianna shook her head as she listened to her brother's teasing comments.

'Certainly not,' she told him firmly, but he was closer to the truth than he knew. She had woken up this morning with a very heavy heart indeed and a deep and gloomy sense of foreboding and dismay at what she had let herself in for.

'Pull the other one,' her brother advised her, showing that he knew her rather better than she liked and informing Janey as she walked into the kitchen, 'I told you she wouldn't go through with it; she's—'

'I *am* going through with it,' Lucianna interrupted him indignantly. 'I just got up earlier than normal because I want to finish a job off before...before I drive over to...'

To prove a point she gulped down her coffee and started to hurry towards the back door before David could make any further teasing remarks. With her back to him she didn't see the look of compassionate sympathy he gave her before exchanging a rueful glance with his wife.

She was his kid sister, damn it, and he loved her, and he could wring that idiot John's neck for the misery he was causing her.

The job Lucianna had pretended was so urgent was

simply a matter of changing an oil filter, and she was on her way back to the house when Jake drove into the farmyard.

'What are *you* doing here?' she challenged him aggressively as he got out of his car. Like her he was casually dressed in jeans, but unlike hers his were immaculately clean and they fitted him properly.

'What do you think?' he retorted calmly.

Lucianna gave him a stubborn look.

'There's no need for you to come and collect me as if I were a…a prisoner. I was going to drive myself over…'

'But now I've saved you the trouble,' Jake told her suavely, 'and that's one of the first lessons you have to learn.'

'What?' Lucianna asked.

'How to accept a man's naturally chivalrous instinct to look after and protect a woman—and,' he added more dryly, 'how not to dent his ego by pointing out that you don't need or want his protection.'

'How? By simpering stupidly and throwing myself at your feet in gratitude?' Lucianna demanded acidly.

'A simple ''thank you'' and a warm smile would be perfectly adequate. You want to thank the guy, not make him think you're desperate,' Jake told her.

Lucianna glowered at him whilst she felt her face grow hot with indignation.

'I am *not* desperate—' she began, but Jake was already shaking his head, telling her directly,

'Don't give me that, Luce… I know you, remember, and for you to go to such lengths…'

'I *love* him,' she told him, tilting her chin determinedly at him as though daring him to argue with her.

'You might think you do but, believe me, you don't even begin to know what love is yet.'

Her brother's emergence into the yard prevented Lucianna from making the kind of retort she wanted to make but she was still seething with resentment and indignation ten minutes later as she sat next to Jake whilst he reversed his car back out of the yard.

'Your timing's out,' she told him critically as she listened to the sound of the engine.

'You're going to have to know me a lot better before you can come out with a comment like that,' he told her in an unfamiliar soft and meaningful voice that made her turn her head and look open-mouthed at him as her senses, more acute and finely tuned than her brain, recognised a message in the dulcet, husky sound of his voice that her brain could not quite pick up on.

'*My* timing is *never* out,' he added even more softly, and then reverted to his normal tone of voice, before she could say anything, to tell her briskly, 'But yes, the *car's* timing is slightly out, Lucianna…

'Tell me something,' he went on conversationally. 'When you and John are alone what do you talk about?'

'Talk about?' Lucianna stared at him.

'You *do* talk, I take it?' Jake questioned dryly. 'Or is your main form of communication on a, shall we say, more basic level?'

It took several seconds for what he meant to sink in, but once it had done Lucianna could feel her face beginning to burn with a mixture of fury and embarrassment.

'Of *course* we talk,' she snapped. 'We talk about all kinds of things…'

'Such as?' Jake demanded, one dark eyebrow raised interrogatively, the profile he was angling slightly towards her uncomfortably reminiscent of the stern demeanour with which he had lectured her on some of her youthful follies.

'Er…lots of things,' Lucianna told him, desperately hunting through her memory for suitably impressive examples of the breadth and erudition of their shared conversations.

'Really? So you'd agree with those who claim that verbal foreplay can be just as erotic and arousing as its physical equivalent, then, would you?' Jake asked her.

'Verbal foreplay!' Lucianna's colour deepened. 'John and I have far better things to talk about than sex,' she snapped bitingly.

'*And* better things to do?'

The soft question slipped very subtly and, yes, sneakily beneath her guard, leaving her totally unable to come up with any safe response other than a taut, 'I don't discuss such personal things with anyone!'

But even that defence could not protect her, as she quickly discovered when Jake unkindly suggested, 'Not even John? You might be able to strip down an engine very effectively and efficiently, Lucianna, but somehow or other I doubt that you have the same skill when it comes to stripping down a man—or *for* a man,' he added with dangerous softness.

Struggling to overcome her mortification, Lucianna stared fixedly ahead through the car windscreen. Little did Jake know it but his scathing remark had echoed an unkind conversation she had recently overheard between two of John's friends—girlfriends.

'Can you imagine it?' one had said to the other,

unaware that Lucianna could hear them. 'She'll be saying to John, "Now this bit goes here and then this bit goes there and then you have to do this." Poor John, I feel so sorry for him. I can't understand what he sees in her, can you?'

Perhaps her sexual experience wasn't all that extensive—at least not in the practical sense—and perhaps, yes, she did rather quail at the thought of having to take the sexual initiative with a man—certainly she had never or *would* never have attempted to undress one. But she could read, and if John had been rather slow to pick up on her hesitant signals that she was ready to take their relationship a few steps further than the kisses and caresses they had so far shared then she had at least, until recently, put it down to the fact that he valued and respected her and their relationship enough to let the sexual side of things develop slowly and naturally. After all, the last thing she wanted was to be wanted merely for sex.

She frowned, suddenly realising that whilst she had been deep in thought Jake had been driving them not towards his home but along the road that led into town instead.

'Where are we going?' she demanded sharply. 'I thought—'

'I'm taking you shopping,' Jake informed her calmly.

'Shopping?' Lucianna tensed, warily remembering all the occasions on which her family had attempted to persuade her to change her style of dress. She knew they thought she was being stubborn and difficult in refusing to listen to what they had to say, but how could she tell them that her refusal to abandon her dungarees and jeans had its roots a long way back in her early teenage years?

Then, as a young schoolgirl, she had desperately wanted to look like her female peers and not like the tomboy she had heard others disparagingly call her.

The gift of some birthday money had given her the opportunity to turn her wishes into reality and she could still remember the excitement with which she had gone shopping with another girl from school, a girl who, in her then youthful and untutored eyes, had seemed to have all the feminine attributes she herself so longed for.

She still shuddered to recall what had followed when, dressed up in her new purchases—the uncomfortable suspender belt and stockings, the tight short skirt and the high heels that had made her wobble perilously as she'd walked nervously at her friend's side—they had encountered a group of boys from school.

The crude remarks which had followed her transformation from tomboy into a girl who they had plainly believed was making herself sexually available had made her ears and her face burn for weeks and months afterwards, her embarrassment and sense of shame so great that she had actually refused to go to school the following week until her father had announced that he was sending for the doctor.

The incident, coupled with her own brothers' derogatory comments about a certain type of girl, had so shocked and shamed her that she had never worn the clothes again, and in the years since, although in her wardrobe there were several rather more formal outfits than her preferred dress of dungarees and jeans, she had steadfastly refused to give in to her family's exhortations to buy or wear 'something feminine'. She had experienced already what happened when she did that, how the male sex reacted, knew that for some reason which was not really clear to herself there was something about her that made it impossible for her to wear the kind of clothes other women wore with such ease and confidence without cheapening herself and making herself an object of sexual contempt and ridicule.

'I'm not going,' Lucianna suddenly announced tersely. 'Stop the car.'

Calmly Jake did so, but the atmosphere inside the car felt anything but calm as he turned to her and asked her critically, 'What is it you're so afraid of, Lucianna? And don't try to deny that you are; I know you—remember? Are you frightened of failure—failing to be enough woman to—?'

'No…'

'No?' One dark eyebrow rose in the interrogative and superior manner she was so familiar with and which so irritated her. 'Then prove it,' Jake suggested quietly.

'I don't need to prove *anything* to you,' Lucianna told him angrily.

'Not to me, no,' Jake agreed, overriding her angry words, 'but you certainly seem to have something to prove to John—and to yourself.'

Lucianna looked away from him, unable to meet his eyes and unable to refute his statement.

'It's your choice,' he told her evenly, 'your decision, but I must say you've surprised me…'

'Surprised you!'

Lucianna gave him a wary look. In her experience surprising Jake took an awful lot of doing.

'Mmm…' he agreed, nodding. 'I thought you had more courage, more guts…more self-respect than to give up without at least making some attempt to fight for what you want.'

'I do have,' Lucianna retorted indignantly, and then added truculently, 'Oh, very well, then, but if you think I'm going to let you bully me into wasting money on some stupid, silly outfit that *you* think a woman should wear—'

'Excuse me, but whilst I may have been guilty of many sins in my time, Lucianna, wanting to see a woman dressed in frills isn't one of them. And besides, you're a long, long way yet from being ready to change your outer image… It's your inner image we're going to be working on today and for many days to come.

'Femininity, womanliness, is something that comes from within. It means being proud of yourself as a woman, being confident about your femaleness and your sexuality; it's showing the world that you value yourself *as* a woman… When a person has that, how they choose to *clothe* their body is really immaterial apart from the fact that what they choose to wear acts like a shorthand message to those who see her.'

Whilst he'd been talking he had restarted the car, and this time Lucianna made no objection as he continued to drive towards the town.

Something about the calm way he had delivered those few unexpected words had for some odd reason or other brought a huge uncomfortable lump of emotion to her throat, an indefinable sense of loss and sorrow, as though he had highlighted something within her which she had secretly felt had never been allowed to flourish and had even more secretly hidden away in shame even from herself.

Yet as she sat silently at his side her thoughts, unexpectedly, were not of herself or even of John but, surprisingly, of her mother.

Might not things have been different if she had not died when Lucianna was so young…? Might not *she* have been different?

'But this is a book shop,' Lucianna protested as Jake determinedly ushered her through the plate-glass doors.

They had arrived in the town five minutes earlier and, having parked the car, Jake had directed her towards the town's main shopping street.

'That's right,' Jake agreed, touching her lightly on the arm as he pointed to a labelled section of books on the far side of the shop. 'I think we'll find what we need over there,' he told her.

Lucianna frowned; the shelves seemed to be filled with diet and self-improvement books so far as she could see. Warily she allowed Jake to propel her in their direction.

'I don't think these will be of much benefit to me,' she told him as she studied the title of the diet book which was prominently displayed.

'I doubt it,' he agreed. 'If anything you need to put weight on.'

'To make me more feminine?' Lucianna suggested, her hackles starting to rise at his implied criticism of her.

'To make you more *healthy*,' Jake corrected her. 'You're naturally fine-boned and delicate—anyone can see that,' he added, startling her as he totally unexpectedly ran his index finger along the curve of her cheekbone, producing an aftershock of sensation on her skin in the wake of his touch something like the kind of feeling she associated with an unexpected rash of goosebumps but with an extra indefinable and unfamiliar something which made her feel peculiarly light-headed and breathless.

'And it naturally follows that your body will be similarly delicately made, long-legged and high-breasted with a narrow waist,' he told her, emphasising his point by reaching out and placing his hands at either side of her body.

Her indignant verbal objection was never uttered as she looked down at where his thumbs met and felt the hard, warm male pressure of his grip through the thickness of her clothes. A suffocating tightness had invaded her chest, far, far tighter and more constricting, more dangerous than Jake's firm grip on her body.

'I can't breathe,' she protested angrily and huskily, reaching out to take hold of his arms as she instinctively tried to force him to release her.

'Can't you?'

The most peculiar and disturbing sensation she had ever experienced in her life seized her as she heard the deeper note in Jake's voice and felt her whole body trembling uncontrollably in response to it in some secret inner vibration. When she looked at him she discovered that his gaze seemed to be focused on her mouth. Probably because he was waiting for her angry objection to his behaviour, she told herself protectively as she fought to control a sudden compulsive need to wet her almost painfully dry lips with the tip of her tongue—and lost.

'Stop it,' she hissed breathlessly. 'Stop it at once…'

'Stop what?' Jake responded mock innocently.

'You know perfectly well what. Stop looking at my…at me like…like you were doing,' she finished lamely, her colour high as she thankfully felt him respond to her agitation and lift his head to meet her eyes at the same time as he removed his hands from her waist.

'You're looking very hot and bothered; what's wrong?' he asked her, outwardly solicitously, but she could see the laughter gleaming in his eyes.

'You know perfectly well what's wrong,' she told him forthrightly. 'It's you…the way you…the way you looked at me.'

'You mean the way a man looks at a woman he wants,' Jake told her calmly. 'It's called body language,' he continued, before Lucianna could take issue with him on the first part of his statement. 'The way a man looks at a woman he wants'—indeed! Well, she knew one thing and that was that he certainly *didn't* want her—and she would never *want* him to want her, she added hastily. It was John she wanted to want her, to desire her, to love her.

'Body language,' Jake repeated instructively as he reached up and removed a couple of books from higher up the shelves and handed them to her. He explained, 'It's a fact that all of us both consciously and subconsciously send out messages to others with every movement we make, every expression we show, and the first step to getting others to be responsive is for you to show them that you are open to that responsiveness.

'For example, just now when I looked at your

mouth, you touched your lips with your tongue, which means—'

'Which means that you were making me nervous and angry.'

'Nervous?' Jake queried with a small half-smile that made her look warily away from him.

'Nervous and angry,' she insisted, but she knew that her voice didn't sound quite as convincing and determined as she would have liked.

'Mmm… I see. So when John looks at your mouth like that what kind of response do you give him?' he asked her placatingly, but Lucianna was too on edge to be placated.

'John *never* looks at me like that,' she answered quickly.

She only realised her mistake when Jake said softly, 'Oh, dear. Well, I'm sure there'll be some advice inside these—' he tapped the books. '—to indicate how you can rectify that situation, and if there isn't—well, I can always…'

But Lucianna wasn't listening. Snatching the books from his hand, she headed determinedly towards the till, head held high as the salesgirl gave the titles a quick, curious glance before taking Lucianna's money and putting them into a bag for her.

'I know her—I serviced her mother's car,' Lucianna hissed angrily to Jake once they were outside the shop. 'I suppose you think all this is very funny,' she added crossly as she fished the books out of the carrier bag, and she read the titles to him in scornful disgust. '*The Science of Body Language and How to Use it Effectively*, and *The Art of Flirtation*.'

'Funny?' Jake repeated. 'No, Lucianna,' he told her curtly. 'I don't think *any* of this is *remotely* funny.'

He looked so grim and unapproachable that the demand to know just what he did think of it and her, which she had been about to voice, died unvoiced.

'This way,' he told her, touching her, indicating the pretty town square which lay ahead of them. Set out with trees and benches and with the sun shining warmly, it was obviously a popular spot with office workers for eating their sandwiches.

One couple were vacating one of the benches as they approached and Jake quickly appropriated the spare seats.

'What now?' Lucianna asked wearily as he indicated that he wanted to sit down.

'Now we're going to do a bit of people-watching,' Jake told her. 'Let's see just how sharp and accurate your instincts actually are and at the same time let's see how much visual experience of the art of body language you can actually recognise.'

'It wasn't called that. It was called *The Art of Flirtation*,' Lucianna snapped back at him.

'Same thing,' Jake told her dryly. 'Now,' he commanded sternly once Lucianna had reluctantly seated herself beside him, 'take a good look around and tell me what you can see.'

Lucianna took a deep breath and mentally counted to ten before telling him irritably, 'I can see the town square and part of the high street and I can see—'

'That wasn't what I meant, Lucianna,' Jake interrupted her crisply, the look in his eyes as he turned to study her the same one he had used to reinforce his older and male status during the years when she had been growing up.

Then it had quelled her and even sometimes made her feel warily apprehensive and, as she now discovered to her chagrin, things hadn't changed all that much. The only difference was that now she felt seriously tempted to ignore his visual warning and see what just *might* happen. After all, what could he really do if she simply got up and walked away?

As though he had read her mind he advised her sharply, 'I wouldn't if I were you. You agreed to this, remember. You're the one who's desperate to prove—'

'I'm not *desperate* to prove *anything*,' Lucianna argued hotly.

'Do you know something, Lucianna?' Jake said wryly. 'Your determination to win John rather reminds me of the same blind stubbornness that a child exhibits in demanding a sweet or a toy simply because it's out of reach and being denied them, and I can't help wondering if it's the fact that he seems out of reach that makes him seem so desirable. There certainly doesn't seem—'

'I'm not a child,' Lucianna began, then realised how neatly and easily she had fallen into the trap Jake had dug for her as he told her sharply,

'No? Well, then, I suggest you cease behaving like one. Now, look around again and tell me what you see, and this time study the people—carefully. Look at that group over there just coming out of the chemist's, for instance, and tell me what you see.'

Heaving a deep sigh, Lucianna painstakingly and dutifully stared in the direction he had indicated.

A man and a woman and two small children were standing on the pavement just outside the chemist's. The woman was leaning towards the man and smiling up at him. The two children were dancing up and down beside them, obviously excited, whilst the man started to remove some papers from his pocket.

At the same time the woman instinctively reached out to draw the children closer to her as a car drove past and the man put out a hand to steady *her* as another shopper looked as though she might barge into them.

They were obviously a family, Lucianna could see that, and a happy one, she acknowledged as she saw their smiles and heard their laughter as they all looked at the strips of photographs the man was holding, the two children barely able to contain their excitement.

But stubbornly she omitted to mention anything of this as she responded to Jake's instruction by simply saying, 'I see a man, a woman and two children.'

'You're beginning to try my patience, Lucianna,' Jake warned her. 'Look again. Look at the way the man is behaving towards the three of them—protectively, lovingly—and the way the woman is responding to *him*, the way she obviously feels that *he's* done something special; and the two children—look at their excitement.

'At a guess I would say that they are a young couple who are just planning their first continental holiday with their children and that they have just been to obtain their family passport photographs. This holiday is probably something they've planned for and saved for for a very long time, something they've had to make sacrifices to afford, especially the man who's probably had to work extra hours to pay for it…'

'That's sexist,' Lucianna objected. 'It might be the woman who's had to do the extra work.'

'It's not sexist at all,' Jake denied. 'I'm simply interpreting their body language. Look at the way the man's almost preening himself. Look at the way the woman's looking at him, the pride and love in her expression, the way she keeps looking at him and touching his arm, and look at the way he's responding. An animal psychologist would probably say they're simply copying an ancient grooming ritual from the animal kingdom and that the one lower down the pecking order is grooming the ones higher up it, so that in this particular instance I would guess that it is the man who's earned the extra money.

'But he's obviously a modern father; look at the way he's bending down now to fasten the elder child's shoes and the way she's leaning against him. It's obvious that fastening her shoes is a task he's comfortably familiar with, just as she's obviously comfortably familiar with him—'

'Very interesting, but I can't really see its relevance for me,' Lucianna interrupted him crossly. Suddenly, for some reason, the sight of the small, happy family was making her feel acutely aware of her own aloneness. 'After all, *I'm* not likely to want to start fastening John's shoes or grooming him,' she added sarcastically.

'You might not want to fasten his shoes,' Jake agreed, 'but as for grooming... It's normally considered to be an important and enjoyable part of the human courting ritual—to touch and be touched, to exchange those but oh, so meaningful caresses... Or am I being old-fashioned? Sex has been stripped of so much of its allure and sensuality these days.

'It's almost as though the race towards orgasm has become a fast-paced motorway requiring intense concentration and a total focus on reaching one's goal, with no opportunity or desire to enjoy the pleasure of a more leisurely meander that allows one to pause and enjoy the moment, the caress.

'Is that what *you* prefer, Lucianna—a sensible, no-nonsense approach to sex that reduces it simply to a biological urge which needs to be satisfied in the most efficient and least time-consuming manner?'

'How I think and feel about sex has *nothing* to do with this *nor* with you,' Lucianna told him fiercely.

'No? Well, if that's what you think no wonder you're having so much trouble. On the contrary, sex has *everything* to do with it—or it should do. When you look at John, if you don't want him to reach out and touch you and if you don't want to reach out and touch him, then—'

'John *never* touches me in public,' Lucianna interrupted him, her colour rising as she told him angrily, 'And nor would I want him to.'

'Well, you certainly should,' Jake told her, as calm as she herself was becoming flustered as he suddenly turned towards her and before she could stop him reached out and curled his fingers around her bare wrist.

His grip, although light, disturbed her. She could feel her heart start to beat faster with what she told herself was anger at his high-handed manner and her pulse was certainly racing because Jake himself was now placing his thumb over it, as though aware of her tension, his thumb beginning a slow, rhythmic stroking of the inside of her wrist which she assumed must be intended to calm and relax her but which, instead, was sending her heartbeat into a crazy, irregular volley of frantic thuds which were matched by the dizzying acceleration of her pulse. No wonder she was finding it difficult to breathe, she told herself hazily.

Through the ragged sound of her own breathing she could hear Jake telling her softly, 'I'm touching you now, Lucianna; I'm touching you the way a man, a lover, the way *John* should want to touch you in public as an indication of his desire to touch you more intimately in private.'

Through the confused jumble of messages assaulting her sensory system Lucianna's brain managed to isolate and hold onto one of them.

'But you aren't John,' she reminded Jake breathlessly.

'No,' he agreed, his stroking thumb suddenly ceasing its inflammatory circular movement against her skin and his voice hardening slightly. 'And I promise you that if I were you would be in no doubt as to *my* feelings for you, Lucianna…'

'I'm not,' she managed to find the robustness to say. 'I do know exactly how you feel about me, Jake,' she told him, and then added succinctly, 'And I promise you I feel exactly the same way about you, only more so.'

Some feminine instinct made her tilt her head determinedly as she threw the words at him, but the look of blazing heat in his eyes as he gazed back at her made her look away again hastily.

She had never seen him look so…so…passionate…so…intense. Normally he was such a calm, controlled man. Too calm and controlled—aggravatingly so at times.

'Luc.'

She turned her head, frowning slightly as she recognised the voice of John's colleague, Felicity. She didn't particularly like Felicity especially since the shopping debacle. She was a tall, leggy brunette with a faintly supercilious manner and a habit of shortening Lucianna's name and pronouncing it as though indeed she had been christened as a boy in the same slightly patronising, sneering manner she was using now.

'Have you heard anything from John yet?' she asked Lucianna, speaking to her but plainly far more visually interested in concentrating on Jake, at whom she was smiling.

Somehow or other she'd managed to stand so that she was facing Jake, keeping her body half turned away from Lucianna, effectively excluding her, and had placed herself closer to Jake than Lucianna herself was. She added, 'We had a fax from him this morning saying that he's settled in safely but that he's missing us.'

'Yes, he faxed me as well,' Lucianna heard herself fibbing, much to her own surprise and shock.

It must be something to do with the lecture Jake had just been giving her about observing other people's body language that was making her so crossly aware of the unsubtle manoeuvres Felicity was using to attempt to create an aura of intimacy between herself and Jake which totally excluded Lucianna.

Well, let her. Let *them*, she decided angrily. She didn't care and it was typical of Jake that he should have attracted Felicity's attention. He was that kind of man.

'Are you one of Luc's customers?' she heard Felicity questioning Jake, her voice low and musical, her laughter a soft feminine gurgle as she added depreciatingly, 'I think she's wonderful doing what she does. To my shame I have to admit I don't even know how to change a tyre...'

'It isn't the tyre you change, it's the wheel,' Lucianna informed her shortly. She stood up and said pointedly to Jake, 'I thought you said we were going shopping…'

'Shopping? Now that is something I *do* know about,' Felicity enthused.

For one appalling moment Lucianna thought that she was going to have to suffer the additional humiliation of hearing Jake invite Felicity to join them, but to her relief he simply smiled at her instead and then turned towards Lucianna, placing his hand beneath her elbow as he rose, and standing firmly close to her.

If someone had told her ten minutes ago that she would actually be grateful to have Jake display such old-fashioned male courtesy and protectiveness towards her she would have denied it with scorn, so it was just as well someone hadn't, because if they had right now she would have been eating her own words, she admitted uncomfortably.

Jake waited until they were out of Felicity's earshot before saying smoothly, 'You never said anything about John getting in touch with you.'

'I don't tell you everything,' Lucianna returned. Jake was still lightly holding her arm, but when she tried to pull away from him she discovered that his hold on her was much firmer than she had imagined and rather than subject herself to an undignified tussle of physical strength which she knew he would win she had to satisfy herself with glowering at him and a brief and, although she didn't know it, betrayingly feminine toss of her head that made Jake fight to hide a rueful smile.

He pointed out dryly, 'Evidently not. Like you didn't tell me you'd acquired a fax machine.'

'Oh!' Lucianna couldn't manage to control the stricken look that crossed her face as he reminded her of the lie she had told Felicity. 'Well, I couldn't let her think that John had got in touch with his office and not me,' she defended herself.

'The office or her?' Jake questioned cynically, and then, to Lucianna's astonishment, he raised his free hand and touched her cheekbone lightly with his thumb as though he were brushing away some dirt or a tear, before saying softly, 'Well, your feminine instincts are there all right. Now let's see if we can unearth a few more of them. When did you last wear something that wasn't a pair of jeans or dungarees, Lucianna?'

'Last night,' she told him smartly as she fought to get back the breath that had suddenly deserted her when he'd touched her face with such mock tenderness. As his eyebrows rose she added sweetly, 'I don't sleep in my work clothes, Jake.'

'No, you sleep in a cotton nightdress,' he agreed sardonically. 'The same one you've been wearing since you were fifteen years old, I imagine.'

'It's still cold at night,' she protested, feeling her face starting to heat up at the taunting note in his voice. 'I like to curl my feet up into it…'

'A woman in love…a woman *with* a lover… wouldn't need a nightdress to keep her warm,' Jake told her mockingly, adding hurtfully, 'But then *you* aren't a woman, are you, Lucianna? Not yet…'

'Not according to you,' she agreed, driven recklessly to answer him back to make him stop taunting her, and she added, 'What's wrong, Jake? Are you having second thoughts, beginning to feel that you've taken on too much, that you can't transform me after all...make me a woman...?'

The look that crossed his face, the utter stillness of his body whilst his eyes turned dark and hot with an emotion she couldn't recognise made her tense warily, not sure what it was she had said or done to unleash the fury she could sense he was trying to control, only knowing that she had suddenly and frighteningly strayed into an area of his personality she wasn't familiar with.

'Don't tempt me,' she heard him saying softly to her. 'Just don't tempt me, Lucianna.'

Don't tempt him to what? she wondered shakily as his hand dropped from her arm as though her skin had burned him. Don't tempt him to wring her neck, probably, she decided unhappily, forced to increase her stride to try to keep up with him as he strode down the street.

Scowling darkly, she flirted momentarily with the idea of telling him that she had changed her mind and that she didn't want or need his help after all, but then she remembered the triumphant mockery she had heard in Felicity's voice when she had told her about John's fax and the slanting-eyed come-hither look she had given Jake, the same look Lucianna had seen her giving John on several previous occasions, and her head lifted and her spine straightened.

Jake, who had turned to wait for her to catch up with him, watched her discreetly.

She looked for all the world like a youthful teenager, her slender body encased in oversized clothes, but she wasn't a child, she was an adult, a woman. A woman whose most basic instincts had been aroused by the threat of losing her man.

Her man. Jake's frown returned as he turned abruptly away from Lucianna. The task he had taken on was fraught with innumerable perils, not the least of which was the fact that he might succeed and that Lucianna would get her way—and her man.

CHAPTER FOUR

'WHAT are you looking at?' Lucianna demanded of Jake as he paused on the corner of the street they were entering to watch something, or rather someone. When Lucianna realised she flushed and gave a rather self-conscious, 'Oh,' as she saw the girl Jake had obviously been admiring come sauntering into view.

Like Lucianna she was dressed in jeans, and like her she also had tawny-coloured long hair, but that was where the resemblance between them ended.

Whereas Lucianna's hair was tied back uncompromisingly this girl's was worn loose and slightly messy, giving the impression that she had been doing something far too pleasurable to waste time grooming her hair before coming out, and she had obviously also neglected to put on any proper underwear beneath the neatly fitting cream stretch jeans she was wearing, Lucianna decided scathingly as she saw Jake's glance move from the other girl's face to her body.

There might not be anything openly tarty about the girl's appearance, Lucianna acknowledged, but there was still definitely an air about her and about the way she was dressed that somehow suggested even to Lucianna's inexperienced eye that she was a person who enjoyed her own sexuality.

'Typical.' Lucianna couldn't quite stop herself from saying this disparagingly as she saw the small, teasing look the girl gave Jake before turning away and strolling across the road—or rather sashaying across the road, Lucianna acknowledged—if that wasn't too old-fashioned a word to use for the provocatively swaying movement of the girl's pert bottom.

'Jealous?' Jake asked her mockingly.

'Certainly not,' Lucianna told him scathingly, adding pithily, 'And I wouldn't dream of coming out without my…not wearing any underwear…'

'Not wearing…?' Jake was frowning slightly as he turned to give the girl another brief look, but when he turned back towards her Lucianna could see that he was struggling not to laugh.

'You really do need educating, don't you?' he told her with a grin that made him suddenly look much younger and made her equally suddenly wonder why she was finding it such a struggle to fill her lungs properly with air.

'If being educated means dressing like a…like that, then I'd rather stay the way I am,' she began crossly, but Jake shook his head.

Still laughing, he told her, 'You're wrong, you know. She's more than likely wearing a string of some type underneath her jeans, and—'

'A string…?'

'Yes, you know, an item of underwear…an item of *female* underwear…that is commonly worn beneath fitted clothing to prevent the unforgivable fashion solecism of VPL…'

'VPL…?' Lucianna repeated in irritation.

'Visible panty line,' Jake explained patiently.

'I know what it means,' Lucianna told him. She might not be fashion-conscious, but she *did* read her sister-in-law's magazines and she knew perfectly well what he meant. Her anger was directed not so much at him for teasing her but at herself for giving him the opportunity to do so.

'I take it that it isn't an item of underwear *you* favour?' Jake said to her as they continued to walk down the street.

'My underwear is not something I intend to discuss with you,' Lucianna told him frostily.

'Pity,' Jake returned, his voice suddenly crisply ominous, 'because, much as it pains me to say it, the male of the species, still at heart being the un-newmanish creature that he is, is still very much influenced and intrigued by women's underwear, let's be honest, is perhaps still regrettably prone to making character and personality judgements on a woman based on her choice of underwear and his idea of what he personally finds exciting and erotic…'

'If you're talking about stockings and suspenders…' Lucianna began warily. She had heard more than enough about the allure and potential of such garments from her brothers during the years they were growing up to have been put off wearing them for life.

'Amongst other things,' Jake agreed. 'Personally, what I find erotic is the knowledge that a woman cares enough for herself and for me to want the act of undressing her to become a sensually special appetiser to our loveplay… Rather like the anticipation and buzz one gets from unwrapping an enticingly wrapped present…'

'Oh, you *would* see a woman like that…as a thing…a toy…a…a present…' Lucianna told him furiously. 'Well, for your information, I would rather die than present myself like that…than humiliate and degrade myself like that…'

'So you expect John to enjoy the sight and act of watching you strip down to the utilitarian and functional underwear you no doubt favour, do you? Tell me something, Lucianna,' Jake challenged her. 'Do you permit him to be equally uncompromising with you? Do you enjoy the sight of him wearing a pair of well-washed baggy boxer shorts, or perhaps the gimmicky jockstrap his pals gave him as a joke for his birthday?'

Lucianna's face had gone scarlet, as much with embarrassment as with anger.

'John and I don't have that kind of relationship, and I don't…'

When she stopped Jake demanded with dangerous softness, 'Yes, do go on; you don't what?'

Stubbornly Lucianna pursed her lips and looked away, refusing to speak. She wasn't going to tell Jake that she had no idea what kind of underwear John favoured any more than she was going to admit that the mental images he had just drawn for her, especially the one of John, had somehow or other rung unpalatably true. His pals were the type who would give him jokey and embarrassing underwear as a present.

Jake, on the other hand, would not doubt— Her thoughts careened to an unsteady halt as she abruptly realised that the mental image she had conjured up of Jake's body, superimposed over the image of an unknown model posing in a pair of immaculate pristine white and very close-fitting undershorts that she had glimpsed in an advertisement in one of her sister-in-law's magazines, was one she most certainly should not be entertaining. One she most certainly should not be entertaining at all, and she had no idea exactly why she was—or, even more importantly, how she was.

After all, the last time she had seen Jake without…wearing very little, she amended to herself hastily, had been the last time they had all gone swimming together before Jake had gone to university. And that had been years ago. She had been a child and Jake had been a young man…a boy…whereas the body she had been mentally visualising had most definitely been that of a man…very definitely that of a man.

'Lucianna!'

Self-consciously Lucianna avoided Jake's eyes as she heard the questioning note in his voice.

'Right,' Jake announced, lifting his wrist to glance at his watch. 'That's enough shopping for today. It's time we were making our way back, I think. I've got some work to do and whilst I'm doing it you can make a start with your homework,' he informed her dryly, nodding in the direction of the books she was carrying.

'I can do that by myself at home,' Lucianna told him spiritedly, not in the least relishing the idea of having to sit reading dutifully beneath Jake's eagle eye like a schoolgirl. 'John might ring,' she added.

'So much the better,' Jake retorted firmly. 'It will do him good to wonder where you are. No more excuses, Lucianna,' he advised her. 'Don't forget you wanted to do this…'

Reluctantly Lucianna had to concede that he had a point. There had been moments during the morning, far too many of them in fact, when she had been in danger of forgetting just why she was putting herself through such a painful process.

As they turned into the car park they were greeted

by the shrill sound of a car alarm ringing. To Lucianna's surprise, Jake halted abruptly and cursed under his breath, muttering feelingly, 'If that's what I think it is, that damn garage…'

Lucianna's eyes widened as she stared across the car park and saw that it was indeed Jake's car alarm that was ringing, the car's indicator lights flashing on and off as though someone had tried to break into the vehicle, and she couldn't resist saying dulcetly, 'Oh, dear, Jake, it looks like something has gone wrong with your car's electronics.'

The look Jake gave her told her that he wasn't in the least deceived by her mock-innocent concern.

'*I* don't have a problem,' he told her forcefully, 'but the *garage* is certainly going to have one. They assured me that they'd found the fault and solved the problem.'

'The electronics systems in these expensive status cars are very complicated and sensitive,' Lucianna told him sweetly, with triumph in her voice.

Only six months earlier, when Jake had first taken delivery of his new car, she had begged to be allowed to familiarise herself with its mechanical and electronics systems, but Jake had sternly refused, telling her in what she had considered at the time to be an extremely bossy manner that the car wasn't a toy and that furthermore it would negate its warranty if he allowed anyone who wasn't an approved mechanic to tamper with its inner workings.

'I don't want to tamper with them,' she had told him through gritted teeth. 'I simply want to look at them…'

'I know your looking,' Jake had reminded her grittily. 'I haven't forgotten what happened when you *looked* at the engine of my TR7.'

Lucianna had grimaced. The TR7 had been Jake's pride and joy, a racy little sports car he had worked hard to buy, and just as soon as his back was turned she had ignored his veto on her touching it. He had returned earlier than expected one afternoon when he had been supposed to be away all day to discover her sitting on the floor of his garage, surrounded by the parts she had painstakingly removed from his car.

It hadn't been *her* fault that he had flustered her so much with his ire that she had muddled up two very similar pieces when she had rushed to reassemble everything. Just as soon as she had realised what she had done and why it wouldn't start, why the heating system was throwing out freezing-cold air instead of hot, she had quickly put matters right—but not, as it turned out, quickly enough to repair the damage the shock of icy cold air blasting over Jake's girlfriend's body had done to Jake's budding romance with her.

It wasn't her fault that his girlfriend had chosen to wear such a stupidly short skirt, Lucianna had defended herself, her already hot face growing even hotter when her amused elder brother had hooted with laughter and told Jake teasingly that it was probably the first time his passionate advances had been frozen off by a faulty car heater.

'The first time and the last,' Jake had replied grimly, then had advised Lucianna tersely, 'Don't you ever, ever tamper with my car again, otherwise you'll be the one in need of a blast of cold air—on your backside, which will be smarting very hotly indeed…'

Lucianna had just been at an age when any reference to almost any part of her anatomy had had the power to raise a deeply mortifying crimson flood of colour through her body—and on that occasion, if she remembered aright, her self-consciousness had outdone itself.

Now she watched in secret glee as Jake tried to silence the car's shrilling alarm, first by using the automatic door key and then, once he had got the car unlocked, by deactivating the alarm itself.

'I thought these things were supposed to stop automatically after twenty minutes,' Jake gritted through grated teeth as all his attempts to stop the alarm met with no response.

'That's house alarms,' Lucianna informed him sunnily, her glee growing as she saw the faint tinge of colour beginning to burn his skin. For the first time in the whole of the time she had known him, Jake was actually beginning to exhibit the tell-tale signs of becoming harassed. His hair was rumpled where he had pushed his hand through it and she could see from his expression that he wasn't enjoying the attention and pity they were attracting from other motorists.

'It could be worse,' she comforted him with pseudo concern. 'I believe the latest model of this car has an optional new alarm system that actually cries, ''Help, I'm being stolen''...'

She managed to keep her face straight as Jake gave her a look that should have turned her to cinders.

'Very funny,' he told her savagely, reaching into the car to pick up his car phone, but Lucianna shook her head and told him gently,

'It won't work, Jake, not whilst the alarm's ringing; there's an automatic bar that means you can't...'

'Where's the handbook?' Jake growled, reaching towards the glove compartment, but once again Lucianna shook her head sorrowfully.

'That won't open, Jake, not—'

'Not whilst the alarm's ringing… I know,' he cut in tightly. Then he asked her grimly, 'What about the engine? I suppose that won't start either…?'

'I'm afraid not,' Lucianna agreed gently.

'All right. You stay here; there's a public call box round the corner. I'll go and ring the garage.'

'All right, but you'd better leave me with the keys,' she told him dutifully, and explained, 'If you don't someone might think that I've tried to break in…'

Silently Jake handed her the keys.

Lucianna waited until he was out of sight and then went into action. Just as well she *had* ignored his veto on her touching his precious car…

Humming to herself, she set to work. Ignoring the alarm and overriding the system to open the glove box and remove the owner's manual, whilst deftly unlocking the bonnet, within three minutes she had silenced the alarm and within another two located the fault, which, as far as she could see, was simply a matter of replacing a fuse. The alarms would have to be re-set, of course, because she had overridden them, but she still felt very pleased with herself as she stood back and enjoyed the consequent silence of her handiwork, patting the car and telling her that she was a very clever girl.

'What the…?'

She smiled as she turned round in response to Jake's ominous voice, telling him calmly, 'It's stopped…'

Out of the corner of her eye she could see a car bearing the insignia of the garage which had supplied Jake with his car. As it came to a halt alongside them Lucianna stepped forward and told the mechanic when he climbed out, 'I've overridden the central nervous system and removed the electronic data coil, but I think the main problem lies with one of the fuses…'

'More than likely,' the mechanic agreed, giving her an initial appraising and then approving look as he lifted the bonnet and checked what she had done.

'It's a problem we're having with these cars, and something that wasn't discovered in the re-testing stage. We suspect it could be caused by changes in the air temperature, but we haven't enough evidence to make a firm decision on that yet…'

That was all the encouragement Lucianna needed; within seconds the pair of them were deep in conversation and it took Jake's grim, 'When the pair of you have finished…' to bring the young mechanic's enthusiastic praise of the manufacturer's latest electronic system to a faltering halt as he turned his attention back to Jake's car.

Ten minutes later, after the mechanic had gone and they were driving out of the car park, Jake turned to Lucianna and demanded coldly, 'All right, Lucianna, you've had your fun. When…?'

Lucianna didn't pretend not to understand what he meant.

'Er…the weekend you had to fly to Brussels. You asked David to drive you to the airport and then collect you when you got back because you didn't want to leave the car parked there because so many had been stolen; so whilst it was at the farm…'

'You ignored what I'd said and decided to start playing around with it… You do realise that it could have been your interfering that caused the fault in the first place.'

She watched his mouth harden as he swung the car out into the road. It felt good to know that there was one area at least where her knowledge was superior to Jake's, and even better to know that he knew it as well—knew it and didn't very much like it, if his thunderous silence was anything to go by.

Lucianna paused in the act of watering the plants she had lovingly rescued, freeing their poor constricted roots from the prison of the over-packed pots in which they had been planted, repotting them in a much more generously proportioned home.

They had repaid her love and care by flourishing despite all the taunting comments of her brother. Her father had been one of the old school of farmers, disdainful and impatient of anything grown for mere ornament and pleasure, and as a girl Lucianna had tended her small garden in secret, guiltily aware that her father would not have approved.

Now things were different, though, and even her brother had been impressed the previous summer when her planters and hanging baskets had not only attracted admiring comments from her customers and visitors, but had also won first prize at the local country fair.

On the other side of the yard her brother and sister-in-law were deep in conversation. Against all her own expectations Lucianna had quickly discovered that the books Jake had persuaded her to buy were giving her a fascinating new insight into other people's reactions and feelings, and now, a week after their purchase, she was discovering that she was becoming something of a people-watcher.

The way her brother was leaning over his wife, the way their bodies were touching, the way she was smiling up at him were all indicative of their love and intimacy, and as she watched them Lucianna felt a painful welling of loneliness and envy.

Why was it that the ability to be attractive to and appeal to a man seemed to come so easily to others but not to her? Surely it wasn't just a matter of looking docile and demure, of deliberately appealing to a man's vanity, to his need to boost his own ego, because if it was she had too much respect for herself ever to adopt that kind of artifice. But no, it couldn't be. She only had to think of how strong Janey could be and how determinedly she held her own against David whenever she felt the need.

Sexual chemistry was easy to recognise but hard to define, according to *The Art of Flirtation*, and without it…

Lucianna turned back to her plants, but this time as she nipped off the dead heads her fingers weren't quite as steady. The relationship she had with John might not be smouldering with sexuality and passion but there *was* more to a good relationship, a meaningful relationship, the kind of relationship she, Lucianna, wanted with a man, than mere sex…

She glanced at her watch. Jake was due back this evening. He had been away on business for the last few days but he had telephoned her from his hotel this morning, instructing her to present herself at the Hall this evening so that they could start work on the new phase of 'The Plan'.

Out of the corner of her eye she suddenly noticed the way her brother's hand had dropped to Janey's stomach.

It was no secret to Lucianna that her brother and Janey had been wanting to start a family for quite some time. Did that small possessive gesture she had just witnessed mean that she had now conceived?

Thoughtfully Lucianna watched the way her brother kept his arm around his wife's shoulders as they walked back to the house together. He was certainly being rather more physically protective and careful of her these days…or was it simply that *she* was more aware of the subtle messages of other people's body language which had hitherto been a closed book to her?

'Jake's still obviously not got around to taking you shopping yet' David teased, as Lucianna joined them in the kitchen tugging affectionately on her hair. 'I can't wait to see what he's got in mind for you. It will have to be black, of course—that way the oil stains won't show.'

'David…' Janey began to warn, but Lucianna shook her head and smiled.

'It's all right, Janey,' she told her. 'I know when I'm being wound up.'

Yes, she knew, but in the past she had always reacted with defensive anger to such teasing, she acknowledged. Overreacted, some might say, but since her eyes had been opened to the power and the potential of using her body language to work for her she had discovered that there were far more subtle ways of getting her arguments across than verbal arguing—and apparently, if the book on flirtation was to be believed, more ways of attracting a man's interest than by dressing provocatively.

In the privacy of her own bedroom she had already secretly been practising the small, telling gestures which were supposed to draw a man's attention…

CHAPTER FIVE

HALFWAY through cross-questioning her on how much time and attention she had given the books she had bought, Jake had had to excuse himself to take a business call in the library. From the way he had been speaking to her since her arrival at the Hall she might have been a schoolgirl, Lucianna decided wrathfully, absently glancing at the TV screen she had just switched on, her eyes widening as she saw the couple on the screen start to kiss one another with passionate intensity. As the camera closed up on their faces Lucianna tensed and watched closely.

When she and John kissed she felt none of the intense passion this couple were so enviably sharing. No, John had certainly never kissed her the way the man on the screen was kissing the woman, holding her face in his hands as he pressed hungry, biting kisses onto her mouth and she responded, twisting and turning in his arms as though she couldn't get close enough to him.

Lucianna felt her heart start to beat faster, oblivious to Jake's return as she stared in fascination at the screen. The couple were kissing differently now, their mouths fused together, their breathing laboured.

'What's wrong, Lucianna? Hasn't John ever kissed you like that?'

At the sound of Jake's voice Lucianna spun round, her face burning hotly, embarrassed at being caught studying the screen as though she had actually been guilty of voyeurism.

'Y-yes, of course he has,' she told Jake fiercely, starting to stammer slightly and somehow unable to meet his eyes.

'I don't believe you,' she heard him challenge her suavely. 'In fact I don't believe you even know how to kiss like that…'

'Of course I do,' Lucianna asserted quickly.

'Yes? Then prove it,' Jake demanded softly. 'Come over here now and prove it to me, Lucianna… Kiss *me*…'

At first Lucianna thought that Jake couldn't possibly mean what he had said—either that or she must have misheard him—but when she searched his face for confirmation she realised with a fierce, sharp thrill of fear that he *had* meant it.

'You can't, can you?' she heard him saying softly to her. 'You can't and you don't—'

'I can,' Lucianna lied immediately.

'Prove it, then…'

How had Jake managed to move so quickly that he was now standing right next to her, one hand already cupping the back of her head, constraining her, preventing her from moving? His mouth was only centimetres away from hers. Nervously she licked her lips and heard him say, 'Well, that's an interesting start, but *you're* supposed to be the one kissing *me*, not enticing me into kissing you…'

Enticing him! Fear and anger, always a dangerously volatile cocktail of emotions, exploded inside her and before she could lose her courage Lucianna closed the distance between them, her lips firmly pressed together as she brushed them against Jake's mouth.

His lips felt cool and smooth and nothing whatsoever like John's, which if she was honest always felt just a little too wet and soft and—

'Call that a kiss? If *that's* the best you can do then no wonder you're having so much trouble with your love life… The wonder is that you've got one at all,' Jake told her succinctly.

Furious now, Lucianna opened her mouth to retaliate and then discovered that it was impossible for her to speak for the very good reason that, despite the fact that she was sure she *had* removed her lips from his, Jake's mouth was now covering hers, covering it and…

Involuntarily Lucianna's eyes widened, her gaze focusing helplessly on Jake's as she recognised that the movement of his mouth against her own felt nothing like John's and, moreover, that her response to it, to *him*, was nothing like anything she had ever experienced in her life before.

Why was her pulse hammering, over-revving so much that her heart felt as though it was going to jump into her throat? Why were her own lips trembling so much? Why did she feel this sudden strange, strong need to get even closer to Jake, so much so that she was, she recognised dizzily, actually pressing her body against his?

Why did she have this urge to make those soft keening, whimpering little sounds she could feel bubbling desperately in her throat?

'Jake…'

To try to protest had been a mistake, she realised seconds later as her lips parted but no sound emerged, for instead of being free to speak, it was Jake who had the freedom to cover her now open mouth with his and to keep it open by pressing his thumb against her chin whilst he slowly stroked the tip of his tongue back and forth against her parted lips.

It must be that the deliberately slow-building rhythm of what he was doing was having some sort of mesmeric effect on her, she decided in shocked bemusement, because instead of trying to stop him she was actually, she was actually…

A vision flashed behind her closed eyelids, a mental image of the couple she had been watching on the television screen and the way they had been kissing.

To her shock, almost as though he had been reading her mind, Jake started to kiss her in the same way—quick, biting kisses interspersed with softer, longer ones that for some reason compelled her mouth to cling helplessly to his.

She felt as though she was lost, adrift, drowning in the unfamiliar torrent of sensation that engulfed her. Beneath her clothes her body was behaving, reacting to Jake in a way it had never reacted to John, nor to anyone else. Jake was caressing the nape of her neck as he kissed her now and his tongue was beginning to make slow, sensual forays into her mouth.

His tongue!

Dizzily Lucianna dug her fingernails into Jake's arms, somehow managing to find the strength to tear her mouth away from his.

'You shouldn't have done that,' she told him stormily, all too conscious of her heightened colour and ragged breathing.

'No,' Jake conceded grimly. 'I shouldn't!'

Jake admitting that *he* was in the wrong? Lucianna could hardly believe it, and neither could she believe the extraordinary way in which she had responded to his kiss. In fact she wasn't going to believe it, she told herself hastily. She was going to forget that the whole incident had ever happened.

She darted a wary look at Jake who had gone to stand in front of the window. He had his back to her.

'Tomorrow afternoon we're going shopping,' he announced abruptly, startling her. 'And this time...' He paused and then told her, 'If you want to be treated like a woman, Lucianna, then you're going to have to learn to dress like one.'

Lucianna was far too relieved that he hadn't made any reference to what had just happened between them to object to his plans for a shopping trip, or to the comment which had accompanied his announcement of them.

And besides, one totally unexpected offshoot from the hours she had stubbornly forced herself to spend people-watching had been a tentative awareness that there *were* other modes of dress for her sex apart from the two completely opposing sides she had previously believed existed.

There had been that woman she had noticed the other day, for instance, wearing neatly pressed, well-fitting jeans, an immaculate white shirt and a caramelly-coloured blazer which Lucianna had just known would feel wondrously soft to the touch, and to her own astonishment, as she'd studied her, Lucianna had experienced a wistful curiosity to know what it would be like to wear such clothes herself and with such confidence.

She had seen other women, of course, wearing garments she would never wear in a million years—tight, short Lycra skirts and equally tight, close-fitting leggings—but they too had exhibited the same careless confidence, a sort of insouciant ease which Lucianna was becoming increasingly aware that she did not possess.

She wore the clothes she did not just for practicality, as she had always insisted, she had been forced to recognise, but as a means of concealing herself, *protecting* herself. Almost as though if she was going to be accused of being unfeminine, unwomanly, then she might as well dress as though she wanted to be judged in that way.

She still wasn't sure where it had come from—this unfamiliar shy yearning for something different, to be someone different—and she was still very nervous and wary of it. But for the first time since she had started to grow up she was aware of a need within her to reach out towards the femininity she had previously fought so hard to deny.

Two hours later, with Jake still questioning her on her reading of the books she had bought, she had all but forgotten the turbulent and passionate moments she had spent in his arms.

Relaying the information she had gathered from the books back to Jake, she'd been surprised to discover just how much she *had* learnt, but if Jake was equally impressed he was concealing it well, his expression impassive, his profile turned slightly away from her, his whole manner towards her rather remote and withdrawn.

Only when she had impishly given him a demonstration of the 'mirroring' technique she had just been reading about did he actually seem to focus on her, but if the brief flash of anger she saw in his eyes was anything to go by he wasn't as surprised by her progress as she had expected.

'Jake…' Instinctively she reached out to touch his arm, unaware herself of just how much her quick mind had picked up from her reading or just how much her new knowledge was already reflected in the way she moved, talked and smiled. Ten days ago she would never have dreamed of touching Jake or any other man—but more especially Jake—to get his attention, and yet now she was doing it as naturally as though it were something she had always done.

She smiled teasingly at him as she said, 'I think perhaps *you* ought to read the books as well. You're supposed to respond to this…' she touched him lightly again and moved slightly closer to him, giving him another teasing smile '…by looking properly at me and moving closer to me.'

'It's John you need to practise your flirting techniques on, not me,' Jake told her harshly, moving away from her. 'I think we'd better call it a night…'

Half an hour later, as she drove home, Lucianna felt an odd sense of let-down and disappointment. What had she been expecting? she derided herself. Not praise from Jake, surely? She knew him far too well for that. For as long as she could remember and certainly since she had been a teenager, he had done nothing but criticise her.

Once Lucianna had gone, Jake poured himself a large glass of whisky. He wasn't normally a drinker, but right now…

Just what the hell had he got himself into? And why? He shook his head in self-resignation. He didn't really need to ask himself *that* question, did he? But until tonight he had managed to convince himself that his motives were, if not a hundred per cent altruistic, then at least ninety-nine per cent so.

Of course, what had happened tonight had blown that self-delusion totally apart. It had all been very well reminding himself at the start of how, as he had watched Lucianna growing up, he had often had to bite hard on his tongue to stop himself from quarrelling with her brothers, his friends, about the way they were treating their younger sister. Not that any of them had meant to hurt or harm her—it was just that because of their own upbringing they were unaware of how they were inhibiting her development as a woman, confident and happy in her femininity and her sexuality. He had seen…known, but then for him it was different. For a start, he *wasn't* Lucianna's brother.

Swearing under his breath, he poured himself another drink, going to sit down in one of the chairs drawn up close to the fire, resting his head back and closing his eyes.

He could still vividly remember the day, the hour, the moment he had recognised just how he really felt about his friends' baby sister, just why, when he was out on a date, instead of enjoying his date's company, he was constantly comparing her with Lucianna, knowing that he would rather be with her, enjoying her wickedly sharp sense of humour and its contrast with her still very naive emotions.

He had gone round to the farm to see David, the kitchen door had been open and he had walked in. The telephone, which was located in the kitchen, had started to ring. Upstairs he had heard a door open and then Lucianna had come running downstairs and into the kitchen, hastily wrapping a thin towelling robe around her wet and totally naked body as she did so.

As soon as she had seen him she had crimsoned with embarrassment, a floodtide of colour which had run up her body, scorching her tender, pale skin, filling her nipples with hot colour which had made them look…

Jake swallowed hard. There were some memories that haunted a man for all his life, some sins. She had been all of sixteen and he… He swallowed again. He doubted he would ever get over the sense of shock and self-disgust he had felt at the urge to take hold of her, to wrap her in his arms and plunder the tight virginity of those thrusting, colour-flushed nipples with the hot suckle of his mouth, until she twisted and arched against him, returning the white heat of passion that was coursing through him, scorching him, torturing him, possessing him with the same overwhelming fury with which he wanted to possess her.

Of course he had done no such thing. Of course he had forced himself to turn away whilst she turned and ran back upstairs, and of course neither of them had ever referred to the incident again. But from then on he had taken good care to distance himself from her both physically and emotionally…especially emotionally.

But, of course, it had been too little and far too late. He had been a man then, more than old enough to recognise what he was experiencing, even if that recognition had been coloured by his own distaste, his disgust with himself for falling in love with someone who was still only a girl…a child.

He had tried to cut himself off from what he was feeling, calling himself a pervert and worse, but none of it had done any good. He had, however, comforted himself that he was at least in control of his feelings, totally and absolutely… Until tonight…

And he still wasn't sure just what it had been about seeing her this evening that had destroyed the barriers he had painstakingly built to protect her. Certainly he hadn't enjoyed hearing her talking about John, and certainly the mental image he had had of her kissing him had stretched his self-control to its limits. But it had been more than that, he recognised. There had also been that new air she had about her, that subtle but oh, so alluring sudden awareness of herself as a woman, which he had returned to find her wearing like a little girl pirouetting proudly in her new dress.

How long would it be before she became even more self-aware, before she realised just *why* he was so determined to hold her at arm's length? And when she did—what then?

He glanced at the telephone. The temptation to ring the farm and say that their arrangement was off was almost overwhelming. It would be easy enough to invent some business trip that would keep him out of the way for a few weeks, but he already knew that he wouldn't do it, that he *couldn't* do it.

If he loved her as much as he claimed, then surely he loved her enough to help her get what she wanted, the *man* she wanted. And perhaps once she was safely engaged to him, married to him, he would finally be able to get on with his life.

Lucianna might not be a child any longer, but her feelings for him were still those she had had as a child. She still disliked and distrusted him and there was no way now that he could tell her just why he had had to make her feel like that towards him—no way, no point.

He closed his eyes again. Had she *any* idea just how close he had come this evening to totally losing control? Just how much he had wanted, ached for her?

'I thought Jake wasn't picking you up until two,' Janey commented with a smile as she caught Lucianna glancing through the kitchen window.

'He's not,' Lucianna agreed, flushing slightly.

'You know, if I didn't know better,' her sister-in-law teased, 'I'd think you were actually looking forward to this shopping trip.'

'Which just goes to show the sacrifices a woman is prepared to make to get her man,' David interjected, saving Lucianna from the need to defend herself and deny Janey's allegations.

They had told her this morning that, just as she had suspected, Janey was pregnant, and she had felt quite pleased to be able to say truthfully to them that she had half suspected as much.

'That sounds like Jake now,' Janey warned her as a car pulled into the yard. 'Looks like he's as eager for this shopping expedition as you are…!'

'Eager to get it over with,' David muttered. 'I hate shopping…'

'If that's the opening shot in a campaign of getting out of going to choose the nursery equipment, then it's one you're not going to win,' Janey told him cheerfully, laughing at his expression. 'And, unlike you, Jake enjoys shopping, and he's got excellent taste, unlike some men I could name.'

To Lucianna's surprise, once they were in the car Jake announced that he wasn't taking her into the local town but to a new shopping complex which had recently been opened several miles closer to the city.

Lucianna had heard about the complex via one of her customers, who had visited it to buy her outfit for her daughter's wedding. And, whereas the old Lucianna would immediately have objected that there was no point in him taking her there, since she had no intention of listening to his dictatorial views on what she should and shouldn't wear, this new Lucianna found that she was actually having to suppress a small bubble of female excitement as well as the sudden rush of apprehension and familiar dread that the thought of having to go into the—to her—unfamiliar and alien world of clothes normally gave her.

From her books she now understood that how a woman chose to present herself visually carried a very strong non-verbal message, and that the male sex was highly receptive and indeed vulnerable to visual messages.

And as for the impulse which had led her the other day to buy a couple of unbelievably expensive and glossy fashion magazines along with her newspaper and the new car magazine she had originally intended to buy, well, she'd told herself that if she had to endure the self-inflicted torture of having Jake boss her around and tell her what to do she might as well grab what extra help she could to make sure she kept her ordeal as short-lived as possible.

Once she had got over the shock at their cost and past her initial reluctance to turn the first page, she had discovered the cut and line of expensive clothes was, in many ways, as interesting to study as the design of a new car, and she had quickly found that, as with cars, her taste ran to the clean and simple, which would endure, rather than the fussy and over-ornamented—styles which were gimmicky.

And already, although Lucianna herself wasn't aware of it, what she had seen not just in the magazines but also through her people-watching exercises had begun subtly to exert an influence over her.

Jake, though, had noticed that the jeans she was wearing were a slightly better fit than the oversized ones she normally favoured, and the crisp white shirt, although still a man's and, he suspected, one she had purloined from her brother's wardrobe, was much more flattering than the heavy checked work shirts she normally wore.

Lucianna was forced to admit to herself that she was impressed by the shopping complex as she and Jake walked across the thankfully not too busy paved piazza area. Sapling trees, shrubs and attractive planters interspersed with seats, along with a good mixture of restaurants, bars and coffee shops, all of which had pleasant outdoor seating areas, all helped to lend a relaxing and almost continental atmosphere to the place, and Lucianna was also impressed by the absence of litter and general air of cleanliness.

'Where do you want to start?' Jake asked her. 'Or would you prefer to have a cup of coffee first?'

The thought of a cup of coffee was tempting, and not just as a means of a delaying tactic, Lucianna acknowledged, but she still shook her head determinedly.

Now that they were here she wanted to get the whole thing over and done with as quickly as possible.

'What's wrong?' Jake taunted her softly. 'Afraid you might lose your nerve?'

Lucianna flashed him a disdainful look and tossed her head, denying fiercely, 'Certainly not.'

Hiding his smile at her predictable reaction, Jake indicated a shop on the other side of the square.

Lucianna started to walk towards it and then stopped, frowning slightly and hesitating.

The understated elegance of the window display seemed to indicate that it would be one of those shops with the kind of assistants who would look down their elegant noses at her and make her wish she were a million miles away, but Jake was walking determinedly towards it and she wasn't going to have him thinking that she was nervous or, even worse, afraid.

'This shop is part of a European chain that specialises in providing a specific look which continues from season to season,' Jake explained.

'Really? How interesting,' Lucianna replied, covering her growing feeling of insecurity and panic with the sarcastic retort, adding, 'Well, that must make things easy for you, I suppose. If you bring all your girlfriends here for their clothes, then at least you won't miss recognising the latest one in the street.'

'And just what the hell is that supposed to mean?'

Lucianna was shocked into instant immobility as, instead of treating her comment with the contemptuous amusement she was used to, Jake suddenly wheeled round to confront her, his mouth a dangerously thin line and his eyes cold with anger.

'It…it wasn't meant to mean anything,' Lucianna denied. 'It…it was just supposed to be a…joke…'

'A joke?' Jake's eyebrows rose. 'Really? Well, I don't find it particularly funny to be accused of being the kind of man who has a chain of interchangeable bimbos dragging through his life, and for your information I have never suggested nor would I ever insult anyone by doing so, that a woman is some kind of doll, a toy, to be dressed up or undressed at my or any other man's whim. And furthermore I find it extremely unamusing, not to say offensive, that you should suggest I might,' Jake informed her acerbically.

Despite the fact that his obvious anger had shocked her, Lucianna fought back valiantly, determined not to be left wrong-footed, as she pointed out, 'Well, I'm sorry if I've got the wrong impression, but you're the one who's always changed his girlfriends more frequently than most men change their…their socks…'

'Really?' Jake challenged her. 'Do go on… It seems to me that you know more about my private life than I do myself.

'What a wonderfully insightful person you must be, Lucianna,' he marvelled sarcastically. 'And there I was thinking you never noticed anything that didn't come with wheels and an engine, and yet here you are, completely au fait with the most personal details of my life…more au fait than I am myself, as it happens, since the last time I had anything even approaching a relationship was—'

He stopped speaking as Lucianna, unable to control herself any longer, interrupted him hotly to say, 'I don't know why you're so angry, or pretending to be so…so… I heard the way David used to boast about the number of girls you and he took out,' she reminded him. Both her eyes and her voice mirrored her feelings, revealing to him far more than she knew as she added defensively, 'I thought it…you were…disgusting…boasting and bragging like that and—'

'Not me,' Jake interrupted her cuttingly. 'I don't recall ever having discussed such a subject in your hearing, and in fact...'

Forced by the sheer grim sternness of his voice to reconsider her own hotly, hastily spoken words, Lucianna was obliged to concede reluctantly, 'All right...I might never have heard you say it, but you were part of it...part of what David was talking about. You and he—'

'He and I might once have behaved with all the boorish stupidity that teenage boys are capable of displaying at times,' Jake interrupted her to agree, 'but the wholesale seduction and abandonment of a series of defenceless, vulnerable teenage girls in the style you were implying was totally and completely fictitious.

'For one thing, you underrate the intelligence and sense of self-preservation of your own sex if you think otherwise, Lucianna...and, for another, teenage boys have a capacity for self-aggrandisement and exaggeration that knows no limits. It's a fault that most of us grew out of very quickly indeed, and the kind of boastful comments teenage boys make shouldn't be taken too seriously, you know...'

Lucianna shivered slightly as she turned away from him, her voice low and slightly shaky as she told him passionately, 'I hated hearing the way you talked about...about girls...and...'

'Sex?' Jake supplied softly for her.

Lucianna could feel her face starting to burn. Why, oh, why had she ever brought up this subject? It was something she found it hard enough to think about herself even in the privacy of her own thoughts, never mind discuss with anyone else—and most especially with Jake.

'Yes, I can understand how some of the things you overheard must have made you feel.'

Pensively Jake watched her. Suddenly an awful lot of things were beginning to fall into place.

'No, you can't,' Lucianna contradicted him wildly, the panic starting to flood through her as she mentally relived the emotions and fears she had suffered through inadvertently listening in on her brothers' macho conversations coupled with the well-intentioned but clumsy lectures they had given her on the wisdom of the way she should behave with boys and the pitfalls that lay in wait for her if she didn't take heed of their advice.

'You're a man and you don't…you can't—' Abruptly Lucianna stopped, conscious that she had been on the verge of saying too much.

Jake, though, was refusing to let the subject drop, prompting gently, 'I can't what?'

Tight-lipped, Lucianna shook her head and looked longingly towards the interior of the shop. What ten minutes ago had seemed an inhospitable, unfriendly, alien place now seemed like a welcome haven when placed alongside Jake's unwanted probings into her most closely guarded thoughts and feelings.

'I can't *what*, Lucianna?' Jake persisted. 'I can understand how destructive, how emotionally and physically blighting it must be for a young girl on the brink of exploring her own sexuality and emotions to overhear a group of young men discussing such subjects without the guards they would normally put on their tongues in the presence of her sex.'

'It didn't do me any harm.' Lucianna immediately defended her brothers. 'In fact, it did me a favour. At least I knew what boys thought…'

'You knew what *boys* thought, yes,' Jake agreed quietly, 'but what about men, Lucianna? Did you…do you know how *they* think and feel, or did the lessons you inadvertently learned from your brothers go so deep that they instilled in you a fear and dread of being talked about as your brothers talked about their first sexual experiences? Did their conversations inspire in you such a dread of having all your dreams violated by the crassness of some boy who might later boast about his sexual conquest of you to his friends that sex is still something you view with distaste and embarrassment?'

'Of course not,' Lucianna denied quickly. 'In fact…' she tilted her chin towards him bravely as she lied '…I don't think anything of the kind… I—actually, I like sex; I like it a lot…'

'I see. So if I were to suggest that instead of continuing with our shopping trip you and I go back to the Hall and spend the afternoon in bed mutually enjoying sex you'd be perfectly happy to agree?'

Lucianna was almost unable to believe her ears, her shock showing in her eyes, her voice quavering betrayingly as she responded, 'No… No, I wouldn't.'

'But you just said you like sex,' Jake pointed out reasonably, 'and since I haven't had a relationship with anyone for quite some considerable time, and of course being a man…'

'I can't go to bed with *you*,' Lucianna protested squeakily.

'Why not? I'm no different from any other man,' Jake told her, adding silkily, with a deliberately sexual downward glance at her body, 'I don't intend to boast, but I think you'll find I'm equally satisfactory as any of the other men you've had.'

'Other men!' Lucianna's eyes rounded. 'I don't... there haven't... I think you're forgetting about John,' she managed to say.

'Ah, yes, John,' Jake agreed, but then added swiftly, 'But he isn't here, is he, and you and I...?'

Lucianna had had enough. Now that she was over the initial shock of Jake's astounding proposition, common sense was pointing out several salient facts to her. Tossing her head, she told Jake forthrightly, 'You're just trying to make fun of me. I know perfectly well you don't want to go to bed with me, you don't want to have sex with me...'

'You're right, I don't,' Jake agreed, but as he watched the emotions chase one another across her face he added mentally to himself, But I sure as hell want to make love to you, again and again and again, and if I had your precious brothers here with me now, friendship or not, I'd wring their wretched necks.

To Lucianna's relief he started to walk towards the shop, but as she made to follow him he stopped and turned back to her, catching her totally off guard as he asked her almost absently, 'Presumably there aren't any problems with the sexual side of your relationship with John...?'

Immediately Lucianna bridled.

'Of course there aren't,' she denied, thankful that Jake wasn't standing close enough to hear the way her heart was hammering. The last thing she wanted was for Jake of all people to discover her most closely guarded and shameful secret...which was that she was still a virgin.

Technically she knew what sex was all about, of course. How could she not do so with her outspoken elder brothers? Elder brothers who had not been merely outspoken in their frank teenage discussions about their own sex lives, when they thought she wouldn't understand or hear what they were saying, but who had been equally outspoken and frank in their fraternal advice to her about the way in which she should respond to any sexual approaches to herself.

'Say no and make sure you keep on saying no,' had been David's stern advice. 'That way they'll know they can't take advantage of you and they'll respect you.'

'Yes, and if they don't they'll have us to answer to,' Lewis had added fiercely.

What they *hadn't* told her, though, Lucianna recognised, was when and how a girl changed her no to a yes and, even more importantly, as she was discovering via her relationship with John, how she should let a man know that she was ready to be given the option to do so.

In the early days of their relationship John had certainly been keen enough to try and coax her into bed, and she, faithful to her brothers' stern lectures, had very firmly said no, but in the weeks before his departure he had seemed quite happy with the tepid kisses and caresses they had exchanged and Lucianna had been at a loss to know how to generate a little more passion between them.

When she had tried tentatively to snuggle up a little closer to him he had simply asked her if she was cold; when she had tried to deepen the kisses they had shared he had seemed oblivious to the hints she was trying to give him.

Hopefully, though, the tips she had picked up via the books she had bought should help her to make things clear to him, but it was a subject she certainly wasn't about to discuss with Jake. Jake, who, despite his surprising announcement earlier about the lack of any current relationship in his life, certainly had far more experience of her sex than she was ever likely to have of his.

Caught up in her thoughts, Lucianna suddenly realised that she had actually entered the shop and that the girl approaching her, far from being the haughty, disdainful type of person she had been dreading, was actually smiling at her with genuine warmth.

'Would you like some help?' she asked Lucianna. 'Or would you prefer to be left alone to browse?'

'We need—'

'I prefer to browse.'

Lucianna overrode Jake firmly, and just as firmly ignored his sardonic comment, meant for her ears only. 'This isn't a jeans shop, you know,' he said as the girl retreated, returning to the pile of jumpers she had been folding when they'd walked in, leaving Lucianna and Jake on their own.

'I *do* know that,' Lucianna returned with pointed emphasis, before turning on her heel and, ignoring Jake, walking over to study a selection of colour coordinated clothes which had caught her eye.

At first sight, the plain, caramelly-coloured coordinates for which she was heading might have seemed dull in comparison to the much brighter range of clothes the shop also carried, but Lucianna had remembered seeing similarly coloured clothes being modelled by a girl with her colouring in one of her fashion magazines.

She reached out and touched the fabric of a pair of trousers uncertainly. It felt cool and silky soft. She frowned as she studied the swing ticket. 'Tencel', it said, which left her none the wiser apart from her instinctive awareness that Tencel, whatever it was, made the fabric feel good and hang well.

There was a brochure on a coffee table beside her turned open at a page depicting the trousers she was currently examining. In the photograph they were teamed with a neatly fitting short jacket casually unbuttoned over what looked like a plain cream silk top.

'This is our newest range,' the salesgirl announced helpfully, suddenly materialising at Lucianna's side. 'It's my favourite and I've really fallen for the shell,' she added enthusiastically, whilst Lucianna looked blank and wondered frantically what on earth 'the shell' was until she saw that Jake had removed a hanger with the cream silk top on it and was holding it out to her.

He said quietly, 'Yes, it would suit you, Luce.'

The top, of course; she remembered now seeing it described as a 'shell' in her magazine. For once she was too grateful for Jake's intervention to object to his interference, but that still didn't quite explain, as she told herself later, quite just how she came to be standing in front of him half an hour later, self-consciously wearing not just the shell but the trousers and the jacket that went with it as well, along with the toning scarf, whilst the salesgirl enthused about the practicality of adding the sleeveless dress that was also part of the collection to the trousers, since the same jacket could be worn over it.

'I don't want…' Lucianna began, and then stopped,

a fiery blush staining her skin as she saw the way Jake was looking at her.

'What is it? What's wrong? Why are you looking at me like that?' she hissed defensively at him whilst the salesgirl went to find the dress.

Jake shook his head.

'Nothing's wrong,' he responded shortly, but he was frowning, Lucianna noticed, and suddenly the burning feeling of self-confidence and heady, unfamiliar pleasure in her own appearance that she had experienced when she had studied her reflection in the changing-room mirrors evaporated, bringing her abruptly back down to earth, making her feel awkward and uncomfortable and longing for the protection of her heavy denims to replace the silk trousers she was wearing.

As he turned his back on her Jake questioned with quiet inner savagery if he was totally sane. Knowing what he did about his feelings for her, it had surely been total madness to bring Lucianna somewhere where he was forced to watch her outer transformation from chrysalis to butterfly. He knew just what effect she was going to have on the rest of his sex when they saw her lovely lissom body dressed in that outfit, was aware that, whilst outwardly perfectly respectable, she seemed to hint with every movement she made at the delicate femininity of the body the suit was supposed to cover and shield.

'You really do have the most wonderful figure,' the salesgirl enthused, coming back with the dress over her arm and pausing to admire the effect of her coaxing and tweaking as Lucianna paused, reluctant to respond, to listen to her.

'And that colour is definitely you as well,' she

added truthfully. 'There's something about clothes like these that makes you feel and look so feminine, isn't there?' she said warmly, and Lucianna, who, after witnessing Jake's reaction, had been on the point of rejecting the outfit, hesitated and then frowned as she glanced into a mirror set at an angle to the shop floor several feet away.

In it she could just glimpse the back view of a woman wearing the same outfit as she was herself but on this woman it looked truly elegant, truly feminine. Lucianna lifted her hand to remove the scarf and then stood staring at the woman in the mirror, immobilised by the shock of realising that the reflection she could see was her own, that *she* was the woman who looked truly elegant, that the unfamiliar back view she had been admiring was, in actual fact, her own.

'I'll take it,' she told the girl positively, before she could allow herself to change her mind. 'All of it...and the dress as well,' she added.

The girl's smile widened.

Ten minutes later, as she paid for her purchases, Lucianna shot Jake a triumphant look.

He might not think she had what it took to be able to wear such feminine clothes but the salesgirl had thought differently and so had she, Lucianna decided firmly. She couldn't wait to see John's face when he saw her wearing her new things.

'I hope you don't mind my saying so,' the salesgirl commented to Lucianna as she handed her a huge carrier bag containing her new clothes, 'but I love the highlights you've had woven into your hair. Would you mind telling me where you had them done...?'

Highlights! Lucianna gave her a puzzled look, whilst Jake, who had overheard their conversation, duly explained for her, 'I'm afraid they're the work of the sun.'

'You mean they're natural? Lucky you,' the girl told her enviously. 'I have to pay a fortune for mine and they don't look anything like as good.'

Lucianna was still frowning as they left the shop. Highlights... Did the salesgirl mean those odd little goldy bits that had always lightened her hair in the summer?

'Coffee?' Jake suggested as he and Lucianna left the shop, but Lucianna shook her head and demanded instead,

'You didn't like it, did you? The outfit I just bought—you didn't like it. I could see it in your face...'

'On the contrary,' Jake assured her truthfully, 'I like it very much.' Where did it come from, he wondered ruefully, this female ability to sense and home in on any unwary male reaction with all the deadly accuracy of a heat-seeking missile?

'But you didn't like it on me,' Lucianna persisted. 'I suppose you think *I'm* not feminine enough, not *womanly* enough to wear it...'

Jake was frowning again now, she observed, his mouth hardening in that dangerous way that always made her heart start to beat just a little bit too quickly. Not that she was afraid of Jake's disapproval—no way...no way at all, she assured herself hastily.

'Anyway, I don't care what you think; it doesn't matter,' Lucianna informed him with a shake of her head before he could reply. 'It's what John thinks that matters...'

'What he *thinks* or what he *does*?' Jake demanded harshly, his own emotions overwhelming the need for caution and good sense. 'What kind of reaction is it you're expecting from him, Luce? What is it you want him to do? Take one look at you and want you so much that he can't wait to start ripping the things off you? Do you expect him to take one look at you and immediately declare his undying love? Because if you do…'

'Because if I do, what?' Lucianna challenged him angrily, her fingers curling tightly over the handle of the carrier bag as her face flushed with mortification. 'Just because *you* don't think I'm…that John loves me. Well, he does love me,' she told him proudly, 'and when he comes back…'

She paused, and Jake could see the tears she was fighting to blink away glittering in her eyes as he cursed himself inwardly for his stupidity. The last thing he'd wanted to do was to hurt her and he ached to be able to make her understand that loving someone, really loving them, had nothing to do with what they wore or how the rest of the world perceived them, and everything to do with what they were, and that a man who could only love a woman he could display on his arm like a pretty trinket wasn't, in his opinion, much of a man at all. But how could he?

CHAPTER SIX

'THIS way; we haven't finished yet.'

Lucianna frowned as Jake took hold of her upper arm in a firm grip and turned her towards the shop facing them.

'New underwear,' he added succinctly, although no explanation had really been needed—not with Lucianna well able to see what kind of apparel the shop he was indicating sold from the items on display in its window—undies which bore absolutely no resemblance whatsoever to the plain, sensible chain-store things she normally wore.

'I don't need any new underwear,' Lucianna denied untruthfully, glowering at Jake as she saw his disbelieving expression.

'No?' he questioned sardonically. 'You surely weren't planning to wear those no doubt sensible but far from sensually appealing items of female apparel you were removing from the washing line when I called round the other week for the welcome-home seduction scene you're planning for John's return, are you? Because if so...' He paused without finishing what he was saying, and added obliquely, 'Besides, they'd show through under those silky trousers.'

Lucianna opened her mouth to argue with him and then closed it again.

She *might* need new underwear to complement her new clothes but there was no way she was going to buy it with Jake there.

'I haven't got time today,' she told him loftily. 'I've got a customer's car booked in for a service at half past four.'

'Really? Well, in that case we'd better make a move,' Jake accepted. 'It's almost four now,' he told her.

They were halfway back to the car when he suddenly said musingly, 'I suppose you could always do without any underwear at all; that way the fabric would certainly hang well and of course, as you'll no doubt have learned by now from your books, from a man's point of view it's a very definite ego boost to know that a woman wants you so much that she's already prepared herself for sex with you and she wants you to know it.'

Lucianna stopped dead and gave Jake a murderous look, her face burning with angry heat as she denied furiously, 'I would *never* do anything like that… How dare you suggest I might?'

The naivety of her angry indignation should have made him feel guilty instead of pleased, Jake acknowledged as they walked on with Lucianna maintaining a stormy silence, because he recognised that he had deliberately used a verbal description to conjure up an image he'd known she would find unappealing.

He could have, for instance, told her that there was nothing a man, and more specifically himself, would have found more erotic and emotional, as well as physically arousing than the knowledge that the only tantalising barrier between his hands, his mouth and her skin was the outward formality of her elegant trousers and top, and that beneath them her skin, her body, was deliciously and wantonly naked. He could have told her that nothing was guaranteed to make him ache more than to be with her in a public place knowing that…

Determinedly he shook his head, reminding himself sternly of the danger of such thoughts.

It had been a shock to see her emerging from that changing room looking both so soignée and glamorous and yet at the same time too vulnerably unsure of herself. He had been hard put to it not to snatch her up into his arms and keep her there, to tell her exactly how he felt about her, how he had always felt about her, and for a moment the temptation had been such that it had been touch and go whether he would be able to control it—and himself.

Broodingly he watched her as she stormed across the car park ahead of him, still obviously angry with him, her head held high, shoulders back. Half of him wanted to take hold of her and show her physically if necessary just why a man who really cared, really loved her, would love her, want her exactly the way she was, and the other half prayed that she would never, ever have to suffer the disillusionment and pain of discovering just how unworthy of her love precious John actually was.

Lucianna hummed softly to herself as she gave the ancient Morris Traveller she had just been servicing a little pat.

Bessie belonged to one of their neighbours, Shelagh Morrison, and Shelagh herself had inherited the car from her grandmother in Dublin, who had, in turn, been given her as a gift by her late husband, Shelagh's grandfather, and Bessie was therefore considered to be more of a family pet than a mere car and had to be treated accordingly.

'She's horrendous to drive and expensive to keep and, if I'm honest, I much prefer my BMW,' Shelagh had confided once to Lucianna. 'And yet I just can't bring myself to part with her. I'm just thankful that you're able to service her for me. They told me at my BMW dealership garage that I was lucky to have found someone who could.'

Lucianna glanced at her watch now. She'd just got time to get Bessie washed and polished before Shelagh came to collect her. Her smile turned to a small frown as she saw a car come racing down the farm lane. Whoever was driving it was driving far too fast for the lane and its country environment and Lucianna's frown deepened as the car swung into the yard and she recognised its driver.

What was Felicity doing out here? She hadn't come to tell Lucianna that they'd had another fax from John, presumably. Lucianna wiped her hands on her dungarees and started to walk towards her.

In contrast to her own sensible mud- and farmyard-proof dungarees and boots Felicity was wearing spiky-heeled, strappy sandals and a short—very short, Lucianna noticed—white dress.

'Oh, Luc, good! I'm glad you're here!' Felicity exclaimed as soon as Lucianna was within earshot. 'My car is making the most peculiar noise; could you look at it for me?'

'I can,' Lucianna agreed, glancing immediately at the car's relatively new number plate, 'but isn't it still under warranty?'

She remembered how impressed John had been when Felicity's then boyfriend had bought her the car as a twenty-first-birthday present, commenting much to Lucianna's chagrin, 'But you can't blame him for going overboard and trying to impress her. She *is* a real stunner…'

Stunner or not, she was certainly not mechanically minded, Lucianna decided ten minutes later, having run the engine of the Toyota and heard it making no noise other than a clean, healthy purr.

'What sort of noise was it making exactly?' she asked Felicity cautiously once she had checked out all the obvious potential faults.

'I don't really know…it was just…you know, a noise…' Felicity told her unhelpfully. 'Heavens, you are clever,' she added. 'I don't know the remotest thing about car engines. Not that I would particularly want to,' she added. 'All that dirt and grease… It must ruin your nails and your hands. Ugh…

'By the way,' she added conversationally when Lucianna made no response, 'who *was* that guy you were with when I saw you in town the other day? I rather thought I recognised him from somewhere but…'

'Jake, you mean?' Lucianna asked her as she closed the bonnet of the car. 'He's…' On the point of launching into an explanation of Jake's background and position in their local society, she suddenly changed her mind, alerted by some female sixth sense as to what was really behind Felicity's seemingly innocent question—which was confirmed by the predatory, eager look in the other girl's eyes. 'Oh, he's just a neighbour,' she said dismissively instead.

'A neighbour?' The other girl's eyes widened slightly and then narrowed as she gave Lucianna an assessing look before starting to smile and then laughing. 'That's typical of you, Luc,' she commented, and then added for no apparent reason, 'I could never do a job like yours.'

'So you've already mentioned,' Lucianna agreed tersely.

'I'd hate having to wear such unfeminine clothes,' she continued, apparently oblivious to Lucianna's increasing desire to bring her call to an end. 'I like to wear soft, silky things next to my skin—silk underwear… Do you ever wear silk underwear, Luc?'

'Not under my dungarees,' Lucianna returned woodenly.

'I don't suppose you ever wear stockings either, do you, Lucianna?' she queried, giving Lucianna a faintly malicious look. 'John often teases me about wearing them.'

Lucianna looked away from her, determined not to let her see how hurtful she found her revelations—revelations which she was beginning to suspect were fully intended to *be* hurtful and to underline the differences between them. Well, anyone could buy a pair of stockings—and wear them. Lucianna's heart suddenly seemed to start beating a little faster.

That was twice now within the same twenty-four hours that she had been told that her choice of underwear lacked man-appeal, and even the book she had been reading on flirtation had stressed that it was perfectly acceptable for a woman to indulge in a small amount of sensually teasing dressing.

She took a deep breath as she came to a sudden decision.

'I can't see that there's anything wrong with your car,' she told Felicity firmly. 'But it might be as well if you took it back to the dealership and got them to check it over just in case.'

She looked at her watch. 'I'm sorry but I've got to get the Traveller washed and polished before its owner comes back for it.' And then, quite deliberately, she turned away from the other girl to show her that she expected her to leave.

If Felicity was so determined to make fun of her then Lucianna couldn't stop her, but she certainly wasn't going to help her, nor was she going to let her use her as a means of trying to get an introduction to Jake.

Did she really think that she, Lucianna, was so stupid, so lacking in female awareness, that she wouldn't realise just what she was really after underneath all that patently untrue concern about her car? If Felicity had been a little bit more open and honest with her, if she hadn't taken such delight in underlining the fact that John found her attractive, then she might have felt more inclined to help, Lucianna decided. And she might even have felt enough female fellow-feeling for her to warn her that Jake was no stranger to female admiration, even though he might have said to *her* this afternoon that it had been a long time since his last relationship.

Determinedly keeping her face averted, Lucianna didn't turn round until she heard the Toyota's engine die away as the other girl drove back the way she had come.

If she was so interested in Jake then let her find another way of bringing herself to his attention. The two of them would be well suited, Lucianna decided angrily.

* * *

'What's wrong with you? You haven't spoken a word all through supper,' David said in concern.

'Nothing's wrong,' Lucianna told her brother quickly.

In point of fact the reason why she had not contributed very much to the suppertime conversation was that she was still reflecting on the events of the day. As she looked towards the window, she was mentally contrasting the visual difference between her own dungaree-clad body and the sultry, deliberately sensual swing of Felicity's hips in the short skirt she had been wearing, the way she had run her fingertips down along her thigh as she'd moved. She recalled the other girl's comment about how John teased her about her stockings.

There had been stockings in the window of that underwear shop Jake had directed her attention to this afternoon—stockings attached to the most frivolously feminine garter, with a tiny pair of briefs to match.

'I'm going over to Ryedales tomorrow. They're taking delivery of a new state-of-the-art harvester and bailer. Want to come with me?'

Lucianna looked at her brother then shook her head.

'I can't,' she told him. 'I've…I've got some shopping to do.'

Behind Lucianna's back Janey quickly and very firmly shook her head in her husband's direction, warning him not to make any comment.

'Lucianna going shopping… I don't believe it,' David commented to Janey later, when they were on their own. 'She's really got it badly for this John.'

'She's a *woman*, David,' Janey reminded him gently. 'And she's just beginning to discover the pleasure of what being a woman means, of taking pride in herself and her femininity.'

'But she's always been such a tomboy…'

'Because that was what all of you *expected* her to be,' Janey told him firmly. 'But she isn't a teenager any more, she's a woman now, and a very, very attractive one…'

'Luce?'

'Luce,' Janey confirmed, shaking her head in faint exasperation at the brotherly disbelief in his voice and adding spiritedly and, so far as David was concerned, very cryptically, 'And if you don't believe *me* then ask Jake…'

'Jake…? What…?'

Shaking her head again, Janey gave him an enigmatic smile.

Men. Why was it that even the nicest of them could be so obtuse at times?

'Jake's been on the phone,' Janey announced as Lucianna walked into the kitchen the following morning. 'He's got to go away for a few days—something about some business matters needing attention. He said to tell you that he'll be back by the end of the week.'

Jake was away. Lucianna's heart gave an unexpectedly intense flurry of small thuds which she told herself quickly were no doubt due to relief that she would be relieved of his odious and demanding presence for a small oasis of time.

She suddenly found herself wondering whether these business matters Jake so unexpectedly had to attend to might involve the presence of a female travelling companion, a someone with whom Jake might share whatever private time these business matters might allow him, a someone who might *enjoy* being taken shopping and dressed up in those same, so silky, frivolous bits of nonsense which had kept manifesting themselves throughout her troubled dreams last night.

Not that *she* cared. No, of course she didn't. Why should she? Jake could buy underwear for as many other females as he chose—it was nothing to her! Nothing at all.

Janey frowned as Lucianna pushed away her cereal virtually untouched. Perhaps David *was* right after all and Lucianna *did* genuinely love John. Janey sincerely hoped not—for several reasons!

'I'd better go upstairs and get changed. I've got some shopping to do this morning,' Lucianna told her sister-in-law, abruptly coming to the decision she had been tussling with.

It was an easy enough task for Lucianna to drive to the shopping complex and find the shop Jake had pointed out to her the previous day. What proved far harder was actually making herself open the shop door and go inside.

In the end it was the friendly and slightly concerned smile of the girl behind the counter inside the shop, who had already glanced in her direction several times, that finally gave Lucianna the impetus to push open the door and go in.

'It *is* hard to choose, isn't it?' the girl commented as Lucianna glanced uncertainly around, thoroughly bewildered not just by the multiplicity of styles and colours in which the underwear was displayed but also by the confusing language in which it was described. 'Would you like some help?' the salesgirl continued.

Lucianna took a deep breath, nodding. Since she was the only customer in the shop she didn't exactly feel comfortable fibbing that she was simply browsing.

'Are you looking for something for yourself?' the salesgirl queried, and when Lucianna nodded again she enquired further, 'Is it for a special occasion or to go under a specific outfit? For instance, we recommend either a string or these to go under trousers,' she explained, taking in Lucianna's jeans-clad figure with a brief but professional glance and pointing to a nearby display.

The 'string', as she described it, made Lucianna gnaw worriedly at her bottom lip. She could just imagine Jake's reaction to the idea of *her* wearing such a delicate feminine wisp of underwear.

'It's far more practical and hard-wearing than it looks,' the salesgirl informed her, taking it off its hanger and proving her point by stretching the skimpy white lace garment.

'I wear them myself, and they're great under even the tightest jeans or anything where you don't want to show any knicker line. My boyfriend thinks they're rather neat as well,' she added with a conspiratorial grin.

'We do sell these as well, of course,' she added, her voice and expression thoroughly professional once more as she replaced the string with its fellows and removed the other pair of knickers she had pointed out to Lucianna.

'Big knickers, we call them,' she explained wryly, 'and of course they do give an equally neat outline, but we do tend to find that they don't sell quite as well as the strings. Men don't like them,' she told Lucianna, before turning away and waving her hand around the shop floor. 'Of course, if you're after something a little bit more frivolous, something that's more flirty than functional, we do several mix-and-match ranges that include everything from silk or satin teddies right through to balconette bras, French knickers…'

Lucianna took another deep, steadying breath and, before she could lose her nerve, blurted out, 'Er…actually, I was wondering… Do you sell suspender belts?'

To her relief the girl didn't betray by so much as a flicker of an eyelash that she found anything unusual in her request.

'Oh, yes, they're over here,' she told Lucianna, indicating and walking towards another display.

'I must say I don't wear them very often myself since I tend to go for trousers rather than skirts, but just once in a while I have to admit there's something rather special and sexy about wearing stockings.

'This is one of our most popular ranges, especially with brides,' she said, removing a delicate garter belt of white silk and lace from the rack and holding it out for Lucianna's inspection. 'We do a matching strapless bustier-cum-corset piece, which is ideal for strapless dresses, but if it's just the belt you want I can definitely recommend this one. And these are the briefs that go with it,' she added, reaching for a pair which Lucianna could see on a display behind her.

'Of course, you'll probably need a small size,' she added thoughtfully, subjecting Lucianna to a professional inspection. 'And if you were thinking of buying a bra to go with them as well, then I'd definitely recommend that we measure you properly to make sure we get the right fit.'

In the end it was a good two hours before Lucianna finally left the shop.

In addition to the suspender belt and two pairs of stockings she had also bought the briefs and a pretty bra that matched the belt and briefs, although she had complained to the salesgirl that there was so little of it that she wasn't sure how on earth it could be so expensive.

'Wait until the man in your life sees you wearing it,' the salesgirl had advised her with a grin. 'Then you'll know it was worth every penny! Trust me…I know!'

She had also purchased two other bras in a shimmery and virtually transparent soft, coffee-coloured Lycra, and their matching strings, which the girl had assured her were just the thing to wear beneath white or any kind of transparent fabric, since, once on, their unusual colour meant that they could not be detected.

Once outside again in the sunshine, Lucianna decided that the odd and unfamiliar sense of lightheartedness and recklessness that seemed to be propelling her across the piazza in the direction of a shoe shop the salesgirl had recommended to her must have something to do with the fact that she hadn't eaten her breakfast—just like the disturbing mental images that kept on popping up out of nowhere, showing herself dressed in all her new finery—including the new underwear—whilst Jake gazed on in stunned awe!

Why on earth it should be Jake rather than John who was stunned speechless by her transformation she had no clear idea… Perhaps it had something to do with the fact that it was Jake who had suggested she buy the stuff in the first place.

The saleswoman in the shoe shop showed every sign of being equally helpful and knowledgeable about the goods she was selling as the girl in the underwear shop had been, but by now Lucianna was well into her own stride and, with an aplomb and sense of assurance which startled herself a little, she very quickly and calmly picked out a pair of light-weight shoes to wear with her new silk suit plus a pair of strappy sandals which, as yet, she had nothing in her wardrobe to wear with—unless, of course, you counted the stockings and suspenders!

It was now definitely time for her to go home, Lucianna decided dizzily as she emerged from the shop clutching her parcels, but first she needed a cup of coffee. And it was whilst she was seated on the pavement under an umbrella to protect her from the heat of the sun that she noticed the banner hanging in the window of the chemist's on the other side of the road, announcing that they were giving free make-up demonstrations and make-overs to anyone who wished to avail themselves of this treat.

Without knowing quite how it had happened, Lucianna found herself inside the chemist's enjoying the cool draught of their air-conditioning whilst she studied the vast array of cosmetics on sale.

Her brothers had teased the life out of her when she had first started experimenting with make-up in her early teens, and David had even gone so far as to make her wash off the garish red lipstick and bright blue eyeshadow which she had secretly saved her pocket money for weeks to buy. But the kind of make-up on sale here was very different from the cheap, brightly coloured cosmetics she had bought as a young girl, she realised. Very different…

'Would you like some help?'

As she turned her head towards the smiling salesgirl approaching her, Lucianna bowed to the inevitable.

Back at the farmhouse David glanced frowningly at his watch.

'Luce can't *still* be shopping,' he told Janey. 'She's been gone for over *four* hours.'

'Of course she can,' Janey replied smugly, adding with a smile, 'She's a woman.'

Thoroughly baffled, David retreated into the farming article he had been reading. *He* might not be an expert on the female sex like Jake was, but he knew when he was beaten!

'It would be just your luck for this—' Janey patted her small bump lovingly '—to turn out to be a girl,' she told him, correctly guessing what he was thinking.

'Girl or boy, I don't honestly mind,' David told her truthfully, putting down his magazine and walking round the table to take her in his arms and hold her, hold them both, tenderly. 'In fact, so far as I'm concerned you can go ahead and produce a whole tribe of girls…'

'*I* can produce?' Janey scoffed. '*You're* the one who decides what sex our offspring are going to be, and as for us having a tribe…'

CHAPTER SEVEN

LUCIANNA frowned critically as she studied her reflection in her bedroom mirror. With David and Janey out of the way on a rare night out together, she had taken the opportunity to experiment with her new make-up purchases, and not just her make-up, she acknowledged as she stared intently into her mirror, trying to gauge if she had followed the salesgirl's advice, or if she ought to add just a touch more depth to the eyeshadow she had so carefully and nervously applied.

'With your colouring, taupes and muted colours will suit your eyes best,' the girl had told her, laughing sympathetically when Lucianna had relaxed enough to tell her ruefully about her unhappy experiments with bright blue eyeshadow.

Now, with the taupe eyeshadow highlighting the size and colour of her eyes, Lucianna was slightly startled to see how both that and the softly pretty coral lipstick she was wearing brought out and emphasised the femininity of her facial features in a way which made her look and feel very different from her normal workaday self.

Would John be similarly surprised?

He had rung her earlier in the day, but she had had a customer waiting to collect her car and so their conversation had been rushed and not very satisfactory. John had sounded distant and on edge, more concerned with telling her all about the way he was being fêted by his colleagues in the Canadian office than interested in talking to her about their own relationship.

Their relationship.

Rather nervously Lucianna stepped back from the mirror and studied her reflection full-length, forcing herself not to look away from what she saw but to examine herself. It was just as well she wasn't wearing any blusher—the rosy glow colouring her skin was more than colour enough—and even though she knew it was ridiculous to feel embarrassed by her own reflection, and in the privacy of her own bedroom, Lucianna couldn't help it. The reflection in front of her was just so very different from the one she was used to seeing.

After she had finished work she had showered and washed her hair, which was still hanging loosely around her shoulders in a thick, silky cloak which she privately deemed rather untidy but which for some reason seemed to highlight the delicacy of her facial bones and the softness of her skin. But it wasn't her face or her hair which was causing her to feel abashed. No, it was the fact that she had taken advantage of David and Janey's absence not just to try out her new make-up but to try on her new undies as well.

What would John think if…when he saw her like this…? Would *he* notice, as she had done herself, how delicate and slender her legs looked clad in such sheer stockings? Would he…? What would he think…say…Lucianna took a deep gulp of air…when he saw the frivolous lacy affair that was holding them up? What would his reaction be to her new bra—a bra which was nothing like any she had ever worn and which it had taken all the salesgirl's earnest professionalism and sincerity to assure her was perfectly respectable and one of their customers' firm favourites?

And, as if all that weren't enough, there was, of course, the string. Lucianna took another gulp of air… From the front it looked if not exactly as sturdy as her normal knickers then certainly not more revealing than a rather high-cut bikini, but from the back…! As yet she hadn't managed to pluck up the courage to study her back view, and the mirror in her room wasn't exactly ideal for doing so.

In Janey and David's room there was a much better full-length mirror which could be angled. Lucianna glanced doubtfully at the high-heeled sandals she was wearing. So far she had only walked across her own bedroom floor in them—and had felt as vulnerable and awkward as a newborn colt.

Taking a deep breath, she reminded herself that sooner or later she was going to have to appear in them in public, so the sooner she learned to walk properly in them the better, and since she could hardly service her customers' cars wearing them she had better make use of every chance she got to practise.

After all, there was no one around to witness her ineptitude, nor her shy awareness of how very different she looked and felt, nor how very much more aware of herself, her body, her womanliness, she suddenly was.

She started to walk tentatively towards the bedroom door.

The business meeting he had been called to in Paris so unexpectedly to attend had proved rather more fraught than Jake had anticipated but, in the end, he had had his way—but not before he had had to argue his point with some force. Along with the estate, he had inherited a considerable portfolio of stocks and shares to which he had, over the years, added other investments of his own, latterly moving into the area of helping others to set up their own small businesses and taking not just a financial but also a managerial interest in those businesses.

It was a high-risk enterprise and one which required steady nerves as well as a good deal of patience and faith in one's own judgement, and Jake's trust in his own judgement had been sorely tested of late.

There had been a delay at Charles de Gaulle and it had been a hot day; he was glad to be free of the stale, fume-filled air of the motorway but the drive home was not giving him its usual sense of release and pleasure. He turned off the main road and into the lane that led both to the farm and then on to his own home; he automatically checked his speed as he drove past the turn-off for the farm and then, instead of accelerating, for some reason he wasn't prepared to analyse, he braked instead.

Braked, stopped, reversed, and then finally took the side turning for the farm.

A little uncertainly at first, then with increasing confidence as she got used to the height of them, Lucianna walked up and down the landing in her new, delicate, high-heeled sandals. It certainly felt most peculiar, but not in the least unpleasantly so.

She frowned a little critically as she caught sight of her unvarnished toenails. The stockings she was wearing were completely sheer, designed to be worn, if necessary, with open-toed shoes, and it seemed now to Lucianna that a pretty but discreet application of a soft shiny colour to her toenails would complement both her shoes and the sheer delicacy of her stockings, rather in the same way that she would have advised a customer that those all-important touches such as keeping the bodywork of their cars clean and polished were also part and parcel of keeping their vehicles in good working order.

Now that she had mastered the art of walking in her new shoes—well, sort of—it was time to venture into David and Janey's room and study her reflection in their mirror.

Once she was inside their room, though, Lucianna found she was having great difficulty in bringing herself to look at what she was wearing. Her heart had started to beat very fast and she was conscious of a mixture of apprehension and nervous excitement churning in her stomach.

Unsteadily, she turned her head in the direction of the mirror and then tensed in shock. Was that really her? That unexpectedly tall, long-legged creature—long-legged woman? she corrected herself shakily. And those curves…that tiny waist, those softly rounded breasts; where had they come from? She didn't normally make a habit of studying her own naked body but surely she would have known, noticed, if her body was really as sensual, as womanly as its mirror image now reflected? Was it the soft light of David and Janey's bedroom that gave her skin its satiny sheen?

Hesitantly, Lucianna touched the smooth swell of her breast above the dainty cup of her bra and then flushed. She looked so different, so… Peeping over her shoulder, she glanced uncertainly at her neatly curved and very provocatively rounded rear.

Totally absorbed in what she was seeing, she didn't hear Jake drive into the yard and stop the engine of his car.

The lights were on in the farmhouse kitchen and upstairs as well and, out of habit, Jake merely knocked briefly on the unlocked kitchen door before pushing it open and walking in. After all, he had been a regular visitor here at the farmhouse from boyhood and had long ago been instructed by David and Janey that he was not to stand on ceremony, that so far as they were concerned he was virtually an adopted member of the family.

The fact that there wasn't anyone in the kitchen wasn't particularly unusual; it was too early in the evening for David and Janey to have gone to bed, and since he had noticed as he'd driven up that their bedroom lights were on he opened the kitchen door and stepped into the hall, intending to call up to warn them of his arrival, but, before he could do so, their bedroom door opened.

The uncertainty in Lucianna's movements as she opened David and Janey's bedroom door and stepped out onto the landing wasn't due as much to her unfamiliar footwear as to her unfamiliar self.

If the reflection of herself she had seen in the dress shop earlier in the week had surprised and pleased her that was nothing to the emotions she had experienced just now. Her reflection might have unnerved her somewhat but there was no doubting its femininity…its sexuality…*her* femininity and sexuality. She paused in the open doorway, arching her neck, standing proudly, a small, secret smile curling her mouth.

Let Jake try telling her now that she needed to look to others to learn how to be a woman; that she needed to adopt their body language in order to make John appreciate her.

Suddenly, and for the first time in her life, Lucianna knew how it felt to be proud of her womanhood, of her body, and it showed in the way she held herself and moved as she started to walk towards her own room.

And how it showed!

Initially, standing in the hallway below her, Jake simply couldn't believe his eyes—or rather his brain was having difficulty in accepting that what he saw, *who* he saw, was Lucianna. His body was experiencing no such problems. *It* had recognised her straight away, recognised her, known her, reacted to her and was still reacting to her, and suddenly all the emotions he had been fighting to control for what, right now, felt like more than half his lifetime, exploded in a self-igniting flash of feral anger that caused him to take the stairs two at a time, blocking off Lucianna's access to her bedroom with his body as he demanded furiously, 'Lucianna…what the hell do you think you're playing at?'

To say she was shocked didn't begin to go anywhere near describing Lucianna's feelings.

The totally unexpected sight of Jake coupled with the intensity of his anger would have been enough to put her on the defensive at the best of times, but to be confronted by it and by him in her present state of undress… It would have been bad enough to have been surprised by anyone, even to be faced by Janey, just at the moment. The only reason she had found the courage to do what she had just done, to try on her new underwear and... Well, the only reason she had done what she had was that she had been secure in the knowledge that she had the house completely to herself.

And if anyone had asked her who the last person, the very last person was whom she would have wanted to see her like this she would immediately have said Jake. And yet here he was, looking at her with such savagery, such fury that...

'Where is he?' she heard Jake demanding furiously as he reached out to constrain her, to grab hold of her wrist, preventing her from fleeing, retreating back into David and Janey's bedroom.

'He...? What he?' Lucianna queried in bewilderment as she tried to prise his fingers free of her wrist.

'What he? The one you've dressed yourself up like that for of course,' Jake told her bitingly. 'And don't tell me there is no "he", Lucianna, because I won't believe you.' His eyes scanned her body, causing her face to burn a hot, embarrassed dark pink and then her whole body to become scorched with the same colour. She suddenly realised that for some totally unfathomable reason her nipples beneath the delicate fabric of her new bra had hardened and were now quite clearly visible in all their pouting provocation, and Jake had seen them; that much was clear from the way he turned his head and looked so intently at her body.

Instinctively, she placed her free arm across her breasts, her eyes flashing daggers of embarrassed fury at him.

'It's a bit late for that,' Jake told her scathingly. 'You might as well be stark naked—you damn well nearly are.'

'I am *not*,' Lucianna denied. 'I'm wearing the new underwear *you* told me to buy,' she defended herself bravely.

'*I* told you to buy?' Jake checked himself and frowned. 'Don't try to tell me you bought this stuff you're wearing—this…these—because of me,' he told her bitingly.

'Why not?' Lucianna challenged him recklessly. 'It's the truth; you were the one—'

Abruptly she stopped speaking, her face going bright scarlet as she realised what she had been about to say, what she couldn't possibly say, and that was that five minutes ago, standing in front of her brother and sister-in-law's bedroom mirror, although it might have been John's reaction to her transformation and her shy realisation of her own sexuality she had first of all been thinking about, to her chagrin, it had been Jake's voice, Jake's face, Jake's reaction she had instinctively pictured.

Just for those few heart-stopping and instantly rejected heartbeats of time it had been Jake's hands, Jake's mouth, Jake's touch she had emotionally imagined caressing her near-naked body. To her horror, even as she fought back the treacherous memory of those few fatal seconds, her body was already wilfully reacting to it, her nipples flouting her fervent plea to them not to betray her, whilst deep down inside her body…

'So you dressed like this because of *me*?' she heard Jake demanding grittily and disbelievingly, releasing her wrist abruptly as he added with a growl, 'Lucianna…'

But as she turned in instinctive response to the harsh command in his voice suddenly his expression changed completely, his hand reaching out towards her again but not this time to restrain her in the old, familiar critical grip he had used on her since her childhood, but, far more dangerously, to gently cup the soft swell of her breast. His thumb caressed the naked flesh above the low-cut cup of her new bra, caressing it and, Lucianna recognised dizzily, edging the fabric even lower so that she could quite clearly see the flushed dusky pink flesh surrounding her nipple and, even more disturbing, feel the urgent pulse of her nipple itself, as though it were silently urging Jake to pull away the fabric altogether.

'*Because* of me?' she heard Jake repeating in a very different voice from the one he had used earlier, a voice which held an unfamiliar, faintly rusty but wholly male message of urgency and arousal. 'Or *for* me?'

For him…? Lucianna opened her mouth to deny any such thing, heard Jake say her name in an excitingly harsh voice she had most certainly never heard him use before, and automatically and instinctively took the small provocative step, the fatal step forward that closed the minute distance between them, her body swaying provocatively, unsteadily, as she tried to balance on her new shoes, throwing her forward against him.

'Oh, God,' she heard Jake mutter under his breath, 'I must be crazy doing this.'

Doing what? she tried to ask, but found she couldn't say a single thing, for the very simple reason that Jake's mouth was now covering hers and silencing every sound she tried to make, including her small shocked squeak of protest.

Later she would try to tell herself that it must have

been the new shoes that caused her to feel so dizzy, just as it must have been the fact that she was only wearing her underwear that made her shiver and draw closer to the warmth of Jake's fully clothed body—fully clothed maybe, but she was not so naive that she couldn't recognise the surging hardness of his body as she pressed her own against him and then pressed herself against him again, carried away by the novel discovery that what she had read in her books had quite patently been correct and that men were responsive to a woman's body language.

Lost in the heady awareness of the power of her sensuality, she was dimly aware of Jake groaning hoarsely as he cupped her face with both hands, but it was only when she felt the urgent thrust of his tongue within the vulnerable cavity of her own mouth that she recognised just what her innocent experimentation had done. By then…by then, inexplicably, all she really wanted to do, all she could actually *think* of doing, was to wrap her arms around Jake just as tightly as she could whilst her senses spun under the sensual assault of his kiss.

When he finally paused to lick the outline of her mouth with the tip of his tongue and command, 'Kiss me back,' it seemed to be the most natural, the most *essential* thing in the world to do just as he had asked, tentatively at first and then with more assurance as she discovered the heady delight of exploring the moist heat of his own mouth with the darting, uncertain tip of her tongue.

But it was when he captured it, held it prisoner and slowly, delicately sucked on it that she finally realised how out of her depth she was and in what dangerous waters—waters in which the only thing she had to cling to, in which her only safety and security lay in trusting herself completely to Jake and letting him take the responsibility for her.

She opened the heavy-lidded eyes she had closed, trembling in his arms as he traced her swollen mouth with his fingertip. He told her huskily, as she shuddered under the sensual caress, her mouth unbelievably sensitive to his touch, 'If that's how you react to being kissed, I can just imagine how you're going to feel when it's your breasts, your nipples—you—that I'm sucking and kissing…'

Lucianna couldn't help it; she felt the shock of his words rip right through her body in a convulsive surge of sensual need and surrender, and without even realising what she was doing she heard herself moaning his name whilst her hands went to her breasts—whether to conceal them or tear away the fabric that covered them, to show him just what effect his words were having on her, she didn't really know; but Jake, it seemed, did, and the cool rush of air that preceded the hard warmth of his hands holding her naked breasts as he pulled away her bra only seemed to increase the hot, spiralling ache pulsing through her whole body.

Jake was kissing the side of her neck whilst his hands caressed her breasts, his mouth, hot and hungry, scorching her naked skin, and yet instead of feeling shocked she actually seemed to be welcoming it, wanting it.

Lucianna heard herself moan again as her body ached against Jake's hands, the rough pads of his thumbs moving against her nipples sending her into a frenzy of taut, aching need and unbelievably intense longing to feel his mouth against her body, caressing her in the way that he had so shockingly described to her.

'Yes…what is it? What is it you want?' she heard him demanding rawly in response to the impassioned plea she hadn't realised she had uttered. And it seemed the most natural thing in the world to tell him, in the sobbing, agonised voice she could barely recognise as her own, 'I want you to do what you said…to kiss me…suck me here,' she told him, putting her own hand where his covered her breast.

Later Jake was to tell himself that if it hadn't been for that, if it hadn't been for the way both her voice and her body had trembled as she'd looked at him with all her newly aroused womanhood in her eyes, he might have been able to stop, to take control of himself and the situation; but he knew he was lying. What was happening had been inevitable, not just from the heart-stopping moment when he had seen her standing there, but from the very first moment he had realised how much he wanted her, how much he loved her.

That, though, was later. Right now, as he felt her hand tremble slightly over his and her body tremble even more, he ruthlessly ignored the stern voice of caution warning him that what was happening must stop, and instead bent to take Lucianna's full weight as he swung her up into his arms. He then walked purposefully towards her bedroom, pausing in the doorway to lower his head and gently nuzzle the exposed peak of one breast with his mouth.

Lucianna felt as though she was going to die from the sheer intensity of the sensation that swamped her as Jake's mouth opened gently over the aching tip of her breast. She had never dreamed there could be such a sensation, such a boiling, turbulent sense of aching need, such a compulsion to lock her fingers in Jake's hair and keep his head, his mouth just exactly where it was.

Her reaction was too much for Jake; the gentle nuzzle became a deep, slow suckle and then an urgent, tugging demand that turned Lucianna's body to a boneless, melting ache of complicity in his arms and made Jake himself shudder from head to foot, his body drenched in a musky, male-scented film of sexually aroused perspiration.

'Do you know what you're doing to me?' he asked Lucianna rawly. 'Do you know what you're making me want to do to you?'

'Show me,' Lucianna urged him in response. 'Show me, tell me…teach me, Jake.'

The look she gave him to accompany her words as she gazed limply and longingly into his eyes was pure feminine seduction and Jake had no defences against it.

'Luce…' he protested hoarsely. 'I…'

'Take off your clothes, Jake,' Lucianna whispered to him. 'I want to see you—all of you,' she told him pleadingly, her face and then her whole body suffused by a tell-tale rosy glow as it reflected her inner shock at her vocal boldness, even if the words she had spoken were the truth and did reflect the longing, the need that was pulsing through her.

Just for a moment Jake hesitated, and then he saw the way she looked at him and the way her mouth trembled.

Very gently he laid her down on the bed, and then,

slowly, he started to remove his own clothes, keeping his glance locked on hers, ready to register the first millisecond that her expression changed, that she betrayed any desire to change her mind.

It never came, and when Jake's hand stilled over the belt of his chinos Lucianna couldn't quite prevent herself from giving a small feminine sound of protest and demand.

She had seen Jake's body before, of course—well, most of it at any rate. As a child she had swum uninhibited with her brothers and Jake in the river that ran through both their properties, and it had only been after her disastrous experiment with her sexuality as a young teenager that she had become reluctant to join the others when they went swimming.

But she had seen Jake working in the field often enough with David, stripped to the waist, wearing an old, faded pair of shorts, and she knew already the broad outline of his torso with its soft covering of dark hair, although she had never before experienced this urge to reach out and touch it…touch him, to bury her fingertips, her *mouth* in its male softness and nuzzle the flesh it covered. And she had most certainly never before experienced this dangerous, heart-stopping, breath-stealing sense of aching sensual excitement and urgency as she waited for him to remove the rest of his clothes. The sexuality of a man's body had never been something that had caused her any missed heartbeats in the past, and it had certainly never caused her to feel the way she was feeling right now.

As he removed the last of his clothes, Jake turned slightly away from her, but immediately Lucianna put out her hand to stop him, her eyes betraying her emotions when he obeyed her silent demand and slid them away from his body, allowing her to see the full maleness of him.

He heard her swiftly indrawn breath, saw the way her eyes widened, almost felt the compulsive shudder that gripped her body, but it was too late now to hide himself from her, and for some reason her soft, slightly shocked but totally awed 'Jake' caused a sharp flare of anger within himself and against himself that manifested itself in an unintentionally harsh retort.

'What is it? What's wrong? You've seen a man before, haven't you?'

'Not one like you,' Lucianna told him honestly, her voice wobbling slightly. 'Not like this!'

'Oh, Luce....' Jake said, torn between laughter and the sharp unexpectedness of tears as he reached out to take her in his arms and hold her comfortingly. He told her gruffly, 'You're not supposed to say things like that to a man. It gives us too big an ego,' he explained, and then added with wry self-mockery, 'Never mind what it does to us physically...'

'Physically?' Lucianna asked him puzzled.

'I want you,' he told her frankly, framing her face in his hands, 'but you've never had a man before...and...'

Instantly Lucianna took umbrage.

'How do you know that?' she demanded.

'You told me...or as good as,' Jake told her dryly. And besides, he added silently, how could he tell her that everything about the way she was responding to him, unaware of just how strongly she was affecting him, pointed to her lack of sexual experience? But the man she really wanted wasn't him, and he knew that even if she, no doubt caught up in the powerful flood of her discovery of her own sexuality, seemed to have momentarily forgotten it.

Lucianna looked at him.

'But I want one now,' she told him truthfully. 'I want you, Jake.' And before he could stop her she leaned forward and touched his body, touched *him*, her fingertips as delicate as a butterfly's wing against his tautly aching flesh but as destructive to his self-control as a sledgehammer.

He heard himself groan, wanted to draw back from her, and yet, as though a part of himself were standing outside himself watching him, powerless to control him or what was happening, he reached out for her, kissing her mouth gently and then less gently. He caressed her body with his hands as he slowly removed the remainder of her underwear, following each caress with a string of delicate kisses which, in Lucianna's now fevered imagination, wove a covering for her as airy and delicate as a cobweb and yet at the same time was as fiery as though he had encased her whole body in a sheet of burning desire.

As she felt him circle her navel with the tip of his tongue, she cried out tormentedly to him, instinctively arching her body, offering it…offering *herself* to him in the age-old, timeless language of feminine desire.

Jake trembled as he gripped her hips with his hands and tried to still her sensual writhing, as unsuccessfully as he tried to subdue his own response to it. And when he felt her innocently fighting against his constraint and trying to open her legs in pleading invitation he knew there was no way he could resist her any longer.

His body ached for the sweet, feminine warmth of

hers so much that he was already shuddering under the impact of trying to control it, and as for the *emotional* impact she was having on him…

It was no good; what was to happen was inevitable, as inevitable as night following day, moon following sun, but first…

Her eyes closed, her hands balled into small, hard fists of agonised need as she cried out against the strictures of aching desperation that possessed her, Lucianna had no awareness of what he intended to do until she felt his hands on her thighs and then the softness of his hair against her skin. And by then it was too late…too late to be shocked by the intimacy of the caresses he was bestowing on her, too late to even think about trying to stop him, and certainly too late to stop her body's sweetly voluptuous, ecstatic response to the touch of his lips, his mouth, his tongue, caressing first her belly and her thighs and then the most intimate, hidden, secret part of her.

The sensation building inside her was so unfamiliar to her, so overpowering and unfamiliar, that she instinctively cried out Jake's name, but by the time he realised what was happening to her it was too late; the sharp, pulsing contractions of her orgasm were already convulsing her.

The shock of experiencing so much intense emotional and physical sensation was too much for Lucianna to bear, and her body started to tremble, her eyes filling with hot tears.

Instinctively, Jake reached out to take her in his arms and soothe her in much the same way he had soothed her when she had been a small child, holding her close, rocking her gently, brushing away her tears.

'What—?' Lucianna started to ask him tearfully, but then stopped.

'You've had an orgasm,' Jake told her.

'I know that,' Lucianna informed him indignantly glowering at him as she saw the way he was looking at her. Didn't he think she knew *anything*...?

'Good...then you'll be able to recognise your second one, won't you?' Jake challenged her softly, and before Lucianna opened her mouth to protest he covered it with his own and started to kiss her. He whispered to her thickly, 'That was nothing... Just wait...you'll see.'

'I don't want to...' Lucianna told him truculently, and then, surprisingly, discovered that, on the contrary, she most certainly did; she wanted to very, very much indeed. And within a very short space of time she was telling Jake just how much she wanted to...just how much she wanted *him*, all of him, deep, deep inside her, moving in her the way he was doing right now, carrying her with him with every powerful thrust to that special magical place she had so recently discovered, that place, as she cried out to him, she so desperately needed. Only *he* could take her.

As she cried out his name Jake reached his own climax, and as he felt the pulse of his orgasm within her Lucianna was dizzily aware of just how pleasurable that small betraying pulse was, of how much her body enjoyed the feel of it, of him, within her. Drowsily she snuggled deeper into his arms.

Carefully Jake smoothed the duvet over Lucianna's still sleeping body. He had already picked up her discarded clothes and carefully folded them before dressing himself and now it was time to go before

Lucianna herself woke up and realised just how much he had betrayed the trust she had placed in him.

Jake was under no illusions. The intensity of her sexual response to him had been activated simply by her discovery of her own femininity and had nothing whatsoever to do with any desire for *him*. How could it when he already knew she believed she was in love with John?

It would have been easy, in the aftermath of their shared intimacy, to use his own experience and her lack of it to convince her that her response to him meant that she cared for him—*loved* him—and God knew he had been tempted, sorely tempted. But how could he have lived with himself if he had done so? He couldn't have. He couldn't steal from her her right to own her own sexuality and her own emotions.

To him, loving her meant allowing her the freedom to be her own woman, and to make her own choices. But it would be a long time, a hell of a long time—if ever—before he could blot out of his dreams the sweet scent and feel of her, the warmth and softness of her, the sound of her ecstatic cries as she reached her orgasm, the small keening sounds of urgency and need she had made in her desire for him. A long time? He would *never* forget. *Never.* Broodingly, he gave her sleeping form one last look before finally turning to leave.

CHAPTER EIGHT

'LUCE, are you all right?'

Lucianna jumped and then flushed, gnawing anxiously on her bottom lip and avoiding meeting Janey's kind, concerned eyes as she lied, 'Yes. Yes, I'm fine.'

'You haven't forgotten that Jake is expecting you to go over there this morning, have you?' David asked her, stressing, 'When he rang earlier he said it was very important that he saw you.'

'No, I haven't forgotten,' Lucianna said hollowly. Forgotten? How could she when…? But right now she dared not even let herself think of all the reasons why she could not possibly forget and *what* she could not forget, not when she knew the tell-tale signs of her own thoughts would be clearly visible in her eyes and on her flushed skin for her astute sister-in-law to see.

She had been woken from the deepest sleep she could remember having in a long time by her family's late arrival home, and at first, still sleepy and confused, she had instinctively turned to the side of the bed where Jake had lain as he'd held her in the aftermath of…of what had happened. But of course Jake had not been there, although her knowledge of what had happened between them had, and abruptly she had come wide awake, her thoughts and emotions chasing one another in frantic unending circles as she'd tried to make sense of not merely what she had done but also what she had said, blush-making though her increasingly cringingly clear memories were. She remembered calling out to Jake to touch her, hold her, imploring him to possess her and, most shocking of all, begging him to… But, far more importantly, she'd tried to make sense of how she had felt and why.

Surely it wasn't possible for the simple act of changing her normal sensible underwear for something much more provocative and sensual to have caused the kind of total personality change she felt she must have undergone to have acted as she had—and with *Jake* of all people?

Not even with John had she ever… She swallowed nauseously on the stomach-churning emotions as she heard Janey asking her again, 'Are you *sure* you're all right? You look awfully pale…'

'I…I do feel a little bit queasy,' Lucianna was forced to admit, adding uncomfortably, 'I think it must have been the fish pie I ate for supper…'

Janey was really frowning now.

'Do you? Well, in that case I'd better throw out what's left…'

'I think I'll go outside and get some fresh air,' Lucianna told her sister-in-law, guiltily aware that the reason for her malaise had nothing to do with Janey's fish pie.

Once outside she walked towards her workshop but made no attempt to so much as even glance at the car she was supposed to be working on.

How could she have been so overwhelmed by passion…by need…by desire that she had…that she had *wanted*…? She swallowed nervously, recalling the panic she had first experienced last night when she'd realised that Jake wasn't there in bed beside her and that she had actually expected and *wanted* him to be…and had *still* wanted him to be this morning.

Her thoughts and emotions were totally confused and frighteningly complex as well. She longed to have someone she could discuss them with, someone she could turn to for help and advice, someone who could help her to unravel the disturbing tangle of her emotions and to reassure her that what had happened, what she had done, did not mean… Lucianna swallowed painfully. Did not mean what?

The needs, the desire, the emotions she had experienced last night, and their intensity, were things she had always expected only to feel with and for a man with whom she was deeply and compellingly in love and who loved her back just as intensely. But the man she had ached for, hungered for, wanted with every single fibre and particle of her body hadn't been John, the man she believed she loved, but *Jake*… Jake…whom she'd never, in her most remotest, wildest dreams or imaginings, had fantasies about, thought of as…

But no, that wasn't quite true, was it? Hurriedly Lucianna opened the bonnet of the car she was supposed to be working on, desperate to avoid the mental confrontation her thoughts were dragging her towards but knowing there was no way she could avoid the collision course she was on.

Her own moral code would not allow her to lie to herself. No, not even for her own self-protection. There had been times recently—brief, startling and shockingly explicit milliseconds of time—when she *had* experienced some very unfamiliar and disturbing sensations when she was in Jake's company, and some even more unfamiliar and disturbing emotions, accompanied by mental images she was blushing to recall now, just as much as she had blushed to remember what had occurred last night when she had first opened her eyes and known what had taken place.

She stiffened as she heard the kitchen door open on the other side of the yard and saw David striding towards her. She knew what he was going to say. He was going to remind her again that Jake wanted to see her.

Her fingers fumbled with the catch of the bonnet as she released it, causing the metal to crash down on her fingers before she had time to snatch them away. The skin wasn't broken but she would definitely bear the bruises of her carelessness for several days, she recognised as she instinctively sucked her sore flesh.

And then she remembered just how Jake had sucked on her vulnerable and responsive body last night, and how it had felt—how she had felt—and by the time David reached her her whole body was burning with the shocked heat of her own thoughts. Not because she now thoroughly rejected and regretted what had taken place, but because…because…

'You do know that Jake wants you to go over to the Hall *this morning*, don't you?' he asked her predictably.

'Yes, I know.' Lucianna knew she was stumbling over the words in her vulnerable emotional state, the colour coming and going in her face.

It was no use trying to delude herself any longer. She *couldn't* have experienced what she had last night—felt how she had last night, done what she had done last night—without at least feeling *something* for Jake, even if it was very difficult for her now, in the harsh light of day, to reconcile those feelings, those needs with the resentment and, yes, even animosity she had previously believed she felt for him.

Recognising that her mind simply wasn't on her work, and that if she didn't want David chasing her tail all day she would be better off simply giving in and going to see Jake, she automatically wiped her hands on a soft rag, wincing at the pain in her swollen fingers, and then headed for the house to get showered and changed.

Abruptly she stopped. Showered and changed...? What was wrong with going round to see Jake dressed as she presently was? After all, she had done so before on countless occasions. Why was this time different? Why did she feel this sudden need to have Jake see her looking her best?

Shyly and uncertainly Lucianna studied her reflection in her bedroom mirror. Her hair gleamed silkily down onto her shoulders, the make-up she had so painstakingly applied brought out the colour of her eyes and the purity of her skin, the lipstick...

She started to reach for a tissue to wipe it off and then stopped herself. The salesgirl had, after all, assured her that the soft colour was perfectly suitable for *any*time wear. It was just perhaps that she wasn't used to seeing it on her mouth and certainly it seemed to make her lips look much fuller, almost slightly swollen, or was that because...? Her hand was trembling as she put the unused tissue down.

Half of her dreaded the thought of seeing Jake but the other half... Her heart skipped a beat and then another. Could it be possible, could she somehow or other, without knowing it had happened, actually have fallen in love with Jake? And was that why...? Jake would know, she comforted herself automatically. Jake would understand...explain... Jake would...

A hot pink film of colour flooded her face as she realised just where her wanton thoughts were taking her. Jake would what? Jake would take her in his arms, kiss her senseless and then…

Suddenly the jeans and tee shirt she was wearing seemed far too heavy and hot. Suddenly her whole body was aching in very much the same way that it had ached last night. Suddenly…

Suddenly she couldn't wait to see Jake, to be with him, to be reassured by him, to have him help her to understand and come to terms with the shock of what had happened.

Jake… He would, she knew, know just how she was feeling, just how shy and uncertain she was…just how much she needed his understanding…his…his love!

Jake frowned as he tried to focus his attention on the work on his desk. His head ached and his eyes felt gritty—no doubt from his lack of sleep last night, but how on earth could he have slept after what had happened? What had Lucianna thought, felt, when she woke up this morning? Did she hate him even more than ever now or…?

Of course she must. Why did he need to ask himself that question? The fact that he loved her was no excuse for the way he had lost his head, not to himself and certainly not to her, and yet lying awake in his own bed last night, thinking about her, remembering how she had felt in his arms, how she had *been* in his arms, remembering the warmth of her, the sheer *essence* of her, a part of him that was unashamedly and wholly male could not totally regret what had happened.

He could not regret either that he had been the first one, the only one, to hear her cries of ecstatic pleasure, to hear her unguarded, untutored words of female arousal, and he knew that, whilst she might not have loved him, last night, for a small space of time, she had been wholly his to love and cherish, his to show the true depths of her own passion and needs as well as his own, his to hold, to cherish…to love…

But this morning, in the cold light of day, he had had to face reality—and her—and so he had rung David and asked David to make sure that she came to see him. What he had to say to her required privacy for them both, and time—time for him to make sure that she listened and fully understood that no part of what had happened between them was in any way *her* responsibility. That burden at least he could release her from. Under other circumstances and in a different relationship with another woman he might have been impelled to ask why, when she claimed to love another man so deeply, she had responded so intensely, so intuitively, so *instinctively* to him, but he suspected he already knew the answer and that was quite simply that Lucianna had responded to him because he had been there, because he had overpowered her, overwhelmed her with his own sexuality and his own needs.

Jake frowned as he saw an unfamiliar Toyota car draw up in front of the house. Turning away from the study window, he went to the front door, wondering if perhaps Lucianna was driving one of her customer's cars. The young woman emerging from the car was vaguely familiar to him and her body language rather more so, although he didn't betray by as much as a single glance that he was aware of the delicate provocation of the way his visitor was walking towards him, nor the way she paused to smooth her completely wrinkle-free skirt down over her thighs, giving him a long, slow smile as she did so.

'I'm sorry,' she apologised as she got within earshot of him. 'I know you won't remember me. I'm a friend of Lucianna's, Felicity Hammond; we met in town a couple of weeks ago.' She tossed her hair and smiled at him again.

'I've just called at the farm but Lucianna wasn't there and I wondered if you could possibly pass on a message to her for me. I wouldn't ask but it is rather urgent. John, her boyfriend, faxed us this morning—I work in the same office—to say that he is coming home earlier than planned… I knew Lucianna would want to know. He's obviously been missing her as much as she's been missing him…'

She paused and glanced towards the door which Jake had pulled closed behind him.

'This is a wonderful house,' she told him appreciatively. 'I'd love to see more of it…'

'We don't hold open days, I'm afraid,' Jake told her impassively, and then added courteously, 'I shall certainly see Lucianna gets your message but now, if you'll excuse me, I'm afraid I'm rather busy…'

As he turned away Jake guessed that the unflattering flush burning her face owed more to anger than embarrassment. He wasn't averse to women taking the initiative—far from it—and the reason he had taken such an intense dislike to her was not so much because of that but because she was the bearer of news he simply didn't want to hear, he derided himself as he firmly closed the door behind himself, leaving her standing in the driveway.

So, John had missed Lucianna, had he? Well, it was a pity that he hadn't appreciated her a little more when he had had the chance, Jake thought. And no doubt Lucianna would be thrilled to hear the news about his imminent return even if he wasn't.

Would she tell John what had happened between them, and if she did would he…? For her own sake he would have to caution her not to do so, Jake told himself sternly. In fact, he would have to caution her not to tell anyone, he acknowledged, feeling fiercely aware of his need to protect her from the judgement of others.

Lucianna saw the Toyota emerging from the drive to Jake's house just as she signalled to turn into it, and recognised both it and its driver immediately. She saw Felicity toss her head and give her a taunting smile, as though… Her whole body stiffening, Lucianna could feel her face starting to burn with the same heat that was savaging her emotions like acid.

The drive to Jake's house wasn't excessively long but it was certainly long enough for Lucianna to recognise immediately and pinpoint the cause of the searing, tearing spasm of anguished fury that had seized her the moment she'd seen the other girl.

She was jealous…jealous of the fact that another girl, another woman, had been with Jake…far more jealous than she had ever been when that same girl had flirted so outrageously in front of her with John.

And she was jealous because…because she and Jake had been lovers? Because she…because she…?

Jake heard the gears on Lucianna's car crashing as her car catapulted to an ungainly stop, its wheels spurting up gravel, its driver shooting from her seat, her eyes flashing, her small hands balled into tight fists as he ran down the steps towards her.

'What was *she* doing here?' Lucianna demanded furiously, not giving Jake time to reply before she added, 'Not that I can't guess.'

Lucianna could barely see Jake for the hot tears stinging her eyes—tears almost as hot as the bitter, corrosive jealousy flooding her body and fuelled by an aching sense of loss and emptiness, coupled with a sick, shocked feeling of agonising despair.

'She came to leave a message for you. Apparently John's coming back earlier than expected.'

'She…? John's coming back…?'

Lucianna's skin turned white and then red, the hot lava flow of her jealousy chilled by the sudden recognition of the appalling way she was behaving, of the feeling she was in danger of betraying, but Jake, seeing that rapid change of colour and the consternation that darkened her eyes, immediately leapt to the conclusion that they were caused by a sense of fear and guilt.

'Come inside,' he instructed Lucianna tersely. 'We need to talk and we can't do so out here.'

'I want—' Lucianna began, but Jake overruled her, opening the door and telling her harshly,

'Oh, I can well imagine what you want, Lucianna, but I'm afraid it just isn't possible for me to give it to you, so…'

He heard her gasp quite clearly over the three yards or so that separated them but luckily, from Lucianna's point of view, she managed to drop her eyelids in defensive protection before he could see the tortured misery in her eyes.

She wanted to tell him that he couldn't be more

wrong and that his cruelty was completely unnecessary. She had not come here intending to tell him that she loved him nor to beg him to love her in return. She had too much pride for *that*, even if… And if he thought for one moment that just because last night…that she might want…that she was here…

'*You* were the one who wanted to see *me*,' she managed to remind him as she followed him reluctantly into the house, not needing any guidance or direction to turn off the elegant rectangular hallway—with its pretty Regency decor and the marble busts of Jake's ancestors which had been commissioned by his great-great-grandfather adorning the shell-backed niches in which they were sited—into the small library which was Jake's favourite room.

For once Lucianna did not sniff the air of the room appreciatively, breathing in the scent of old leather and wood, neither did she pause to admire the wonderfully crafted mahogany furniture as she drew in the ambience of the room and briefly envied Jake such a wonderful home.

'What exactly did you want to see me about?' she demanded instead, deliberately avoiding looking at Jake as she asked the question to which she suspected she already knew the answer.

Jake, it seemed, was equally unimpressed.

'I shouldn't have thought you'd need to ask. *Do* you really need to ask?' he challenged her tersely. 'Last night—'

'Last night was nothing,' Lucianna interrupted him hurriedly, still avoiding looking at him and so missing the look of stark pain that crossed his face as he listened to her.

'Nothing to *you*, perhaps,' he agreed quickly once he had himself back under control.

'And nothing to *you* either,' Lucianna cried out, unable to hold back the words—words which Jake incorrectly interpreted as a plea from her to be reassured that it had *not* meant anything to him, that he was *not* going to embarrass her with his unwanted protestations of love.

And so, bowing his head, he continued brusquely, 'Nothing to either of us, maybe, but to others… I think it might be a wise and sensible course of action if what happened between us last night remained exactly that—between us…'

Now Lucianna *did* look at him.

'You mean you don't want anyone to know?' she demanded scornfully.

'Do you?' Jake argued back angrily, and then pushed his fingers into his hair. 'It isn't a matter of what *I* might or might not want people to know, Lucianna. It's *you* I'm thinking of. Your John will soon be home and the last thing he's going to want to hear is that you… I'm telling you this for your own sake and not…

'After all, the whole point of everything you've done…we've done,' Jake told her doggedly, 'has been to help your relationship with John…'

'Is *that* why you took me to bed and made love to me?' Lucianna cried, unable to endure any more. 'Because it would help me to make John *love* me?

'I hate you, Jake,' she told him passionately. 'I hate you more than I've ever hated anyone else in my whole life…'

And before Jake could stop her she ran out of the

room, pulling open the front door and flinging herself back into her car.

'Lucianna,' Jake protested, but she had already got the engine started and short of dragging her out of the vehicle and forcibly manhandling her back into the house Jake knew he had no option other than to let her go.

He had been right to dread Lucianna's reaction to last night and more than right to guess that she would blame him; that she would be distraught with guilt and despair over what to her would be a betrayal of the love she believed she felt for John. But he'd been wrong, it seemed, to think he could talk to her about it—help her, reassure her.

Halfway back to the farm Lucianna suddenly pulled up and stopped the car. There was no way she could return home looking and feeling as she did right now.

Dry-eyed, she stared unseeingly into the distance. What she felt hurt too much for tears. What she felt right now went so deep into her heart and body that she knew the pain would never ease, that she would *never* get over Jake's rejection of her, that she loved him so much, that…

Lucianna's teeth chattered as her body shuddered under the uncontrollable waves of pain that struck her. She loved Jake and suddenly, like someone whose vision had previously been blurred and distorted without them being aware of it, now that she had the benefit of true clarity, real vision, she could see and understand how shallow and childish, how laughable in so many ways the love she had claimed she had had for John had actually been.

She hadn't loved John at all, *didn't* love him at

all... What she had *loved* had been the idea of being in love, of being loved in return, and she had imagined love between a man and a woman as something gentle and passive, something that would be a comfortable, simple part of her life without really touching her or changing her.

She couldn't have been more wrong. Love wasn't like that at all; love wasn't sweet and gentle, easily malleable, allowing itself to be manipulated and set neatly into the controlled framework of one's life.

This love, *her* love, was a tumultuous force, an overpowering, overwhelming surge of emotion and need that affected every single part of her life and every single particle of *her*. Love was pain and despair, a helpless sense of longing and need, an endless grieving for what she could never have, the *person* she could never have.

Love was...Jake.

But Jake didn't love her. Jake didn't want...Jake didn't need her. He didn't even particularly like her. He hadn't been able to wait to remind her that John was her boyfriend.

John. Lucianna frowned as she tried to summon up a mental image of him and discovered that she couldn't, that his features simply refused to form, that behind her tightly closed eyelids the only features which would form were those belonging to Jake.

Jake frowned as he watched Lucianna's car disappear in a cloud of dust. She was an exceptionally good driver and very little other traffic used the quiet country lane which linked his home to the farm, but even so, in her present mood, she was all too likely...

He reached into his pocket for his own car keys

and had just got to the door when the telephone rang. For a moment he was tempted to ignore it but he knew it would be the call he had been expecting regarding a joint venture he had recently entered into and which hopefully, if necessary, would bring the estate some valuable extra income.

Reluctantly he replaced his car keys in his pocket and went to answer his call.

It was almost an hour before Lucianna felt composed enough to return to the farm. The anger and hurt pride which had fuelled her furious flight from Jake had been replaced by a dull, numbing emptiness which enclosed her in a protective but oh, so fragile bubble—so fragile that she was instinctively cautious about allowing anything or anyone to get close to her in case they accidentally damaged it and allowed all the pain it was holding at bay to swamp back over her.

Janey, who had seen her park her car, watched her walk slowly and carefully towards her workshop, all her female instincts aroused by the pall of despair that seemed to hang over her like an invisible cloud. Putting aside the pastry she had been mixing, she made two mugs of coffee and carried them both out to where Lucianna was working.

Lucianna looked up apathetically as her sister-in-law knocked and then walked into her workshop, carefully placing the tray of coffee on an empty space on the workbench.

'I don't know what I'm going to feel like in five months' time,' Janey groaned conversationally as she sat down. 'I feel huge and worn out already…'

'You don't look it,' Lucianna assured her, putting

down the manual she had been trying to read and studying Janey instead.

In fact if anything her sister-in-law looked positively blooming, her happiness at having conceived so apparent that she positively glowed with it. Already, too, Lucianna had noticed a difference in her brother. It had always been obvious how much David loved Janey but now…now he treated her as though she was the most precious, fragile, wonderful woman who had ever walked the earth.

As she looked at Janey, suddenly, for no reason at all that she could think of, Lucianna felt her eyes fill with sharp, hot tears. Quickly she turned away before Janey could see them, pretending to busy herself with some papers whilst Janey continued lightly, 'Jake rang about half an hour ago wanting to know if you were back. He sounded rather concerned…'

Jake, concerned about her? That would be the day… Concerned, more like, that she would ignore his warning and tell Janey and David just what had happened.

'He mentioned that John's coming home earlier than expected.'

'Yes,' Lucianna agreed stiffly and uncommunicatively.

Janey frowned a little as she drank her coffee. Something was quite obviously upsetting Lucianna, but knowing her sister-in-law as she did she felt reluctant to pry too deeply. On the other hand, if Luce wanted someone to talk to…

'I expect you're feeling a little bit nervous and uncertain about seeing him again. In the circumstances that's quite natural…and—'

'Nervous…of seeing Jake? Why should I be?'

Lucianna demanded savagely, forgetting the tell-tale signs of her tears glittering in her eyes as she wheeled round and glowered miserably at Janey. Despite everything he had said to her Jake had obviously said something to Janey about what had happened between them, probably to get Janey to reinforce what he himself had already said to her. Poor Janey. Even though she might not realise it, she was being used by Jake just as mercilessly as Lucianna herself had been, albeit in a very different way…

Janey's eyes widened in confusion as she listened to Lucianna's angry tirade.

'Luce, I was talking about *John*,' she managed to intervene gently, 'not Jake.'

Too late Lucianna realised her own mistake and just what she might have betrayed.

'Have you and Jake quarrelled?' Janey questioned her softly.

Lucianna shook her head, unable to give her any answer, and wisely Janey did not pursue the subject.

CHAPTER NINE

'I APPRECIATE your advice, Jake.' David thanked his friend gratefully as he stood up. He had spent the morning over at Jake's house discussing with him the pros and cons of a new pension plan he was considering taking out.

'The farm provides us with a reasonably good income, but you never know what the future is going to bring.' David shook his head. 'And with the baby to consider...'

'You and Janey must be looking forward to your holiday,' Jake commented. 'Not long to go now before you're off.'

'Yes, we can't wait. Thanks for agreeing to move into the farmhouse to keep an eye on things whilst we're gone. Luce is capable enough, but neither of us likes the idea of leaving her there on her own. In fact...'

He frowned and paused before saying self-consciously, 'Janey's a bit worried about her at the moment. She seems to think the two of you might have quarrelled and...well, Luce certainly does seem to have been unusually subdued. I know, of course, that she's worrying about this business of having to see Rory Simons from the bank—she took out an overdraft when she first set up to equip her workshop and, well, to be quite frank...' David shook his head. 'It's like I keep telling her: it's not that she isn't a first-rate mechanic—she is—but men just don't like the idea of a woman tampering with their cars…'

'You mean men don't like the idea of a woman knowing a good deal more about what goes on inside the engine of their cars than they do themselves,' Jake corrected him dryly.

David gave him a wry look and advised him, 'You try telling that to Luce. You know what she's like…it's like a red rag to a bull, and she's off like a firecracker… Or at least normally she would be. As I said, she's been very subdued recently. How are the lessons going, by the way?'

'They aren't,' Jake told him grimly, and then added, 'A mutual decision…'

'So Luce said,' David said.

He and Jake had virtually grown up together but, close though they had always been, there were times when Jake made it uncompromisingly clear that certain areas of his life, certain things, certain subjects were not open for discussion. And, whatever had transpired between him and Luce to provoke their mutual silence, this was obviously one such subject. David knew better than to pursue a lost cause or provoke Jake's ire by continuing to press him.

'Janey said to remind you that you're always welcome to join us for supper,' was what he said instead as Jake accompanied him to the door.

'Thanks,' Jake returned, frowning before he asked abruptly, 'David, Lucianna's business…just how bad are things?'

'Pretty bad,' David told him. 'She's just about managing to keep her head above water but only because she lives rent-free with us. I've offered to help her out but you know what she's like, how stiff-necked and proud she can be… It's like watching a kid trying to cross a flooding river swimming doggy-paddle,' he told Jake feelingly. 'You just ache to jump in and give them a hand, but Luce…

'She lost another customer this week…a woman whose car she's been servicing… Apparently her husband is buying her a new model and the distributors have told her that it will have to be serviced by a nominated garage. It's the same when someone brings a car to her that's been involved in an accident. She can do the work easily enough, and at a highly competitive price, but because she isn't on any of the insurers' lists of accredited garages she doesn't get the work.

'Janey says Luce has reapplied to a couple of the big dealers in the city for an apprenticeship and she's even been talking about looking further afield, moving away.'

'Moving away?' Jake questioned sharply. 'Why would she want to do that? John's due back at the end of this week, isn't he?'

'Yes, he is,' David agreed. 'And to judge from the number of phone calls Luce's received from him these last few days it seems as though we were wrong in thinking that he didn't want her.'

Luckily David was looking away from Jake as he spoke and so didn't notice the spasm of pain that crossed his friend's face.

What the hell was he doing punishing himself like this? Jake asked himself savagely once David had gone. Why didn't *he* just sell up and move somewhere else—somewhere as far from Lucianna as it was possible for him to get? But you couldn't simply turn your back on two centuries of family history and family tradition just because you couldn't bear the thought of seeing the woman you loved with another man... At least, you didn't if you were a Carlisle, and his great-uncle had passed the house on to Jake because he had trusted Jake to take care of it.

But a house, no matter how beautiful, couldn't compensate for not having the woman you loved, had loved, did love, would love.

Would Lucianna remember him when she lay in John's arms? Would she think about how it had felt to be with him, in his bed, her body possessed by his, her womanhood totally responsive to his manhood? Would she?

What was the point in torturing himself with such thoughts? Jake asked himself bitterly. Torturing himself wasn't going to change things... How could it?

God knew, he had had time enough over the years—and to spare—to grow accustomed to the fact that Lucianna didn't love him. But just why in hell did she have to go and give her love, *herself*, to a man like John who quite plainly neither appreciated nor valued her? And why the hell had he, Jake, ever been moronic enough to agree to help her reveal herself to him as the precious, sensual, loving woman Jake had always known she could be?

Well, he might not have been totally successful in getting her to value herself, or to realise how unworthy of her her vain and weak boyfriend actually was, but there were still other ways in which he could help her, protect her...

He went back to the library and quickly dialled the number of the farm manager he employed, tersely giving him some instructions before hanging up and then dialling the number of his solicitor.

What he was doing could never save Lucianna from suffering any emotional loss but it would certainly help to prevent her from enduring a financial one, even if he had been able to tell from the tone of their voices that both his farm manager and his solicitor quite plainly thought he was crazy.

Tiredly Lucianna pushed her fingers into her hair—hair which increasingly these days she wore soft and loose around her face whenever she was not actually working. And just as automatically and instinctively she found she was wearing make-up and more neatly fitting clothes, but the reasons why she looked so different whenever she caught sight of her own reflection had nothing really to do with her new clothes or even her new awareness of her femininity. No, the soft blue shadows that gave her eyes their haunting vulnerability owed their existence not to Jake's teachings but to Jake himself.

Hard enough to bear were the daylight hours when she fought valiantly to suppress every thought of him, but even harder were the nights and the longings, the emotions, the love that surfaced through her subconscious in her dreams to bring her wide awake with tears pouring down her face. She dreamed of not having Jake's love or, even worse, of being back in his arms, once again experiencing the ecstatic pleasure of his lovemaking, only this time believing that he actually loved her.

Those were the most cruel dreams of all—more cruel even than the realisation that her hopes of running her own small business successfully and proving to her doubters and detractors that a woman could be just as good a mechanic as a man—indeed better—

were never going to become a reality. No longer a dream—it was in truth more of a nightmare, she acknowledged as she stared dispiritedly at the figures in front of her.

In three hours' time her bank manager would be arriving to remind her that it was time for her to start repaying the overdraft facility he had granted her, and he would, of course, want to look at her books and check on the progress of her small business.

What progress? Lucianna swallowed grimly. There *was* no progress. And it wasn't as though she hadn't tried and tried desperately hard to build up her client base. She had, but to no avail. The figures in front of her said it all and she knew already what the bank manager was going to tell her. Her business simply wasn't viable, even with the benefit of rent-free premises and the fact that she made no drawings from the business at all, relying increasingly on her savings and the interest on an inheritance she had shared with her brothers to fund her day-to-day living.

Janey, who had been watching her sympathetically, tried to console her by saying, 'Try not to worry; I'm sure Rory will understand. After all, you couldn't have done any more than you have done to get more business in…'

'Maybe, but it hasn't been enough. Perhaps Dad's right after all; perhaps I should never…' Lucianna stopped and bit her lip and then shook her head. 'I'd probably have been better off going to university and then getting a more orthodox job…a more feminine job,' she declared bitterly.

'Oh, Luce,' Janey protested gently, but Lucianna wasn't in any mood to be comforted.

'It's no good. Rory Simons is going to tell me that

I've wasted my own money and that now I'm wasting the bank's and he's quite right.'

Janey's heart went out to her.

'Perhaps David…' she began.

But Lucianna shook her head immediately and told her fiercely, 'No. If I can't make the business pay by myself—for myself—then I don't want…I don't deserve… It isn't money, a loan, that I need, Janey,' she told her sister-in-law dispiritedly. 'It's work. David was right. Men *don't* trust a female mechanic.'

'But there are lots of women drivers,' Janey said, but Lucianna shook her head again.

'Women *drivers*, yes,' she agreed, 'but not *women* car owners. Not when it comes down to it… Not where it counts.'

'Well, at least John will be home soon,' Janey reminded her warmly, 'and to judge from the number of times he's telephoned recently he's obviously missed you.'

'A case of absence making the heart grow fonder,' Lucianna quipped wryly. If only she could say the same about her own emotions, that it was Jake's absence that made her heart ache, Jake's missing presence that was causing her sleepless nights and an aching heart and body, not John's.

Lucianna glanced at her watch as the bank manager drove into the yard right on time.

David had offered to cancel a meeting of his own to give her the support of his presence, but she had shaken her head, for once not taking umbrage, but instead telling him gratefully, 'It's kind of you, but no, this is something I have to do myself.'

As David had later remarked to Janey when they

were alone, Lucianna had changed dramatically over the last few weeks, and not just in the way she looked and dressed. She had matured.

'Turned from a girl to a woman,' Janey had supplied gently for him.

'Yes,' David had agreed ruefully. 'Very much a woman.'

When Rory Simons stepped out of his car he too was surprised by the physical change in her. Gone were the shabby, oversized dungarees and in their place Lucianna was wearing an immaculately clean, neat-fitting pair of tailored trousers and a soft knitted top—an impulse buy if he had but known. It had been chosen to bolster her confidence and caused her to spend virtually the last of the birthday money she had received from her father and her aunt.

'Lucianna,' he greeted her with a fatherly smile. 'You look well.'

It was a lie, he recognised as he saw her face for the first time. She looked *different*, unfamiliarly well turned out and certainly unfamiliarly femininely appealing, causing him to realise what an extraordinarily beautiful young woman she actually was—but she most certainly did *not* look well. In fact…

As he studied her more closely he started to frown. Her face bore all the signs of someone undergoing the kind of crisis he, as a bank manager, was becoming increasingly familiar with. His heart sank. He had come here hoping against hope that her small business had started to turn the corner and might yet prove to be a viable proposition, as much for her sake as the bank's. After all, he had known her and her family for a good many years, but he suspected that his worst fears were about to be realised.

Half an hour later his suspicions were a certainty. Closing the books she had shown him, he sighed.

'Lucianna,' he began, 'I'm very much afraid—' And then he stopped as a car being driven into the yard distracted Lucianna's attention, causing her to stare hungrily through the window, a fixed expression on her face, her body tense.

Curiously he too looked towards the window, and immediately recognised Jake as he emerged from the driver's seat of his car.

He knew, of course, that Jake and David were old and close friends, but Jake wasn't heading for the farmhouse; instead he was walking towards Lucianna's workshop.

As he pushed open the door Lucianna retreated to the other side of the workbench, hoping that the shadows would mask the hot colour burning up painfully over her skin. Just seeing him made her whole body ache with a feverish need so intense that she could feel herself actually starting to shake.

'Sorry I'm late,' Jake began incomprehensibly as he nodded acknowledgement in Rory Simons' direction before unzipping the leather document case he was carrying and removing from it a thick wad of papers. 'I got held up in town by the traffic. I've got all the service contracts here now, Lucianna.

'I'm glad you're here, Rory,' he commented to the bank manager. 'Perhaps you wouldn't mind witnessing Lucianna's signature for us...?'

The service contracts? What service contracts? Lucianna had been about to demand, but her voice deserted her as Jake took half a dozen steps towards her and the ache in her body became a tormented flood of agonising longing. He was dressed formally today in a dark suit, the jacket open over an immaculately white shirt, the tie he was wearing as dark as his suit but with a small design on it that almost exactly matched the colour of his eyes—a tie bought for him, bought for him by a woman, Lucianna guessed jealously—and, as it happened, incorrectly.

'The contract cover for all the estate's farm vehicles, plus Henry Peters' car, and, as we agreed, it runs for five years. During that time, *you* will be responsible for servicing and maintaining all the estate's machinery and equipment,' Jake continued formally, ignoring both Lucianna's shocked expression and the bank manager's look of pleased relief as though he were totally unaware of the full import of what he had said.

'My own car, of course, will be subject to a separate contract,' he went on. He glanced at his watch. 'I don't want to rush you, but I've got a directors' meeting this afternoon, so if we could get these agreements signed...'

Lucianna couldn't take her eyes off him. What on earth was Jake *doing...saying...*? He had *never* discussed with her giving her a service contract to maintain the estate's vehicles, never mind indicated that he intended to have her service the estate manager's and his own car... She shook her head, convinced that she must be dreaming, imagining things, half expecting—and then she closed her eyes totally, convinced that when she opened them again he would have disappeared. Only when she did he hadn't.

'Jake—' she began in a wobbly voice, but before she could ask him what on earth was going on Rory Simons overrode her, demanding eagerly.

'Jake, am I to understand that you're giving

Lucianna an *exclusive* service and maintenance contract for all your estate machinery?' he asked.

'She submitted the best tender,' Jake told him offhandedly, shrugging as he did so. 'And certainly so far as I'm concerned I couldn't find a better mechanic…

'Oh, by the way,' he added casually, 'Lucianna mentioned to me that she's having a bit of a cash-flow problem at the moment. I've suggested that one way around the problem could be for me to inject some capital into the business and to guarantee the current bank borrowing.'

From the look on Rory Simons' face Jake might have just offered him the winning numbers on a lottery ticket, Lucianna decided, still in too much of a state of shock herself even to begin to query what Jake was saying.

'Right, Lucianna,' Jake was instructing her now. 'If you could just sign here and then Rory could witness your signature. I might still be able to make it to my meeting on time…just…'

In a complete daze Lucianna found herself taking the pen Jake was holding out to her, weak tears starting to burn behind her eyes as her fingers reacted sensitively to the fact that the pen still held the warmth of Jake's touch, a touch that, almost in another life now, or so it seemed, she had actually felt against her own body, her own flesh, her own most intimate…

Quickly she bent her head so that neither of the two watching men could see the hot flush that burned her skin, but she knew that Jake must have witnessed the way her hand trembled as she signed her name where he had indicated.

She had no idea what was going on, nor why Jake had chosen to pretend to her bank manager that he was giving her what she knew to be a completely fictitious contract, and if she'd had anything about her she would have challenged him right there and then, she told herself. But somehow she simply couldn't find the strength of will to do so… Not because of her business… No, not because of that. It was because of her emotions, her need…her *love*…that she was afraid to confront him, because she was mortally afraid that simply to stand there and look at him would cause her to break down and tell him how she felt, to beg him.

Rory Simons was signing the papers now, smiling happily as he did so, but Lucianna couldn't share his happiness. Stiffly she stood apart from the two men, watching as Jake gathered up the signed papers and then, with a brief look in her direction, started to stride towards the door.

'Why didn't you tell me that Jake Carlisle was giving you his business?' the bank manager mock scolded her after Jake had gone. Lucianna couldn't say anything. All she could do was shake her head and try to blink away her weak, foolish, yearning tears.

It was only later, as Lucianna turned the whole incident over in her mind and tried despairingly not to linger longingly on her mental image of Jake in his expensive suit, looking very, so very disturbingly male and so hopelessly out of reach, that one possible and very unpalatable explanation for Jake's extraordinary behaviour struck her. Far from being some altruistic and even chivalrous attempt to come to her rescue and save her failing business, as it had originally seemed, could Jake perhaps be thinking that in guaranteeing her debts he was also guaranteeing her silence on the subject of the night of their secret intimacy? He had, after all, made it very plain to her that he *wanted* it to be kept a secret.

The thought that he might actually feel he could buy her off, *pay* her off like some…like a…made Lucianna feel physically ill. And not just ill but bitterly hurt and bitterly angry as well. Well, she would show him—and she would show him what he could do with his precious contracts as well, she decided.

She would rather starve in a gutter, sacrifice her precious business, *and* her independence with it, than accept his help and allow him to think… Oh, how could he? How dared he? Did he really find the thought, the memory of what had happened between them so obnoxious that he felt he had to expunge it, destroy it and her by reducing her precious memories to the status of some kind of…? Lucianna swallowed painfully.

She had worked hard to establish her small business and she was loath to lose it, but she *couldn't* allow Jake to think…to believe what she was now convinced he did think and believe.

Purposefully Lucianna removed the list of her current clients from the file she had prepared for the bank manager's visit but as she dialled the first number on the list her hand was shaking very badly.

Two hours later it was done; every single one of her clients had been advised that she was no longer in business. Now all she had left to do was to arrange to withdraw what was left of her savings and cash in on her investments in order that she could repay the bank all that she owed them. After that…

Proudly Lucianna squared her shoulders. She would have to find herself a temporary job and then, at the end of the summer, she could re-start her studies, go to university perhaps as a mature student, find herself something to do that was more 'suitable' for a woman.

The view beyond her workshop window blurred and swam as she blinked fiercely to disperse the tears.

She had equipped this workshop with such high hopes, such faith and belief not just in herself but also in others, in the surety that they would ultimately accept that she was every bit as good a mechanic as any male. And she *was* as good. Nothing could change *that*, just as nothing, apparently, could change the male pride that meant that they could not and would not accept her.

She would have to tell her family, of course—David and Janey first and then her father. And now that David and Janey were expecting a child it might also be a good time for her to look for somewhere else to live. Fresh tears filled her eyes and, before her resolve could break and desert her completely, she picked up the papers Jake had left her and ripped them neatly into four pieces, her fingers trembling very badly as she stuffed them into an envelope, addressed it to him, then sealed it. No doubt he would be able to make his own interpretation of her actions, just as she had of his.

'You're doing what?' David demanded, too stunned to keep the shock out of his voice when Lucianna broke her news to him over supper.

'Not doing...*have* done,' Lucianna informed him, doggedly refusing to look directly at him as she pretended to be busily eating the food in front of her.

Behind her back, Janey shook her head warningly at her husband. She too had been shocked by Lucianna's news, but one look at her sister-in-law's white face and set expression had informed her that it would be wiser not to pursue the subject.

'She's obviously very upset about the whole thing,' Janey counselled David later when Lucianna had returned to her workshop, explaining quietly that she had to catalogue her equipment so that she could put it up for sale.

'*She's* upset...' David expostulated, pushing his hands into his hair. 'Why on earth didn't she discuss it with us first?'

'Perhaps because she wanted to be allowed to make her own decision and handle things by herself,' Janey told him quietly.

'But that damned workshop meant so much to her; it was her whole life,' David reminded Janey in male confusion. 'I can't believe she'd just give it up like that.'

'Perhaps she's discovered something or someone that means more to her,' Janey suggested, sighing ruefully to herself as he struggled for comprehension. David was a darling and she loved him dearly but when it came to women's emotions, especially his sister's, he did tend to be rather obtuse... Despairingly so at times, she acknowledged five minutes later as David spoke again.

'You mean John's *making* her give it up?' he asked her, puzzled. 'I know he wasn't keen on her work but...'

'John may have been the catalyst but somehow I doubt that he's the cause,' Janey responded mystifyingly—at least so far as her husband was concerned. Women! How was a mere man supposed to understand them?

As a result of his afternoon meeting, Jake had to fly to New York later in the day to discuss a takeover bid for one of the companies in which he had a major shareholding. As his plane was crossing the Atlantic, the four quarters of the contracts he had so lovingly and time-consumingly had drawn up and which Lucianna had ripped into so many useless shreds were crossing town on their way to him.

CHAPTER TEN

'I WONDER what's happened to Jake?' David commented curiously to Janey as he replaced the telephone receiver. 'That's the third time I've tried him today and got no reply...'

'Oh, didn't I tell you? I bumped into the farm manager in town this morning and he said that Jake had had to fly to New York on business.'

Lucianna's head was bent over the advertisement she was writing, to advertise not just the contents of her workshop but in addition the ancient racing car she had been lovingly restoring and which Jake had taunted her over what seemed like a lifetime ago now. Her hand started to tremble. *When* was it going to end? When was she going to stop overreacting to the mere sound of Jake's name?

'Isn't it today you're picking John up from the airport?' Janey asked her.

'Yes, this afternoon,' Lucianna informed her joylessly.

It seemed almost laughable now that she had ever believed herself in love with John. A small frown pleated her forehead. She would have to tell him, of course, that their relationship was over. Not that she could believe that he would be *too* upset, she decided hardily. After all, he had been happy enough to leave her.

There. Lucianna glowered into the mirror at her prettily made up face and shining hair. In an hour's time she would be picking up John at the airport and she supposed that she might as well make use of the skills she had so recently learned even if the man who was going to be given the benefit of them was no longer the man she wanted… *Wanted*…ached for, craved, needed…loved… And would go on loving until the day she died. But what was the point in dwelling on the agony and misery of her unwanted feelings? Jake did *not* love her. In fact Jake wanted her so little, *valued* her so little that he had been prepared to offer her *money* to keep her distance from him.

Swiftly she stood up. Her new jeans showed off her tiny waist and long legs and the crisp checked cotton shirt she had knotted at her waist gave her whole appearance a sharp top note of chic casualness—a far cry indeed from the image she had presented three weeks earlier when she had seen John off at the airport. The swift appraising and admiring look the salesgirl had given her when Lucianna had instinctively knotted the checked shirt instead of more plainly tucking it into her jeans had proved just how far she had come, just how much she had learned.

Rather to her own surprise she had discovered that she didn't simply possess the flair to assess and judge what kind of clothes suited her best, but that she actually enjoyed doing so as well. But if the admiring glances she collected nowadays whenever she went out boosted her ego they still couldn't do anything to relieve the agonising ache that was her love for Jake.

In a couple of days the local paper would come out, carrying the advertisement for the sale of her equipment. Quickly she went downstairs. Janey was in the kitchen ironing clothes for her and David's holiday.

'How many suitcases are you taking?' Lucianna teased her as she walked towards the door.

The arrivals hall wasn't particularly busy and Lucianna spotted John before he saw her. However, it wasn't shyness or insecurity that made her hold back as she watched him look around, his gaze searching the hall for her.

Where had those feelings she had thought were so strong gone? They certainly didn't exist any longer—at least not for John. And even odder than their complete disappearance was her sudden awareness of the petulant sulkiness of his expression and the way he focused rather longer than was necessary on the two pretty girls crossing the concourse in front of him. Squaring her shoulders, Lucianna took a step forward.

She recognised the exact second that John spotted her from the almost ludicrous change in his expression. His eyes widened and his jaw dropped and there was no doubt at all from his reaction that not only was he surprised by her metamorphosis but he was also very visibly impressed by it.

'Luce!'

Lucianna grimaced and then stiffened as John reached her and grabbed hold of her, insisting on kissing her with a great deal of public swagger. Like a little boy showing off a new and much coveted toy, she reflected wryly.

'You look *wonderful*,' he told her as she firmly turned her face to one side so that his kiss landed on her cheek instead of her mouth. 'No need to ask if you've missed me,' he added with a satisfied smile as they walked towards the exit. 'I can see for myself how much trouble you've gone to to look good for me. And you *do* look good, Lucianna,' he told her. 'I'll show you how good later.'

'I'm afraid I've got some work to do later, John,' Lucianna said quickly, deftly stepping to one side as he made to place his arm around her.

'*Work*? You mean you're trying to stick together someone's beat-up old banger,' he commented disparagingly.

'No, that *wasn't* what I meant,' Lucianna denied. She had forgotten the way John loved to make depreciatory remarks about her work, putting both it and her down, but whereas once they had hurt her now they simply irritated her.

'You haven't said yet that you're pleased I came back from Canada early,' John reminded her.

'You haven't told me yet why you're back ahead of time,' Lucianna parried, and then realised that she had obviously hit a hidden and very raw nerve as John's face suddenly turned brick-red and he turned away from her.

'There was a bit of a problem—a clash of personalities… I don't want to talk about work,' he said, then turned back to smile at her. 'I'd much rather talk about *us*… I've been thinking about us a lot whilst I've been away, Luce…missing you a lot…'

Lucianna's heart missed a beat. She had known when she'd agreed to collect John from the airport that sooner or later she was going to have to tell him that their relationship was over, but then she had not expected him to behave as though…as though their relationship had a great deal more meaning for him than he had ever previously given her cause to believe.

Had she misread the situation before he'd gone away—the growing distance between them and John's increasing tendency to treat her as though he was growing tired of her? Or was she being overly suspicious in thinking that there was more to his sudden interest in her than met the eye?

And then, as she looked away from John, she suddenly froze as, totally unexpectedly, she saw Jake walking across the airport concourse. At her side John's voice was a distant, monotonous blur—just like John himself—her whole attention, yes, her whole *being* focused on Jake through the waves of anguished longing and pain that rocked through her.

How was it possible to love someone so much and yet at the same time almost hate them for the hurt they had caused you? Abruptly Jake stood still and Lucianna felt as though her heart had stopped beating as he turned his head slowly, searching the concourse for someone. She held her breath and then released it on a sharp, rattling sob as she saw him look directly at her.

Across the distance that separated them she could still see his expression, and his eyes and mouth hardened as he looked at her.

Desperate to salvage something of her pride and self-respect, Lucianna acted entirely on instinct, grabbing hold of John's arm and snuggling up close to him as she smiled at him through her pain.

It seemed almost grotesque now to think that once the immediacy and enthusiasm of John's appreciative response to her gesture would have meant so much to her, whilst now it meant so little.

'Let's get out of here,' she heard John muttering ardently, and through her tears she could just about see Jake turning on his heel and walking contemptuously away as John urged her towards the exit.

'Look, Luce, if you want to give your business another go, Janey and I…' David began awkwardly the day after John's return, but Lucianna shook her head as she smiled wanly at him.

'Thanks, David, but no… Anyway it's too late,' she told him quietly. 'I've already put the ad in the paper—it comes out tomorrow.

'Hopefully by the time you and Janey get back from holiday the barn will be empty. What's happening about the stock whilst you're away, by the way?' she asked him incuriously.

'There's no need for you to worry about that,' David assured her. 'That's all sorted out… You could do with a holiday yourself,' he added. 'Perhaps you and John…?'

Lucianna shook her head. 'John's too busy at work to take any time off at the moment,' she told her brother, not untruthfully, but what she didn't add was that the last thing she wanted was to place herself in a position where she would have to spend time alone in John's company.

'Are you sure you don't want me to drive you to the airport?' she asked David.

'No, it's all right; Janey's booked the taxi.' He glanced at his watch. 'Just think, another twelve hours and we'll be away from all this.'

'Stop trying to make me jealous.' Lucianna smiled, trying to enter into his playful mood and not wanting to spoil his anticipation of their holiday with her own unhappiness and despair. Tonight John was taking her out for a meal, not that she particularly wanted to go, not in fact that she wanted to see him at all really. Despite the fact that he was full of fulsome praise for the change in her outward appearance, Lucianna sensed that he was at heart no more emotionally involved with her than she was with him.

'Right, that's it,' Janey announced as she came into the kitchen. 'The cases are finally packed… Have you got the passports and our tickets ready, David? The taxi will be here soon…'

'They're safe in my jacket pocket,' David assured her. 'I'll go and bring down the cases.'

Half an hour after David and Janey had gone Lucianna went upstairs to get ready for her date with John.

With a wry smile she removed her new trouser suit from her wardrobe. She had changed immeasurably in countless ways from the girl who had been dragged so reluctantly and defiantly on that shopping trip with Jake. Gently she touched the fabric of the suit. Like a faded rose packed carefully in tissue to protect it from the damaging light of the sun she had stored away her own precious memories, and one of those was the look on Jake's face when he had seen her wearing the silk suit.

As she showered and dressed and put on her make-up Lucianna acknowledged that she was not looking forward to the evening ahead at all.

What amazed her almost more than anything else was what she could possibly have seen in John in the first place. He was, she realised, everything she most disliked in a man—immature, self-centred, wholly lacking in sensitivity or any genuine warmth; nothing whatsoever like…

Shakily she put down the brush she had just picked up to apply her lipstick.

That was an avenue down which her thoughts must not be allowed to go.

She had just slipped on her suit when she heard a car drive into the farmyard. Frowning, she went downstairs to open the door.

John was half an hour too early for their date, but fortunately she was virtually ready. However, as she opened the back door into the yard she realised that it wasn't John who had just driven in but Jake.

'You're too late,' she told him abruptly as he strode towards her. 'David and Janey have already left.'

'It's you I've come to see, not them,' Jake replied bitingly, walking into the kitchen and closing the door behind him, whilst Lucianna retreated to the other side of the kitchen table, watching warily as he reached into his jacket pocket and produced a familiar envelope.

'I found *this* waiting amongst my post,' he told her tersely. 'Would you like to explain to me, Lucianna, what's going on?' he demanded as he tipped the pieces of the contract onto the table in front of her.

'I should have thought it was self-explanatory,' Lucianna told him proudly, her eyes flashing, emotion giving her voice a mature huskiness as she added, 'I *know* what you were trying to do, Jake, but it won't work—you can't buy me or… I'm not for sale,' she told him fiercely.

'But your business is,' Jake retorted curtly.

'I've decided to re-train…do something else,' Lucianna informed him.

'*You've* decided?' Jake challenged her. 'Or did someone else make the decision for you, Lucianna…? John perhaps? You really must love him one hell of a lot,' he said savagely, and then added with what to Lucianna felt like unbelievable cruelty, 'Certainly one hell of a lot more than he does you.'

'You have no right to say that,' she responded fiercely. How dared he question John's feelings for her when his own…when he…?

'No right?' she heard him mutter fiercely, and he strode round the table and totally unexpectedly grabbed hold of her, his fingers biting painfully into the tender flesh of her upper arms as he gave her a small shake. 'Lucianna… I…'

'Don't touch me.' Lucianna panicked, almost screaming the words at him, her body reacting with helpless intensity to his touch and his proximity, her aching need for him filling her with a heat, a hunger that caused her to tremble violently and visibly. Half of her ached to close the distance between them and to feel the longed-for sensation of his body close to her own, against her own, *within* her own, whilst the other half…the other half was gripped by a terrified headlong flight into total panic as she tried to pull away from him and put a safer distance between them.

'Don't touch you?' she heard Jake repeating harshly through gritted teeth. 'I've heard you singing a very different song…'

Instantly Lucianna went completely rigid, her face paper-white, her eyes huge, bruised pools of feminine pride and pain as she asked him piteously, 'How could you? How *dare* you bring that up now?'

'Oh, I can and I dare,' Jake assured her. 'I can and I dare because…'

He was mesmerising her with his voice and his eyes, Lucianna decided dizzily; he must be, otherwise she would have been fighting to pull free of him instead of simply standing there, mute and bemused, as his hands travelled up over her arms to cup her face and hold it still. He bent over her, his body blocking out the light as he lowered his head towards hers, his mouth unerringly finding hers... His mouth...

Too late Lucianna tried to move, to avoid the descent of his head and the hot, savage pressure of his kiss, because her lips were already clinging helplessly to his, remembering, returning their passionate caresses, trembling, parting, her whole body shuddering in despairing pleasure as she felt the first swift thrust of his tongue inside her mouth.

She wanted him so much. *Loved* him so badly. She wanted him to pick her up right now and carry her upstairs, lay her on her bed and tell her he loved her whilst he...

Tell her he loved her? But he *didn't* love her...and he had already made that more than plain to her...

Abruptly Lucianna came to her senses, pushing Jake away as she struggled to suppress the small sob of desolation rising in her throat.

'Just in time,' Jake told her cynically as they both heard the sound of a car pulling into the yard. 'But I can tell you this, Lucianna...'

'No,' Lucianna denied, covering her ears with her hands in a gesture that was almost childish, her voice distraught with pain as she told him, 'I don't *want* to hear *anything* you have to say, Jake...*anything*...' And then, before he could reply, she opened the kitchen door and hurried into the yard towards John's car.

'What's he doing here?' John asked her as he opened the car door for her, frowning in Jake's direction as he saw Jake standing in the doorway.

'Oh, he came over to see David,' Lucianna fibbed. She had no qualms about leaving Jake in the farmhouse. She knew he had his own key, an arrangement David had made with him years ago, and she knew that despite their own quarrel and the enmity which now existed between them he would be scrupulous about locking the farm door behind him when he left. Fortunately she had instinctively reached for her bag as she'd left the kitchen, so at least she would be able to get back in again.

'I'm really looking forward to this evening,' John told her as he drove out of the yard, turning his head to give her a meaningful glance that made her heart sink. 'You mean a lot to me, Luce,' he said warmly, reaching out to take hold of her hand before she could stop him and giving it a damp squeeze. 'An awful lot,' he emphasised in a voice she assumed was meant to sound sincere and sexy but which in fact to her sounded almost exactly the opposite.

As she firmly extracted her hand from his and looked away, she couldn't help wondering how he would react if she reminded him that for someone who claimed to think an awful lot of her he had found it remarkably easy to walk away from her. And she hadn't forgotten all those hurtful criticisms he had made before he had left for Canada, but since she had no wish to provoke a quarrel with him she kept her thoughts to herself, merely saying quietly and with a certain cynicism in her voice, 'I take it, then, that there were no particularly attractive girls at the Canadian office?'

* * *

John certainly was out to impress her, Lucianna admitted half an hour later as he pulled into the car park of a particularly prestigious and expensive local restaurant. However, once they were inside she discovered that his actions were not quite as generous as she had initially assumed. She had learned quite early on in their relationship that John had a thrifty streak, and *that*, it seemed, was something about him which had not changed.

John was not taking her out for a meal *à deux* as she had initially believed; instead they were joining a party of his colleagues who were celebrating the fiftieth birthday of the senior partner.

'J.J. is paying for everything,' John whispered to her enthusiastically as he slipped his arm around her waist in a proprietorial fashion and urged her forward.

It was odd to think that once—and not so very long ago at that—the looks of disbelief on the faces of John's work colleagues as they stared at her would have filled her with joy that at last she had proved herself worthy of being with John. Now it meant nothing—just as John himself meant nothing.

She saw the look of hostility that Felicity gave her as she clung to the arm of a much older, overweight, balding man, teetering slightly in her too high heels. Quickly Lucianna looked away.

J.J., whom she had only met previously at the firm's Christmas dinner dance, smiled benevolently at her as John propelled her forward and re-introduced her.

'So you're John's girlfriend. Excellent, excellent,' he commented, giving her a warm smile and John an oddly probing, hard-eyed look. 'John tells us that it will soon be wedding bells,' he added jovially.

Lucianna tried not to let her shock show. 'Wedding bells?' she questioned John abruptly as a waiter ushered them to their places. 'What was he—?'

'Not now,' John told her curtly. 'Hello, Basil,' he greeted the man standing listening to them.

'So how does it feel to be back? Rather a shorter stay in Canada than was originally planned. Still, if I had a fiancée as pretty as yours waiting at home for me I expect I'd have been eager to get back too…'

'Fiancée?' Lucianna expostulated as soon as he was out of earshot. 'John, what's going on? You and I aren't engaged, and—'

'We'll talk about it later,' John interrupted her. 'Just don't say anything, there's a good girl, and I'll explain everything later.'

Lucianna stared at him. Be a good girl…? How *dared* he adopt that kind of tone, that kind of *manner* with her…?

'John…' she began warningly, but he was shaking his head, and since the other guests at either side of them were taking their seats Lucianna acknowledged that she had no option but to wait until they had more privacy to both demand an explanation and to tell him that, far from being his fiancée, as of this evening their relationship was well and truly over!

The meal dragged on interminably. A small frown creased Lucianna's forehead as she saw how much John was drinking. Sweat beaded his upper lip and his fair complexion looked unhealthily flushed. Suddenly Lucianna could see how he would be in twenty years' time. How on earth had she ever thought him attractive?

Automatically she stood up.

'Where are you going?' John demanded.

'To the ladies,' Lucianna informed him quietly.

There was only one other girl in the ladies' cloakroom when Lucianna pushed open the door and her heart sank as she saw who it was.

Felicity and her 'boyfriend' were seated almost opposite Lucianna and John and Lucianna had noticed that she too was drinking heavily.

'You think you've got it made, don't you?' she sneered to Lucianna. 'You really think that the reason John's come back ahead of time is because of you. Well, you couldn't be more wrong...' She gave Lucianna a pleased smirk before toying with her already thick lipgloss.

'The real reason he's come back...sorry, been *sent* back...ahead of time is because our John...*your* John...has been having an affair with the wife of one of the Canadian partners. And *he* found out about it and John's been sent home in disgrace, although of course it's all been played down. The wife is insisting it was all a mistake and that her husband's got it wrong, and as for John—well, John's claiming that far from getting himself involved with another man's wife he's actually been counting the days until he got home to his own little wife-to-be.

'He doesn't really want to marry you at all...but he knows that unless he toes the line and produces a wife p.d.q. he's going to be out of a job.

'Nothing to say?' she challenged Lucianna dulcetly. 'Well, if you don't believe me why don't you ask John? Not that he'll tell you the truth. John's got quite an eye for our sex on the quiet, you know. The Canadian partner's wife wasn't his first indiscretion. He likes them older and married...it makes them so much more grateful and so much easier to get rid of when the affair has lost its lustre…

'Oh, dear, have I shocked you?' she cooed with patent insincerity when Lucianna made a small shocked sound. 'But surely you must have been suspicious? After all, before he went away he'd made it pretty obvious that he'd lost interest in you, hadn't he? So you must have wondered what was going on when he came back very much the adoring lover… Not, of course, that the two of you *have* been lovers, have you? He told *me* that the night he and I… Whoops! I don't suppose you know about that either, do you?'

Lucianna waited until she had gone before going to the foyer to use the payphone to ring for a taxi, and to ask the receptionist for a small piece of paper so that she could write John a note. She kept it short and succinct, telling him that their relationship, such as it was, was over and adding that she would prefer it if he did not make any attempt to get in touch with her.

Strangely, as she climbed into the taxi and gave the driver the address of the farm, her strongest feeling was one of intense relief, a sense of having escaped—John's affair or affairs meant nothing whatsoever to her, and she was simply quietly thankful that the fact that they had never had an intimate physical relationship meant that she need have no fears for her own health and well-being.

As the taxi turned into the farm lane, she instructed the driver to drop her at the normally seldom used front door instead of driving round into the yard.

John was a part of her life that was now—thankfully—over. She only wished she could say the same about the pain that loving Jake was causing her, but instinct told her that Jake and her love for him were things that she would never be able to forget or ignore.

CHAPTER ELEVEN

JAKE had just stepped out of the shower when he heard the taxi draw up outside the front of the farmhouse. Grabbing a towel, he hurried downstairs, reaching the hallway just as Lucianna was pushing open the front door.

'Jake.' Lucianna whispered his name in shock, fully intending to ask him what on earth he was doing in her home and quite obviously making himself *at* home, his body slick and wet from his shower and the towel, which he had wrapped around his hips, leaving little to conceal the fact that…that he was Jake…and she…she was…

But, before she could open her mouth, to her chagrin, and for no reason that she could really think of—unless you counted the fact that she was desperately, despairingly in love with him and just the sight of him made her ache so badly inside with the need to fling herself headlong into his arms and to be held tenderly and lovingly there, whilst he—Lucianna discovered that she had started to cry.

Not delicate, neat, tidy little dewdrops of tears that could easily be sniffed away, either, but huge great tearing sobs that blocked her throat and made her whole body shake with the anguish of what she was feeling.

'What is it? What's wrong? What has he done…? Where the hell is he?' She heard Jake growling with increasing ferocity as he totally unexpectedly fulfilled at least one part of her fantasy by grabbing hold of her and, if not cradling her tenderly and lovingly, then at least offering her the comfort of his arms and the solid proximity of his body. He demanded, repeated, 'What the hell has he done to you, Lucianna, and where is he?'

'Having dinner at a restaurant,' Lucianna told him in between hiccuping sobs. 'I left him there. He couldn't have driven; he'd had too much to drink.

'He'd told people that we were engaged, that we were going to be married,' Lucianna explained, still sobbing as Jake's arms tightened almost painfully around her. 'But it wasn't true; he didn't want to marry me at all—it was just because he'd had an affair with someone else… He just wanted to *use* me to protect his job. He didn't love me at all really.'

Now she was crying in earnest, although she had no real idea why, unless it was because Jake was holding her more like a brother than the lover she wanted him to be.

She shivered suddenly.

Against her cheek she could feel the hard warmth of his shoulder, smell the clean, damp, freshly showered male smell of him, and her body was reacting to it as though she had inhaled the headiest and most intoxicating of drugs. Forget the alcohol, her brain decided dizzily—being close to Jake like this was having a far more dangerous effect on her senses. She wanted to stay close to him like this for ever—no, longer than for ever—for eternity and beyond eternity—but already Jake was starting to move her away, holding her off with one hand whilst he reached out with the other to push open the sitting-room door.

'What you need is a hot drink and the chance to

calm down…' Lucianna heard him saying pragmatically.

Suddenly she had had enough. What she needed was most definitely *not* a hot drink; what she needed, what she wanted…

Later she would swear to herself that if she hadn't been genuinely overwhelmed by a sudden fit of shivers she would *never*, for one minute, have behaved in the way that she did. For the fit of shivers was genuine and unplanned, and it seized her body with such force that Jake immediately frowned, releasing the open door to take hold of her with both hands as he told her grimly, 'You're in shock. You need—'

'I need *you*, Jake,' Lucianna heard herself saying to him shakily. 'I need you so much right now that I…'

She wasn't the one who had suggested buying the book that told her how to flirt with a man, she was to tell herself self-righteously later. All she had done was do as she was told, buy it and read it. And if she had read that to reach out and touch a man's bare forearm with one's fingertips and, moreover, to draw those same fingertips oh, so gently down the bare skin in a soft stroking motion was a definite and provocative come-on that very few men would be able to resist, then whose fault was that? Not hers.

Whoever had written that book obviously knew what they were talking about, she acknowledged in heady triumph half a dozen seconds later when she had felt the whole of Jake's arm jerk in response to her touch and had heard the soft, stifled groan he had made in his throat.

'Lucianna, I *know* that John's hurt you and that right now you're—'

'I'm cold, Jake,' Lucianna told him, overriding him. 'I'm so cold, please hold me,' she begged him piteously.

'What you need is a hot bath and then bed; things will seem much better in the morning, you'll see,' Lucianna heard Jake telling her gruffly.

'Mmm…' Lucianna agreed, snuggling deeper in his arms. 'But you'll have to help me, Jake; I'm just so cold…'

From her position, cuddled up against his body, Lucianna could feel the groan that shuddered through his chest.

'I *know* you don't know what you're doing, Luce…or what you're inviting…but…'

Very slowly Lucianna lifted her head from his chest and looked up at him, deliberately moistening her lips with the tip of her tongue.

'What am I inviting, Jake? Tell me…*show* me…' she whispered provocatively.

Surely it couldn't be the three glasses of wine she had had to drink that was responsible for her extraordinarily out-of-character behaviour? Lucianna questioned herself dizzily as she let her glance drop very slowly and very, very deliberately—another hint she had picked up from that book—from Jake's eyes to his mouth.

It worked. She could actually see the muscles in his face tense, *feel* the sensual hardening of his body as he tried to pull away from her, and then, with a speed and ferocity that took her off guard, he dragged her back down against his body, cupping her face with one hand whilst he pressed the other to the base of her spine, urging her against his own body as he told her between the fierce, hungry kisses he was pressing against her eager mouth, 'Feel what you're doing to me, Luce… Feel how much I want you.'

Instinctively Lucianna moved closer to him, wrapping her arms tightly around him as she returned his kisses with unashamed intensity, opening her mouth to him and to the sensual probe of his tongue, moaning soft, sweet sounds of pleasure into his mouth as his kiss deepened and his hands roamed her body, stroking, moulding, shaping, caressing.

She cried out in swift, sharp pleasure as his hand cupped her breast, his thumb rubbing demandingly against her already stiff nipple.

'Jake!'

As she breathed his name into his mouth, Lucianna reached impatiently towards the towel he was wearing, but Jake got there first, holding her upper arms as he kissed her with increasing passion and urgency, her own heartbeat starting to race as her body picked up on his arousal and excitement—and shared it as he demanded thickly, '*What* is it you want, Lucianna? *Who* is it you want? Is it me…?'

'Oh, yes, it's you…you I want, Jake,' Lucianna averred frantically, kissing his throat and then his shoulder as she felt herself starting to spin crazily out of control, her emotions, her arousal bringing her flesh out in a betraying rash of goosebumps. She pleaded, 'Take me to bed, Jake…please, please; I want you so much.'

'Nowhere near as much as I want you,' she heard Jake telling her forcefully as he swung her up into his arms, but, to her astonishment, instead of carrying her upstairs, Jake was heading for the front door.

'Jake,' she protested, suddenly apprehensive and afraid that after allowing her to believe he wanted her he was simply going to walk away from her, to abandon her as he had done the last time… The last time… 'Where are you going?' she demanded huskily.

'I'm taking you home,' Jake responded fiercely. 'To *my* home, to *my* bed, and once I've got you there I'm…'

As she saw the look in his eyes, Lucianna started to tremble, but not from fear…

Later she would have no clear recollection of the short drive to Jake's house—only of her awareness that it was just as well it was a private lane since all Jake was still wearing was the towel. Jake's home and even Jake's bedroom were already familiar to her, but as he carried her from the front door towards the stairs the sensations, the *emotions* filling her totally obliterated the fact that Jake's home was a familiar part of her own childhood. Instead…

At the bottom of the stairs Jake set her on her feet and slowly, cupping her face, started to kiss her, gently at first and then with increasing passion until she was writhing frantically against him, calling his name with small sobbing cries of need as she pressed herself closer and closer to him.

Was it Jake or was it her own hands that dragged the buttons of her jacket from the buttonholes? She didn't know, but she knew well enough that it was Jake's hands that caressed her naked breasts, stroking and kneading them as she pushed them eagerly into his caressing palms, and Jake's lips, Jake's mouth that took her to even greater transports of sensual pleasure when they stopped halfway up the stairs and Jake knelt down in front of her. For slowly he started to suckle on first one and then the other taut nipple before very deliberately tracing a line of hot, thrilling kisses down to the waistband of her silk trousers and then below it as he unfastened and let them fall to the floor. His tonguetip circled her belly button, causing her to cling helplessly to his shoulders, torn between wanting to beg him to stop and aching to urge him to go on.

But, even so, despite knowing how much she wanted him and how much she loved him and how aroused he was himself, it was still a shock to hear him tell her gratingly, 'If we don't make it to my bedroom soon, I'm going to have to have you right here and now where we are…'

'On the stairs?' Lucianna blurted out, betraying her innocence as she added, 'But we can't…'

'Oh, yes, we can,' Jake assured her, his teeth gleaming in an almost boyish smile as he flushed and then looked enquiringly at her. 'No, don't ask me to explain, not right now… The way I want you…need you right now is on a bed…on *my* bed…where we can take our time and I can show you…'

He stopped, frowning as Lucianna gave a small sharp cry, her eyes suddenly going very dark, and his expression was very male as he realised the cause of her audible moan of pleasure was the sight of his naked body.

As Lucianna looked a little self-consciously from him to the towel which lay on the stairs beside him, she asked him, 'When did you…?'

'I didn't…you did,' he told her softly, adding when she shook her head, 'Yes, you did; it was just now when I kissed you right here.' He touched one fingertip to the place just above the line of her briefs where his mouth had only seconds before been caressing her sensitive skin and sending frantic pulses of pleasure darting through her.

'Jake…' Lucianna started to say, and then stopped as she closed her eyes. What she wanted to say, what she ought to be saying, was that they shouldn't be doing this, that *she* shouldn't be here with him like this, not when… But as she raised her hand she inadvertently brushed her fingertips against his thigh and as she felt the hard, warm sensation of his skin, followed by the flooding sweetness of her own longing for him, she knew those words would never be spoken. Instead she looked up into his eyes and then down at his body, and then, with a low moan, opened her arms to him.

They might not have made love on the stairs as Jake had threatened but it was a pretty close thing. By the time they reached the bed both of them were naked and as he lowered her onto it bending over to kiss first her mouth and then one breast and then her mouth again and then the other, before sliding his hands over her body, cupping her hips and then stroking her thighs and gently easing them apart, Lucianna knew that she didn't want to wait any longer for him.

The book on flirtation hadn't had any helpful hints on how one might best deal with such a situation but in truth Lucianna didn't need any, and if Jake's reaction to the way she touched him and the soft, encouraging sounds of need she made were anything to go by she was managing very well without them.

This time, perhaps because her body already knew the pleasure his would give it, the sensation of having him within her was so overwhelming, so explosive that the shudders of pleasure and completion started to pulse through her right from Jake's first thrust, the intensity and swiftness of her climax leaving her shuddering in his arms. She was so sensitive to him that she could actually feel the hot, thick pulse of his own release within her body, could feel it and, unbelievably, react to it with a softer, gentler echo of her own earlier orgasm, a quick, delicate throb of her body as though it wanted to draw him even closer and deeper within it as she took from him that final, life-giving male pulse of desire.

'John…' Lucianna began sleepily as she cuddled up in Jake's arms, her body and emotions totally exhausted after the events of the evening but still wanting to explain to Jake that she hadn't really been upset to realise that John didn't love her. But her eyes were already closing, her breathing slowing, and suddenly, as sleep claimed her, it was too much of an effort to say anything.

Jake, on the other hand, was suddenly very much awake.

John. She had called *him* John! As he lay there in the darkness with Lucianna's body nestled so trustingly and lovingly in his arms, he knew with bleak certainty that there was no pain worse than hearing the woman you had just loved calling you by another man's name. The man she really wanted.

Lucianna woke up abruptly, confused at first by her surroundings. And then she remembered. Shivering, she tried to blink back her tears as she realised that once again Jake had left her alone in bed. *His* bed, though, this time, not hers. Pushing back the bedclothes, she slid her feet to the floor and started to walk towards the half-open bedroom door.

There was a light on downstairs and instinctively

she made her way down, frowning as she reached the hallway and heard the sound of someone using a computer in Jake's office… Pushing open the door, she walked in, oblivious to the fact that she was completely naked.

Jake was seated at his desk, dressed in a shirt and jeans.

Still frowning, she studied the screen in front of him.

'Jake, what are you doing down here?' she asked him tremulously.

'Working!'

'Working!'

All the emotions she had been fighting to suppress welled up inside her.

'What is it with me…what is it that's *wrong* with me?' she demanded furiously. 'What is it about me that makes it impossible for a man to love me…? First John and now you… Oh, I don't care about John. I realise now I *never* loved him really at all…in fact I'm actually glad that he doesn't want me…but *you*…' Tears rolled down her face and she shook them away impatiently. 'I *love* you, Jake, but I know you don't love me.

'You've even tried to bribe me, to buy me off so that no one would ever know that you and I… But you didn't *need* to do that… I would *never* have told anyone… I suppose you thought that just because you'd…because we'd been lovers…that I'd expect… But I'm not that naive…I do know *some* things. And I suppose you're down here working now because you didn't want me to think…because you don't want me to think…' She started to correct herself and then stopped as Jake strode out from behind his desk, his face white and an expression in his eyes which…

Nervously Lucianna gulped and swallowed, protesting feebly as he reached her and took hold of her, 'Jake…'

'What do you mean, you love me?' she heard him demanding rawly.

'What do you mean what do I mean?' Lucianna countered tremulously. 'I suppose you don't want me to say it but it's the truth and I'm not going… I love you, Jake, and I'm sorry if you don't want me to…'

'You're *sorry*? Oh, my God,' he muttered piously under his breath. 'Lucianna, I—' He stopped and took a deep breath, his skin drawn tight across the bones of his face as he shook his head and told her abruptly, 'Come with me…'

Docilely, Lucianna followed him as he guided her out of his study and towards the stairs, walking so fast that she had trouble keeping up with him.

Halfway up the stairs he turned round to wait for her, and as she reached him Lucianna heard him saying helplessly, 'Oh, Luce…Luce…Luce…' And then she was in his arms and he was kissing her as fiercely as though they hadn't kissed in years, decades, centuries, as though they hadn't kissed for a lifetime. And in between his kisses he was telling her that he loved her, that he had always loved her and that he always *would* love her.

Somewhere along the line Lucianna realised that she and rationality had parted company, but that no longer seemed to matter, not when she had Jake's kisses, Jake's hands, Jake's body…

'Oh, you *can* do it here on the stairs—you were

right,' she managed to gasp as her body responded to the shuddering thrust of Jake's within her.

'The stairs, the kitchen, the table, the floor…anywhere…anywhere you like, anywhere you want…' Jake moaned sensually to her as he carried her with him to a climax that was a fierce starburst of sensation, the response of her womanhood to his manhood.

'Don't you ever, ever again tell me that I don't love you,' Jake told her thickly ten minutes later as he wrapped her in his arms and carried her back to bed and joined her there, holding her close to his heart as he whispered the words to her.

'But I thought you didn't…you said…' Lucianna began, and then fell silent as he kissed her gently.

He told her softly, 'I've loved you from the day I was old enough to know what love was—when you were too young to even begin to be burdened with such feelings. I've loved you and I've hated myself for it, and sometimes, I admit, I've come close to hating you for it as well.'

Lucianna sat up in bed, her eyes sparking indignantly. 'You've loved me all that time and you've never said anything, never shown me…told me…? You let me think you didn't care, you didn't want me, even made me feel you were trying to *pay* me to stay out of your life by coming up with that contract to keep the bank at bay…'

As she paused to take a deep breath, Jake interrupted firmly, 'Now hang on; let's take one thing at a time. For a start, when I first realised how I felt about you, you were way, way too young for me to tell you, and if I had…well, legally you might have been able to enter into an adult sexual relationship with me but mentally, emotionally, and in just about every way I could think of, to persuade you to give yourself to me then, to *commit* yourself to me, would have been as much a crime against you as it would have been against my love.

'I didn't say anything, Luce, quite simply because I loved you enough not to… Now what are those for?' he chided her gently as he saw the quick, emotional tears filling her eyes.

'Oh, Jake, I've been so wrong about you; all those years, all those times when you seemed so aloof and uncaring, when I…'

She bit her lip and stopped, and Jake said rawly, 'When you…? Go on. What were you going to say? Or can I guess? All those times when you treated me as though you loathed the very sight of me?'

'Is that why you decided to…to help me learn how to become a woman?' Lucianna asked him tentatively.

His reply surprised her.

'No,' he told her firmly. 'No, it wasn't…and, whilst we're on the subject, I did *not* help you *learn* how to become a woman, you already *were* a woman…very much a woman…the woman I loved,' he insisted sternly. 'And if other men—another *man*—didn't have the maturity or intelligence to appreciate that fact then I was damned if I was going to point it out for him.

'No.' He leaned forward, cupping her face, kissing her lingeringly on the mouth and murmuring appreciatively, his hand starting to move towards her breast, until, a little reluctantly, Lucianna reminded him that he hadn't finished his explanation.

'No, I haven't, have I?' he agreed, apparently unable to resist the temptation to drop a teasing ring of kisses around her now quivering nipple before tugging the duvet back around her and telling her, 'And with you looking like that I doubt that I'm ever going to. All right, all right. Now, where was I? Oh, yes. The main reason I decided to pick up what my common sense told me was a challenge I shouldn't go within a million miles of accepting was because of you—for you…

'I hated to see the way you were hurting so badly,' he told her tenderly, 'and I hated as well to see how little others valued you when I knew that if they'd only take the time, look a little closer… Love—*real* love—has nothing to do with physical attractiveness—at least not for me. It goes deeper, much, much deeper than that. After all, a person's physical appearance is only their outer shell and it's the inner personality, the inner person that really counts.

'No, I wanted to help you to discover the real power of your womanhood, of *yourself*, for your *own* sake. If the only gift I could ever allow myself to give you was the gift of your own self-confidence, your belief in yourself as a woman, the sense of self-worth that those idiotic brothers of yours should have—'

He paused and broke off, shaking his head. 'There were so many times when you were growing up when—'

'They didn't mean to hurt me,' Lucianna acknowledged ruefully. 'I was just too sensitive…too aware, perhaps, of the way boys of a certain age talked about and reacted to certain things about a girl.'

'You hid away your femininity because you were afraid of the consequences of it,' Jake told her gently. '*I* could see that but—'

'If you loved me so much then why did you leave me…reject me after…when…the night…?'

'I felt I'd taken advantage of you, broken my own code of morals, used your vulnerability and need, and your growing awareness of your own sensuality, in a way that went totally against everything I'd promised myself the relationship between us would be. And the worst of it was I knew damn well that given the whole situation over again I *still* wouldn't have been able to stop myself…to resist…

'Making love with you was like a drug: one taste wasn't anywhere near enough and simply served to whet my appetite for even more. All I could feel was the need within me that previously I'd been able to keep under control only because my body hadn't ever experienced the sweetness of…of you…

'In the morning, I couldn't believe that you and I…that we'd…that I… I never knew it could be like that…that I could want…need…feel…'

Lucianna looked away shyly and then told him huskily, 'In your arms…with you…like that…it felt…it was all the things I'd ever dreamed making love should be but had felt never could be for me. But what hurt me even more than waking up without you then was when I came to your house the next day just as Felicity was leaving. She'd already been round to see me to try and get your name and address. John was always talking about her and I knew…' She swallowed. 'I felt so jealous, so full of despair and anger and self-loathing.'

'You had no need,' Jake told her lovingly. 'I'd already made it more than plain to her that I wasn't interested in what she had to offer…in *anything* she had to offer…'

Very slowly Jake bent his head to kiss her and Lucianna held her breath, her whole body quivering with suppressed longing and expectation, and then, shockingly, he stopped and looked into her eyes.

'I nearly forgot,' he told her sternly. 'That contract you sent back to me in so many pieces… I could have wrung your pretty little neck for doing that, after all the trouble I'd been to. What on earth made you think I'd done it to buy you off?' He shook his head. 'I did it because I wanted to help you… You worked so damned hard to get your business going, and you are a good mechanic, a better than good mechanic, Luce—and don't ever let anyone else tell you differently,' he chided her.

'You realise, of course, that our children are bound to turn out to be little geniuses, don't you?' he added, laughing into her eyes at her expression. 'What with my business brain and your mechanical skills, they'll probably end up ruling the world…'

Lucianna gave a small shudder. 'I hope not. That's the last thing I'd want for them,' she told him quietly.

'Then what would you want for them?' Jake asked her tenderly as he started to stroke her skin, and then he bent his head to nibble on the delicate cord that began just behind her ear, causing her to quiver visibly and longingly, her eyes closing in mute pleasure.

Finally she whispered unsteadily, 'What I want is for them to be happy and loved…to grow up with confidence, to know that they are worthy of being loved and giving love in return…'

'They will,' Jake promised her softly. 'After all, with our example to follow, how could they do anything else?'

'Jake, it's almost morning,' Lucianna told him as

she saw the first signs of light pearling the sky beyond his bedroom window.

'Good… I love looking at you whilst we make love, Lucianna… I love seeing the expression in your eyes and on your face… I love knowing that I'm pleasing you and I love—'

'I love you, Jake,' Lucianna interrupted him huskily. 'I love you so much.'

'Do you? Come here, then, and show me,' Jake challenged her.

Laughing up at him, Lucianna fully discarded the duvet and, proudly glorying in the nudity of her body and Jake's reaction to it and to her, she crossed the small space that divided them and went into his waiting arms.

Miranda Lee is Australian, and lives near Sydney. Born and raised in the bush, she was boarding-school educated and briefly pursued a career in classical music, before moving to Sydney and embracing the world of computers. Happily married, with three daughters, she began writing when family commitments kept her at home. She likes to create stories that are believable, modern, fast-paced and sexy. Her interests include meaty sagas, doing word puzzles, gambling and going to the movies.

Don't miss Miranda Lee's latest seductive story:
THE TYCOON'S TROPHY WIFE
On sale in October 2005, in
Modern Romance™!

AT HER BOSS'S BIDDING

by

Miranda Lee

PROLOGUE

SHE was perfect, Justin thought from the first moment Ms Rachel Witherspoon walked in to be interviewed.

Perfectly plain and prim-looking, dressed in a very unsexy black suit, mousy brown hair severely scraped back and anchored in a twist. No make-up and no perfume, he realised with relief, the absolute opposite of the blonde bombshell who'd been wiggling her way around his office for the last month, pretending to be his personal assistant.

No, that was probably unfair. The girl had been efficient enough. The company who'd sent her over straight away after his previous PA quit on short notice didn't have dummies on their books.

But she'd made it clear within a few days that her services could easily extend beyond being just his PA. She'd used every opportunity—and every weapon in her considerable physical arsenal—to get this message across. He'd been bombarded with provocative clothes, provocative smiles and provocative comments till he couldn't bear another second. When she'd come in last Monday, showing more cleavage than a call-girl, Justin had cracked.

He didn't sack her as such. He didn't have to. She was just a temp. He simply told her that this would be her last week, saying that he'd hired a permanent PA and she was starting the following Monday.

A lie, of course. But a necessary one for his sanity.

Not that he was sexually tempted by her. Oh, no. It

was just that every time she came on to him, he was reminded of Mandy and what she must have got up to with that boss of hers. What she was *still* getting up to every single day, jet-setting around the world and being his personal assistant in every which way there was.

Justin's jaw clenched down hard at the thought. It had been eighteen months since his wife had confessed what had been going on, then added the shattering news that she was leaving him to become her boss's mistress.

Eighteen months! Yet the pain was still there. The pain of her betrayal and deception, plus the sharpest memory of the hurtful things she'd said to him that final day. Cruel things. Soul-destroying things!

Most men who'd been so savagely dumped might have soothed their battered egos by going out and bedding every female in sight. But Justin hadn't been to bed with a single woman since Mandy walked out. He simply hadn't wanted to. Just the thought of being physically intimate with another female made him shudder.

Of course, none of his male friends and colleagues knew that. You didn't confess such things to other men. They would never understand, or sympathise. His mother had an inkling, though. She knew how hurt he'd been by Mandy's deception and desertion. She kept telling him that someday he'd meet a really nice woman who'd make him forget about Mandy.

Mothers were eternal optimists. And incorrigible matchmakers.

So when his mum—to whom he'd been complaining about his office situation—rang last weekend to say that she had the perfect PA for him he'd been understandably wary. Only after he'd struggled without a secretary for a week, and been repeatedly reassured that this Rachel was nothing like his temptation of a temp, did Justin agree to interview Ms Witherspoon.

And here she was. In the flesh.

What there was of it.

She was so thin! And terribly tired-looking, with huge black rings under her eyes. Nice eyes, though. Nice shape. And an interesting colour. But so sad.

She was supposed to be only thirty-one, according to the birthdate on her résumé. But she looked closer to forty.

Understandable, he supposed, after what she'd gone through these last few years. Sympathy for her washed through Justin and he decided then and there to offer her the job. He already knew she had the qualifications, even if she might be a bit rusty. But someone as smart as she obviously was would have no trouble brushing up on her secretarial skills.

Still, he supposed he had to go through the motions of a proper interview, otherwise she might think it a bit fishy. Nobody liked charity. Or pity.

'So, Rachel,' he said matter-of-factly once she'd settled herself in the chair. 'My mother has told me a lot about you. And your résumé here is very impressive,' he added, tapping the two-page work history which had been faxed to him the day before. 'I see you were finalist in the Secretary of the Year competition a few years back. And your boss at that time was very high up in the Australian Broadcasting Corporation. Perhaps you could tell me a little about your work experience there...'

CHAPTER ONE

'THIS is just like old times, isn't it?' Rachel said to Isabel as she jumped into bed and pulled the pretty patchwork quilt up to her chin.

'True,' Isabel returned, and climbed into the matching single bed, her memory racing back to those old times.

Rachel and Isabel had attended the same boarding-school, and become best friends from day one. After Rachel's parents were killed in a freak train accident when Rachel was only fourteen, the girls had grown even closer. When Rachel's upbringing had been taken over by her mother's best friend, a nice lady named Lettie, Isabel had been thrilled to discover that Lettie lived in the same suburb of Sydney as her parents did. During the school holidays Rachel had often slept over at Isabel's. Sometimes, she'd stayed for days. Lettie hadn't minded. The girls had become inseparable, and liked nothing better than to lie awake in bed at night and talk for hours.

Rachel smiled over at Isabel. 'I feel like fifteen again.'

Well, you don't *look* like fifteen, Isabel thought with an inner sigh. Rachel looked every one of her thirty-one years, and then some. Which was a real pity. She'd once been drop-dead gorgeous, with glossy auburn hair, flashing eyes and a fab figure which Isabel had always envied.

But four years of nursing her terminally ill foster-mother had taken its toll. Rachel was a mere shadow of her former self.

Isabel had hoped that Lettie's finally passing away—the poor love had been suffering from Alzheimer's—and Rachel getting back into the workforce would put some oomph back into the girl.

But that hadn't happened yet.

Still, it had only been a few weeks.

She *had* put on a couple of pounds, which was a start. And when she smiled as she had just then you could catch a glimpse of the vibrant beauty she'd once been.

Hopefully, tomorrow, at the wedding, she'd smile a lot. Otherwise, when she saw the photographs of herself at a later date she'd be in for a shock. Isabel knew that she herself was looking her very best. Love suited her. As did pregnancy.

She was glowing.

Isabel was glad now that she'd taken *some* measures to make sure her chief bridesmaid didn't suffer too much by comparison.

'Promise me you'll let my hairdresser have his wicked way with you tomorrow,' Isabel insisted. 'Red hair will look much better with your turquoise dress than brown. And its bare neckline needs curls bouncing around on your shoulders. None of that wearing your hair pulled back like you do for work. Or up in any way. Rafe hates hair worn up on a woman, anyway. I've also hired a make-up artist to do our faces and I don't want to hear any objections.'

'I won't object. It's your day. I'll do whatever you want. But just a temporary rinse in my hair, please. I don't want to show up at the office on Monday morning with red hair.'

'Why not?'

'You know why not. One of the reasons Justin hired me as his PA was because I was nothing like my predecessor. She'd been flashy and flirtatious, remember? Alice told us all about her.'

Isabel rolled her eyes. 'I don't think a bit of red dye in your hair constitutes flashy and flirtatious.'

'Maybe not, but I don't want to take any chances. I like my job, Isabel. I don't want to do anything to risk losing it.'

'You know, when I first heard about Justin McCarthy I thought he was being sensible, not wanting a glamour-puss secretary who obviously had the hots for him. Office affairs rarely end well, especially for the woman. Now I'm beginning to agree more with Rafe's opinion of him. He says any divorced guy who fires a beautiful PA for flirting with him has to either be paranoid about women, or gay.'

'He did not fire my predecessor,' Rachel said, rather defensively, Isabel thought. 'She was just a temp. And Justin is not at all paranoid about women. He's very nice to me.'

'You said he was difficult and demanding.'

Rachel sighed. 'That was only on the day I somehow stupidly deleted a file and it took him six hours to recover it. Normally, he's very even-tempered.'

'Not all bitter and twisted?'

'I don't see any evidence of it.'

'OK, that leaves gay. So, what do you think? Is your boss gay? Could that be the reason his wife left him?'

'I honestly don't know, and quite frankly, Isabel, I don't care. My boss's private life is his own business.'

'But you said he was good-looking. And only in his

mid-thirties. Are you saying you're not attracted to him, just a little?'

'Not at all. *No*,' Rachel repeated firmly when Isabel gave her a long, narrowed-eyed look.

'I don't believe you. You told me a little while back that you were so lonely you'd sleep with anything in trousers. Now here you are, working very closely with a handsome hunk of possibly heterosexual flesh and you're telling me you don't have the occasional sexual fantasy about him? You might be a bit depressed, Rach, but you're not dead. This is me you're talking to, remember? Your best friend. Your confidante in matters up close and personal over the years. I haven't forgotten that you lost your virginity at the tender age of sixteen, and you were never without a boyfriend after that till Eric dumped you. You might not like men much any more, given what that bastard did, but—'

'Oh, I still like *some* men,' Rachel broke in. 'I like Rafe,' she added with a cheeky little grin.

'Yes, well, all females like Rafe,' Isabel returned drily, 'even my mother. But since darling Rafe is already the father of my babe-to-be, and about to become my husband tomorrow, then you can't have him, not even on loan. You'll have to find some other hunk to see to your sexual needs.'

'Who said I had sexual needs?'

'Don't you?' Isabel was startled. She must have after four years of celibacy!

'I don't seem to. I rarely *think* about sex any more, let alone need it.'

Yes, that was patently obvious, now that Isabel came to think about it. If Rachel felt like sex occasionally, she'd do herself up a bit, and to hell with her paranoid boss. There were plenty of other secretarial jobs in the world, and plenty of other men to go with them. The business district of Sydney was full of very attractive men of all ages. Of course, with her looks on the wane, Rachel might not be able to catch herself a seriously gorgeous hunk like Rafe, but there was no reason for her to be lonely, or celibate.

'Actually, I'm not sure I ever did need it, as such,' Rachel went on thoughtfully. 'Sex was just another facet of my being in love. Losing my virginity at sixteen wasn't a sexual urge so much as an emotional one. I'd fallen in love for the first time and I wanted to give myself to Josh.'

'But you enjoyed it. You told me so.'

'Yes, I certainly did. But it wasn't just sex I was after. It was that lovely feeling of being loved.'

Isabel smiled. 'You know, it's possible to have very good sex without love, Rach.'

'Maybe for you, but not for me. When I said I'd sleep with anyone after Lettie died, that was just my grief and loneliness talking. I can't just sleep with anyone. I have to be in love and, quite frankly, since my experience with Eric I don't think I'm capable of falling in love any more. I just don't have the heart for it. Or the courage. Eric hurt me more than I could ever explain. I honestly thought he loved me as much as I loved him. But, looking back, I don't think he loved me at all.'

'He didn't, the selfish rat. But that doesn't mean that one day you won't meet a man who will love you the way you deserve to be loved.'

'You're only saying that because you were lucky enough to find Rafe. Not so long ago, you didn't have such a high opinion of the male sex.'

'True.' Isabel couldn't deny that she'd been a classic

cynic for ages where men were concerned. She'd spent most of her adult female life falling in love with Mr Wrong. She knew where Rachel was coming from and, honestly, she couldn't blame her for feeling the way she did. Eric had treated her shamefully, dumping her after he found out Rachel was quitting her job to look after Lettie. That, coming on top of Lettie's own husband heartlessly abandoning his increasingly vague wife, must have been the final straw. It was no wonder Rachel's faith in the male sex had been seriously dented.

'I'm quite happy as I am, Isabel,' Rachel went on, '*without* a man in my personal life. I'm really enjoying my job. It's very interesting working for an investment consultant. I'm learning a lot about the stock market, and money matters, which hasn't exactly been my forte till now, as you know. I'm thinking of going to university at night next year and doing a business degree, part-time. I have plans for my life, Isabel, so don't you worry about me. I'll be fine.'

Isabel sighed. That's what she always said. Rachel was one brave girl. But a rather unlucky one. When Lettie died they'd both thought she'd at least have some financial equity in Lettie's house, despite it being mortgaged. Rachel was the sole beneficiary in Lettie's will, made after Lettie's husband had deserted her. Rachel had been going to sell the house and put a deposit on an inner-city apartment with the money left over after the loan had been repaid. So she'd been shattered to find out the house was still in Lettie's husband's name.

When Rachel went to the solicitor who was looking after Lettie's estate and explained that she'd personally paid the mortgage for the past four and a half years with money she'd earned doing clothes alterations at home, the solicitor had countered that Lettie's ex had paid the mortgage for fifteen years before that and had no intention of giving her a cent.

She was also informed that Lettie's ex was thinking of contesting Lettie's last will as well, since it was made after she was diagnosed with a mentally debilitating illness. Rachel was advised she could go to court to fight for a share of the house and contents if she wished, but her case was shaky. Even if she won, the amount of money she'd be awarded would undoubtedly be exceeded by her court costs.

So Rachel had walked away with nothing but a few personal possessions, her clothes and a second-hand sewing machine.

She'd temporarily been living with Isabel in her town house at Turramurra, and had agreed to house-sit whilst Isabel and Rafe were away on their honeymoon. Isabel had offered her the use of her place on a permanent basis for a nominal rent, since she was moving into Rafe's inner-city terraced house on their return, but Rachel had refused, saying she would look for a small place of her own closer to the city.

Silly, really, Isabel thought. She should let her friends help her in her hour of need. But that was Rachel for you. Independent and proud. *Too* proud.

But the nicest person in the world.

Isabel hoped that one day a man might come along worthy of her. A man of character and sensitivity. A man with a lot of love to give.

Because of course that was what Rachel needed. To be loved. Truly. Madly. Deeply.

Just as Rafe loves me, Isabel thought dreamily.

God, she was so lucky.

Poor Rachel. She did feel terribly sorry for her.

CHAPTER TWO

RACHEL hurried down the city street the following Monday morning, anxious not to be late for work. She'd caught a slightly later train than usual, courtesy of the longer time it had taken her to get ready for work that morning. Now she was trying to make up for lost time, her sensibly shod feet working hard.

Turning a corner into a city street which faced east, Rachel was suddenly confronted by the rays of the rising sun slanting straight into her eyes. But she didn't slacken her pace.

The day was going to be warm again, she quickly realised. Too warm, really, for a black suit with a long-sleeved jacket. Spring had been late coming to Sydney this year, but it was now here with a vengeance. October had had record temperatures so far and today looked like no exception. Not a cloud marred the clear blue sky, making the weather forecast for a southerly change today highly unlikely.

There was no doubt about it. She'd have to buy some new work clothes soon. What she'd been wearing would not take her right through the spring till summer. She should never have been stupid enough to buy all long-sleeved suits to begin with. She'd buy something other than black next time too, though nothing bright or frivolous. Something which would go with black accessories. Light grey, perhaps. Or camel. That colour was very in.

Unfortunately, such shopping would have to wait till

Isabel got home from her honeymoon in three weeks' time. Rachel didn't have a clue where the shops were that Isabel had taken her to last time, and which catered brilliantly for the serious career girl. Admittedly, a large percentage of the clothes in those shops was black, but they also had other colours.

Till then, however, she was stuck with black. And long sleeves.

Thank heaven for air-conditioning, she thought as she pushed the sleeves up her arms and puffed her way up the increasingly steep incline.

A sideways glance at her reflection in a shop window brought a groan to her lips. Her hair was still red, despite several washings yesterday and a couple more this morning. Maybe not quite as bright a red as it had been for the wedding on Saturday, but bright enough. She wished now she'd gone out yesterday and bought a brown hair dye. But at the time she'd been hoping the colour would still wash out.

If Isabel hadn't already been winging her way overseas on her honeymoon, Rachel would have torn strips off her mischief-making best friend. That hairdresser of hers must have used a semi-permanent colour on her hair, Rachel was sure of it.

Admittedly, she'd ended up looking pretty good for the wedding. From a distance. Amazing what a glamorous dress, a big hairdo and a make-up expert could achieve. But that was then and this was now, and bright red hair did not sit well with Rachel's normally unmade-up face, or her decidedly *un*-glamorous work wardrobe.

She was thankful that the repeated washings yesterday had toned down the colour somewhat. Hopefully, the way she was wearing it today—scraped back even more severely than usual—would also minimise the effect. She would hate for Justin to think that she was suddenly trying to attract his attention in any way.

As she'd told Isabel the other night, she liked her job. And she didn't want to lose it. Or even remotely risk the good relationship she'd already established with her boss, which was very professional and based on mutual respect. Justin had told her only last week what a relief it was to come into work and not be overpowered by some cloying perfume, or confronted with a cleavage deep enough to lose the Harbour Bridge in.

Rachel was out of breath by the time she reached the tall city office block which housed the huge insurance company where she worked.

When she'd first heard about the job as Justin's PA Rachel had been under the impression that Justin was an AWI executive. That wasn't the case, however. He was an independent hot-shot financial analyst under contract to AWI to give them his exclusive financial advice for two years, after which Justin planned on starting up his own consultancy company. Preferably in an office away from the inner-city area, he'd explained to her one day over a mutual coffee break, ideally overlooking one of the northern beaches.

Meanwhile, AWI had given him use of a suite of rooms on the fifteenth floor of their building, which was high up enough to have a good view of the city and the harbour.

But the view wasn't the only good thing about this suite of rooms. The space was incredible. Rachel had sole occupancy of the entire reception area, which was huge, and boasted its own powder room and tea-cum-store room, along with a massive semicircular work station where three secretaries could have happily worked side by side without being cramped.

Justin's office beyond was just as spacious, as well as having two large adjoining rooms, one furnished for meetings, the other for relaxing and entertaining. Rachel had never seen a better-stocked bar, not to mention such a lavish bathroom, tiled from top to bottom in black marble, with the most exquisite gold fittings.

Justin had confided to her during her first interview that this suite of rooms had previously been occupied by an AWI superannuation-fund manager who'd redecorated as if he owned the company, and been subsequently sacked. No expense had been spared, from the plush sable carpet to the sleekly modern beech office furniture, the Italian cream leather sofas and the impressionistic art originals on the walls.

Clearly, Justin being allotted this five-star suite of rooms showed how much his skills were valued by his temporary employers.

Rachel valued him as her boss, too. She admired his strong work ethics and his lack of personal arrogance. Most men with his looks and intelligence possessed egos to match. Justin didn't. Not that he was perfect, by any means. He did have his difficult and demanding moments. And some days his mood left a lot to be desired.

Still, Rachel already knew she'd like nothing better than to go with him when he left to set up his own company. He'd already implied she could, if she wanted to. He seemed as pleased with her as she was with him.

A shaft of sunshine lit up Rachel's red hair again as she pushed her way into the building's foyer through the revolving glass doors. The top of her head fairly glowed in the glass and she groaned again. She would definitely be going out at lunch time and buying that brown dye. Meanwhile, she would explain to Justin the reason behind her change of hair colour, and that it was as good as gone. Then he couldn't jump to any wrong conclusions.

No one gave Rachel a second glance during the lift ride up to the fifteenth floor, which was because none of the smartly dressed men and women in the lift even knew her. Few people who worked in the building knew her. Justin worked alone, with only the occasional fund manager actually dropping in for advice, face to face. Mostly they contacted Justin by phone or email, and vice versa.

So far, he hadn't held a single meeting around the boardroom-like table in his meeting room, and only once to her knowledge had he entertained an AWI executive in the other room. Sometimes, he had a nap in there on one of the two sofas after he'd been working all night. He did attend monthly meetings upstairs with all the fund managers, but he never attended the company's social functions, and he resolutely refused to become involved in AWI's internal politics.

The truth was her boss was a loner.

Which suited Rachel just fine.

She'd found that since her lengthy stay-at-home absence from the workforce—and the outside world in general—she'd become a bit agoraphobic. She liked the insular security of her present office situation, plus the little contact with strangers which her working day held. She no longer seemed to have the confidence she'd once had to make small talk with lots of people. She'd actually become quite shy, except with her very close friends, like Isabel and Rafe, which wasn't like her at all. She'd once had a very outgoing personality.

Isabel kept saying she'd get back to her old self eventually.

But Rachel was beginning to doubt it. Her experiences over the last few years had definitely changed her. She'd become introverted. And serious. And, yes, plain.

That was one of the biggest changes in her, of course. She'd lost her looks. And dying her hair red wasn't going to get them back. All it made her feel was foolish.

The lift doors opened and Rachel bolted down the corridor, hopeful of still arriving before Justin. He worked out in the company gym every day before work, and occasionally lost track of time. Hence his tardy arrival at the office on the odd morning.

The door from the corridor was still locked, heralding that this was one of those mornings. Rachel sighed with relief as she found her key, already planning in her mind to be sitting at her desk, looking coolly composed and beavering away on her computer when Justin finally came in.

She was doing just that when the door burst open fifteen minutes later. Her heart did jump, but not for any sexually charged reason, as Isabel had fantasised the other night, just instant agitation. What would her boss say when he saw her hair?

Justin strode in, looking his usual attractive but conservative self in a navy pinstriped suit, white shirt and bland blue tie. His damp dark hair was slicked back at the sides, indicating that he'd not long showered. He had the morning papers tucked under one arm and was carrying his black briefcase in the other. He was frowning, though not at her, his deeply set blue eyes quite distracted, his thick dark brows drawn together over his strong, straight nose in an attitude of worried concentration.

'Morning, Rachel,' he said with only the briefest sidewards glance as he hurried past. 'Hold the coffee for ten minutes, would you?' he tossed over his shoulder as he forged on into his private sanctuary. 'I have something I have to do first.'

When he banged the door shut behind him Rachel glared after him, her hazel eyes showing some feminine pique for once.

'Well!' she huffed at the closed door. 'And good morning to you, too!'

So much for his having noticed her red hair. It came to Rachel that she could have been sitting there stark naked this morning, and Justin would not have noticed.

Not that her being naked was anything to write home about these days. Despite having put on a couple of pounds during the past month, she was still thin, her once noteworthy breasts having long ago shrunk from a voluptuous D-cup to a very average B plus. She'd complained about it to Isabel on Saturday when they were getting dressed before the wedding.

'You still have bigger boobs than me,' Isabel returned as she surveyed Rachel in her underwear. 'OK, so you're thin, but you're in proportion. Actually, you look darned good in the buff, girl. You've surprised me.'

Rachel had laughed at the time. She laughed now, but with a different type of self-mockery. What on earth was she doing, even thinking about what she looked like naked? Who cared? No one was going to see her that way, except herself.

Again, it was all Isabel's fault, putting silly thoughts into her head about Justin and sex.

Sex! Now, that was a subject not worth thinking about.

So why was she suddenly thinking about it?

Rachel filled in the next eight minutes trying to work through her irritability, before giving up and rising to go pour Justin a mug of coffee from the coffee maker, which she kept perking all day. Justin liked his coffee. She figured that ten minutes would have passed by the time she carried it in to him. Any further delay was unacceptable. The sooner he noticed her red hair, and the sooner she explained the reason behind it, the sooner she'd be able to settle down to work, and put aside the fear of looking ludicrous in her boss's eyes.

'Come in,' Justin snapped when she tapped on his office door exactly ten minutes after his order.

She entered to find him sitting at the bank of computers which lined the far side of his U-shaped work station. His back remained to her as he rode his swivel chair down the long line of computers, peering at each screen for a couple of seconds as he went. His jacket was off and his shirtsleeves rolled up. His tie, she knew without being able to see it, would be loosened.

As Rachel made her way across the room Justin slid down in front of the furthest computer on the right.

'Just put it down here,' he directed, patting an empty spot next to his right elbow without looking up.

Grimacing with frustration, Rachel put the coffee down where ordered and was about to leave when she stopped.

'Justin...'

'Mmm?'

He still didn't look up.

She sighed. 'Justin, I need to talk to you,' she said firmly.

'What about?' Again, no eye contact.

'I wanted to explain to you about my red hair.'

'What red hair?' He spun round from the computer, his eyes finally lifting. He frowned up at her, his head tipping slightly to one side. 'Mmm. It's a bit bright for you, isn't it?'

Rachel winced. 'It looked all right for the wedding on Saturday,' she said, her pride demanding she say something in her own defence.

His blue eyes widened. 'Wedding? What wedding? My God, Rachel, you didn't go and get married on the weekend without telling me, did you?'

Rachel almost laughed. As if.

'I don't think you need worry about that ever happening, Justin,' she said drily. 'No, I was a bridesmaid at my best friend's wedding on Saturday and she insisted on having my hair dyed red for the day. It was supposed to wash out afterwards but, as you can see, it didn't. I just wanted to reassure you that I'm going to dye it back to brown tonight.'

He shrugged his indifference, then picked up his coffee. 'Why bother?' he said between sips. 'It doesn't look *that* bad. And it'll wash out—or grow out—eventually.'

Rachel's shoulders stiffened. It would take two years for it to grow out. Did he honestly think she had such little personal pride that she'd walk around with half-red, half-brown hair for two *years*?

Clearly, he did.

'It looks dreadful and you know it,' she said sharply, and whirled away from him before she did something she would regret.

Rachel could feel him staring after her as she marched towards the open doorway, probably wondering what was wrong with her. She'd never spoken to him in that tone before. But when she turned to close the door behind her he wasn't staring after her at all. Or even thinking about her. He was back, peering at the maze of figures on the computer, her red hair—plus her slight outburst—clearly forgotten.

Rachel didn't realise the extent of her anger till she tried to get back to work. Why she was so angry with Justin, she couldn't understand. His indifferent reaction to her hair should have made her happy. It was all rather confusing. But there'd been a moment in there—a vivid, *violent* moment—when she'd wanted to snatch the coffee out of his hands and throw it in his face.

It was perhaps just as well that her boss didn't emerge for the rest of the morning, or call her for more coffee to be delivered. Clearly, he was steeped in something important, some sudden programming brainwave or financial crisis which required his undivided attention.

In the month she'd been his PA, Rachel had discovered that Justin was a computer genius as well as a financial one, and had created several programs for following and predicting stock-market trends, as well as analysing other economical forces. Aside from her general secretarial duties, Rachel spent a couple of hours each day entering and downloading data into the extensive files these programs used. They needed constant updating to work properly.

She was completing that daily and slightly tedious area of her job shortly before noon, when the main door from the corridor opened and Justin's mother walked in.

Alice McCarthy was in her early sixties, a widow with two sons. She'd been one of Rachel's best customers during the four years she'd made ends meet by using her sewing skills at home. A tall, broad-shouldered woman with a battleship bust and surprisingly slender hips, Alice had difficulty finding clothing to fit off the peg. But she loved shopping for clothes, rather than having them made from scratch, and had more than enough money to indulge her passion. Mr McCarthy had been a very successful stockbroker in his day, and, according to Alice, a bit of a scrooge, whereas Alice veered towards the other extreme. Consequently, she was in constant need of a competent seamstress who could cleverly alter the dozens of outfits she bought each season.

Till recently that person had been Rachel, whom Alice had discovered when Rachel had distributed brochures advertising her sewing skills through all her local letterboxes. Alice lived only a couple of streets away from Lettie's house.

Despite the thirty-year age gap, the two women had got along well from the start. Alice's natural *joie de vivre* had brought some brightness into Rachel's dreary life. When her foster-mum passed away and her friends thought Rachel needed a job working outside of the home Alice had been generous enough to steer her into her present position, despite knowing this meant she had to find another person to alter her clothes. Fortunately, a salesgirl in one of the many boutiques Alice frequented had recommended an excellent alteration service in the city, run by two lovely Vietnamese ladies who were extremely efficient as well as inexpensive.

After Rachel had gone to work for her son Alice had

rung her at the office a couple of times to see how she was doing, but this was the first time she'd made a personal appearance.

'Alice!' Rachel greeted happily. 'What a lovely surprise. You're looking extremely well. Blue always looks good on you.'

Alice, who was as susceptible to a compliment as the next woman, beamed her pleasure. 'Flatterer. Nothing looks all that good on this unfortunate figure of mine. But I do my best. And my, aren't you looking a lot better these days? You've put on some weight. And you've changed your hair colour.'

Rachel's hand went up to pat the offending hair. 'Not for long. It goes back to brown tonight. I had it dyed for Isabel's wedding on Saturday. You remember Isabel, don't you? You met her at Lettie's funeral.'

'Yes, of course I remember her. Very blonde. Very beautiful.'

'That's the one. She wanted my hair red for the day. Of course, it wasn't done like this. It was down and curled. I also had more make-up on than a supermodel on a photo shoot.'

'I'll bet you looked gorgeous!'

'Hardly. But I looked OK for the occasion. And for the photographs. I'm well aware this colour red doesn't look any good on me normally.'

'But it might, you know, Rachel, if you wore some make-up. It's just that against your pale skin it looks too bright. And without any colour in your face that black suit you're wearing is too stark, by contrast. Now, if you were wearing blue,' she added, her own blue eyes sparkling, 'like the blue I've got on, and a spot of make-up, then that red hair just might be perfect.'

Rachel really wasn't in the mood for another woman to start trying to make her over. Isabel had been bad enough on the weekend. On top of that, she was still upset over Justin ignoring her this morning.

He wouldn't ignore her, however, if she started seriously tarting herself up. He'd think something was really up and then there would be hell to pay.

'Alice,' she said, slightly wearily. 'You were the one who told me about my predecessor, that flashy, flirtatious temp your son was so relieved to eject from his office. The reason Justin gave me this job is because he *likes* the way I look. He *likes* me *au naturel*.'

Alice rolled her eyes. In her opinion, no man liked women *au naturel*, even the ones who said they did. They all liked women to doll themselves up. You only had to watch men's eyes when a glamour-puss walked into a restaurant, or a party. Justin was simply going through a phase, a post-Mandy phase.

The trouble was, this phase was lasting far too long for her liking. It wasn't natural. Or healthy, either, for her son's mind or his body.

'That boy doesn't know *what* he likes any more,' she grumbled. 'That bitch of a wife of his certainly did a number on him. If ever I run into her again I'd like to…'

Whatever it was Alice was about to vow to do to her son's ex-wife was cut dead when the door to Justin's office was suddenly wrenched open, and the man of the moment appeared.

'Mum! I thought I heard a familiar voice. What are you doing here? And what were you talking about just then? Not gossiping about me to Rachel, were you?'

Alice's cheeks flushed but she managed not to look

too guilty. 'I never gossip,' she threw at her son defiantly. 'I only ever tell the truth.'

Justin laughed. 'In that case, why are you here? And no white lies, now. The truth, the whole truth and nothing but the truth.'

Alice shrugged. 'I came to the city early to do some shopping, didn't see a single thing I liked and decided on the spur of the moment to pop in and take you to lunch. Rachel too, if she'd like.'

'Oh, no, no, I can't,' Rachel immediately protested. 'I have some shopping that I simply have to do.' Namely, some brown hair dye.

'And neither can I,' Justin informed his mother. 'There was some unexpected bearish rumblings on the world stock markets last night and I have to have a report ready for the powers that be here before trading ceases today. So I'll be working through lunch. I was going to get Rachel to pop out and bring me back some sandwiches.'

'Poor Rachel,' Alice said. 'I thought the days of secretaries doing that kind of menial and demeaning job were over. I dare say you have her bring you coffee twenty times a day as well. I know how much you like your coffee. What else? Does she collect your dry-cleaning too?'

Justin looked taken aback. 'Well, yes, she has collected my dry-cleaning. Once or twice.' His eyes grew worried as they swung towards Rachel. 'Do you object to doing that kind of job, Rachel? You've never said as much.'

Rachel sighed. Of course she didn't object. If Alice thought those jobs were menial and demeaning, let her try changing urine-soaked sheets every morning.

'No, I don't mind at all. Really, Alice,' she insisted when Justin's mother looked sceptical. 'I don't.'

Now it was Alice's turn to sigh. 'No, you wouldn't. Just make sure you don't take advantage of Rachel's sweet nature,' Alice warned her son.

Rachel wished Alice would simply shut up.

Justin's eyes met hers again and she knew by their exasperated expression that he was thinking exactly the same thing. Rachel gave him a small smile of complicity, and his blue eyes twinkled back.

'I would never take advantage of Rachel,' he told his mother. 'I value her far too much to do anything to risk losing the best PA a man could have.'

Rachel's cheeks warmed at his flattering words.

She didn't realise at the time how ironic they were.

CHAPTER THREE

MOST city singles loved Friday afternoons. Their moods would lift as the working week drew towards an end, anticipation building for that wonderfully carefree moment when they poured out of their office buildings and into their favourite bars and drinking holes for the traditional Friday-night drinks-after-work bash. Even the non-drinkers liked Fridays, because there was still the weekend to look forward to, two whole days without having to sit at their desks and their computers; two whole days of doing exactly as they pleased, even if that was nothing.

Rachel was one of the exceptions to the rule. Since coming back to work she hated the week to end because she hated the prospect of two whole days of doing just that. Nothing.

As she made her way to work the following Friday morning Rachel began thinking she might have to go shopping by herself this weekend after all, just for something to do. Last weekend had been OK, because of Isabel and Rafe's wedding. But this weekend was going to be dreadful, with Isabel away and that strangely soulless town house all to herself.

She could hardly fill the whole weekend with housework. She already kept the place spotless on a daily basis. She could read, of course, or watch television. But, somehow, indoor activities did not appeal. She felt like getting out and about.

It was a pity that the town house didn't have a garden. Unfortunately, the courtyard was all paved and the few plants dotted around were in pots. Rachel liked working with her hands. That was why she'd first taken up sewing as a teenager.

But sewing was on the no-no list for Rachel nowadays. She never wanted to see her sewing machine again. It was packed away at the back of a cupboard, never to see the light of day again. After the funeral, whenever she looked at it she thought of Lettie's illness, and all that had happened because of it. No nice associations at all.

Sometimes, she wished Justin would ask her to work overtime on the weekend. She knew he went into the office on a Saturday, so surely there was something she could do. Extra data entry, perhaps. Justin often had to farm some of that work out to an agency.

But he never asked, and she wouldn't dream of suggesting it. He might see her offer as evidence of a desire for more of his company, rather than the result of chronic loneliness.

Rachel glanced up at the sky before she entered her building. The clouds were heavier than the day before, the southerly change predicted earlier in the week having finally arrived yesterday, bringing intermittent showers.

The thought of more rain over the weekend dampened Rachel's enthusiasm for shopping by herself. Maybe she would wait till Isabel returned. There was no real hurry, now that Sydney's weather had changed back to cooler. Her black suits would do a while longer.

Yes, she decided as she swung through the revolving glass doors. Her shopping expedition could wait.

Justin was already in when she arrived. Surprisingly,

he'd put on the coffee machine and was in the act of pouring himself a mugful when she walked into the tea room. He was wearing one of her favourite suits, a light grey number which looked well against his dark hair and blue eyes, especially when teamed with a white shirt and blue tie.

'Morning,' he said, throwing her a warm smile over his shoulder. 'Want me to pour you one as well?'

'Yes, please,' she answered, her spirits lifting now that she was at work. She shoved her black bag and umbrella on the shelf under the kitchen-like counter, then took the milk out of the fridge, preferring her coffee white, though she could drink it black, at a pinch. Justin always had his black.

'What's it like outside?' he asked, and slid her mug along the counter to where she was standing.

'Overcast,' she said as she added her milk.

'Not actually raining, though?' he queried just before his mug made it to his lips.

'Not yet. But it will be soon.'

'Mmm.'

Rachel detected something in that 'mmm' which made her curious.

'Why?' she asked. 'Do you have something on this weekend which rain will spoil?'

He took the mug away from his mouth. 'Actually, no, just the opposite. I won't be here in Sydney at all. I'm flying up to the Gold Coast this afternoon to spend the weekend at a five-star ocean-front hotel.'

'Lucky you,' she replied, wondering who he was spending the weekend with.

'No need to feel jealous. You're coming with me.'

Rachel was grateful that she hadn't lifted her own

coffee off the counter, because she surely would have spilt it.

Justin chuckled. 'You should see the look on your face. But don't panic. I'm not asking you to go away with me for a dirty weekend. It's for work.'

Rachel closed her mouth then. Well, of course it was for work. How could she, even for a split-second, imagine anything else?

Silly Rachel.

'What kind of work?' she asked, finally feeling safe enough to lift her coffee off the counter and take a sip.

'A different kind of investment advice from my usual. Apparently, this holiday hotel—it's called Sunshine Gardens—is on the market and all potential buyers—of which AWI is one—are being flown up free of charge so they can see and experience first-hand the hotel's attractions and assets. Generally speaking we can do our own thing, except for tomorrow night, when we'll be wined and dined by management, after which there'll be a video shown, along with a presentation of facts and figures to con everyone into believing the hotel is a rock-solid investment. Guy Walters was supposed to go, but he can't, so he asked me to go in his place.'

Rachel frowned. 'Guy Walters. Who's he? I can't place him.'

'You must know Guy. Big, beefy fellow. Fortyish. Bald head. Exec in charge of property investments.'

Rachel searched her memory. 'No. No, I don't think I do. I'd remember someone who looked like that.'

Now Justin frowned. 'You're right. Guy hasn't been down here to see me personally since you started. Anyway, I do weights with him every morning. When I arrived this morning he wasn't there. He raced in half an hour later and explained that he was off to the airport to fly to Melbourne because his dad was ill, after which he explained about where he was supposed to be going and begged me to go in his place. Apparently, the CEO of AWI is super-keen on buying this place and is expecting a report on his desk first thing Monday morning, no excuses. Guy said I was the only one he could ask to go in his place whose opinion he would trust. He said he knew an old cynic like me wouldn't be blinded by surface appearances and would look for the pitfalls. At the same time, he also wanted a woman's opinion. He said women see things men don't always see.'

'So what woman was *he* going to take? His secretary? Or a colleague?'

'No, actually, he'd been going to take his wife. When I pointed out I didn't have a wife he said that shouldn't present a problem for a man-about-town like me, and I got all that male nudge-nudge, wink-wink crap. Guy's always implying I must have a little black book filled with the phone numbers of dozens of dolly-birds available for dirty weekends at a moment's notice.'

Rachel stopped sipping her coffee, her curiosity piqued. 'And you don't?'

'God, no.' The distaste on his face was evident. 'That's not my style.'

Rachel didn't know what to think. Maybe he simply didn't like women. Or maybe he just had old-fashioned principles and standards.

The thought that he might be right off sex—and women—was swiftly abandoned. The sceptic in Rachel couldn't see any heterosexual male of Justin's age and health being totally off sex no matter what. It went against everything she and all her female friends had come to believe about the human male animal.

'I told Guy I would be taking my valued and very astute PA,' Justin added. 'If you're available to go, of course. Are you?'

'Yes, but…'

'But what?'

'What about the accommodation? If this chap had been going with his wife, then…'

'I've already thought of that and there are no worries there. AWI's been allotted a two-bedroom apartment with two separate bathrooms, so there's no privacy issue. Also, you don't have to spend every minute of every day with me. You're free as a bird. I'd expect you to accompany me to the dinner on the Saturday night, however.'

'Er—what would I have to wear to something like that?'

'Guy said it's black tie. Lord knows why. Someone's being pretentious as usual. Probably their PR person. Do you have something suitable in your wardrobe? If not, I'm sure AWI can spare the expense of a dress. You could buy one up there tomorrow. Tourist towns usually have loads of boutiques.'

'No, I've got something suitable,' Rachel returned, thinking immediately of her bridesmaid dress, which Isabel had chosen specifically because it was the sort of dress you could wear afterwards. At the time, Rachel hadn't been able to imagine where, but it would be ideal for wearing to this dinner. As much as Justin might not like her coming into the office done up to the nines, surely he wouldn't want her to accompany him to a dinner looking totally colourless and drab.

A tiny thrill ran down her spine as she thought of

how surprised he might be if she wore her hair down and put on a bit of make-up. Nothing overdone, of course. A classy, elegant look.

'Great. And don't forget it's going to be a lot warmer up there at this time of year,' Justin went on. 'You'll need very light clothes for day wear. Very casual, too.'

Rachel saw the expression in his eyes as they flicked up and down the severely tailored black suit she was wearing.

'It's all right, Justin,' she said wryly. 'I do have some other more casual clothes.' Again, thanks to Isabel.

When Isabel's ex-fiancé broke off their engagement earlier this year Isabel had given Rachel her entire honeymoon wardrobe, bought to be worn on a tropical island. Rachel had thought at the time she would never have an opportunity to wear any of them, same as with the bridesmaid dress.

Now, suddenly, she did. What a strange twist of fate!

'So when is the flight?' she asked.

'It departs at four, which doesn't leave all that much time to do what has to be done here before we go. Unfortunately, I can't abandon my other work today entirely. I still need to check last night's markets and you'll still have to update the files. So, let's see, now…you live at Turramurra, don't you?'

'For the moment.'

He frowned. 'What do you mean, for the moment?'

'It's my friend's place. I've been staying with her temporarily since my foster-mum's funeral. Don't you remember? I told you all about Lettie and her illness at my interview.'

He slapped his forehead with the ball of his free hand and shot her an apologetic glance. 'Of course you did. You also said you'd be selling her old house and buying yourself a unit closer to the city. Sorry. I did listen to you that day. Honest. I'd just forgotten for the moment. So how's all that going? Found a buyer yet?'

Rachel sighed. 'Unfortunately, things haven't worked out the way I thought they would. Lettie did will me everything she owned, but it turned out she didn't own the house and contents in the first place. It was all still in her husband's name. I could have taken the matter to court but I just didn't have the heart. The solicitor said I probably wouldn't end up with much, anyway.'

'He's right there. Litigation is to be avoided at all costs. But gee, Rachel, that's a damned shame. And not fair, after all you did for your foster-mum. But then, life's not fair, is it?' he added with the bitterness of experience in his voice. 'So what are you going to do about a place to live?'

'Well, I'm house-sitting Isabel's town house whilst she's on her honeymoon. She won't be back for another fortnight. But I plan on renting a place of my own closer to the city after she does get back.'

'Flats near the city are expensive to rent,' Justin warned. 'Even the dumps.'

'Tell me about it. I've been looking in the paper. I can only afford a bedsit. Either that, or I'll have to share.' Which was a last resort. The idea of moving in with strangers did not appeal at all.

'Can't see you sharing a place with strangers,' Justin said, startling Rachel with his intuition. 'Can't you stay where you are in your friend's place? She won't be needing it, now that she's married.'

'She did offer it to me for a nominal rent.'

'Then take it and don't be silly,' he pronounced

pragmatically. 'So, how long do you think it would take you to go there, pack, then get back to the airport? I'll pay for taxis both ways, of course.'

'I don't think I could do it in less than two hours, and that's provided I don't hit any traffic snags. It is Friday, you know.'

'True. That means you'll have to leave here by one at the latest. Guy gave me the plane tickets, so I'll give you yours before you go and we'll meet at the allotted departing gate. OK?'

'Yes. OK.'

Justin smiled over the rim of his coffee mug. 'I knew I could count on you not to make a fuss. Any other woman would have had hysterics about how she'd need all day to get packed and changed, but not you.'

Rachel gave a rueful little laugh. 'I'm not sure if that's a compliment or a criticism.'

'A compliment,' Justin said drily. 'Trust me. Come on, let's get back to work. I want to have a clear desk and a clear head by the time that plane takes off this afternoon. I don't know about you, but I'm rather looking forward to having a break away from this office, not to mention this rotten weather. I've always been partial to some sun and surf. Which reminds me. Don't forget to pack a swimming costume. Even if you don't like the surf, the hotel has a great pool, I'm told.'

He plonked down his empty mug and marched off, leaving Rachel to stand there, staring after him, her stomach revolving as she recalled the bright yellow bikini amongst the clothes Isabel had given her.

The thought of swimming in a bright yellow bikini in front of her boss sent her into a spin.

'Hop to it, Rachel,' he threw over his shoulder.

She hopped to it, but she still kept thinking about

that bikini. Though modest by some standards, it was still a bikini. That, combined with the colour, would not present the non-flashy, non-flirtatious image Justin had of her and which he obviously felt comfortable with. She knew it was a stretch of the imagination that he would ever be sexually attracted to her—especially if he didn't like women—but in the end Rachel decided that the bikini would be accidentally left at home. She had a good thing going with her job and she didn't want to risk changing the status quo.

With this thought in mind, she decided not to wear her hair down for the dinner tomorrow night, either. It could go up as usual. And her make-up would be confined to a touch of lipstick. That was all she owned, anyway. It would be crazy to race out and buy a whole lot of stuff for one night. For what? Just to satisfy her feminine pride? Because that was all that was at stake. *Her* pride. Nothing to do with Justin. He obviously didn't give a damn how she looked.

Feeling much better with these decisions, Rachel put her mind to her job. At one o'clock on the dot she was off, the taxi making good time to Turramurra. Packing was a breeze. Isabel's discarded honeymoon gear was already in a very nice suitcase. It was just a matter of taking some things out, and adding some, namely her bridesmaid gear, along with her toilet bag. She did also add some white sandals from Isabel's wardrobe, knowing her friend wouldn't mind.

She didn't have time to change but she did put a simple white T-shirt on under her black jacket so that she could take the jacket off once they reached Coolangatta.

By two-ten she was back in a taxi, heading for Mascot, but this time the going was slower, because it had started to rain quite heavily. They fairly crawled down the Pacific highway. There was an accident at an intersection at Roseville, which caused a back-up, and they moved at a snail's pace again right down to Chatswood, after which the flow of traffic improved, courtesy of the new motorway. But her watch still showed five after three when she climbed out at the domestic terminal at Mascot. By the time she'd waited in line, been booked in and gone through Security, it was twenty-five to four, only ten minutes from the scheduled boarding time.

As she hurried along the long corridor towards the nominated gate Rachel hoped Justin wasn't worrying. She knew he'd already arrived because the lady on the check-in counter had been left instructions on her computer to give her the seat next to him.

Gate eleven came into sight at last, and so did Justin. He was sitting on a seat at the end of a row in the waiting area, reading an afternoon newspaper, and not looking at all anxious, though he did glance up over the top of the pages occasionally. When he spied her walking towards him he folded the newspaper, smiled and patted the spare seat beside him.

'You made it,' he said as she dropped down into it.

'Just. The traffic back into town was horrendous. I was wishing I had a mobile phone to call you and tell you my progress.'

'No worries,' he said. 'You're here now.'

'Yes. Yes. I'm here now.' Breathless, relieved and quite excited, now that she wasn't stressing about her clothes, or how she would look at tomorrow night's dinner. It had been years since she'd gone anywhere for the weekend and here she was, flying off to the Gold Coast in the company of a very attractive man.

OK, so he was only her boss, and there was nothing remotely romantic between them. But other people didn't know that. Other people might look at them and think that they *were* going off for a dirty weekend together.

Not likely, you stupid girl, a quite savage voice reprimanded inside her head. *Just look at him. He's gorgeous! The epitome of tall, dark and handsome. And just look at you. Talk about drabsville. A few years ago, things might have been different. You were a real looker then. Now you're a shadow of your former self. No, not even a shadow. A shell. That's what you are. A cold, empty, sexless shell!*

Rachel sagged back against the seat, a huge wave of depression swamping her earlier excitement.

'I think this trip'll do you good,' Justin said suddenly by her side.

'Oh?' she replied wearily. 'Why do you say that?'

'You've been a bit down-in-the-mouth since your friend's wedding last weekend. I dare say you're missing her. And it can't be much fun, working for a workaholic bore like me.'

She stared over at him. 'You're not a bore. I like my job. And I like working for you.'

He smiled at her. 'And I like you working for me. You are one seriously nice woman. Which is why what my mother said the other day has been bothering me. Tell it to me straight, Rachel. Do you object to bringing me coffee and running little errands for me? If you do, then I want you to say so. Right now.'

'Justin, I don't mind. Honestly. It's a change sometimes to get up and do something physical instead of just sitting at the computer, updating files.'

He frowned. 'That's a good portion of your job, isn't

it? Updating the files. That *must* be boring for someone of your intelligence. I should involve you more in what I do, explain my programs, show you how to analyse the data yourself, make proper use of that good brain of yours. Would you like that?'

'Oh! I…I'd *love* it! If—er—you really think I could do it, that is,' she added, her chronic lack of confidence not quite keeping up with her instant enthusiasm over his proposal.

'Of course you can. That way, when I set up my own company, I'll promote you to being a proper personal assistant with a salary to match, and we'll hire another girl to work on Reception and data entry.'

'Justin! I…I don't know what to say.'

'Just say yes, of course.'

She beamed at him. 'Yes, of course.'

'That's another thing I like about you. You don't argue with me. Aah, there's the boarding announcement. Come on, let's be one of the first on board. Then I can settle back to reading the newspaper and you can read that book you've got in your bag.' He was on his feet in a flash and off.

'How do you know I've got a book in my bag?' she asked after they'd been through the boarding-pass check and were striding down the tunnel towards the plane.

'Rachel, give me credit for *some* powers of observation,' he said drily. 'I do realise I have my nose buried in computer screens most of the day but I'd have to be a total moron not to notice some of your habits. You read every single lunch-hour. And I imagine every day on the train to and from work. Am I right?'

'Yes.'

'What kind of books do you like?'

'Oh. All kinds. Thrillers. Romances. Sagas. Biographies.'

'I used to read thrillers obsessively when I was at uni,' he said in a happily reminiscent tone. 'But I have to confess my reading rarely extends beyond the newspapers and business-based magazines these days.'

'I think that's a shame. Reading's a great pastime. And a good escape.'

'A good escape, eh? Yeah, you're right. It is. Maybe I should try it,' he muttered under his breath, 'instead of the gym.'

Rachel just caught this last possibly meant-for-his-ears-only remark, and wondered what he was trying to escape from. The memories of his marriage?

If his mother was to be believed then his ex-wife had been the bitch from hell. But if that was the case, then why would Justin have married her in the first place? He didn't strike Rachel as being a fool, or a pushover.

Relationships were a minefield, Rachel mused as she trailed after Justin past the welcoming flight attendants and into the body of the plane. And most marriages were a right mystery to all but the people involved. Justin's mother would naturally blame her son's wife for their break-up, but did she really know what had happened between the pair of them?

Justin stopped abruptly next to row D and turned to her. 'You have the window seat,' he said. 'I don't mind sitting on the aisle. Actually, it gives me a bit more leg room.'

'Thanks,' she said gratefully, and slid into the window seat. She liked to see where she was going.

Once settled, Rachel took out her book then stowed her black shoulder bag under the seat in front of her, ready for take-off. 'I hope it's not raining up there too,' she said as she peered out at the rain-soaked tarmac.

Justin looked up from the newspaper. 'It isn't according to the radar weather map I looked up on the internet just before I left the office. It's fine on the Gold Coast today with a top temperature of twenty-seven degrees. And more of the same is forecast for the week-end.'

'Sounds lovely,' she said with a happy sigh.

When Justin resumed reading his newspaper, Rachel opened the family saga she'd been reading the last couple of days. It wasn't riveting so far, but she liked the author and trusted her to get her in eventually.

Soon, she was off in that imaginative world of the story, so she didn't see the man who boarded the plane shortly afterwards. Or his female companion. If she had, Rachel would have recognised both of them.

She missed seeing them again at Coolangatta Airport, as it was so easy to do in crowds. Though, admittedly, she had been occupied chatting away with Justin at the luggage carousel and hadn't looked round at the other people waiting to collect their bags. She missed them again in the foyer of Sunshine Gardens, because she and Justin were already riding the lift up to their ocean-view apartment by the time they arrived.

Rachel might not have seen them at all till the following night at the dinner—which would have been an even greater disaster—if she hadn't discovered on reaching the door of their apartment that her door key didn't work.

'It must be faulty,' Justin said when his worked fine. 'I'll call the front desk when I get inside and they can bring you up another one.'

'No, I'll go back down now and get one myself,' Rachel said. 'You saw how busy they were.'

'Rachel, you're much too considerate sometimes.'

'Not really. I've always found it's quicker and less irritating to just do things myself, rather than wait for someone else to do it.'

'True. That's why I carried the luggage up myself instead of leaving it to the porter. I'm like you, I think. I can't stand waiting for things. When I want something I want it *now*. Off you go, then. I'll put your case in your bedroom and find the coffee-making equipment. Or would you rather I pour you a drink drink?'

'Coffee for now, I think. But you don't have to make it.'

'I know that. Call it repayment for services rendered.'

'Justin, you are much too considerate sometimes,' Rachel quipped as she hurried off, smiling when she heard his answering laugh.

Rachel had no sense of premonition as she rode the lift down to the ground-floor level again. Why should she have?

The lift doors opened and she walked out into the terracotta-tiled foyer, glancing around again at the décor as she made her way over to the reception desk.

Actually, this hotel reminded her of an island resort she'd gone to once with Eric. High ceilings, cool colours and glass walls overlooking lush green gardens with lots of water features.

Eric…

Now, there was a right selfish so-and-so if ever there was one. If she'd known how shallow he was she'd never have fallen in love with him in the first place, let alone agreed to marry him.

Rachel gave herself a swift mental shake. She wouldn't think about Eric. Ever again.

But, perversely, when she walked up to the reception desk the man booking in reminded her strongly of Eric, despite only viewing him from the back. He had the same sandy blond hair. The same way of holding his shoulders. The same elegance.

The attractive brunette standing next to him seemed familiar as well. Rachel listened to them chatting away together as they checked in, their voices horribly familiar.

And then, suddenly, they both turned around.

CHAPTER FOUR

JUSTIN was suitably impressed the moment he stepped inside the apartment. It had a cool, comfy feel, with plenty of space, even to having its own foyer, which was unusual in hotel apartments.

As he dropped their two suitcases next to the hall stand—a sturdy yet elegant piece with a smoked-glass top and carved oak base—Justin caught a glimpse of himself in the matching mirror above. His hair, which possibly needed a cut, was all over the place. That's what happened when you had to walk across windy tarmac, as they had at Coolangatta airport. No tunnels to spoil you.

Straightening, Justin smoothed back the wayward top and sides with the flat of his hands, then moved a little closer to the mirror to peer at the bags under his eyes.

Could do with a good eight hours' sleep, he thought as he turned and went over to slot his room key into the gizmo beside the door. The lights came on automatically, as did the air-conditioning. That done, Justin strode into the main living area, where he stripped off his jacket and tie, tossed them over the back of one of the nearby dining chairs then took himself on a quick tour of the rest of the apartment.

Absolutely everything met with his approval, even the crisp citrus colours they'd used on the walls and soft furnishings. Normally, lime and yellow and orange would not be to his taste but the brightness was offset by the wall-to-wall cream carpet, the cream woodwork and the extensive use of pine. The kitchen was all pine, with white counter-tops and white appliances, and the bathrooms—thank heaven—were white as well. Justin had had about enough of that all-over black marble in the hideously pretentious bathroom at his office.

He contemplated giving Rachel the main bedroom, then decided she would only protest, so he put her bag in the second bedroom, which suffered little for size. Both bedrooms also had access to the balcony that stretched the full length of the apartment and had a view that looked pretty spectacular, even from inside.

How much better would it look from the balcony itself?

Justin decided to find out before making the coffee, and wasn't disappointed. You could see for miles, from Tweed Heads on his right to Surfer's Paradise in the northern distance with its tell-tale skyline of skyscrapers. The sea was looking breathtakingly beautiful, even now, with the sun having set and the sky darkening from its earlier bright blue to a dusky grey. Admittedly, first thing in the morning the sun might be a bit too brilliant as it rose over the horizon and slammed straight into the windows behind him, but in the afternoon and evenings it would be wonderful to sit outside here in one of the deckchairs, sipping some chilled white wine.

'I wonder if Rachel likes white wine,' he said to himself, and seriously hoped so, because the scenario he'd just pictured in his mind didn't seem quite so appealing on his own. He would ask her when she got back, and if she did he'd see about having Room Service send up a bottle or two. Then later he'd take her to the swankiest restaurant in the place for dinner.

Hotels like this always had at least one à la carte eating establishment.

Rachel deserved a bit of spoiling, he decided, after all she'd been through these past few years.

Justin breathed in the refreshing salt-sea air for thirty seconds longer before returning to the living area and going in search of the coffee-making equipment. It crossed his mind whilst he rummaged around in the cupboards that Rachel was taking a good while. Presumably, the front desk was still busy. Or maybe they couldn't find another key to this room. He made a mental note to find out what had actually happened. Guy would want to know what he thought of the service. The last thing a new owner needed to do was to have to sack staff then find replacements. Far too expensive and time-consuming an operation.

The electric jug found, Justin filled it and put it on, then set about emptying a small packet of—wow!—*quality* coffee into each of the two white mugs he'd located. No cheap muck. That was good. Very good. He hated hotels that supplied low-grade products. He'd have to remember to ask Rachel what the shampoo and conditioner were like. He could actually never tell the good from the bad in that department, but a woman would know. Guy was right in that regard.

The water had boiled and Justin was standing there, deciding whether to pour his or wait for Rachel to come back, when there came a knock on the door. He hurried over to answer it, tut-tutting to himself on the way.

'You don't have to tell me,' he said when he wrenched open the door to find Rachel on the other side. 'They didn't have another key.'

Rachel just stood there, her face ashen, her eyes anguished, her hands clutched tightly in front of her.

Justin, despite not being the most intuitive male in the world, was quick to appreciate her distressed state.

'Rachel!' he exclaimed. 'What is it? What's happened?'

'I...I...'

Clearly, she could not go on, her throat making convulsing movements as she struggled for control.

'Come inside,' Justin said and, taking her left elbow, steered her quite forcibly into the apartment. Her hands remained clutched tightly in front of her and she looked as if she was going to burst into tears, or faint.

Once Justin had kicked the door shut behind them, he guided her over to the three-seater opposite the television and plonked her down into the middle cushion, then sat on the pine coffee-table, facing her.

'Rachel,' he said softly, taking her still clasped hands within his. 'Tell me what happened?'

She gave a small laugh that held a decided edge of hysteria.

'What happened?' she repeated. 'They didn't recognise me, that's what happened. *He* didn't recognise me. Can you believe that?'

'Who's he?'

'Eric.'

'Who's Eric?'

'My fiancé,' she choked out, 'till I told him I was leaving my job to stay home and mind Lettie.' She started shaking her head as though still not quite believing the situation she found herself in. 'I thought I knew why he broke our engagement,' she went on in shaken tones. 'I thought he didn't love me enough, or care enough to support my decision. It never crossed my mind that there might have been another woman in the wings all along, and that I'd given him the perfect excuse to call our wedding off.'

'What makes you think there was another woman at the time?'

'Because I've just seen the bitch,' she said, surprising Justin with the unexpected flash of venom. 'She was downstairs just now, checking in with him.'

'And she is...?' Justin probed, knowing it couldn't be Rachel's best friend, since she was overseas on her honeymoon. Thank God.

'The real-estate agent who sold him the fancy unit which was supposed to be our marital home,' she elaborated bitterly.

'I see. And are *they* married now?'

'No. Living together, I presume from the conversation I overheard at the desk. Either that or they just go away together on what he called weekend junkets associated with her job.'

'I see,' Justin said again, trying to think of something to say to pacify her. But he knew how hard that was, when your emotions were involved. 'Look, you don't really know he was carrying on with this woman before he left you, Rachel. You're just jumping to conclusions.'

'No, I'm not. I know I'm right. I had a feeling about them at the time but I ignored it. I told myself that I was imagining the intimate little looks which used to pass between them, and the many excuses he made to meet up with her at the unit when I was busy at work. Eric's a top lawyer, you see, and can pretty well come and go as he pleases.'

'OK. So he's a two-timing rat as well as a shmuck.

What does it matter now? You can't possibly still be in love with him. Not after…how long ago was it?'

'Four years, give or take a month.'

'See? Now, if you'd said a year maybe, or eighteen months…' like in his case with Mandy '…then I'd understand why you're so upset.'

'Love doesn't stop simply because you want it to, Justin. Even if I didn't love Eric any more, I wouldn't be human if I didn't hate seeing him with another woman like that. But I'm doubly upset because neither of them *recognised* me!' she finished on a strangled sob.

Sympathy *and* empathy consumed Justin as he realised what she was saying. Her hurt was not solely because of this Eric's former betrayal, but because he hadn't recognised her physically.

Justin understood that type of humiliation well and his heart went out to her.

'Maybe he wasn't really looking at you,' he tried excusing. 'Maybe he was off in another world.'

'I wish. But no. He bumped into me when he turned away from the check-in desk. Almost knocked me over. He actually grabbed my shoulders and looked right at me for a second or two. He saw me well enough and there was not a hint of recognition. *She* didn't recognise me, either. Though I can't really blame her. She didn't know me all that well. We only met a couple of times. And I know I've changed a lot. But Eric should still have known me. We were lovers, for pity's sake!'

'Did you say something to him? Call him by name?'

'*Speak* to him? No.' She shuddered. 'I bolted into the ladies' room in the foyer and stayed there till I was sure they'd have left the area and gone up to whatever floor they're staying on. That's what took me so long.'

What probably took her so long, Justin believed, was the time she'd spent in there, weeping and looking in the mirror to see what it was this Eric had seen, and *not* seen.

'Do you think he…um…might have been pretending not to know you?'

'No. There was nothing like that in his eyes. Just blankness. He didn't recognise me.'

'Have you changed *that* much in four years, Rachel?'

Her shoulders sagged, her eyes clouding to an expression of utter misery. 'I guess I must have.'

'So what do you want to do?' he asked, his own spirits sagging at the realisation that this weekend wasn't going to be such a happy or relaxing getaway after all.

'About what?' she asked wearily.

'Presumably this couple will be at the dinner tomorrow night. That must be the junket you heard mentioned.'

Horror filled her face at the prospect.

'You don't have to go,' he said quickly.

'Are you sure? I mean…I don't like to let you down but I…I don't think I could bear it. Eric might recognise me after I do myself up a bit. But, there again, he might not. Either way, I'm going to be terribly uptight, and very poor company with few powers of observation.'

'It's all right, Rachel. Truly. I'll go by myself.' He let her hands go and straightened.

She stared up at him, and he realised her hazel eyes were really quite lovely. How could that fool have not recognised her, if he'd been her lover? Eyes were the one thing which never changed. How many times would this Eric have stared down into Rachel's eyes when they'd been in bed together?

Hell, Mandy's beautiful blue eyes were imprinted on his brain!

His sigh carried a wealth of emotions of his own. 'I'll go finish making us that coffee.' And he stood up.

'You are such a nice man,' she choked out, then burst into tears, burying her face in her hands.

Smothering a groan, Justin sat himself down next to her and took her into his arms, cradling her weeping face against his shirt front.

'No decent human being,' he said gently as he stroked her back, 'could be anything but nice to you, Rachel. This Eric is scum. You're better off without him.'

'I know that,' she sobbed. 'But it still hurts to see him with another woman.'

'I'm sure it does,' Justin murmured soothingly. God knows how *he'd* react if he ever ran into Mandy with that swine who'd stolen her away from him, he thought. Murder was too good for the pair of them.

'Maybe seeing him again like that is a good thing,' he tried, though not quite believing it himself. 'It should give you the motivation to forget him once and for all and get on with your own life. After all, life isn't too bad for you now, is it? You have a job you like, with a considerate boss. Or so you said,' he added wryly. 'And soon you'll have an even better job with enough of a wage coming in to afford a seriously nice place to live in of your own. What more could you possibly want?'

'To still be beautiful,' she mumbled into his chest.

Justin reached down and took her hands away from where they were jammed under her chin, then tipped her face up so that their eyes met. 'You *are* still beautiful, Rachel,' he said softly. 'Where it counts.'

'Right,' she said ruefully. 'Pardon me if I don't get too excited by that compliment. I've found that beauty on the inside is highly overrated as an asset, especially when it comes to the opposite sex.'

'Not all men are as shallow as your Eric,' he countered, confident that he didn't judge a woman so superficially.

'Is that so? Might I ask you a rather personal question?'

'Shoot.'

'Was your ex-wife beautiful?'

Justin opened his mouth, then closed it again. Mandy had been drop-dead gorgeous, there was no doubt about it. She had a very pretty face, big blue eyes, long blonde hair. A *great* figure. And she'd known how to showcase herself to perfection, from the top of her glossy blonde head to the tips of her pink-painted toes.

Rachel, on the other hand, was a far cry from drop-dead anything. Yet she wasn't ugly. She couldn't even be called plain. Aside from having genuinely lovely eyes, she had regular features in her oval-shaped face and an interesting mouth, now that he bothered to really look. Wide, and tilted up at the corners, with a very full bottom lip.

It was just that she always looked so colourless, like a picture that had faded badly. The black suits she wore to work looked extra-drab on her, as did the clunky mid-heeled black shoes.

As for her hair…

He could not think of a good thing to say about her

hair, except that it was far better not red, as it had been last Monday, because any attention brought to it could only create a more negative impression.

'Case closed,' Rachel said succinctly, and stood up. 'God, I feel terrible. I must look terrible too. I think I'll go and have a shower and change. Which way to my room?'

'What about coffee?'

'Thank you but I don't feel like it just now.'

Me neither, he thought. He needed something much more potent in the drinks department. Some food was in order as well. Time was getting on and he hadn't had anything to eat since breakfast except that on-board snack. He wouldn't mind betting Rachel hadn't had any lunch either. No wonder she was so thin.

Though not *that* thin, he'd realised when he was holding her close just now. She had some reasonable breasts hiding there underneath that black jacket. Either that, or she'd been wearing a padded bra.

'Showering and changing sounds like a good idea,' he agreed, determined not to spend all weekend wearing a suit. Bad enough he had to tog up in a tux tomorrow night. 'Your room's on the right down that hallway. The bathroom's opposite on the left. I left your case at the foot of the bed. I'm going to pop into the shower too, but first I'll order us something to eat from Room Service, since going out to dinner tonight is out of the question now. You wouldn't want to run into yours truly and his lady-love. And no, please don't say again what a nice man I am.'

She gave him a faint smile. 'All right.'

'Go, go, go.' He waved her off.

Once Rachel went, he crossed to the desk, which held the leather-bound folder that listed all the hotel's services, plus the in-house menu. He ran his eye swiftly down and decided on something cold. A platter of mixed seafood and a couple of different salads, followed by strawberries and cream, all washed down with a bottle of their best white wine.

Most women liked white wine and Rachel needed cheering up.

Frankly, so did he.

He always did after thinking about Mandy.

Room Service arrived half an hour later, with Justin able to answer the door totally refreshed and dressed in beige cargo shorts and a dark red polo shirt. His feet he'd happily left bare for now. With the food safely deposited in the fridge, and the waiter tipped and dispensed with, Justin set about opening the bottle of wine, a Chablis, after which he popped it in the portable wine cooler provided.

The wine glasses supplied weren't exactly top-drawer crystal but they were nice enough. He placed two of them in the fridge to chill then wandered down the hallway to see how Rachel was progressing. He'd heard her shower going for ages earlier on.

'You ready yet, Rachel?' he asked, stopping in the hall between both shut doors, her bedroom and the bathroom. He didn't know which room she was in.

'Not really.' Her voice came from the bedroom.

'What do you mean, not really?'

'I have a slight problem.'

'What's that?'

'I—er—washed my smalls in the shower before I realised I'd forgotten to pack any more.'

Justin had to struggle not to laugh. But Rachel without underwear was so *un*-Rachel. 'That's OK. Just put on a robe for now. They'll dry by morning, then you can go shopping for more.'

'Er…'

'Don't tell me you didn't pack a robe, either.'

'No, no, I do have a robe but it's a bit…um…'

'What?'

'Nothing. I suppose I'm silly to worry,' she muttered.

'Put it on, then, and get yourself out here. Your pre-dinner drink awaits.'

'OK. I…I'll just be a minute.'

'I'll be out on the balcony, waiting. Don't be too long. I hate drinking alone.'

Justin was lounging back in a deckchair, sipping his wine and thinking life wasn't too bad after all, when he heard the glass door slide back from down Rachel's end. His head turned just in time to see her step out onto the balcony.

Justin did his best not to do a double take, or to stare. But, hell, it was hard not to.

The robe Rachel was wearing was not a modest little housecoat by any means, but a very sexy emerald-green satin number which clung as only satin could. Admittedly it had sleeves to the elbow and did reach down to her ankles. And she *had* sashed it tightly, but this only seemed to emphasise the surprisingly shapely and obviously naked body underneath it.

Clearly, she hadn't been wearing a padded bra earlier, Justin realised as his gaze took in the natural fullness of her breasts, which were very nice indeed. Actually, her body was very nice all round. She had a deliciously tiny waist and enough curve to her hips to look very feminine and, yes, almost sexy.

Amazing what had been hiding underneath those awful black suits she'd been wearing to the office!

Amazing what that awful hairdo had been hiding as well. Having her hair down and curling damply onto her shoulders took years off her face. There was some much-needed colour in her complexion as well, possibly from the heat of the shower, which gave him a glimpse of what she might look like with some make-up on.

Maybe still not a beauty queen but one hell of a lot better than her usual colourless façade. With the right kind of dress she could look quite fabulous. That figure of hers was a knock-out.

When she started coming towards him the robe flapped back at the knees, revealing a full length matching nightie underneath, which was perhaps just as well. He didn't want to stare too much or she was sure to get embarrassed. Even so, it was a very sexy outfit and not the sort of lingerie Justin would have expected Rachel to own, let alone wear.

Still, seeing her in it gave him an idea which just might salve some of Rachel's pride and give him some personal satisfaction as well. He already hated this Eric creep for what he'd done to such a nice woman. Dumping her was bad enough, but fancy not recognising her!

Of course, Rachel was her own worst enemy when it came to her appearance. Obviously, she could look a whole lot better than she did every day.

If she'd do what he was going to suggest, however, then, come tomorrow night, dear old Eric was bound to recognise her. And Rachel would never have to scuttle off and hide in a ladies' room again, weeping with hurt and humiliation. She'd be able to hold her head high in any company and show her pathetic ex-fiancé that he'd made a big mistake in dumping her.

A *big* mistake.

Just as Mandy made a big mistake dumping you? came the dark and caustic thought. *Is it vengeance for Rachel you want here, or some vengeance for yourself?*

Mandy, he thought angrily. Always, it came back to Mandy!

CHAPTER FIVE

WHEN Rachel saw Justin's sudden scowl she stopped walking towards him. She hadn't minded his surprise on first seeing her dressed as she was. Surprise was fair enough. But a scowl was another matter entirely.

'I…I think I'd better go back and find something else to put on,' she said. 'This just isn't appropriate, is it?'

'Certainly not!' he exclaimed, then astonished her by laughing. 'No, no, that's not what I meant. I meant don't go back inside and change. You look perfectly fine as you are. Heavens, Rachel, you're wearing more clothes than most girls wear walking down the street up here. Here, sit down and get some of this wine into you.' He swept up a bottle of white wine from the portable cooler standing by his chair and poured her a glass.

'I hope you like Chablis,' he said as he placed the glass on the white outdoor table and pushed it across to where she was settling herself in one of the matching white chairs.

'Yes, I do. Thank you.' Rachel was grateful for the drink, but more grateful to be sitting down, and no longer on show. That short walk along the balcony had felt like a million miles. Talk about embarrassing!

The whole situation was embarrassing. Fancy forgetting to bring any underwear.

She picked up the wine glass, cradled it in both her

hands to stop them shaking and took a sip. 'Oh, yes,' she sighed. 'This *is* good.'

'It ought to be,' Justin said with a smile in his voice. 'It cost a small fortune. But no sweat. Everything's on the house, according to Guy. I aim to take full advantage of it. And so should you. Which gives me an idea. Wait here.'

He put down his wine and levered himself up from the chair. 'Won't be long,' he said, and hurried back inside through the sliding glass doors, leaving Rachel to do a spot of staring of her own.

It was strange seeing her boss in a bright top, casual shorts and bare feet. She'd always known he sported a nice shape and tan, but she'd never seen so much of it before. Even his bare feet were brown, which made her wonder what a man who wore shoes and socks all week did to achieve that. Lie in one of those sunbeds at the gym? Or swim a lot in an outdoor pool? If so, where? She knew he lived in a high-rise apartment in an exclusive complex down on the harbour foreshore at Kirribilli, so it probably sported a pool. Exclusive ones usually did.

'I thought as much,' Justin was saying as he returned through the open glass doors, carrying an open black leather folder. 'They do have a beauty salon in this place.'

'A...a beauty salon?' Rachel repeated, not sure what Justin was getting at.

'Yes. Seeing you wearing that gorgeous green and with your hair down has shown me, Rachel Witherspoon, that you have been hiding your light under a bushel. I don't know if anyone has ever told you before but black does nothing for you, and neither does the way you wear your hair to work. You also have a damned good figure, which your working wardrobe doesn't show to advantage. With a different hairstyle, some make-up and the right clothes, Rachel, you could look more than good. You could look great.'

'But…'

'But what?'

'But I thought you didn't want me looking great, especially at work.'

'What?'

'Your mother told me all about your previous PA long before you ever did.'

He grimaced. 'Oh, God, she didn't, did she?'

'Afraid so.'

He frowned over at her. 'So you *deliberately* made yourself look like a plain Jane to get the job.'

Not really, an amazed Rachel was thinking. She'd just come *au naturel*. She *was* a plain Jane. But she wasn't about to say so. She rather liked the thought that Justin believed she'd been down-playing a whole host of hidden attractions.

'Well…' she hedged, not sure what to say at this juncture.

'Oh, Rachel, Rachel, you didn't have to do that. I'd have given you the job, anyway, because I saw right from the start that you were nothing like that other girl. It wasn't just the way she dressed, you know, but the way she acted. Like some oversexed vamp all the time. She drove me insane.'

'So you wouldn't mind if I did myself up a bit for work?'

'Why should I mind?'

'I was worried that if I suddenly came into the office with a new hairdo and a new wardrobe you might think I was…um…'

'Tarting yourself up for me?'

'Yes,' she said sheepishly.

He laughed. 'I would never think that of you. Silly Rachel.'

Rachel tried not to be offended. But she was, all the same. Yes, silly, *silly* Rachel.

'Which brings me right back to my original suggestion,' he went on. 'Now, tomorrow I want you to go down to that beauty salon and get the works. Facial, massage, pedicure, manicure, waxing, hair, make-up. The lot. It says here they do all that.'

'That seems excessive.' Even for me, she thought ruefully.

'No, it's not. It's necessary.'

'Oh, thank you very much,' came the waspish comment.

'Now, now, this is no time for over-sensitivity, Rachel. The truth is you've let yourself get into bad habits with this plain-Jane nonsense. I can understand that you might not have bothered with your appearance much when you were at home all the time, but I'll bet there was a time when you went to a lot of trouble with your hair and make-up and clothes.'

'We-ll...'

'Well?' he probed forcefully.

'I always suspected I didn't become a finalist in the Secretary of the Year competition on my office skills alone,' she said drily.

'I don't doubt it. I'll bet you were a looker back then.'

'I was...attractive.'

'And you never wore black.'

'Not often.'

'How did you wear your hair?'

'Down,' she admitted. 'With auburn highlights.'

'No wonder people from your past didn't recognise you today. But, come tomorrow night, Eric the Mongrel will recognise you all right.'

'Eric the Mongrel?' she repeated on a gasp.

'Yeah. That's what I've nicknamed him. Do you like it?'

'Oh, dear. I *love* it.'

'So you'll do it? Come to the dinner with me?'

Rachel swallowed. It would take every bit of courage she owned to face Eric and that woman once more, even if she was dolled up to the nines. But, by God, she would!

'Yes,' she said, and Justin beamed.

'Fantastic. Here. A toast is in order.'

He held his glass out towards her and she clicked it with hers.

'To the comeuppance of Eric the Mongrel,' Justin pronounced.

Rachel's stomach flipped over. 'Comeuppance?'

'Oh, yes. Your ex deserves a few serves. And I'm just the man to deliver them!'

Justin paced up and down the living room, impatient for Rachel to make her appearance. She'd stayed hidden ever since her return from the beauty salon around five, letting herself in whilst he'd been in the bathroom, shaving. Now it was getting on for seven and he was dressed in his tux and ready to go down for the cocktail party that preceded the dinner at eight, an arrangement Rachel was well acquainted with. They'd discussed it last night.

So when seven came and went without her showing,

Justin strode down the hallway and knocked firmly on her door.

'Enough titivating in there, Rachel. It's seven o'clock. Time you faced the music.'

'Coming,' she called back. But nervously, he thought.

The door opened and Justin's blue eyes rounded.

'Wow, Rachel. You don't just look great. You look fabulous!'

Even that was an understatement. Where had his plain-Jane PA disappeared to? In her place stood a striking creature. No, a stunning creature. No, a striking, stunning, *sexy* creature.

Justin found himself standing there, just staring at her, trying to work out what she'd done to cause such a dramatic transformation.

It couldn't just be her hair, though it was very different. And very red, he noted wryly. Cut in layers, it fell from an off-centre parting to her shoulders, framing her face and her *eyes*, her always lovely eyes, which now looked not just lovelier but larger. Was it the smoky eye make-up which had achieved this effect, or some other subtle change? Whatever, when he looked into her face he couldn't stop looking at her eyes.

They looked back at him, heartbreakingly hesitant. She still didn't know how beautiful she was. How amazingly, incredibly beautiful.

'You honestly think so?' she asked. 'You don't think I look…foolish?'

'Foolish?' he echoed in disbelief. 'In what way could you possibly look foolish?'

'My hair colour bothers me for starters. It's too red,' she said, touching it gingerly with her equally red nails.

'Honey, you can carry off red now,' he reassured softly.

'Oh…' She blushed prettily. 'But don't you think the make-up girl put too much foundation on me? I look like a ghost.'

'No, you don't. That's the fashion. You know, that's the slinkiest bridesmaid dress I think I've ever seen,' he remarked, shaking his head as his gaze ran down the dress again.

It was a turquoise silk sheath, with thin shoulder straps and a fitted waist that showed off Rachel's nice bustline and tiny waist to perfection. The skirt was straight and slender, and fell to mid-calf, with a slanted hem from which hung strands of crystal beads. Under this rather provocative feature her legs were bare, yet looked as smooth and shiny as they would if covered in the most expensive stockings. Her feet were shod in turquoise high heels, which matched the colour of the dress and had open toes, showing scarlet-painted toes. She smelled faintly of jasmine, possibly from a scented oil used to massage her skin. Her arms, Justin also noted as his eyes travelled back up to her face, looked as soft and shiny as her legs, probably the result of a full body massage today.

That beauty salon deserved a medal for the miracle it had managed in one short day. Not that he'd tell Rachel that. Despite her fab new look, her self-esteem was still wavering, which was a problem. Frankly, he'd been looking forward to exacting some well-deserved revenge on rotten exes tonight, and he needed Rachel's full co-operation to achieve that end. Clearly, her confidence still needed some more boosting.

'You look good enough to eat, Rachel. Eric the

Mongrel is going to be jealous as sin when I walk into that dinner party with you on my arm.'

'I think it's Eric's girlfriend who might be the jealous one,' Rachel returned as she looked him up and down.

Justin was surprised but pleased that she thought him attractive. It would make his plan for the evening run smoother. 'Yes, we've both cleaned up rather well, haven't we? Come on, let's go and put a cat amongst the pigeons. Do you have a bag?'

'No, I don't.'

'No need. It's not as though we have to go outside. There'll be no wind to mess up your hair. If you feel in the need for any repairs during the night you can always whip up here in the lift. I'll have my key card with me.'

'Yes, I might need to do that after dinner. I always eat off my lipstick, though the make-up girl who did me up said this particular brand is renowned for not coming off. She said it's the one the actresses use who make blue movies.'

Justin laughed and started shepherding Rachel towards the door. 'That's handy to know. So if you disappear under the tablecloth at any time tonight I'll feel confident you'll resurface still looking immaculate.'

When she looked scandalised Justin tut-tutted. 'Come, now, Rachel, try to get with the spirit of this occasion. Remember, I'm not just your boss for tonight. I'm your lover as well.'

'What?' She ground to a startled halt.

Justin was taken aback. 'I thought you understood that was part of my plan. Look, how else are we going to get up Eric the Mongrel's nose, unless he thinks we're a hot item? We want him to believe you haven't missed him one bit, that you've survived his callous dumping; you did your duty to Lettie like the angel you are and are now moving on to a much more exciting and fulfilling life than you would have had married to him. You're looking better than ever. You live in a fantastic town house at Turramurra. And you have this great new job, with a handsome, successful, besotted boss who can't keep his hands off you.'

'But…but I wouldn't *like* having a boss like that!'

'You might not, but it's some men's fantasy. And some women's. Trust me on that. I would imagine it was right up Eric the Mongrel's alley.'

'You have to stop calling him that or I'm going to giggle all night.'

'That's all right. Giggling's good.'

'But it's not *me*.'

'It can be. You can be anything you want to be tonight. The point of this exercise is to show your ex that he doesn't know you at all, if he ever did. And to make him want the new you like crazy!'

'I…I don't think…'

'Now, thinking's a definite no-no for this evening as well. Thinking rarely does anyone any good. Just follow my lead, honey, and everything will be fine.'

When he took her elbow he felt her resistance and stared down at her. She stared back up at him.

'You called me honey.'

'Well, I'm not going to call you Rachel all the time. Sounds far too platonic. OK, so honey's out. How about the occasional darling? Yes, that's much better. Much classier. Come along, Cinders, darling,' Justin said with a rueful smile. 'It's time to go to the ball.'

CHAPTER SIX

RACHEL stood silently by Justin's side in the ride down in the lift, her stomach twisted into nervous knots.

How could she possibly carry this charade off? It was...beyond her. She might be looking good on the outside but inside she was still the same Rachel who'd run into Eric yesterday and bolted like a frightened horse. Fear rippled down her spine and invaded every pore in her body. The thought of confronting her ex with his new lady-love held nothing but a sick-making apprehension.

'I...I can't do this, Justin,' she whispered just as the lift stopped at one of the floors on the way down to the lobby.

'Yes, you can,' he reassured firmly.

The lift doors whooshed back and there, waiting for the lift, were the objects of her fear.

Rachel sucked in sharply.

'I gather that's Eric the Mongrel,' Justin whispered.

'Yes,' she choked out, not feeling at all like giggling at the silly nickname this time. Eric the Magnificent would be more like it. He really was a drop-dead gorgeous-looking guy, especially in a dinner suit. Charlotte was no slouch in the looks department, either, the passing years seeming to have enhanced her darkly striking beauty. Tall and supermodel-slim, she was chic personified with her concave-cut dark brown bob and elegant black dress.

'Charlotte, come on,' Eric said impatiently, stepping

forward to hold the lift doors open whilst not giving its occupants a second glance.

Charlotte, who'd been checking her hair and make-up in the hall mirror when the lift doors opened, finally swung round. 'Keep your shirt on, lover,' she said. 'These things never start on time.'

As Charlotte walked past Eric into the lift he glanced up over her shoulder and finally noticed Rachel in the corner, his face registering instant recognition this time, plus considerable shock.

'Good lord!' he exclaimed. 'It's Rachel. You remember Rachel, Charlotte. Rachel Witherspoon.'

Rachel would later wonder where her courage—and her composure—came from. Possibly from the look of surprise on that bitch's face as she surveyed Rachel from top to toe.

'So it is,' Charlotte said. 'Fancy seeing you here, of all people.' Her sexily slanting black eyes soon slid over to Justin. Women like Charlotte never looked at other women for long when there were attractive men around.

Meanwhile, Eric kept staring at *her* as though she were a little green man from Mars.

'I was just thinking the same about you two,' Rachel returned, proud as punch of her cool control. 'I gather you're together? This is my boss, Justin McCarthy,' she swept on, not giving either of them the chance to answer. 'Justin, these are friends of mine, Eric Farmer and Charlotte—er—sorry. I can't seem to recall your second name, Charlotte.'

'Raper.'

'Oh, yes. Raper...' A ghastly surname. 'So what brings you two up to the Gold Coast this weekend? Business, or pleasure?'

Eric muttered 'Pleasure' the same time as Charlotte said 'Business'. After Charlotte shot him an angry look he changed his answer to 'Both'. But he looked far from happy.

Rachel had to smile at having rattled Eric so easily. Justin was right. A spot of revenge was a good salve for old wounds. But she still wasn't sure about pretending she and Justin were lovers.

'And you?' Eric finally thought to ask. 'Are you here for business or pleasure?' He too was assessing Justin on the quiet, Rachel noticed. And perhaps not feeling his usual male superiority. For, as glamorous as Eric still looked at first glance, up close there was some evidence he was beginning to go to seed. He was becoming jowly, his crowning glory was thinning on top and his stomach was no longer athletically flat.

Frankly, he was looking a bit flabby. Of course, he had to be going on forty nowadays, whereas Justin was in his earlier thirties. Justin was taller than Eric, too. Taller and fitter and possibly more attractive, Rachel was surprised to discover.

'We're just here on business, aren't we, Justin?' she said, and touched him lightly on his nearest arm, her eyes pleading with him not to say differently.

Justin covered her hand with his and gave it an intimate little squeeze. 'Oh, absolutely,' he agreed, whilst his glittering blue eyes gave an entirely different message. 'Rachel's my new PA, and such a treasure. Only been with me for five weeks or so, but I already wouldn't know what I'd do without her.'

Oh, God, Rachel agonised. Somehow, without saying a word to that effect, Justin was making it sound as though their relationship extended way beyond the office.

'Really,' Eric said coldly, one eyebrow arching as he stared at her cleavage.

Rachel could feel heat gathering in her cheeks because it was perfectly clear what Eric was thinking.

'Eric,' Charlotte said sharply. 'Will you please move your butt inside the lift so that the doors can close?'

He flashed his lover a caustic glance but took a step inside.

'Have you known Rachel long?' Justin asked him whilst they waited for the lift to resume its ride down.

Rachel immediately tensed over what answer he would give.

'We were engaged once a few years back,' Eric bit out. 'But things didn't work out at the time, did they, Rach?'

Everything inside Rachel tightened further at his use of that once affectionate shortening of her name. But she'd be damned if she'd show any reaction on her face other than indifference to the role he'd once played in her personal life. 'Oh, I think things worked out just fine, Eric,' she said with a casual shrug. 'I did what I had to do and you did what you had to do. Anyway, there's no point in talking about the past. You've obviously moved on, and so have I.'

The lift doors closed at that juncture, as though emphasising her point.

'You still let a good one get away,' Justin remarked on the way down. 'But your loss is my gain.'

'I thought she was only your PA,' Eric shot back.

'Oh, she *is*. But a good PA these days is worth her weight in gold. Rachel leaves the girl I had before her for dead. She's not only beautiful but bright as a button, and such a sweetie. Just think, if you two hadn't broken up Rachel would be your wife by now. Instead, she's working for me, making my life run like a breeze. Amazing the little twists and turns in life, isn't it? Aah, here we are at the lobby.'

Rachel did her best not to flinch when Justin slid a highly intimate arm around her waist and steered her smoothly from the lift in Eric and Charlotte's wake. *They* weren't touching at this point, Rachel noted. They weren't even holding hands. Charlotte's body language showed anger, and so did Eric's.

Rachel tried to be scandalised with what Justin had just done, and she was a bit, but at the same time she felt a strange elation. And some vengeful satisfaction. Now she knew what Justin had meant by putting a cat amongst the pigeons.

'I presume you're going along to the special presentation dinner tonight?' Justin asked Eric before he could make his escape with Charlotte.

'Yes, we are. Charlotte's in real estate and is here representing a wealthy client of hers.'

'I can speak for myself, Eric,' Charlotte snapped. 'Actually, my client is more than wealthy. He's a multi-multimillionaire. Trust me, if he decides to buy this place whoever you're working for won't stand a chance. What this man wants he gets. So who is it that *you* work for, anyway? And what is it that you actually do?'

Justin delivered an intriguingly enigmatic smile. 'Now, that would be telling, wouldn't it? I can confess to being an investment adviser, but, as I'm sure you are aware, client confidentiality is important in matters such as this. Property-development deals are rather like a game of poker. You don't ever put all your cards on the table, not till after the game has been done, or won.'

'My client never bluffs,' Charlotte said smugly. 'He

doesn't have to. When he wants something he simply makes sure he's the top bidder. Money overcomes all obstacles.'

'Is that so? Your client might not ever bluff, but if he keeps making business decisions that way he might end up with a house of cards rather than a solidly based portfolio. One day, it'll come crashing down around him.'

'Well, that's no concern of mine,' Charlotte said with an indifferent shrug of her slender shoulders. 'He's just a client. As long as I get my commission on a sale, I don't care what happens afterwards.'

'Spoken like a real-estate agent,' Justin said with a dry laugh.

She didn't bat an eyelid at the barb. 'Property's a tough business.'

'But you're well up to it.'

'Oh, I'm not *that* hard,' she returned. 'Not once you get to know me.' And she flashed him an almost coquettish smile.

Rachel could not believe it. Charlotte was making a play for Justin right in front of her and Eric's eyes!

But what's new? she realised bitterly. That was what she'd done with Eric when he'd been engaged to her.

A quiet fury began to simmer within Rachel. Charlotte had seduced Eric away from her, but no way was Rachel going to let Charlotte get her claws into Justin! He might only be her boss but he was far too nice a man for the likes of that alley cat to play with.

'I hate to interrupt this conversation,' she piped up with a saccharine smile, 'but we really must be getting along, Justin. The dinner starts at eight and you promised to meet Mr Wong at the main bar at seven-fifteen. And it's way past that now.'

'You're right. See what I mean? What would I do without her? No doubt we'll run into each other again during the dinner. Maybe we can even sit at the same table. Mind us a spot if you can. Meanwhile, I must away and meet my—er—meet Mr Wong. And no, don't ask me who he is, sweetheart,' he threw at Charlotte, then pressed his index finger to his lips. 'Client confidentiality, remember.'

'Who the hell is Mr Wong?' he whispered to Rachel after a sour-faced Eric grabbed Charlotte's arm and started steering her forcibly past Reception in the direction of the main conference room, the venue for the dinner.

'No idea,' Rachel confessed. 'I made him up.'

'But why? The idea is to stay in Eric and Charlotte's company if we're to achieve our aim for the night.' And nodded towards the departing couple's backs.

'She was flirting with you,' Rachel pointed out indignantly.

'So? That was good, wasn't it? It'll make Eric the Mongrel jealous and insecure.'

'I was afraid you might be liking it.'

'I was. But not the way you're thinking. I wouldn't touch that cold-blooded bitch in a million years. God, Rachel, you don't know me very well if you'd think that.'

'But I *don't* know you very well, do I? You have an unexpectedly wicked streak in you, Justin McCarthy. Yet before tonight I thought you were…um—er—er…' She struggled to find a word other than 'nice'.

'Staid?' he suggested drily. 'Boring?'

'No! Never boring. Maybe a little staid. No, you're not really staid, either. Oh, I don't know what I mean. I guess I just didn't think you'd ever conceive of something so devious as to make them think we're lovers even whilst you're claiming we aren't. That was incredibly conniving of you, and manipulative.'

'If you can't beat 'em, then join 'em, Rachel. People like Eric and Charlotte are devious, and conniving, and manipulative. They're also shallow and selfish and truly wicked. They don't care who they hurt or betray. All they care about is themselves and what suits them at the time. If you think I'm the first man Charlotte has flirted with, then think again. She hasn't been faithful to your Eric, nor he with her. That's the way they both are.'

'Maybe, but not *everyone* is like that, Justin,' she pointed out, unwilling to embrace the self-destructive philosophy of total cynicism. Isabel had been like that with men for ages, till she met Rafe. And, really, Rachel hadn't admired that about her one bit. She was a much nicer person now that she was living her life with love and hope in her heart.

'True,' Justin said, his gaze softening momentarily on her. 'Some people are decent and kind. But the two people we were unfortunate enough to fall in love with *weren't*. Eric treated you abominably, Rachel. And he shouldn't be allowed to get away with it!'

Rachel stared up into her boss's bitter blue eyes and realised he wasn't only talking about Eric. He was talking—and thinking—about his wife. Justin was deeply wounded.

Rachel wanted to ask him about his wife and what she'd done to him, but knew it was not the right time, or the right place. For one thing, his wounds were still way too raw. Maybe there would never be a right time or a right place. Maybe he'd loved her far too much, and would never get over her.

At least *she* had the comfort of knowing she no longer loved Eric. Seeing him again tonight had at least proved that to her once and for all. He might be successful and superficially handsome, but 'handsome is as handsome does', she'd discovered first-hand this evening. He was welcome to the likes of Charlotte. They were made for each other, in her opinion.

'Promise me you won't flirt with Charlotte when we finally get to that dinner?' she asked.

Justin laughed. 'I promise. But you shouldn't worry about me, you know, Rachel. I can take care of myself where female vampires are concerned. How are *you* doing, meeting up with lover-boy again? Does he still turn you on with those smooth, golden looks of his?'

'God, no.' She half laughed, half shuddered. 'No, not at all.'

'I suspect he still has the hots for you.'

She blushed. 'Don't be ridiculous!'

Justin frowned. 'You think it's ridiculous for a man to have the hots for you, especially the way you look tonight?'

'Well, no… I mean…yes… I mean… Look, I still can't compare with Charlotte. She's one seriously sexy lady.'

'She's about as sexy to me as a dead skunk.'

Rachel was startled. 'Really?'

'Really. But to ease your concern I will consign all of my flirting for the rest of the evening to yours truly. Make Eric the Mongrel's teeth gnash some more.' He glanced at his watch. 'Mmm. Twenty to eight. Look, let's go to that main bar you mentioned, where I'm supposed to be meeting the mysterious Mr Wong. We can fill in the time till eight with a couple of pre-dinner drinks.'

Rachel bit her bottom lip. 'Oh, I—er—made that up about the main bar as well. I have no idea if there is such a place.'

Justin grinned. 'And you said I had an unexpectedly wicked streak in me. I think you're the one who has the unexpectedly wicked streak, Ms Witherspoon. Come on, we'll go ask at Reception where the bars are located. They have to have at least one or two in a place this size.'

They had three, one connected with the à la carte restaurant on the mezzanine level, one on the first floor in the disco-till-you-drop room and a third up on the top floor, which had a more sedate dance floor and a view to die for, or so the clerk behind the desk said. It also wasn't open to the public, just the clientele of Sunshine Gardens and their guests.

Ten minutes later they were sitting at a table on an open-air terrace, sipping Margaritas by moonlight and drinking in that view to die for, which was spectacular, even at night. Most of the buildings along the foreshore were lit up, outlining the curved sweep of the coastline for as far as the eye could see. The night air was still and balmy, with Rachel's bare arms and shoulders not proving a problem.

'This is so lovely,' she said with a wistful sigh. 'But we won't have time for a second drink. Not if you want us to make that dinner on time.'

Actually, she hated the thought of going down to that dinner now. As much as she'd enjoyed her moment of vengeance in the lift, she didn't want to keep pretending she and Justin were lovers, or to have Justin acting like some sleazebag boss who couldn't keep his hands off her. She knew he meant well, but in a way it was demeaning for him to act out of character like that.

'What if I said we'd skip the presentation dinner entirely, and order some food to have right here?' he startled her by suggesting. 'They do serve light meals. They're listed on the other side of the drinks menu.'

'But don't you *have* to go to the dinner?'

'It's not strictly essential. They're making a video of the promotional presentation after the dinner for potential buyers who couldn't make it tonight. I'll buy a copy in the morning and view it when I get home tomorrow night, in case there's anything remotely informative in it, which is doubtful.'

'But what about Eric and Charlotte?'

'What about them? You said you didn't give a toss about Eric any more.'

'I don't.'

'Well, then we've done what we set out to do,' he said. 'Made Eric the Mongrel see you've survived without him. Also made him see he gave up a truly fine and, might I say, very attractive lady for a total bitch like Charlotte. Frankly, it could prove a more successful and devious strategy not showing up to the dinner at all. Eric will stew over the thought that I've whisked you back up to our room for a long night of hot sex, and darling Charlotte will worry her material little heart out that my mysterious Mr Wong might be some mega-rich businessman from Singapore who'll bid more for Sunshine Gardens than the ego-maniacal fool she's representing. Your revenge is already complete, Rachel. Why risk spoiling it?'

'But…'

'You have a penchant for buts, Rachel. There are no buts in this case, not even business buts. I guarantee I won't get into trouble over not going to that dinner. I made my own private enquiries around town today and I won't be recommending that AWI buy this place, anyway. Reliable sources tell me the occupancy rate here is way down, except in peak tourist season, and even then not a patch on a couple of their nearby competitors. Another little birdie told me that, despite the quality of the building and the décor, the management here is less than the best and staff turnover is very high.'

'What reliable sources? What little birdie?'

'The people who live here in Coolangatta, and work here. Shop owners. Suppliers. Taxi drivers. They have no reason to lie, whereas the present owners of Sunshine Gardens have every reason to misrepresent the truth.'

'I see.'

'So what do you say? We miss the dinner and stay up here?'

'Yes, please,' Rachel said eagerly as relief overwhelmed her.

Justin smiled his own pleasure at the change of plan. 'We'll order a bottle of wine with our dinner,' he suggested on picking up the menu. 'And then we might have a dance or two. That dress has dancing written all over it.'

Rachel's heart jolted. She hadn't danced in years. The last time had been with Eric, the week before he'd broken off with her, and the day before she found out the awful news about Lettie. They'd been to a Christmas party and she'd got very tipsy on the punch. He'd whispered hot words of love and desire in her ears whilst he danced with her, holding her very close, making her want him to put his words into action.

When she'd been beyond resisting him he'd whisked her into the bathroom and made love to her up against the door.

Or so she'd thought at the time. Now she knew he hadn't been making love at all. He'd just been having sex. Because he'd never really loved her.

'I…I haven't danced in years,' she said, her voice shaking a little at the memory. As much as she no longer loved Eric, the damage he'd perpetrated on her female psyche was still there.

'You didn't dance at your friend's wedding?' Justin asked on a note of surprise.

'No.'

'Why not? I'll bet you were asked in that dress.'

'Yes, I was.'

'Why did you say no?'

'I…I just didn't want to.' In truth, she'd felt far too emotionally fragile at the time to do something as potentially destructive as dance with a man. When she'd watched the bride and groom dance their first dance together she'd been consumed with a pain so sharp, and a misery so deep, she'd fled into a powder room—one of her favourite escapes—and cried for ages.

Justin frowned. 'This has something to do with Eric the Mongrel, hasn't it?'

Her smile was sad. 'How did you guess?'

'You told him in the lift you'd moved on, Rachel. And you told me just now he no longer mattered to you. I think it's time you put your feet where your mouth is. You're going to dance with me tonight and I don't want to hear another word about it. I won't take no for an answer.'

'Yes, boss,' she said, rather amused by his tough-guy attitude. It was so un-Justin. Same as with his earlier pretending to be a sleazebag boss.

'That's a very good phrase,' he pronounced firmly. 'Practise saying it.'

'Yes, boss.'

'Again.'

She laughed. 'Yes, boss.'

He grinned. 'By George, she's got it!'

CHAPTER SEVEN

JUSTIN sat there, watching Rachel really enjoy herself, possibly for the first time in years. She'd relished the food, despite the meal being a simple one, and she'd certainly swigged back her fair share of the wine. Now she was looking totally relaxed, leaning back and peering up at the stars.

He'd just ordered their after-dinner coffee but it probably wouldn't arrive for a while. Whilst the setting and ambience of the bar was great, the service was slow. The place was clearly understaffed, especially for a Saturday night. Management were probably cutting costs to make their profit margin look better, a common strategy when a business was for sale.

Time to ask Rachel to dance, Justin decided. The music coming from inside the bar was nice and slow, the rhythm easy to follow.

He rose to his feet, walked round her side of the table and held out his hand towards her. 'Shall we take a turn around the terrace, Ms Witherspoon?' he asked with feigned old-fashioned formality.

She smiled up at him. Such a lovely smile she had. Pity she didn't use it more often. Still, maybe she would after tonight.

'Why, thank you, Mr Darcy. Oops. Mr McCarthy, I mean.' When she stood up she swayed back dangerously on her high heels. He grabbed her upper arms and pulled her hard against him.

'Oh,' she gasped, her eyes startled as they jerked up to meet his.

'Methinks you've had too much to drink, Ms Witherspoon,' he chided gently. 'Just as well you find yourself in a gentleman's company this evening, or you might be in a spot of bother.'

'Yes. Just as well,' she murmured even whilst her eyes remained locked to his and her woman's body stayed pressed up against him.

Justin could not believe it when his own male body suddenly stirred to life. Neither could Rachel, by the look on her face.

Nevertheless, she didn't move. Or say a word. Just stared up at him with those lovely eyes of hers, her lips still parted. Yet for all that, she didn't look disgusted, or repelled by his arousal. Neither did she attempt to push him away, not even when his arms developed a devilish mind of their own and stole around her waist, one hand settling in the small of her back, the other sliding down to play over the soft swell of her buttocks. Instead of wrenching away from him in outrage, her own arms actually slipped up around his neck, and she sank even more closely against him.

'Rachel,' he breathed warningly.

'Yes, boss?' she said in a low, husky voice, her hazel eyes having gone all smoky.

'You're drunk.'

'Yes, boss.'

'Maybe dancing together isn't such a good idea.'

'Just shut up, boss, and move your feet.'

Her uncharacteristic assertiveness surprised him, but he shut up and moved his feet. Still, he'd been right. It wasn't a good idea. The slow, sensual rhythm of the music got further into his blood, as did the scent—and softness—of the woman in his arms. Of course, it didn't help that her fingertips started stroking the back of his neck in a highly provocative fashion, or that she kept gazing up at him with eyes full of erotic promise. By the time the music stopped he was in agony, his erection straining against the fly of his suit trousers.

At least he had a jacket on.

'I need to go to the gents',' he ground out after depositing her back in her chair. Fortunately, their coffee had finally arrived. A potful, as ordered. Hopefully, after a couple of strong cups Rachel might sober up and stop trying to seduce him.

His normally very proper PA was going to hate herself in the morning, Justin thought ruefully as he strode back inside the bar and over to the gents'. Alcohol could make even the most sensible woman behave a bit stupidly. Add her tipsy state to all that had happened earlier this evening, and he had a very different Rachel on his hands tonight.

Of course, he had to shelve some of the blame himself. He hadn't realised when he'd encouraged her to make herself over today that her transformation would be quite so dramatic. When a woman looked as seriously good as Rachel did tonight she was apt to find her flirtatious side.

Still, what was *his* excuse for responding so powerfully? Since he didn't fancy Rachel in that sense, he could only conclude he was suffering from acute frustration.

Maybe his male body was finally rebelling against its long stint of celibacy. Possibly it was time for him to search out an accommodating female who'd give him regular sex without any emotional strings involved. *Definitely* no strings involved. The last thing he wanted was a serious relationship. Or being told he was loved.

Definitely not. Sex was all he needed, something that was painfully obvious when he went into a cubicle in the gents' and confronted his wayward flesh.

Justin sighed and waited till the worst had subsided. But he was still aroused when he emerged from the cubicle to wash his hands. The sight of a condom dispenser on the wall next to the basins immediately caught his attention, with temptation not far behind.

Before he could think better of it, he dropped a couple of single dollars in the slot provided and slipped two condoms in his trouser pocket. Who knew? He might come back up here after Rachel was asleep. It was still only early. He'd already noticed an attractive redhead sitting all by herself at the bar, who'd given him the eye as he walked past. He just might return and take her up on her none-too-subtle invitation, since getting to sleep tonight in his present state of mind and body might prove difficult.

Difficult? More like bloody impossible!

Once Justin left her alone, Rachel's conscience—and common sense—returned with a vengeance. What on earth did she think she was doing, flirting with her boss and dancing with him like that, winding her arms around his neck like a clinging vine and moulding her body to his like some neglected nymphomaniac?

Justin's getting turned on wasn't his fault. He was just a man after all, a man who possibly hadn't had sex for some time. His leaving her to race off to the gents' had been too embarrassing for words.

Rachel cringed with humiliation, and guilt. If she could have bolted back to her hotel room right now without consequences she would have. If Justin hadn't been in possession of the door key she might have. As things stood, she had no alternative but to sit there and wait for his return, when she would apologise for her appalling behaviour, and beg his forgiveness and understanding. She would blame the wine, then throw herself on his mercy by explaining that she wasn't herself tonight.

Not her recent self, anyway. The Rachel Justin had employed would never have acted as she just had. In a way, it amazed her that she'd had the gall. Being sexually aggressive took courage, and confidence. Either that, or being turned on to the max.

This last thought bothered her the most. Because during those moments when she'd felt his hardness pressing into her stomach she'd wanted him in the most basic way; wanted to feel him, not against her but inside her. It was a startling state of affairs for a girl who'd always believed she had to be in love to want to be made love to. Clearly, she'd come to a point in her life when that wasn't the case any more. Perhaps that was what happened to a single woman when she got to a certain age, or when she'd been so lonely for so long that any man would do.

Rachel hated that idea but she could not deny it just might be true.

Crossing her arms with a shiver that had nothing to do with being cold, Rachel peered anxiously through the plate-glass window into the more dimly lit bar, both wanting and fearing Justin's return.

But there was no sign of him. He was certainly taking his time.

Desperate for distraction from her increasing agitation, she poured herself some coffee and gulped it down, black and strong. Unfortunately, this only served to sober her up and make her agonise further over the folly of her earlier actions.

She was refilling her empty cup when her boss finally showed up, but he didn't sit back down. He stayed standing by the table, his expression grim as he frowned down at her.

'I think I should take you back to the apartment,' he said abruptly. 'What you need is sleep, not coffee.'

'I'm not *that* drunk,' she replied sharply before remembering that being intoxicated was to be one of her excuses for behaving badly.

'I didn't say you were. But you've had a long and emotionally exhausting day. Come along, Rachel, be a good girl, now, and don't argue with me.'

Perversely, Rachel now felt like arguing with him, his patronising tone having really rubbed her up the wrong way. Any thought of apologising went out of the window.

He'd been equally to blame for what had just happened, she decided mutinously. If he hadn't insisted she tart herself up she would never have had the confidence to do any of the things she'd done tonight. *He'd* never have asked her to dance, either. When she'd been a plain Jane he hadn't given her a second glance.

She'd be damned if she was going to feel ashamed of her behaviour. Considering how long it had been since a man had taken her in his arms, it was no wonder she'd lost her head there for a while. She was only human.

A soon-to-be unemployed human, if you keep this attitude up, came the dry voice of reason.

With a sigh of surrender to common sense over rebellion, Rachel put down her coffee-cup and levered herself carefully out of the chair. This time, she was much more steady on her feet.

'I didn't think Cinderella had to go home till midnight,' she muttered with a glance at her watch. 'It's only half-past ten. Still, if you say it's time for me to go to bed then it's time for me to go to bed. You're the boss after all.'

Justin wished she hadn't said that, his mind immediately filling with various lust-filled scenarios associated with his taking this particular Cinderella to bed, none of which involved his playing the role of Prince Charming. More like the Black Prince. When he went to take her arm he thought better of it, deciding to keep his hands to himself till she was safely ensconced in her bedroom. *Alone.*

'Let's go, then,' he grated out, and stepped back to wave her ahead of him.

Unfortunately, Rachel walking ahead of him in that highly provocative dress stimulated him further. If she'd had eyes in the back of her head she'd have been disgusted by his suddenly lascivious gaze as it gobbled up her rear view, which, whilst not quite as delicious as her front, had the bonus of its owner not being aware of being ogled. He could ogle to his heart's content.

Justin didn't even notice the redhead at the bar this time as he passed by, his attention all on Rachel's *derrière* in motion. The tinkling sounds of the crystal-drop hem brushing against her legs dragged his eyes down to her shapely calves, then further down to her slender ankles and sexily shod feet.

Justin didn't normally have a shoe or foot fetish, but that didn't stop him imagining Rachel walking in front of him in nothing but those turquoise high heels. Nothing. Not a stitch.

His stomach crunched down hard at the mental image, blood roaring round his body and gathering in his nether regions. The end result was an erection like Mount Vesuvius on the boil. It surprised him that there wasn't smoke wafting from his trousers.

Their ride down in the lift was awkward and silent, Justin keeping his hands linked loosely over his groin area in a seemingly nonchalant attitude, but inside he was struggling with the most corrupting thoughts.

She probably wouldn't stop you if you started making love to her. She wants it. You know she does. Understandable under the circumstances. She probably hasn't been to bed with a man since Eric the Mongrel left her. And she certainly hasn't looked this good since then, either. She wants you to want her. That's why she was stroking your neck like that. And that's why she wasn't all that happy a minute ago when you brought her Cinderella night to an abrupt halt. You'd be doing her a favour if you slept with her. You'd be delivering the whole fantasy. A man in her bed for the night. A man wanting her again. A man finding her beautiful and desirable and, yes, sexy.

Which he did find her tonight. What man wouldn't? She looked gorgeous.

But what about in the morning, Justin? What about next week when you have to work with her? What then?

Justin smothered a groan. He couldn't do it. No matter what. It was unacceptable and unconscionable and just plain wrong. She might not be dead drunk but she was decidedly tipsy, and extra-vulnerable tonight. She needed compassion, not passion. Understanding, not underhanded tactics.

'You're angry with me, aren't you?' she said wretchedly when they finally made it into the apartment, neither having said a word since they'd left the bar.

Justin sighed. 'No, Rachel, I'm not angry with you.'

'You're acting as though you are.'

'I'm sorry if it looks that way. If you must know, I'm angry with myself.'

She blinked her surprise. 'But why? I'm the one who's been behaving badly.'

'That's a matter of opinion. If you could see into my head right now then you wouldn't think that.'

She stared at him and he stared right back, his conscience once again raging a desperate war with his fiercely aroused body. He tried to recapture the gentle and platonic feelings Rachel usually engendered in him; tried to recall how she'd once looked. But it was a losing battle. That sexless creature was gone, and in her place was this incredibly desirable woman. All he could think about was how she'd felt in his arms upstairs and how she'd feel in his bed down here.

'This is an even worse idea than dancing with you,' he muttered as he stepped forward and cupped her startled face with his hands. 'But I haven't the will-power to resist. Don't say no to me, Rachel. Not tonight.'

He was going to kiss her, Rachel realised with a small gasp of shock. No, not just kiss her. He was going to make love to her.

She almost blurted out 'no', his carnal intentions fuelling instant panic. But before her mouth could form any protest his lips had covered hers in a kiss of such hunger and intensity that she was totally blown away.

His tongue stabbed deep, his fingers sliding up into her hair, his fingertips digging into her scalp as he held her mouth solidly captive under his. It was a brutally ravaging, wildly primitive, hotly demanding kiss.

And she loved it, her moans echoing a dazed, dizzying pleasure.

'No, don't,' she choked out ambiguously when his head lifted at long last, leaving her mouth feeling bruised and bereft. She actually meant, No, don't stop. But he naturally took it another way.

'I told you not to say that,' he growled, and swept her up into his arms. 'There will be no "no"s tonight.'

He kissed her again as he carried her down to his room, then kissed her some more whilst he took off all her clothes. Once she was totally, shockingly naked, he spread her out on the bed and kissed every intimate erogenous part of her body.

And she never once said no. Because she never said a word. She was beyond words. Beyond anything but moaning with pleasure.

Yet she didn't come. He seemed to know just how much she could endure without tipping over the edge. Time and time again she would come incredibly close, and tense up in expectation of imminent release. But each time he would stop doing what he was doing, and she'd groan and writhe with frustration. As often as not he'd just smile down at her, as though he was enjoying her torment.

By the time he deserted her to strip off all his own clothes she would have done anything he asked. But he didn't ask. Instead, he drew on one of the two condoms he pulled from his trouser pocket, and just took. Swiftly and savagely.

'Oh,' Rachel gasped, coming within seconds of his

entering her. She'd never climaxed as quickly as that before, her flesh gripping his as he continued to thrust wildly into hers. He didn't last long, either, his back arching as his mouth gaped wide in a naked cry of primal release. Afterwards, he collapsed across her, his chest heaving, his breathing raw.

Rachel just lay there under him, stunned and confused. For a woman whose body had just been racked by a fierce and fantastic orgasm, she didn't feel at all satisfied, just primed for more.

'Don't talk,' he commanded when he finally withdrew and scooped her still turned-on body up in his arms. 'Talking will only spoil everything.'

His *en suite* bathroom was as white and spacious as hers, with a shower cubicle built for two. Holding her with one strong arm, he adjusted the water on both shower heads then deposited her in there before leaving to attend to the condom.

Rachel stood under the warm water and watched him through the clear glass of the shower cubicle, thinking that he really had a fabulous body. When he'd undressed earlier she'd been too caught up with her own excitement and apprehension to notice him in detail. Now her eyes avidly drank in his perfect male shape; the broad shoulders, slender hips, tight buttocks. Muscles abounded in his back, arms and legs. He also sported an all-over tan, except for the area that had been covered by a very brief swimming costume. Justin was built very well indeed. His wife certainly hadn't left him because he was inadequate in that department. Or in the lovemaking department either. He knew what to do with a woman's body all right. He made Eric's idea of foreplay look pathetically inadequate.

Thinking of Justin's wife and Eric reminded Rachel

that what she was doing here—and what Justin was doing here—had nothing to do with love and relationships, and everything to do with need. Need for sex, and the need to be needed, even if only sexually.

At least, that was the way it was for her. Justin's wanting her, even for this one night, had done more for her feminine self-esteem than all the physical makeovers in the world. He'd brought out the woman in her again. If nothing else, after tonight she could not go back to being that pretend plain Jane who'd been playing the role of his prim PA in such a piteous fashion.

Even if it meant having to resign, she would truly move on from this point, and live her life as she once had. There would be no more wimpishly making the least of herself. No more hiding behind dreary black suits and spinsterish hairdos. Definitely no more being afraid of other people, and men in particular. That sad, lonely chapter in her life was over.

'You're thinking,' Justin grumbled as he joined her under the water and turned up the hot tap.

'And you're talking,' she reminded him as she lifted her hands to slick her dripping hair back from her face.

'That's my prerogative. I'm the boss. Keep your arms up and your hands behind your head like that,' he ordered thickly. 'Lock your fingers together. Keep your elbows back.'

Rachel was staggered by his request. But she obeyed, and found the experience an incredible turn-on. By the look in his eyes, Justin did too. His gaze roved hotly over her body, which felt extra-naked and extra-exposed as she stood there like that. The now steaming water kept splashing over her head and running down her face, into the corners of her by now panting mouth. Down her neck it streamed, forming a rivulet between her breasts, pooling in her navel before spilling down to the juncture between her thighs, soaking the curl-covered mound and finally finding its way into the already hot, wet valleys of her female flesh.

'Beautiful,' he murmured, his voice low and taut. 'Now close your eyes and don't talk. Or move.'

Her eyes widened but then fluttered closed, as ordered. Rachel was far too excited to even consider not obeying him. She'd never played erotic games before, and the experience was blowing her mind.

Now, within her self-imposed prison of darkness, she could only imagine how she looked, standing there so submissively, with her elbows back and her breasts thrust forward, their nipples achingly erect. Was he looking at her and despising her for her unexpected wantonness, or delighting in her willingness to play slave to his master?

The shocking part was she didn't seem to care, as long as he looked, and touched, and satisfied her once more. By the time his hands started skimming lightly over her body, she was already craving another climax, her mind propelling her forward to that moment when he'd surge up into her, filling her, fulfilling her.

She moaned softly when something—not his hand—rubbed over her nipples. Soap, she soon realised. A cake of soap. He wasn't washing her as such, just using the soap, caressing her with its slippery surface, making her nipples tighten even further. Every internal muscle she owned tightened along with them. When the soap started travelling southwards Rachel sucked in sharply.

No, not there, she wanted to warn him. But before her tongue could formulate her brain's protest the soap was between her legs, sliding back and forth, back and forth, back and forth. She tried to stop the inevitable from happening, but it was like trying to stop a ski-jumper in mid-jump. When her belly grew taut and her thighs began to tremble she knew the struggle for control had been futile.

She came with a violent rush, her knees going to jelly and her arms falling back down to her sides. She might have sunk into a wet heap on the floor had he not snapped off the water and swept her back up into his arms. Her eyes must have conveyed her shocked state as he carried her back to his bedroom, but he just ignored them and spread her dripping body face down across the bed, pushing a pillow up under her hips.

Was she too shattered to stop him at that moment? Or was this what she secretly wanted as well? For him to take her like that. For him to take her over and over in every position imaginable. To make her come again and again. To show her…what?

That she could be as wickedly sexy as the next woman? As Charlotte, perhaps?

When he didn't touch her—or take her—straight away an impatient Rachel glanced over her shoulder, only to see he was busy with a condom. She was tempted to tell him that he didn't really have to use protection. Not unless he was a health risk. Perversely, she was on the Pill for reasons which had nothing to do with contraception. It simply stopped her from having dreadful PMT, which she hadn't been able to cope with on top of the stress of minding Lettie.

She didn't tell him, in the end. Not right then. She wasn't *that* brazen. But she told him later, after she realised he had no more condoms and she'd moved way beyond brazen, way beyond anything she thought she could ever be.

CHAPTER EIGHT

JUSTIN stared down at the sleeping woman in his bed with disbelieving eyes. Was that really his prim and proper PA lying there in the nude, looking wickedly sexy with a sheet pulled suggestively up between her legs? And had it been himself who'd ravaged and ravished her amazingly co-operative body all night long?

The answer was yes, to both questions.

He groaned, his hands lifting to clap each side of his face then rake up into his hair. Whatever had possessed him? With Rachel, of all women!

Bosses who seduced their secretaries were top of his most despised list of men.

But seduce Rachel he had. The fact that she'd enjoyed herself enormously in the end had little bearing on the fact that initially he'd taken advantage of her drunken and vulnerable state, blatantly using his position as her boss to pressure her into sex. When he thought of the things he'd asked her to do in the shower his mind boggled. That she'd done everything he wanted, without question, was testament to her not being her usual sensible self. It was a particularly telling moment when she'd confessed later in the night to being on the Pill. No girl these days made such a rash revelation, not unless they were totally out of their minds with lust!

Which Rachel had been by then. No doubt about it.

Astonishing, really. He would never have believed it of her. Not with him, anyway. Still, given the circumstances, possibly any man would have done last night. He'd known that subconsciously. Hell, no, he'd known it *consciously*. He'd thought about her vulnerable state *before* he'd crossed the line. And what had he done? Still crossed that line, then wallowed in her unexpected sensuality and insatiability, urging her on to arouse him repeatedly with her mouth till he was ready to take her in yet another erotically challenging position.

His body stirred just thinking about it. Groaning, Justin dragged his eyes away from Rachel's tempting nudity and headed straight for the bathroom, plunging his wayward flesh into the coldest of showers.

She'll have to go, he began thinking, despite the icy spray doing the trick. I can't possibly work with her. She'll make me feel guilty all the time. Or worse.

The prospect of spending every weekday having cold showers at lunch time would be untenable. Aside from the constant distraction and frustration, it would remind him of Mandy, and what Mandy was up to on a daily basis with that bastard boss of hers.

Yet to sack Rachel would make him an even bigger bastard of a boss. Justin was trapped by the situation. Damned if he did and damned if he didn't!

'Bloody hell,' he muttered, and slammed his palms hard against the wet tiles.

Rachel woke with a start, her eyes blinking as she tried to focus on where she was. She didn't recognise the ceiling. Or the walls. Or the bed, for that matter.

And then, suddenly, she remembered.

Everything.

'Oh, God,' she moaned.

The sound of the shower running was some comfort,

because it gave Rachel the opportunity to jump out of the bed, gather up her clothes and escape back to her own room without having to face Justin, naked, in his bed.

Grimacing, she dived into a shower of her own without delay, where she stayed for some time, doing her best to wash away all the evidence of what she could only describe as a night best forgotten.

But forgetting the way she'd acted was nigh on impossible when she was constantly confronted with the physical consequences of her amazingly decadent behaviour. Her nipples ached. Her mouth felt like suede. And she probably wouldn't be able to walk without discomfort for a week.

As much as she hadn't felt ashamed of her behaviour last night—she'd blindly viewed it as an exciting liberation from her drab, lonely and celibate existence—in the cold light of day she could see that having her own private orgy with her boss had not been a good career move.

He would not be pleased, she knew, either with her or himself.

Rachel was sitting on the side of her bed half an hour later and wishing she were dead, when a knock on the door made her jump.

'Rachel,' Justin said through the door in a business-like voice. 'Are you dressed?'

'Not quite,' she croaked out. A lie, since she'd just pulled on an outfit from Isabel's discarded resort wardrobe, white capri pants and a matching white and yellow flowered top, *with* underwear, thank God. She'd bought a couple of bra and pants sets the previous day. But her hair was still wrapped in a towel and she hadn't a scrap of make-up on.

Despite regretting going to bed with Justin, no way was she going to revert to plain-Jane mode again. If nothing else, yesterday's make-over had propelled her out of that pathetic state.

'We have to talk,' Justin went on. 'And we have to eat. In case you haven't noticed, it's after eleven and the breakfast buffet downstairs has long closed.'

'I'm not very hungry,' she said wretchedly.

'Maybe not, but you still have to eat something. We'll only get a snack on the flight home this afternoon. Look, why don't I order sandwiches from Room Service whilst you get dressed? Then we can talk over brunch on the terrace. We have plenty of coffee and tea in the room, so a hot drink is no problem. See you out on the terrace in, say…half an hour?'

'All right,' she agreed, thinking with some relief how very civilised he was sounding. Maybe he wasn't going to sack her after all.

Any hope of Justin's that she might appear dressed in dreary black again was dashed when she stepped out onto the terrace looking delicious in tight white trousers and a bright yellow top that hugged her breasts. For a girl he'd recently thought of as skinny, she had some surprising curves.

And some surprising moves, he recalled, doing his best not to stare at her pink glossed mouth.

Gritting his teeth, he waved her to her seat at the table, then got straight down to brass tacks. No point in putting off the unpleasant.

'Before you say anything,' he began, 'let me immediately apologise for my appalling behaviour last night. I have few excuses, except possibly eighteen months of celibacy and half a bottle of wine. Then, of course, there was the way you looked last night…' Not to mention the way you look this morning, he could have added when his gaze swept over her again.

On top of the figure-fitting clothes, her hair was swinging around her face in a sleek, sexy red curtain, and her scarlet-painted toes were peeping out at him from her open-toed white sandals. She also smelled like fresh green apples, a scent he'd always liked.

'I owe you an apology as well,' she returned with what sounded like relief in her voice. 'I led you on when we danced together. I know I did. And I certainly didn't say no at any stage. I guess I must have been drunker than I realised.'

Justin was happy to play it that way, if it made her feel better. It certainly made him feel better. Or did it? Was she implying she must have been plastered to go to bed with him? Did she need reminding just how many times she'd come last night? And how often she'd begged him not to stop, long after the effects of that wine had worn off?

She'd been drunk all right. Drunk on desire.

You wanted me, baby, was on the tip of his tongue.

But, of course, he didn't say that.

'Fine,' he said instead. 'We're both to blame. That's fair. So let's forgive each other, forget last night ever happened and just go on as before.'

He saw her shoulders snap back against the seat and her chin jerk up in surprise. She fixed frowning eyes upon him. 'You can really do that? Forget last night ever happened?'

Not with you sitting next to me, sweetheart. And looking good enough to eat.

Justin shrugged. 'Yes, why not? It didn't mean anything to either of us. You needed a man and I needed a woman. It was simply a case of being in the wrong place at the wrong time. It's obvious that both of us need to get out more,' he finished up with a bitter little smile.

'So you're not going to sack me?'

'Sack you! Of course not. The thought never occurred to me.'

Which was possibly only the first of a host of lies he'd be telling Rachel in future.

'I…I was worried that you might. Isabel always says that to have an affair with the boss is the kiss of death, job-wise. The girl always ends up being given the boot.'

Not always, he wanted to say. Not when the woman in question is my beautiful blonde ex-wife. She's been her boss's assistant-cum-mistress for two years and they're still together, at it like rabbits on desks and in private jets and on yacht decks.

'But we're not having an affair, are we?' he reminded Rachel ruefully. 'We made the mistake of going to bed together. *Once.* But we won't be making that mistake again, will we?'

'What? Oh, no. No, certainly not,' she said firmly, but her eyes remained worryingly ambivalent.

Justin knew then that she was experiencing at least a little of the leftover feelings which were still haunting him.

Damn, damn and double damn! His own dark desires he could cope with. And hide. But he was a goner if she started coming on to him again.

'One thing, though,' he went on brusquely.

'Yes?'

'Your appearance…'

'Yes?'

Justin wasn't sure if what he was about to say would work. But it was the only way out of the bind he'd got himself into.

'I—er—wondered if you're intending to dress differently for work from now on. I mean…I'm only human, Rachel, and I wouldn't want you coming into the office in clothes which I might find…distracting.'

She closed her eyes for a few seconds and pursed her pretty lips. 'Justin…' Her eyes opened again and her chin lifted in what could only be described as a defiant gesture. 'I'm sorry,' she said firmly, 'but I refuse to go back to the way I used to look. I couldn't. I'd rather resign than do that.'

'There is no question of your resigning!' he pronounced heatedly. Surprising, when this was what he'd been trying to make her do. Resign. But the moment she said she might he knew that was not what he wanted. He wanted Rachel to stay on, working for him. He wanted… God, he didn't know what he wanted any more.

He smothered a weary sigh before it left his lungs. 'You can wear what you like,' he said. 'Within reason, of course.'

'I've *never* been the type of girl to dress provocatively at work, Justin. I simply won't be wearing those awful black suits again, except perhaps tomorrow. I don't have any other work clothes till I buy some more. I'll pop out and buy a couple of brighter outfits during my lunch hour.'

'Not too bright, I hope,' he muttered, dreading anything which would constantly draw his eyes and rev up his hormones. 'What about your hair?'

'What about it? Don't tell me it's too bright as well.'

No, just too damned sexy the way you're wearing it today.

'Would you consider wearing it back up again?' he suggested in desperation. 'I've always thought that a suitable look for work.'

She sighed. 'Very well, I'll put my hair up.'

'And not too much make-up.'

'I have *never* worn too much make-up, either. I only have lipstick on at this moment.'

'Really?'

He would have sworn she was wearing much more. Her skin looked so pale and clear, yet her cheeks were glowing. As for her eyes... He'd always known they were her best feature but had they always had such long lashes?

'Don't worry, Justin,' she said with more than a touch of irritation in her voice. 'I won't waltz in to work looking like the office slut. And I promise I'll wear underwear.'

His stomach jolted at the thought of her walking around the office without anything on underneath her clothes. What a shockingly appealing idea!

Justin suppressed a sigh and wondered how long it would be before Rachel stopped being the object of his sexual fantasies. A week? A month? A year?

Damn, but he wished he'd resisted temptation last night. And he wished he'd never suggested that bloody make-over. He wanted his old Rachel back. She didn't stir his blood or challenge his conscience. She was sweet and kind and calming. This new Rachel was anything but calming. Even now, he wanted to say to hell with all this conciliatory chit-chat, let's just go back to bed and stay there all day. And to hell with underwear in the office as well. I *want* you buck-naked under your clothes. And no bra. Never a bra. I want your beautiful breasts accessible to my touch at the flick of a button. I want to be able to lift your skirt at any time and lean you over my desk and just do it. I want…

Justin's fantasies were really running away with him when a sudden appalling realisation reined them in. What he wanted to do with Rachel was exactly the sort of thing Mandy's rapacious boss had been doing with her!

Justin's blood ran cold at the thought, which was good. Very good. And very effective.

His burgeoning arousal ebbed away immediately.

That was what he'd do in future. Think of Mandy whenever these unacceptable desires struck. Pity he hadn't thought of the bitch last night. But better later than never!

Rachel realised that her attempt at a little joke about her underwear had backfired when Justin's back stiffened and his face took on an icily disapproving expression. Truly! It was getting difficult to remember him as the red-hot lover who'd made her do all the deliciously wicked things he'd made her do last night.

All of a sudden, he was acting like some prude!

Still, maybe that was what he basically was. A prude. Maybe he *had* been drunker last night than he seemed at the time.

Whatever, it was clear he deeply regretted having sex with her and was doing his level best to return their relationship to its previous professional-only status, even going so far as to want her to go back to looking much the same as she used to.

Fat chance of that, buster, she thought with private mutiny. If you want me to revert to plain-Jane mode, how about you doing something about *your* looks?

Why don't you stack on twenty kilos, and put a paper bag over your head for good measure? Oh, and start wearing grotty, nerdy clothes, none of those super-suave suits you wear into the office, or that coolly casual outfit you've got on at the moment. After all, sexual attraction—and distraction—was a two-way thing.

From the moment she'd set eyes on him again this morning, her heart had quickened and her eyes had surreptitiously gobbled him up. Frankly, it had been an effort so far not to keep staring at him in those smart beige trousers and that sexy black open-necked shirt. She supposed she should be grateful that he wasn't wearing shorts, but she was still brutally aware of what lay beneath his clothes. All that working out in the gym had produced a fantastic body. Talk about toned and honed! She hadn't been able to stop touching it last night.

In fact, she *hadn't* stopped touching it. If truth be told, she wanted to touch it again. Right now.

Rachel gave herself a savage mental shake and rose to her feet.

'I'll make us some coffee to go with this food,' she said, glancing resignedly at the two plates of mixed sandwiches that were sitting on the table. She still didn't have any appetite and would definitely need help in washing bread down her throat.

'You don't have to wait on me,' he said curtly, and rose to his feet as well. 'I'll help.'

Getting the coffee together was awkward. When Justin brushed her arm Rachel jumped away as though she'd been stung by a bee. When he glared at her she winced inside.

Lord, but she was like a cat on a hot tin roof around him. The lightest of touches and her skin felt scalded.

Rachel could only hope that time would lessen this sudden and intense physical awareness. After all, last night *was* still fresh in her mind. And her body was still harbouring some solid reminders as well. She felt tender in some places and rock-hard in others. On top of that, her whole system was suffering from a general feeling of agitation, which was perverse, since all that sex should at least have relaxed her nerves, not fired them up.

Hopefully, things would improve when they were back into their normal working-day routine. It wasn't helping that they were still alone together in this hotel, well away from their real lives. Perhaps that was another reason why they'd both acted so out of character last night. A romantic setting was well-known for undermining people's sexual defences. A woman's, anyway.

Rachel's hand shook as she picked up her cup and saucer, some coffee slopping into the saucer. Justin shot her another impatient look, which irked her considerably.

'OK, so I'm clumsy this morning,' she snapped. 'We can't all be perfect all the time.'

'I would have thought that was obvious after last night,' he retorted, and carried his coffee back to the terrace without spilling a drop.

Rachel fumed as she followed. What a pig, she began thinking. And she'd always imagined him to be kind. Why, he was nothing but a typical male. Trying to put the blame on her for last night. He'd been the one to kiss her first! He was the one to open Pandora's box. And now he was trying to shove her back in there again and close the lid.

Well, she was not going to go. She was free now.

Free of Eric. Free of the past. Free to be the woman she wanted to be.

Which was not some mealy-mouthed creature who was too afraid to speak up or be herself lest she lose her job. There were plenty more PA positions to be had. And plenty more men out there who could turn her on. She didn't need Justin McCarthy to provide her with either a salary *or* sex.

Despite her disgruntled state, Rachel decided that in deference to having to tolerate Justin's constant company for the next few hours, she would hold her tongue for today. But, come tomorrow, if he started pressuring her to be something she wasn't she'd start looking around for another job.

Because there was no going back after this. The die had been cast and she intended to roll with it!

CHAPTER NINE

JUSTIN could not believe it when he walked into work the following morning—a cowardly half an hour late—and found Rachel wearing what he'd always thought her dreariest black suit, yet looking so sexy, it was sinful.

The severely tailored jacket with its long sleeves and lapelled neckline seemed tighter, and more shapely, hugging her small waist and full breasts. Had she taken it in at the seams? She'd definitely taken the skirt up, he realised when she brought in his morning coffee, the hem now a couple of inches above her knees instead of sedately covering them. And she was wearing black stockings. Not the thick, opaque, sexless kind. The sheer, silky, sexy kind which drew a man's eye and made him picture them attached to suspenders.

When he started wondering just that he wrenched his eyes back up to her face, which wasn't much help. OK, so she *had* put her hair up, as he'd requested. But not the way she'd used to, scraped back severely into a knot. It was caught up very loosely with a long black easily removable clip. Several strands had already escaped its ineffectual clasp to curve around her chin, drawing his gaze to her mouth, a mouth which bore no resemblance to Rachel's usual workaday mouth. It was more like that mouth which had tormented and teased him on Saturday night. Blood-red and full and tempting. Oh, so incredibly tempting.

Justin clenched his teeth hard in his jaw and dropped

his gaze back to his work. 'Just put the coffee down there, thank you, Rachel,' he said brusquely, nodding to a spot near his right hand.

When she lingered in front of his desk without saying a word he was finally forced to look up. 'Yes?' he said sharply. 'What is it?'

'Could I have a longer lunch hour than usual today, Justin?' she asked. 'I have some clothes shopping to do. I'll work late to make up for it.'

Justin no longer cared what clothes she bought. She couldn't look any sexier to him if she tried, anyway.

'Yes, yes.' He waved her off impatiently. 'Take all the time you need.' The rest of my life, preferably.

'Are you sure?'

'Yes, Rachel,' he bit out. 'Quite sure. Now, if you'll excuse me, I have to write this report for Guy.'

'Did I hear my name mentioned?' the man himself said as he strode in.

Justin welcomed the distraction. 'Aah. You're back from Melbourne earlier than I expected,' he said, glad to have an excuse to ignore Rachel. 'How's your father?'

'Much better. It was one of those nasty viruses. He was rotten on Friday and Saturday but on the improve by yesterday. So what did you think of Sunshine Gardens?'

'Take a seat and I'll tell you. Close the door as you go out, would you, Rachel?'

Justin noticed that Guy's eyes followed her as she did so.

He gave a low whistle after the door clicked shut. 'So that's your new PA,' he said, with meaning in his voice. 'You lucky dog, you. I *love* pretty women in black. Though, of course, I prefer them in nothing at all.'

'There's nothing between Rachel and myself,' Justin lied staunchly, his face a stony mask.

Guy chuckled. 'That's your story and you're going to stick to it. Wise man. Office affairs are best kept behind closed doors. And hotel-room doors. So how was your weekend junket? Everything to your satisfaction?' And he grinned lecherously.

Justin decided to ignore Guy's none-too-subtle innuendoes and plunged into giving him a brisk report on the hotel as a property investment. Naturally, he didn't mention their not having been to the presentation dinner. He let Guy think they had. Justin had watched the video last night and hadn't changed his mind about the place, despite the glowing marketing spiel.

'So that's my professional opinion,' Justin finished up. 'Added to the fact I think it's a lemon, I also gleaned some valuable inside information from a lady real-estate agent there for the free weekend. Apparently, the client she was representing is intent on purchasing the hotel at any price. I never think it's a good idea to get into a bidding war with that kind of buyer.'

'This agent could have been bluffing.'

'Yes, but I don't think so.'

'Mmm. Do you happen to know who this interested party is?'

'No. Just that he's filthy rich and has an ego the size of his cheque-book.'

'I heard a whisper that Carl Toombs is thinking of going into the property market up that way.'

Justin struggled to keep his face unreadable. No one at AWI knew the circumstances behind his divorce. No one knew that his ex-wife was Carl Toombs' secret mistress. No one except him and Mandy and his mother.

Justin's own ego had kept their secret for them.

So of course he could not be seen to react to Carl Toombs' name in any way other than a professional one.

'The man certainly fits the description the agent gave of him,' he said coolly. 'She said her client always gets what he wants, money no object.'

And wasn't that the truth? He'd set his sights on a married woman who'd been deeply in love with her husband at the time—Justin still believed that—and totally corrupted her, with his money, his charisma and his supposed sexual prowess.

Justin hated the man with a passion. As did quite a lot of other people in Australia, people who'd invested in some of his previous entrepreneurial get-rich-quick schemes. Some had succeeded, but a good few had failed. Yet somehow Toombs always managed to extricate himself with his own fortune intact. He had brilliant lawyers and accountants, and the best of contacts, both in the political and social scene. Married twice, with an adult daughter from his first marriage and two teenage sons from his present wife, Carl Toombs was in his early fifties, but looked a lot younger, courtesy of his personal dietician, trainer and cosmetic surgeon.

When Mandy had first gone to work for Carl Toombs she'd made jokes about his vanity and massive ego. Justin had joined in. But the joke had been on Justin in the end. Carl Toombs had come out on top. Literally.

Thinking about that swine and Mandy inevitably put Justin in a foul mood. 'I hope Toombs buys the place,' he went on testily. 'And I hope he loses a packet. Of his own money for a change.'

Guy looked taken aback. 'Sounds as if you lost some of your money in one of his famous ventures.'

Justin gritted his teeth. He'd lost something he valued much more than money. 'Let's just say he wouldn't want to meet me in a dark alley on a dark night.'

Guy laughed. 'And there I've been, thinking you'd never put a foot wrong financially.'

'We all make mistakes, Guy. That's how we learn.'

'And what did tangling with Toombs teach you?'

'Never to underestimate a man who has more money than I have.'

'True,' Guy said, nodding sagely. 'OK, so you don't suggest that I recommend Sunshine Gardens to the CEO.'

'Not if you value your job.'

Guy laughed, then stood up. 'See you tomorrow morning at the gym?'

'Absolutely.'

'Don't work too hard.'

'You don't really mean that.'

Guy smiled. 'Nope. I hope you work your butt off. Profits have been up since you came here. I even sleep at night sometimes.'

'Get out of here. And tell Rachel to bring me another coffee when you go past, will you? This one's gone cold.'

'Will do. I might stay and watch her do it, too. That girl has an incredible walk. And a *derrière* to die for. But I suspect you already know that, McCarthy,' he threw over his shoulder as he walked towards the door. 'No wonder you work out every morning till you're ready to drop. Can't be easy keeping your hands off that nice piece of skirt out here.'

Justin groaned. 'For pity's sake, Guy, keep your voice down. She might hear you. Haven't you heard of sexual harassment in the workplace?'

Guy shrugged and put his hand on the door knob, but he didn't turn it. 'I could be mistaken, mate, but I caught a glimpse of something in your PA's very lovely eyes a few minutes ago which indicated she might not be averse to a little sexual harassment from you.'

'Don't be ridiculous!'

'I'm not being ridiculous. I studied body language when I did a sales and marketing course recently, and she fancies you, mate. I guarantee it. But I guess if you're not interested, then you're not interested. Poor girl. I guess she'll just have to go find herself some other tall, dark, handsome jerk to give her a bit. Pity I don't fit the bill. I'd give her one, I can tell you. OK, OK, you don't have to say it. Get lost. And I won't forget the coffee on my way out.'

He didn't. Unfortunately. Soon, Rachel was undulating towards his desk with the coffee and Justin found himself mentally stripping her again. Oh, God. This was how it all began back there in that bar, with him watching her walk in front of him and imagining her without any clothes on. The trouble was, this time he *knew* what she looked like without any clothes on. And the reality far surpassed the fantasy his imagination had conjured up. She was all woman. And she could be all his, according to Guy.

Was he right? Did she really fancy him, not as some rebound substitute for Eric the Mongrel, but as a man in his own right? Was she secretly hoping he'd keep their affair going?

The thought both excited and worried him. He didn't love her. He'd never love her. He wasn't capable of that kind of love any more. He wasn't capable of any relationship of any depth. All he would want—or need—from any woman for a long time was what she'd given him the other night. Sex without strings.

He watched her put the coffee down then glance up at him, her face expectant. 'Is that all for now?'

Was it? What would she do, he wondered, if he told her to go close the door, then lock it?

A shudder of self-loathing—or was it arousal?—ricocheted through him. He could not do it. *Would* not.

'Rachel…'

'Yes?'

'Nothing,' he bit out. 'That's all. You can get back to your work. Oh, and you can take the whole afternoon off for your shopping, if you like.'

'The whole afternoon?' she echoed in surprise.

'Yes, why not? You deserve it after the weekend.'

He'd meant she deserved some time off because, technically, she'd been working overtime. But when her face darkened he immediately saw how his words could be interpreted.

'You mean in exchange for services rendered?' she threw at him.

'No, of course not. Look, if you're going to bring that up all the time, I'm not sure we *can* go on working together.'

Justin didn't need to have studied body language to gauge her reaction to that charming little announcement. Her whole body stiffened, and her eyes…her eyes stabbed him right in the heart.

'I see,' she said frostily. 'It's nice to know where things stand. You'll have my resignation on your desk *before* I leave at lunch time. And yes, I will have the whole afternoon off, thank you very much.' Spinning on her heels, she stalked from the room, banging the door behind her.

Justin slumped back into his chair with a groan. He'd done it now. And he'd never felt lower in all his life. He dropped his head into his hands and called himself every name under the sun.

Rachel could not sit down at her desk and go calmly back to work. She paced the outer office for a couple of angry minutes, then marched into the tea room and poured herself a fresh coffee, more for something to do than because she wanted it. In fact, the steaming mug remained untouched on the counter whilst she just stood there, tapping her foot and trying to gather herself.

Isabel had been so right about office affairs. Not that she needed her best friend to tell her that. Hadn't it always been the case in the workplace? The male boss got away with sleeping around and the female employee got the push.

She had an urge to go back in there and give Justin a piece of her mind. But pride wouldn't let her. Pride and common sense. Given her lack of recent work experience, she needed a reference. Not that Justin would dare not give her a reference. She could make real trouble for him over this, if she had a mind to.

But Rachel had no stomach for such an action. No, she would simply resign and to hell with Justin McCarthy. In fact, to hell with him for the rest of the day. She was going to write out her resignation right now and leave. And then she was going to go out and spend every cent in her savings account on a brand-new wardrobe!

Leaving her coffee still untouched, Rachel stormed back to her desk and set to work on her resignation letter.

Justin was in front of one of his many computer screens, pretending to work, when his office door was flung open and Rachel marched in with flushed cheeks and her head held high.

'There's my resignation,' she announced, and slapped a typed page down in front of him. 'I'll work out my notice and I'll expect a glowing reference, though lord knows how I'm going to explain leaving my present position after so short a time. But I guess that's my problem. Oh, and I'm taking the rest of the day off, starting right now!'

'Rachel, don't…'

'Don't what?'

'Don't resign,' he said wearily.

'Too late,' she snapped, and Justin winced. 'And please don't pretend this isn't what you want. You've been working towards this moment ever since you woke up yesterday morning and found me in your bed.'

Justin could not deny it.

'I'm beginning to wonder if the same thing happened with your previous girl. Or do you only screw the plain ones?'

'Rachel, I didn't mean t—'

'Yes, you did,' she broke in savagely. 'You screwed me good and proper. But I'll survive. I'm a survivor, Justin McCarthy. Watch me.'

He watched her walk with great dignity out of his office, and he'd never admired her more. But he didn't call her back, because she was right. He had screwed her good and proper. And he wanted to do it some more.

Best she leave before he really hurt her.

Best he crawl back into his celibate cave, and best he go back to work!

Rachel felt tears begin to well up in the lift ride down to the lobby. Her anger was swiftly abating and in its place lay a misery far greater than she had anticipated. At the heart of her dismay lay the fact she'd really liked Justin. And she'd really liked working for him.

And you *really* liked having sex with him, came another quieter but more honest voice. That's why you're feeling so wretched. All your silly female attempts to look attractive for him this morning were a big waste of time. You vowed you'd never get that horrible sewing machine out again and what did you do last night? Hauled the damned thing out of the bottom of the wardrobe and worked till midnight practically remaking this wretched suit.

And what did he do? Hardly looked at it, or at you. He doesn't want you any more. He never really did. How could you possibly have started imagining he might? You were just there, when he needed sex. He said as much yesterday. And now you're a nasty reminder of behaviour he'd rather forget.

Rachel's eyes were swimming by the time the lift doors opened, so she fled to the ladies' room in the lobby and didn't come out till she was dry-eyed and back in control.

But she no longer felt like shopping for clothes. What did it matter what she wore around Justin?

Hooking her black carry-all over her shoulder, she headed for the exit. Straight home, she decided.

'Rachel!' a male voice shouted, and her heart jumped. 'Wait.'

Her heart began to race as she turned.

But it wasn't Justin hurrying towards her across the lobby.

It was Eric.

CHAPTER TEN

'ERIC!' Rachel exclaimed, startled. 'What...what are you doing here?' Possibly a silly question when he'd always worked in the Central Business District in Sydney. It was inevitable that one day, now she was working in the city, she might run into him.

But to run into him only three days after running into him on the Gold Coast seemed to be stretching coincidence too far.

'I was looking for you,' he explained. 'I asked around about your boss and found out he worked in this building.'

'How enterprising of you,' she said coolly.

'I am, if nothing else, enterprising,' he returned, and smiled what she'd once thought of as such a charming smile.

She no longer thought anything about Eric was charming.

She no longer thought he was all that gorgeous, either, despite his grooming still being second to none. His sleek black business suit would have cost a fortune. And he would have spent half an hour blow-drying his hair to perfection this morning. It must be killing him, she thought a bit spitefully, to find that it was receding at a rapid rate.

'Why were you looking for me?' she asked in a less than enthusiastic tone.

'I was worried about you.'

She could not have been more surprised if he'd proposed marriage.

'Good lord, why?'

'Can we go somewhere and talk in private? There's a coffee shop just off the foyer facing the street. How about in there?'

She shrugged with seeming indifference. 'If you insist.'

He didn't enlighten her till the coffee arrived, and she refused to press, despite being curious. The days when she'd hung on Eric's every word had long gone.

'You didn't come to the dinner on Saturday night,' he began, throwing her slightly. What to say to that? Rachel cast her mind back to the night in question and decided to go with the fiction Justin had created.

'We had no need after my boss met with his client.'

'Mr Wong decided against Sunshine Gardens?'

Rachel maintained her cool. 'You don't honestly expect me to discuss my boss's business with you, do you? If that's why you've come, to pump me for inside information for your girlfriend, then you've wasted your time. *And* the price of this coffee.'

'That's not the reason,' Eric said hastily when Rachel made to rise. 'I came to warn you. About your boss.'

Rachel sat back down, blinking. 'Warn me. About *Justin*?'

'Look, I know I hurt you, Rachel. I'm not a fool. The way you look at me now…you probably hate my guts and I can understand that. But I don't hate you. In fact, I think I made a big mistake breaking up with you. You are one special lady and you deserve better in life than getting tangled up with the likes of Justin McCarthy.'

Rachel opened her mouth to deny any involvement with Justin, but after their performance on Saturday night it would be difficult to claim they weren't lovers. Not that it was any of Eric's business who she slept with.

'I don't know what you're talking about,' she said stiffly. 'Justin is a wonderful boss, and wonderful in every other way. What could you possibly be warning me about where he's concerned?'

Eric laughed. 'I have to give him credit. He puts on a good act. But he's not in love with you, Rachel. He's just using you.'

'How kind of you to tell me that,' she said, struggling now to control her temper. 'Might I ask what right you have to say that, what evidence? Or is it just that when you look at me you see a pathetic, foolish woman that no man could really love?'

'There's nothing pathetic or foolish about you, Rachel, and you know it. You're still as beautiful and bright as you always were. But you do have one fatal female flaw. You fall in love with bastards.'

'I am *not* in love with my boss,' she denied heatedly.

But when Eric's eyes searched hers she felt her face flame.

'I hope not,' he said. 'Because he's one bitter and twisted guy. Not that he doesn't have a right to be. I'd be bitter and twisted if my wife did to me what his wife did to him.'

Rachel's mouth went dry. 'What…what did his wife do?'

'I thought you wouldn't know about that. It's not the sort of thing a man would spread around. Charlotte didn't put two and two together on Saturday night when you first introduced him. After all, his is not such an unusual name. But she got to thinking about it last night and made some discreet enquiries, and bingo, he was the one all right.'

'Eric, would you kindly just say what it is you've come to say?'

'Your boss's ex-wife has been Carl Toombs' personal assistant for a couple of years now. And I mean *very* personal. He pays for her apartment and she travels everywhere with him. Their relationship is a well-kept secret but that's the reason she left her husband, to shack up more often with her high-profile boss. You do know who I'm talking about, don't you?'

'Yes, of course I do,' Rachel snapped. 'I might have been out of the workforce for a few years, but I wasn't dead. I don't know of anyone in Australia who wouldn't know who Carl Toombs is.'

'OK, OK, don't get your dander up. Anyway, Toombs is Charlotte's client, the one who wants to buy Sunshine Gardens. Because of their business association, Charlotte's had quite a bit to do with his beautiful blonde PA over the past few weeks, and you know girls. They like to chat. Anyway, the ex-Mrs McCarthy confided in Charlotte over lunch and a few Chardonnays the other day. Apparently, darling Mandy is still suffering great gobs of guilt over her ex-hubby. She told Charlotte how cut up he was when she left him. She confessed she said some pretty dreadful things so that he would hate her and forget her, but that *she'd* never forget the look on his face when she told him she'd been having sex with Toombs for some time. She said she did love her husband and he was mad about her, but she simply couldn't resist Carl's advances. She said Carl wanted her and nothing was going to stop him having her. She said she thinks she broke her husband's heart.'

Rachel didn't say a word. She was too busy absorbing the full ramifications of Eric's news.

'From what I gather he's one very bitter man,' Eric went on. 'Knowing you, Rachel, you probably think he's in love with you. You're not the type of girl to jump into bed idly. But it's not love driving your boss these days. More like revenge.'

'You don't know what you're talking about, Eric. For one thing, I'm not in love with Justin. And I don't imagine for one moment that he's in love with me.'

Eric frowned. 'Then...what is it between you two?'

'That's my business, don't you think?'

'You are sleeping with him, though.'

'That's my business, too.'

'Look, I've only got your best interests at heart, Rachel. I care about you.'

She laughed. 'Since when, Eric? Are you sure you didn't seek me out today to tell me this because you're getting bored with Charlotte and think you might have a bit more of what you once used to take for granted?'

'I never took you for granted, Rachel. I loved you in my own way. I just couldn't see our marriage working with you becoming a full-time home carer. I'm a selfish man, I admit. I wanted more of your time than that. I need a wife whose first priority is me.'

'Then you chose a strange partner in Charlotte. Her first priority is her career. And her second priority is herself.'

'I always knew that. Why do you think I didn't marry her? It was you I wanted for my wife, Rachel. I still do...'

'Oh, please. Spare me. Thank you for the coffee,'

she said, rising without touching a drop. 'And thank you for your very interesting news. You might not know this but you did me a huge favour in telling me about Justin's ex. It's made everything much clearer.' Which it had. She might not know the full details of Justin's thoughts and feelings. But it wasn't revenge driving him. Revenge would have acted very differently at the weekend, and today. Revenge *would* have used her.

Rachel walked away from Eric without a backward glance, her mind wholly and solely on Justin. Alice hadn't exaggerated. Her son's wife certainly was a cold-blooded bitch. Either that, or terribly materialistic and disgustingly weak.

He was better off without someone like her in his life. The trouble was…did he realise that yet?

Maybe. Maybe not. Clearly, he'd been deeply in love with this Mandy. Possibly, he still was. It was hard to say.

Still, time did heal all wounds. Just look at herself. She'd once thought the sun shone out of Eric. She'd been devastated by his dumping her. Today, she hadn't turned a hair at his declaring he still wanted her as his wife. The man meant nothing to her any more, and being free of him felt marvellous.

Rachel suspected, however, that Justin was not yet free of his ex. His beautiful blonde ex, Eric had said. Naturally, she would be beautiful. *Very* beautiful. Men like Carl Toombs didn't take ugly women as their mistresses. They chose exquisite creatures with perfect faces and figures, women with a weakness for money and a fetish for the forbidden.

It was no wonder Justin had an aversion to sex in the office. Rachel understood completely. But it was time for him to forget the past and move on, as she had decided to do.

Of course, she'd had four years to come to her present state of heart and mind. Justin's wife had betrayed and abandoned him much more recently. Only two years ago. And she'd said truly dreadful things to him, according to Eric.

What kind of things? Rachel wondered during the lift ride back up to the fifteenth floor. Had she criticised his skills in bed? Hard to imagine that. Justin left Eric for dead as a lover. And every other boyfriend she'd ever had. Perhaps the wretched woman had told him he wasn't rich enough, or powerful enough? Who knew?

Rachel didn't dare ask him, but she dared a whole lot more. She dared to go back and tell him she'd changed her mind about resigning. She dared to stay. And she dared to go after some more of what they'd shared on Saturday night.

If truth were told, she couldn't stop thinking about it. Surely he had to be thinking about it, too. Rachel could be wrong but she suspected she was the first woman Justin had had sex with since his wife left him.

The thought amazed, then moved her to anger. Selfish people like Eric and Mandy had a great deal to answer for. But you couldn't let them get away with trampling all over your emotions, and your life. You had to stand up and fight back. You had to stop playing the victim and move on. There were other people out there. Other partners. But you had to be open to finding them. You had to embrace new experiences, not run away from them.

Rachel left the lift at her floor and hurried along to her office, her new-found boldness waning a little once she approached the door she'd slammed shut less than an hour ago. Suddenly, she was biting her bottom lip and her stomach was churning. Was Justin still there behind that door, sitting at his computers, slaving away? Probably. It wasn't lunch time yet, and her boss had no reason to go home. He had nothing in his life except his work, a bruised ego and a broken heart.

Till now, that was. Now he had *her*. Her friendship and companionship. Her body too, if he still wanted it.

Her hand was shaking by the time she summoned up enough courage to knock. But it was a timid tap. Annoyed with herself, she didn't knock again. Instead she turned the door knob and went right in.

'Oh, no,' she groaned, her gaze darting around Justin's empty office.

Rachel was battling with her disappointment when she heard a banging noise coming from inside one of the adjoining rooms, the one with the bar and the sofa in it. Before her courage failed her again she marched over and flung open the door.

Justin almost dropped the ice-tray he was holding. He hadn't expected to see Rachel again. Not that day, anyway. After she'd left he'd tried to work, but he'd been too distracted, and too depressed to concentrate. In the end, he'd come in here in search of some liquid relaxation.

'What on earth do you think you're doing?' she threw at him.

Her accusing tone—plus her unexpected reappearance—didn't bring out the best in him.

'What does it look like I'm doing?' he countered belligerently. 'I'm getting myself some ice to put in my Scotch. But the bloody stuff's stuck.'

'But…but you never drink during the day!'

'Actually, you're wrong there,' he said drily. 'I often drink during the day. Just not usually during the week.' He gave the ice-tray another bang on the granite bar-top and ice cubes flew everywhere.

'Don't do that!' he roared at her when she hurried over and began picking up the ice cubes. Damn it all, the last thing he wanted was for her to start bending over in front of him.

She ignored him and picked them up anyway, giving him a good eyeful of her *derrière*-to-die-for. 'You shouldn't drink alone, you know,' she said as she straightened and dropped several cubes into his glass.

'What do you care?' he snapped, irritated by her presence beyond belief. 'You're not my keeper. You're not even my PA any more.'

'I am, if you still want me to be. I came back to tell you I don't want to resign. I want to keep working for you.'

He laughed. 'And you think that's good news? What if I said I don't want you working for me any more? What if I said your resigning was exactly what I wanted?'

'I don't believe you.'

'She doesn't believe me,' he muttered disbelievingly, and quaffed back a mind-numbing mouthful of whisky. 'So what do I have to say to *make* you believe me?'

'There's nothing you can say,' she pronounced, and gave him one of those defiant looks of hers. Damn, but she had a mouth on her. What he wouldn't like her to do with it!

He tossed back another decent swig and decided to shock her into leaving again.

'What if I told you that since Saturday night whenever I look at you I'm mentally undressing you? What if I confessed that after you made that joke about you not wearing any underwear it became my favourite fantasy, you not wearing any underwear around the office? What if, when you accused me of having screwed you good and proper, my first thought was that I hadn't screwed you nearly enough?'

She just stared at him, clearly speechless.

'That's only the half of it,' he went on after another fortifying swallow of straight Scotch. 'When you brought me that coffee this morning after Guy left it wasn't coffee I wanted from you but sex. I wondered what you'd do if I asked you to lock the door and just let me do it to you right then and there across my desk. From behind,' he added for good measure.

Her eyes grew wider but she still hadn't said a word. She seemed rooted to the spot, frozen by his appalling admissions.

The trouble was, giving voice to his secret sexual fantasies about her had also had the inevitable effect on his body. Or was it just her, standing there in front of him, within kissing distance?

'Well? What *would* you have done?' he demanded to know, his raging hormones sparking more recklessness.

She finally found her tongue. 'I…I don't know,' came her astonishing answer.

'What do you mean, you don't know?' he shot back, floored by such an ambiguous reply.

'I mean I don't know. I was angry with you back then. Why don't you ask me now?'

My God, she meant it. She actually meant it.

His hand tightened around his glass and his head spun. So that was why she'd come back, was it?

Because she wanted him to seduce her again. He'd suspected this might be the case when she'd come in this morning looking good enough to eat, but he'd been hoping he was wrong.

Any hope of that, or that he could keep resisting temptation disappeared as swiftly as the rest of his Scotch. Emptying the glass, he banged it back down on the bar-top and faced his nemesis.

'Would you go and lock the door, Rachel?' he asked in a gravelly voice. 'Not the one that separates this room from my office. Or the one separating my office from yours. The one out in your office. The one that lets the outside world in.'

She did it. She actually did it. Justin's mind reeled with shock. But nothing could stop him now.

'Now come here to me,' he ordered thickly when she reappeared in the open doorway, looking both beautiful and nervous.

She came, her cheeks flushed with excitement and her eyes glittering brightly.

'I've been wanting to do this,' he growled, and reached up to release the clip. As her hair tumbled down around her face and shoulders Justin knew that he wasn't simply crossing a line here, he was about to propel them both into a world from which there was no turning back, a word where lust ruled and love was nothing but a distant memory. She had no conception of the demons in his mind, or the dark desires that had been driving him crazy since Saturday night. She probably thought he loved her.

Now, that was one transgression he would not be guilty of. Deception. The games he wanted to play with her were sexual, not emotional.

'You do realise I don't love you,' he said as he flicked open the buttons on her jacket.

'Yes,' she surprised him by admitting, though her voice was trembling and her eyes had gone all smoky.

'I will *never* fall in love with you,' he added even as his hands slipped inside her jacket to play with her breasts through her bra. God, but her nipples were hard. So incredibly hard.

And so was he.

'I…I don't expect you to,' she replied somewhat breathlessly.

'You don't have to do anything you don't want to do,' he told her before his conscience shut down entirely.

'But I want you to,' she choked out.

'Want me to do what?' he murmured as he slipped the jacket off her shoulders and let it fall to the carpet.

'Wh…whatever,' she stammered.

Justin suspected she was too turned on to know what she was saying. He was rapidly getting to the point of no return himself.

For a split-second, he almost pulled back and saved her from herself. And from him. But she chose that moment to reach round and unhook her bra herself. Blood roared into his ears as she bared her beautiful breasts to his male gaze. And then she did something even more provocative. She dropped the wisp of a bra on the floor then reached up and rotated her outstretched palms over her rock-like nipples.

Any hope of salvation fled. He was lost, and so, he realised when he looked down into her dilating pupils, was she.

CHAPTER ELEVEN

THE phone was ringing when Rachel arrived home that night around seven. She raced to answer it, thinking—no, *hoping*—it might be Justin.

'Yes?' she said as she snatched it up to her ear.

'Rach, I was just about to give up and hang up.'

'Isabel!' Not Justin. Of course not. Silly Rachel. 'What…what are you doing, ringing me on your honeymoon?'

'Oh, don't be silly, Rach. We can't have sex *all* the time.' And she laughed.

Rachel almost cried.

'Not that we haven't given it a good try,' Isabel burbled on. 'I think I've worn him out. The poor darling's having a nap so I thought I'd use the opportunity to give you a call and find out how things are going at home. I've already rung Mum and Dad, so don't start lecturing me.'

'I never lecture you, Isabel. Not any more. The boot's on the other foot these days.'

'You could be right there. But you need lecturing sometimes. So tell me, how's things with your job?'

'Fine,' she said with pretend lightness.

'You still getting along with grumpy-bumps?'

'Justin is not a grumpy-bumps. He's just serious.'

And how, Rachel thought with a shiver, trying not to think about the day she'd spent with him.

'In that case, he's probably not gay,' Isabel pronounced. 'Gay men are never serious.'

'Justin is definitely not gay,' Rachel said, her tone perhaps a tad too dry.

'Really? Is that first-hand experience speaking there?' her best friend asked suspiciously.

Rachel decided that some sarcastically delivered truths would serve her purpose much better than heated denial. Because no way could she ever tell Isabel what was going on between herself and her boss. Isabel would be scandalised. She was pretty scandalised herself!

'Yes, of course. Didn't I mention it? He can't keep his hands off me. We've been doing it everywhere. On the desk. In the little-men's room. On the boardroom table. Standing up. Sitting down. Frontwards. Backwards. Haven't tried it upside-down yet. But give it time.'

'OK, OK,' Isabel said, sighing exasperatedly. 'I get the drift.'

No, you don't, Rachel thought with an erotically charged shiver. I'm telling you the shocking truth. 'But let's not talk about me,' she went on hastily. 'Can I know where you went on your honeymoon now?'

'Yes, of course. Hong Kong. And we're loving it. The clothes shopping is fantastic. I've been such a naughty girl. Bought a whole new wardrobe. But you know Rafe. He likes me to dress sexily, and all my clothes at home are a tad on the conservative side.'

Rachel had never thought Isabel's wardrobe at all conservative. Just classy.

'You can have them, if you like,' Isabel offered.

'What? All of them?'

'Everything I left behind. Provided you wear them, of course. That's the deal. You have to wear them. To work as well. It's time you bit the bullet and threw out those dreary black suits. I'm sure your boss could cope. It's not as though any of my old outfits are provocative. You can even have the shoes to go with them. We're the same shoe size.'

'Yes, I know. But are you sure, Isabel?' she asked, amazed by her friend's generosity.

'Positive. Actually, there's nothing in that place that you can't have. Take the lot. Handbags. Jewellery. Make-up. Beauty products. Whatever you can find. I won't be needing any of it.'

'You can't mean that, Isabel. You used to spend a small fortune on all your accessories. As for cosmetics and skin products, both bathrooms here are chock-full of them.'

'And I don't need any of it. Look, I brought everything I really like with me, and that includes my best jewellery. The stuff I left behind is just costume jewellery, bought to go with the clothes I've just given you. You're welcome to whatever you can find. If you don't use them they'll only go to waste. I have a new look now, from top to toe. Speaking of new looks, I've also bought some great maternity clothes for when I begin to sprout. Oh, I can't wait to get home and show everything to you.'

'So when exactly will you be home?'

'Next Saturday week. The flight gets in around midday. I'll ring you when we arrive home at Rafe's place and you can come over that evening for dinner.'

'But you won't want to cook after travelling.'

'Who said anything about cooking? We'll order something in. Is that all right by you?'

'Perfect.' There was no worry that she'd be spending any time with Justin on a Saturday. That was one of the many stipulations he'd made during their marathon afternoon of sex and sin. He wasn't offering her a real relationship. He didn't think it was fair to her to build her hopes up in that regard. Meeting each other's sexual needs was what they were doing. But dating was out. So was going to each other's places. Sex was to be confined to the office, but not till after five in future. Today was an exception.

She'd agreed to stay behind after work for a while every day till they were both satisfied. She'd agreed that he would not take her out to dinner afterwards, or take her home. She'd agreed that they wouldn't see each other at weekends.

In hindsight, Rachel could see she would have agreed to anything at the time.

But she knew, deep down in her heart, that she was skating on thin ice where Justin was concerned. She had underestimated the extent of his broken heart, and the darkness that had invaded his shattered soul. If Eric had hurt her, Justin could very well destroy her. But she felt helpless against the power of her need to have him make love to her as he had today. Primitively. Erotically. Endlessly.

There was nothing she wouldn't agree to to continue their sexual relationship.

'Uh-oh, I'd better go, Rach. The lord and master is stirring. Now, don't do anything I wouldn't do till I get home,' Isabel said happily, and hung up.

'No worries there,' Rachel muttered ruefully as she replaced the phone in its cradle. 'Whatever you're doing with Rafe, I'm doing one hell of a lot more with Justin. Much, much more.'

An image flashed into her mind of her straddled over Justin's lap, her back glued to his chest, her arms wound up around his neck. They were seated on his office chair, their naked bodies fused and beaded with sweat, despite the air-conditioning. He was making a pretext of showing her how his programs worked whilst he idly played with her breasts. If he'd expected her to learn anything, he was sadly mistaken. All she'd learned was that she was rapidly becoming addicted to his brand of sex, and rapidly becoming obsessed with him.

If Isabel thought Rafe's body was great, then she hadn't seen Justin's. She quivered just thinking about how he felt, all over. She couldn't get enough of touching him. And whatever else he wanted her to do.

And he'd wanted her to do everything today. There wasn't an inch of his beautiful male flesh that hadn't enjoyed the avid attentions of her mouth, or her hands. She'd been shameless. Utterly shameless.

Yet shame wasn't her overriding emotion when she thought of the woman she became in his arms. The memory evoked the most intoxicating excitement. Her heart thundered and a wave of heat flushed her skin.

There was no way she could voluntarily give up having sex with Justin. No way she could quit now and get another job. She was his, till he decided otherwise. His to admire and desire. His to have and, yes, to hold.

But never to marry, she reminded herself.

Her heart twisted at this last thought. But that didn't stop her racing down to Isabel's walk-in wardrobe and seeing what was there for her to wear for Justin tomorrow. Something classy but sexy, she wanted, her eyes scanning the long rows filled with outfits, most of them suits in pastel shades. She pulled out a pale blue silk trouser suit, then put it back. Trousers did not appeal. She needed something with a skirt, either long and floaty, or short and tight. Something that would draw Justin's eye and recharge his hormones. She wanted him well and truly fired up by five. She wanted him as desperate for her as she already was for him.

A cream linen suit caught her eye, matched with a mustard-gold camisole. The jacket still had long sleeves but that didn't matter yet. Sydney's weather was still overcast and cool.

She laid it across the bed then rummaged around till she found matching cream shoes and bag. The jewellery box on the dressing table revealed a pearl choker with matching earrings. Not real pearls, of course, but still classy-looking. This time she would put her hair up in a more severe fashion, showing her throat and ears. To compensate, she would wear more make-up, paying particular attention to her eyes and mouth. Rachel knew she had nice eyes. And Justin seemed fascinated with her mouth.

Oh, and she would wear perfume. One of the expensive French fragrances Isabel had always favoured. Rachel had already noticed several not quite empty bottles in the wall cupboard above the main vanity unit. She would experiment with a new one each day and find out which one Justin seemed to like the most, then go and buy herself a bottle.

Stripping down to her underwear, she tried on the cream linen suit, pleased to see that it fitted very well, a surprise, considering she was considerably slimmer around the hips and waist than Isabel. Perhaps Isabel had bought it last year when she'd been dieting. The cami was much too tight around the bust, however, so Rachel took it off, discarded her bra and tried it on again.

With her full breasts settled lower on her chest the top felt less tight, but, as Rachel walked over to check her reflection in the cheval mirror on the back of the wardrobe door, the satin rubbing over her naked nipples had them puckering into pebble-like peaks. She winced at the sight of their provocative outline, which screamed her lack of underwear, plus her constant arousal. Would she dare wear it like this? And would she dare take off her jacket?

Oh, yes, she accepted as another wave of heat flooded her body.

She dared.

She would dare anything after today!

CHAPTER TWELVE

JUSTIN glanced up at the office wall clock for the umpteenth time that afternoon. Almost five. His pulse quickened at the thought that soon he could abandon any pretence of working and do what he'd been desperately wanting to do all day: have sex with Rachel.

Just the thought of it sent his blood racing through his body.

But then another less happy thought intruded. It was Friday again. For the next two days he would not see Rachel at all; could not thrill to the exquisite anticipation of knowing that at the end of the day she would let him remove all her clothes to draw her naked and trembling into his arms.

Last weekend had been almost unendurable without her. This weekend would probably be worse. Justin resolved to keep her with him later than usual tonight. She wouldn't mind. She enjoyed what they were doing just as much as he did, a fact that soothed his conscience somewhat. If he ever thought that what they were doing together was hurting her in any sense he would have to stop.

But *could* he stop, even if his conscience demanded it? That was the question. He had difficulty at the moment doing without her for two days. The prospect of never having sex with Rachel again was an idea he didn't want to address.

Another glance at the clock showed it was finally five o'clock.

His heartbeat took off.

It was time.

Rachel's head snapped up from her computer with a gasp when Justin wrenched open his office door right on the dot of five. She'd been pretending to herself that she hadn't noticed the time, pretending to be working.

But that was all it was. Pretence. She lived for this moment every day. It was what she dressed for. And undressed for. It was why each afternoon at four-thirty she rose to lock the outside door, then go to the ladies' room to make preparations for just this moment. For the last half-hour she'd been sitting there with her panties stuffed in her top drawer and no underwear of any kind covering her bare buttocks and upper thighs. Stay-up stockings had long replaced her pantyhose. She also rarely wore a bra these days, having quickly grown addicted to the feel of silk linings against her bare skin, plus the aphrodisiacal effect of knowing she was naked underneath her clothes.

Their eyes locked across the room and her surroundings slowly began to recede. Suddenly there was only him, and the way he was looking at her.

'Get yourself in here, Rachel,' he ordered, his impatience echoed in the tightness of his neck muscles.

Her legs felt like lead as she levered herself up from her desk and walked, like some programmed robot, into his office. Yet inside she was anything but a cold-blooded machine. She was all heat and hyped-up nerve-endings. Her head was spinning like a top and her heart was pounding behind her chest wall.

The speed with which he yanked up her skirt then hoisted her up onto his desk punched all the breath from Rachel's body. He was between her legs in a flash, unzipping his trousers and freeing his rather angry-looking erection. Her body was ripe and ready for him, needing no foreplay. His hands grasped her hips, his fingertips digging into her skin as he scooped her bottom to the very edge of the desk and drove into her to the hilt. With a grunt of satisfaction he set up a powerful pumping action, his eyes grimacing shut, his lips drawing back over gritted teeth. Rachel leant back and braced herself by gripping the back edge of the desk, but even so her bottom slid back and forth across the smoothly polished desk-top.

Something—possibly the fact he hadn't even kissed her first—got to Rachel, and suddenly she wanted him to stop.

The trouble was…her body didn't want him to stop. It had a mind of its own. Frantic for release, it was. And ruthlessly determined in its quest, pushing aside any gathering qualms and ignoring the danger warnings. Her libido remained recklessly separated from her heart as pre-climactic sensations began to build and the need to come became all-consuming.

Her belly tightened. As did her thighs. Her bottom. Her insides. He groaned in response to her involuntary squeezing and then they were both splintering apart, their cries of erotic ecstasy echoing in the stillness of the room. His back arched back as he shuddered into her whilst she gripped the edge of the desk so hard her fingers went white.

But the spasms of pleasure passed, as they always did, and this time Rachel came back down to earth with a terrible thud.

The reality of what they were doing together could no longer be denied. It was beneath her, carrying on like this. So why was she settling for such an arrangement? *Why?*

The reason was obvious, she accepted with considerable anguish. The reason had always been obvious, if she'd looked for it. The reason was at this moment still inside her body, his arms wound tightly around her waist, his head resting between her sweat-slicked breasts.

It was then that she started to cry.

CHAPTER THIRTEEN

'I THOUGHT you said you were never going to take me out to dinner,' she said with curiosity—and something else—in her voice. Was it hope?

Rachel's unexpectedly breaking down into tears after the episode on the desk had jolted Justin out of his selfish desires, and made him take a long, hard look at what he'd been doing. He wasn't a complete fool, or a bastard, even if he'd been acting like one. It didn't take him long to realise that a woman of Rachel's standards and sensitivity couldn't indulge her sexual self indefinitely without her emotions—and her conscience—eventually becoming involved. She claimed she was all right, and that she often cried after she came.

But she never had before.

She'd said through her sobs that she didn't want him to stop, but to continue in the face of her distress was something he simply could not do. He hadn't sunk *that* low.

So he'd comforted her as best he could, then announced that he was starving and couldn't possibly go on till they'd eaten, adding that he didn't want any of the take-away muck they sometimes had delivered to the office. He wanted a decent meal. And decent wine.

Despite a momentary look of surprise, she hadn't made any protest, so he'd booked a table in a nearby restaurant whilst she'd made whatever repairs needed to be made after sex, and retrieved her panties from where she always put them in her top drawer. Fifteen minutes later, here they were, sitting opposite each other at a candlelit table, with Rachel finally giving voice to what was a very fair question over his changing the rules of their arrangement.

He stared across the table at her and thought how lovely she looked in the soft candlelight. The simple mauve dress she was wearing was very classy and elegant. There again, all the clothes she wore to work these days were classy and elegant.

'So I did,' he said quietly. 'But things change, Rachel. I thought it was time we talked.'

Was that panic in her eyes? Or fear? Fear of what, for pity's sake? Of his stopping the sex? Or changing the rules?

Maybe she hadn't been lying to him when she said she was all right. Maybe she liked things the way they were. Maybe she'd become as addicted to his body as he was to hers.

Such thinking threw him. He didn't want her feeling nothing but lust for him. He wanted… He wanted… What *did* he want, damn it?

He wants to call it quits, Rachel was thinking.

Oh, God, she couldn't bear it if he did that. Which was perverse, considering. It should be her telling him that, yes, things *had* changed, and that she wanted out. Out of his office and out of his life.

But she stayed silent and waited for him to say what he had to say, nausea swirling in her stomach at the thought he might not want her any more.

'We really can't go on like this, Rachel,' he said, and a great black pit opened up inside her.

'Why's that?' she said, struggling to sound calm and reasonable whilst her world was disintegrating.

He sighed. 'Look, it's been fantastic. I grant you that. Every man's fantasy come true. But I can see things are in danger of becoming…complicated.'

'In what way? I've done everything you asked.'

He stared at her. 'Yes, you certainly have. Just excuse me for a moment whilst I order the wine.'

She sat there numbly, with Justin and the wine waiter's voices nothing but distant murmurs. Her mind was going round and round and so was her stomach. What was she going to do when he told her it was over? How would she survive?

'Rachel…'

'What?' She blinked, then made an effort to gather herself.

'The waiter's gone.'

'Oh. Yes. So he has.'

'The thing is, Rachel, I don't want to continue with what we've been doing.'

She nodded, her mouth as dry as a desert. 'Yes, I rather gathered that.' Her voice sounded dead. Hollow.

'I want to try something a little more…normal.'

Her head snapped back, her eyes rounding.

'I know I said I didn't want a real relationship with you, and I meant it at the time. And, to a degree, that still holds true. Love and marriage are not on my agenda, so I won't pretend I am offering you any hope of that. But I do want you in my life, Rachel, not just as my PA and not just for the sex. I want to go out with you and, yes, go home with you sometimes. My weekends are terribly lonely. Last weekend was… intolerable.'

'Mine too,' she agreed readily, her spirits lifting with what he was suggesting.

'So I was thinking, if you'd like, that we could try that kind of a relationship.'

She struggled not to cry.

'I...I'd like that very much,' she managed, and found a smile from somewhere.

He smiled back. 'I can't promise not to ravage you occasionally in the office.'

'I won't mind.'

He laughed. 'You're not supposed to say that.'

'What am I supposed to say?'

'*No* might be a good start.'

'You're not much good with no.'

'It's not my favourite word, I confess. Not where you're concerned. But it really isn't right, you know, doing it on my desk. I'm finding it increasingly hard to concentrate on my work.'

'Poor Justin,' she said.

'You don't sound all that sympathetic.'

'I'm not.'

'Would you believe I've actually been feeling quite guilty?'

'Not guilty enough to stop, though,' she pointed out with a wry little smile.

He smiled back. 'No. Not nearly *that* guilty.'

The arrival of the wine gave Rachel a few moments to hug her happiness to herself. Justin might not be offering her the world, but being his special lady friend was a big improvement on the role of secret sex slave.

'This is the best wine,' she said after the waiter left and she took a sip.

'Hunter Valley whites are second to none,' Justin replied, sipping also.

'Can…can I tell Isabel about us?' Rachel asked tentatively. 'She'll be home from her honeymoon tomorrow.'

'If you want to. But I'd rather you didn't mention what we've been up to these past two weeks.'

'Heavens, I wasn't going to tell her about *that*!' she exclaimed.

Rachel doubted Isabel would be shocked as such. But she would be furious. With Justin, for treating her best friend in such a fashion. At least now Rachel would be able to say that she was Justin's proper girlfriend. They might even be able to go out with Rafe and Isabel sometimes as a foursome.

Justin's head tipped to one side as he searched her face. 'You have enjoyed what we've been doing, haven't you, Rachel?'

'How can you ask that?' she exclaimed, blushing now. 'You know I have.'

'And your tears tonight… Did you tell me the truth about them?'

She swallowed, then looked him straight in the face. 'Why would I lie?'

'I was worried you might think you're in love with me.'

'Not at all,' she said without batting an eyelid. And it wasn't really a lie, because she was *sure* she was in love with him. 'I…I confess I was bit upset because you hadn't kissed me first. You just…you know…'

He grimaced. 'You're right. It was unforgivable of me. But I refuse to take all the blame. That perfume you're wearing today should be banned. I just couldn't wait.'

Rachel made a mental note to buy a king-sized bottle

of that one. If she couldn't have Justin's love, she could at least ensure his ongoing lust.

'So when are we going on our first date?' she asked eagerly.

'We're on it now.'

'Oh. Yes. So we are. And where to after dinner?'

'I thought I'd take you home to my place for the night.'

Now Rachel was seriously surprised. When he'd said he would like to come home with her sometimes she'd thought he was still keeping his own place out of bounds.

'If you like, that is,' he added.

'I'd like it very much.'

'I lease a furnished apartment at Kirribilli,' he went on. 'No point in buying a place when I plan on setting up my future business out of the city. I'd like to buy some building with a couple of floors and then I can live above the office. I resent the time I waste travelling to and from work. Not that Kirribilli is all that far from here. Just over the bridge. But you know what I mean. Parking in the CBD is appalling and public transport is the pits.'

'I know just what you mean. I don't mind my train trip too much when I get a seat. But that's not always the case. So what's it like, your place in Kirribilli?'

'Very modern. Very stylish. But a bit on the soulless side. Could do with a spot of colour. Everything's in neutral shades.'

'Sounds like the place I live in. It's all cream and cold. I much prefer warm colours and a cosy, almost cluttered feel to a room. That's why I'd like my own place, eventually, no matter how small. Then I could decorate it exactly as I want, with lots of interesting pictures on the walls, and knick-knacks galore.'

'Sounds like Mum's place. Truly, there's hardly a spare space on the walls, or on any of the furniture. She's a collectorholic. You'll have to come over and see her collection of teapots one day. They fill up two china cabinets all by themselves.'

Rachel blinked her surprise. 'You mean you're going to tell Alice about us?'

'Is there any reason you want to keep our friendship a secret?'

'No. I guess not. But you know mothers. She might start thinking we'll get married one day.'

'I can't worry about what she might think,' he said a bit sharply. 'She should know me well enough to know that is never going to happen. Now, why don't you think about what you're going to order for dinner? The waiter's on his way over.' And he picked up his menu.

Rachel was happy to do likewise, aware that her face had to be registering some dismay over his curt remark that he would never marry her. As much as Rachel tried telling herself that she was pleased with the kind of relationship Justin was offering her, deep down in her heart she knew it was a second-rate substitute for marriage and a family.

Isabel would think her a fool for accepting such a go-nowhere affair. What on earth are you doing, Rach, she'd say, wasting more of your life on another man who's never going to marry you or give you children? You're thirty-one years old, for pity's sake. Soon you'll be thirty-two. Grow up and give him the flick. And get yourself another job whilst you're at it.

Easier said than done.

Love made one foolish. And eternally hopeful.

Even whilst cold, hard logic reasoned she *was* wasting her time, Rachel kept telling herself that maybe, one day, Justin would get over his ex-wife and fall in love with her. Maybe, if she was always there for him, he'd wake up one morning and see what was right under his nose. A woman who loved him. A woman who would never leave him. A woman who'd give him a good life. And children, if he liked.

He would make a wonderful father, she believed. And she…she would dearly love the chance to be a wonderful mother.

'So what do you want?' he asked, glancing up from the menu.

You, she thought with a painful twist of her heart. Just you.

CHAPTER FOURTEEN

RACHEL woke mid-morning to the sun shining in the bedroom window and the smell of fresh coffee percolating. Justin's side of the bed was empty, but she could hear him whistling somewhere.

He sounded happy. And so was she. Relatively.

Spending last night in his bed had given her some hope that Justin hadn't changed the rules of their relationship just so he could have more of what he'd been having at the office. When he'd brought her back to his apartment after dinner he'd been incredibly sweet, and his lovemaking incredibly tender. He'd held her in his arms afterwards, stroking her hair and back. Strangely, she'd felt like crying again at the time, but she'd kept a grip on herself, thank the lord. Justin wouldn't have known what to make of that. She'd finally fallen asleep and here she was, totally rested and…totally surprised.

'Goodness, breakfast in bed!' she exclaimed as a navy-robed Justin carried one of those no-spill trays into the room.

Sitting up, she pushed her hair back from her face and pulled the sheet up around her nakedness just in time for him to settle the tray down across her lap.

'My, this is lovely,' she murmured, eyeing the freshly squeezed orange juice and scrambled eggs on toast, along some fried tomato and two strips of crispy bacon on the side. 'I usually only have coffee and toast. So what are you having?'

'I've already had it,' he said, sitting down next to her on the side of the bed then leaning across where her legs were lying under the bedclothes.

He looked marvellous, she thought, despite the messy hair and dark stubble on his chin. His vivid blue eyes were sparkling clear, with no dark rings under them. He must have slept as well as she had.

'I'll bet you didn't have anything as decadent as this,' she chided.

'I surely did. And I enjoyed every single mouthful. I'm going to enjoy watching you eat yours, too. You need a bit of fattening up, my girl.'

'Oh? You think I'm too thin?' she asked, that dodgy body image raising its ugly head again.

'Not unattractively so, as I'm sure you are aware. But you don't have anything much in reserve.'

'But if I put on weight I won't fit into my lovely new wardrobe. And my boobs will start sprouting. That's where fat always goes on me first.'

'Nothing wrong with a bit more weight on a woman's boobs. Though yours are already a gorgeous handful. Pity any extra weight I gain doesn't go where it would do me the most good. It usually becomes entrenched around my middle.'

'How can you say that? You don't have an extra ounce of fat on you.'

'You didn't see me eighteen months ago. I was the original couch potato with a sprouting beer gut.'

'I don't believe you. You have the best body I've ever seen on a man in the flesh, with a six-pack to envy. And you certainly don't need any extra inches in that other department. You have more than enough for me.'

His laugh carried a dry amusement. 'Being with

someone like you seems to have made a permanent difference to the size of my equipment.'

'So I noticed. But you know what they say. Size doesn't matter. It's what you can do with it that counts. And I certainly have no complaints over what you do with yours.'

'So I noticed. You are seriously good for my ego, do you know that?'

As opposed to his ex-wife, Rachel guessed. Justin's revelation about being a bit overweight and less than fit eighteen months ago gave rise to the speculation that the vain puss he was married to might have criticised him over his physical appearance, as well as his sexual performance. Rachel recalled Justin once implying he thought himself staid, and boring. Had that woman undermined Justin on every level, simply to excuse her own disgusting and disloyal behaviour?

More than likely. Guilt in a human being often searched for any excuse for their own appalling actions.

As much as Rachel understood how such criticisms would have been crushing, Justin must surely now know the woman never really loved him. True love wasn't based on superficial things like gaining—or losing—a few wretched pounds. Or on knowing every position in the Kama Sutra.

Again, she wanted to ask him what Mandy had actually said when she left him, but once again this wasn't the right moment. Hopefully, in time, he might confide in her himself. Meanwhile, she had to play a waiting game.

Wrapping the sheet more firmly around her bare breasts, she tucked into the breakfast whilst Justin watched her with a self-satisfied smirk on his face.

'You're really enjoying that, aren't you?' he said and she nodded, her mouth full of egg.

'I'm brewing some very special coffee for afters.'

She swallowed the last mouthful of egg and smacked her lips. 'If it tastes half as good as it smells, I'll be in heaven.'

'That's what I was thinking about you all yesterday,' he said drily, and she laughed.

'I aim to buy a really big bottle of that perfume this very day.'

He groaned. 'Sadist.'

'Takes one to know one. Now you know how I've been feeling every day in that office, waiting for five to come round. Only a sadist would make a rule like that.'

'Trust me, it was much harder for me, with the emphasis on ''harder''. Hopefully, we might both have a bit more control at work if we spend every night together.'

Rachel blinked her surprise. '*Every* night?'

'Too much for you?'

She wanted to say no, of course not. But she didn't want to be that easy. She'd been far too easy with Justin so far. Men never appreciated women who were easy.

'Yes, I'm afraid so,' she said. 'We women do have personal things we have to do sometimes, you know. Also, once Isabel gets back I will want to spend some time with her. She's my best friend, after all. Actually, I'm having dinner with her and her husband tonight. Her husband, Rafe, has a terraced house in Paddington. He's a photographer.'

'I see,' Justin muttered, his face falling.

Rachel decided that faint heart never won fat turkey.

'You can come too, if you like,' she said, and was rewarded with a startled smile.

'Seriously?' he asked.

'Of course. There's no way I'm going to be able to keep you a secret from Isabel. I wouldn't even try.'

'But won't she mind having someone extra thrust upon her on such short notice?'

'No, and she's ordering food in anyway.'

'I would have thought she'd be too tired to entertain on the first night back from an overseas honeymoon.'

'I said much the same thing to her on the phone but she insisted. I guess it's not all that long a flight from Hong Kong and I dare say they'll have flown first class. Probably slept all the way. But I'll check with her when she calls me. Which reminds me, I will have to go home this morning to await her call and get fresh clothes.'

'I'll drive you,' he offered.

'Gosh, you mean you have a car?' she teased. 'I thought you lived in trains and taxis.'

He certainly did have a car, a nice new navy number. Not overly flash; more of a family car, with easily enough room for two adults and two children.

Rachel wished she'd stop having such thoughts about Justin, but it was impossible not to dream.

They pulled up at the town house in Turramurra shortly after one, Justin accompanying Rachel inside as she knew he would. And they ended up back in bed, as she knew they would. So much for her resolve not to be easy! But it was so hard to resist him once he started kissing her. They were still in bed together when Isabel's call came shortly after three p.m.

'Yes?' Rachel answered in a slightly croaky voice.

'Rach, is that you?' Isabel asked, sounding doubtful.

'Yes, yes, it's me. Justin, stop that,' she hissed under her breath. 'I have to talk to Isabel.'

'Is that the TV on in the background, or are you talking to someone?' Isabel asked.

'I...um...I'm talking to someone.'

'Oh? Who?' Now she sounded surprised.

Rachel gave Justin a playful kick and he laughed before climbing out of bed and heading for the bathroom, Rachel wincing at the sight of the red nail marks she'd dug into his buttocks. Truly, she'd turned into a wild woman in bed!

'Sounds like a man,' Isabel said.

'It is.'

'Oh, my God, you've gone and got yourself a boyfriend!'

'You could be right.'

'Who? Rafe, Rafe, Rachel's got herself a man!' she called out before returning her attention to her friend. 'Where did you meet him? What's he like? Have you been to bed with him yet?'

Rachel had to smile. Trust Isabel to get down to the nitty-gritty straight away. 'I met him at work. He's gorgeous. And yes, I've been to bed with him.'

'Oh, wow, this is such great news. How old is he?'

'Early thirties.'

'Presumably, he works for AWI.'

'Yes.'

'What's he look like?'

'Tall, dark and handsome.'

'What's he like in bed?'

'Makes Eric look like a moron.'

'Single or divorced?'

'Divorced.'

'Oh. Pity. But you can't have everything, I suppose. So, does Casanova have a name?' she added.

Rachel's stomach swirled. This was going to be the sticky part. 'Um…Justin McCarthy.'

Dead silence at the other end for at least ten seconds. Hearing Justin switch on the shower was a blessing. He wouldn't be returning for a while. Time enough, hopefully, to smooth things over with Isabel.

'Justin McCarthy,' Isabel finally repeated in her best I-don't-believe-you-could-be-such-an-idiot voice. 'Your boss. You're sleeping with your boss. Your obviously not gay but pathetically paranoid boss.'

'Um… Yes.'

'But why? How? *When,* for pity's sake?'

Rachel did her best to explain the circumstances leading up to their first going to bed together, as well as where their affair had gone since then, without it all sounding as though she was desperate and Justin was simply using her for sex.

Her friend's sigh told it all. 'You are just setting yourself up for more hurt, love,' Isabel said.

'Maybe. Maybe not. Either way, it's my choice.'

Isabel sighed. 'True.'

'He's really a very nice man.'

'I suppose I'll have to take your word for that.'

'No, you don't. If you'll let me bring him over to dinner tonight then you can judge for yourself.'

'What a good idea,' she said in a tone that worried the life out of Rachel.

'Promise me you won't say anything sarcastic.'

'Who? *Me?*'

'Yes, you, Miss Butter-wouldn't-melt-in-your-mouth. You've got a cutting tongue on you sometimes.'

'I'll do my best to keep it sheathed.'

'You'd better.'

'Where is lover-boy at the moment?'

'In the shower.'

'Good, because I have something I want to say to *you*.'

Rachel rolled her eyes. Here it comes. 'What?'

'Now, don't take that tone with me, Missy. Someone has to look after your best interests and that someone is me. I know you, Rach. You probably think you love this man. But I seriously doubt it. It's just a rebound thing after running into Eric like that. You've also been very lonely. And loneliness can make a girl do incredibly stupid things. From the sound of things, your boss has been very lonely too, not to mention having had the stuffing kicked out of him. Not too many men could come through an experience like that without a seriously damaged soul. How do you know he's not living out some sort of sick revenge, doing to you what he imagines Carl Toombs is doing to his wife? Have you thought of that?'

'Yes.'

'And?'

'It doesn't fit his character. He's too decent for that.'

'Decent! Reading between the lines, he's been screwing you silly all over your office. I haven't forgotten that little joke you made during our last phone call. Only that wasn't a joke, was it? That was the truth!'

'Sort of. But things have changed.'

'Huh. He's just changed the scene of his crimes, that's all. He's probably afraid you'll slap a sexual-harassment suit on him if he keeps doing it on his desk. He's thinking ahead.'

'Thinking ahead to what?'

'To that day when he gets bored and gives you the bullet.'

'He's not like that.'

Isabel groaned. 'You *do* think you love him.'

'I do love him, OK? So shoot me.'

'For pity's sake, girl, it could just be lust, you know. Even on *your* part.'

'Like it was on yours? With Rafe?'

'That was different.'

'How?'

'It just was.'

'Wait till you meet Justin. Then tell me if you still think that.'

'All right. I will!'

CHAPTER FIFTEEN

'I STILL can't believe it,' Isabel said to Rafe as the returned honeymooners made the after-dinner coffee together in the kitchen.

'What can't you believe, darling? That you've come back home to find Rachel looking utterly gorgeous and glowing? Or that her creep of a boss—the one you've been ranting and raving about all afternoon—is actually a genuinely nice guy?'

'Both. Frankly, I don't know what to think any more. If I didn't know Justin McCarthy's history I'd say he just might be in love with her. The way he looks at her sometimes… As for Rachel, I've had to abandon any desperate hope I was clinging to that she might only be in lust with the man. She's obviously mad about him.'

Rafe glanced over the kitchen island at the woman *he* was mad about. 'Then why are you still so worried?' he said.

'I just couldn't bear to see her get hurt again. She's had such a rotten deal in life so far, Rafe. She deserves to be happy.'

'I know, sweetheart,' Rafe said soothingly. 'I know. But she's a grown woman. She has to make her own choices and decisions in life. You can't make them for her. Even if you could, what would you say? Leave him before he leaves you? You saw for yourself the physical transformation in her. Whatever happens between them in the end, that can't be a bad thing.'

'No… No, you're right. If nothing else, falling for Justin McCarthy has done wonders for Rachel's looks. It's difficult to believe she's the same girl who was worried about having a bit of red dye put in her hair three weeks ago today. I wonder what Alice makes of all this.'

'Alice?' Rafe frowned.

'Justin's mum. She was the one who got Rachel the job as Justin's PA in the first place.'

'Aah, yes. I remember now. Well, maybe Alice doesn't know that her son's new Girl Friday has been promoted to Girl Saturday and Sunday as well.'

'If she doesn't then that would be telling, don't you think? You told your mother about us quick smart. Maybe I'll try to find out over coffee.'

'Isabel,' Rafe said sharply. 'Don't interfere.'

'But…'

'No buts, darling, except butt out. It's their life.'

'Oh, don't be so typically male! The trouble with you is you don't really care. Rachel's not *your* best friend.'

'No. She's not. Which is possibly why I'm a better judge of what you should and shouldn't do. Now, let's take this coffee out to our guests and finish this very pleasant evening chatting about non-inflammatory subjects.'

'Such as what?'

'How about Rachel's new look? That should keep you two girls going till after midnight, talking about hair and make-up and clothes.'

'Very funny.'

'Justin and I could discuss manly things, such as money and football and sex.'

'You're a male chauvinist pig, Rafe St Vincent.'

'Not at all. Just a typical male, as you so cleverly pointed out. And, speaking of typical males, I wonder if Rachel would consider accidentally on purpose getting pregnant to the marriage-shy Mr McCarthy. It's amazing how the thought of your own cute little baby-to-be can focus even the most commitment-phobic people.'

Isabel's eyebrows arched. 'Now, that's an idea. But a bit too soon, I think. Though I might mention it to her later on. Trust you to come up with that one,' she finished ruefully.

'All brilliantly successful ideas should be shared. Come along, darling. If we don't get out there with this coffee, it'll be stone-cold!'

Rachel knew Isabel was out there in the kitchen gossiping to Rafe about her and Justin. But nothing her friend could say would stop her from continuing with her relationship with Justin. The more time she spent with him, the more deeply she fell in love with him. And it wasn't just the sex bewitching her. It was definitely the man. He was everything Eric had never been. Kind. Considerate. Caring. And funny, when he wanted to be. She'd been amazed at what a witty conversationalist he'd been over dinner with people he hadn't met before. It was obvious Rafe liked him. And Isabel too, if she'd put aside her personal prejudice long enough to admit it.

'I like your friends,' Justin said whilst they were sitting there at the dining table alone, waiting for the coffee. 'And I like their house,' he added, glancing around the cosy dining alcove which came off the main lounge room upstairs.

'They'll probably buy a bigger place after their baby is born,' Rachel remarked.

'They're expecting a baby?'

'Didn't I say so? I thought I had. Yes, Isabel was already expecting before they got married. But that wasn't why they got married. They planned it that way. Or Rafe did. Actually, Isabel wasn't going to get married at all. But she wanted a baby. Oh, dear, I'm not explaining this very well. It's a bit complicated.'

Justin smiled. 'It sounds it.'

'Let me try to explain it better. Now, let's see...a few months back Isabel decided to have a baby using artificial insemination, then raise it by herself, because she was sick to death of falling in love with Mr Wrong. You know the kind. Not exactly good husband or father material. She'd already tried the idea of marrying with her head rather than her heart, and was engaged to this really nice architect who felt the same way, but two weeks before their wedding he fell head over heels for another girl and called the wedding off. It was around this time—only a couple of months back really—that Isabel met Rafe. He was going to be her wedding photographer. Right from their first meeting, she was very attracted to him. No, that's understating things. She fancied him like mad. So much so that when she found out he was single and unattached she asked him to go away with her on her pre-booked and pre-paid honeymoon, on a strictly sex basis with no strings attached. Naturally, Rafe agreed.'

'Naturally,' Justin said laughingly.

'Well, yes, what man wouldn't?' Rachel concurred. 'Isabel's drop-dead gorgeous. Anyway, to cut a long story short, Rafe fell in love during their fling and didn't like the idea of Isabel having a baby all by herself. So he set about deliberately getting her pregnant without her knowing, hoping that then she'd marry him.'

'How on earth did he get her pregnant without her knowing it was on the cards?'

'I gather he doctored the condoms.'

'That was an extremely bold move.'

'Love can make you bold, I guess. And wanting something badly enough.'

'I guess,' he said, his eyes clouding over, then drifting off somewhere distant.

'Did you want children when you were married, Justin?' Rachel asked before she could think better of it.

'What?' He stared at her for a second as though he had no idea what she was talking about. But then his eyes cleared. 'Yes, yes, I did. Mandy did, too, till she…' He broke off abruptly. 'Can we discuss something else, please?'

Isabel and Rafe's return with the coffee was a blessing, though Isabel's intuition antennae seemed to pick up on something straight away, and she flicked Rachel a frowning glance.

Rachel gave a little shake of her head and dredged up a covering smile. 'You haven't shown me all the lovely things you bought in Hong Kong yet,' she said brightly.

'I was just saying that to Isabel,' Rafe replied. 'Why don't you two girls take your coffee into the bedroom and do just that? We two men can stay here and talk about man stuff.'

Isabel rolled her eyes as she handed the stylish blue and white mugs of steaming coffee around. 'In that case, you have a deal. Two arrogant, self-opinionated males exchanging macho bulldust is not my idea of a fun time. Come on, Rach, let's get out of here and leave these two to play one-upmanship all by themselves.'

'I'll have you know that I never play one-upmanship!' Rafe called after the girls as they retreated, mugs in hand.

Rachel and Isabel's laughter lasted till the bedroom door was safely shut behind them.

'What happened out there?' Isabel asked straight away. 'You were both happy as larks when Rafe and I left to go make the coffee, and as tense as anything when we came back.'

Rachel sighed. 'The conversation came round to you and Rafe expecting a child and I stupidly asked him if he'd wanted children when he was married.'

'*Stupidly* asked!' Isabel exclaimed, her expression one of outrage. 'What's stupid about a normal question like that? Truly, Rachel, you're not going to turn into one of those women afraid to ask their boyfriend anything about his past. Or your future together, for that matter. I, for one, would like to know *exactly* what his intentions are towards you.'

Rachel had to smile. Dear Isabel. She really was a good friend. When she wasn't playing bossy mother. She didn't know it but she was just like her own mother in some ways, a fact which would pain Isabel if she realised it.

'He wants me to be his lover, his friend and his PA,' Rachel answered patiently. 'But not necessarily in that order of priority. He doesn't want me to be his wife. And obviously not the mother of his children. He doesn't love me. Neither does he want to remarry. He told me so upfront. He's been very honest with me,

Isabel, and I have no right to cross-question him, or try to change the status quo.'

'Oh, Rachel, that's just so much crap.'

'No, it's not. I've gone into this affair with my eyes wide open. I know the score. Justin doesn't want my love. He wants my friendship, my companionship and my body.'

'And you can live with that?'

'For the time being. That doesn't mean I don't have a very different long-term agenda. I'm not that self-sacrificing. I love Justin more than I ever loved Eric and I aim to marry him one day.'

'Wow. Now, that's more like my old Rachel. So what are you going to do? Get pregnant accidentally on purpose after a little while?' Isabel asked excitedly.

Rachel was taken aback. 'Are you insane? That strategy would never work with Justin.'

'How do you know? Rafe said it's a winner if the guy cares about you at all, and you obviously think he does.'

'Yes, I do. But he hasn't totally got over his wife yet. I'm hopeful he will, though, the same way I eventually got over Eric. Time does heal all wounds, you know.'

'No, it doesn't,' Isabel countered sharply. 'Sometimes people get gangrene. On top of that, it took you damned years to get over that rotter, my girl. By the time Justin is ready to move on from his slutty ex, you might be too old to have children. Don't wait, I say. Take a chance and get preggers and see what happens.'

'Uh-uh, Isabel. That worked for you and Rafe because you loved each other. Justin doesn't love me yet. He wouldn't marry me at this point in time and I don't want to be a single mum. I want any child of mine to have it all. Both parents who love him or her, and who love each other.'

Isabel frowned, and cocked her head on one side. 'Are you sure he doesn't? Love you, that is?'

'What? Look, what are you playing at now, Isabel?'

'Just looking at the situation from a different angle. To be honest, if I didn't know Justin's personal history I would have said he was quite besotted with you.'

Rachel could feel herself blushing. 'You really think so?'

'Absolutely. He might very well be in love with you. He just doesn't know it himself yet. Rafe didn't realise he loved me for ages. So tell me one thing. Is Justin going to tell his mother about you, or is your sleeping together to be kept a tacky little secret?'

'Funny you should ask that. I thought he'd want to keep our affair a secret. But no, he's already told Alice over the phone and we're going to her place for lunch tomorrow. Apparently, he has lunch with his mother practically every Sunday.'

'Well, well, well,' Isabel mused. 'That's good news. That's very good news indeed.'

'I thought so too.'

'We have reason to hope, then, don't we?' Isabel said, feeling more optimistic over this relationship than she had all evening.

'We do, Isabel,' Rachel agreed and smiled at her best friend. 'Now, no more talk about Justin. I want to see all the goodies you brought back from Hong Kong.'

CHAPTER SIXTEEN

'WHAT are you thinking about?' Rachel asked dreamily.

They were in bed together, post-dinner with Isabel and Rafe, post-coitus, both on their backs, both staring up at the bedroom ceiling.

Justin didn't answer immediately, since the truth was out of the question. How could he possibly tell her he was thinking that if she wasn't on the Pill they might have just made a baby together, or, even more amazingly, that he wished that were the case?

Ever since Rachel had told him that story tonight about Rafe deliberately getting Isabel pregnant to get her to marry him, he'd been having the most incredible thoughts. He knew he didn't love Rachel. Hell, how could he when he still loved Mandy? Yet here he was, wanting her to be the mother of his child. And maybe even his wife!

Was he losing his mind? Or had Rachel's also asking him if he'd wanted children when he was married to Mandy made him realise just how much he *had* wanted children? Losing the woman he loved to another man didn't mean he had to lose the chance of having a family of his own, did it?

Another remark of Rachel's tonight came back to tantalise his mind, and torment his conscience.

Wanting something badly enough can make you bold.

Would it be bold to tell Rachel he'd fallen in love

with her and wanted to marry her? Or was that just plain bad?

'Justin?' Rachel prompted, but Justin closed his eyes and pretended to be asleep. Better not to answer right now. The lies could wait. Till the time was right.

He heard Rachel eventually sigh, then turn over and go to sleep, but he didn't sleep for quite a while. He was too busy planning his strategy for getting Rachel to fall in love with him.

Taking her to his mother's for lunch tomorrow was an excellent first move. But it would only be the first of many.

Justin hadn't realised till that moment how bold he could be when he wanted something badly enough. Or how ruthless.

'Rachel, my dear!' Alice exclaimed shortly after opening her front door to them. 'I hope you don't take offence but you look simply marvellous! I can hardly believe it.'

Rachel laughed and didn't take offence. 'It's a bit of an improvement from the last time you saw me, isn't it? No more dreary black for starters.' In deference to Alice's suggestion that blue would suit her, she was wearing a blue silk trouser suit that did look very well against her colouring. Her hair had taken ages to do that morning, and so had her make-up, but it was worth it to see the expression of surprise and pleasure on Alice's face.

'And Justin, love,' Alice said, her gaze swinging over to check out her son from top to toe. 'You're looking ten years younger yourself. Whatever you've been doing with Rachel, keep it up.'

'Mum. *Really.*'

'Oh, don't go all prudish on me. You know I can't stand it when you do that. It reminds me of your father, who, might I add, was not in any way prudish behind closed doors. He just liked to act that way in public. Come along, you two. Come through to the back terrace. I've got a nice cold lunch all set out there, with a couple of delicious bottles of Tasmanian wine for us to try.'

'Like father, like son,' Rachel whispered to Justin when he took her arm and guided her down the long central hallway.

'Behave yourself,' he rasped back. 'Or I'll put you over my knee when I get you home tonight.'

She shot him a cheeky look. 'Would you? You promise?'

'Have some decorum,' he said, but smilingly. 'We're at my mother's.'

'What are you two whispering about?' Alice shot over her shoulder.

'I was telling Justin how much I like your house,' Rachel said.

'Which reminds me, Mum. I want you to show Rachel your teapot collection later. She's into pottery and knick-knacks.'

'Oh, wonderful. I'll take her to a few auctions with me. We'll have such fun.'

They emerged onto the sun-drenched back terrace that looked like a new addition to the house, which was federation-style and inclined to be a little dark inside with smallish windows. Cosy, though, from what Rachel had glimpsed during her journey down the hallway. The terrace, however, looked like something that belonged to an Italian villa, with a lovely vine-covered pergola overhead and large terracotta tiles providing an excellent floor for the rich cedar-wood outdoor setting.

The lunch set out on the table looked as if it would feed an army, with all sorts of seafood and salads, and two already opened bottles of white wine resting in portable coolers. The wine glasses waiting to be filled were exquisitely fine, with small bunches of grapes etched into the sides.

'I'll just get the herb bread out of the oven,' Alice said. 'Justin, pour the wine. I don't mean to rush you into eating but a storm's been forecast for this afternoon and I'm worried it might spoil everything. We haven't seen the sun for some time and I wanted to take advantage of it whilst it was there.'

She hurried off, leaving Rachel to openly admire the rest of the huge back yard with its large tract of lawn and neat garden beds along the side and back fences.

'You were lucky to have such a lovely big back yard when you were growing up,' she commented. 'My parents were inner-city apartment people. Career people, too. Frankly, I often felt like the odd man out. I wasn't surprised when they sent me to boarding-school. I was often in their way. Of course, I was upset when they were killed, but it wasn't till I lived with Lettie that I knew the kind of love and attention that a child cherishes. She wanted me. She really did. She was always there when I needed her. I never felt that with my parents. So it was impossible to let her down when she needed me.'

A wave of sadness hit her as she thought of Lettie and the cruel illness that had taken her. She didn't realise Justin was there till he took her into his arms. 'You are the kind of person who would never let any person down,' he said softly. 'A very special person. I am so lucky to have found you, Rachel.' He tipped up her chin and kissed her so tenderly that it brought a lump to her throat.

Was this the kiss of love? Could her heart's desire be coming true this quickly?

Alice clearing her throat had them pulling apart, but Rachel didn't feel at all embarrassed. She was too happy for that. Alice looked happy too. Perhaps she was also hoping for what Rachel was hoping for.

Rachel didn't have the opportunity to find out till after lunch was finished. With Justin retreating to the family room to watch the final round of a golf tournament on TV, Alice was able to draw Rachel into the living room on the pretext of showing her the famous teapot collection. But the conversation soon turned from pottery to personal matters.

'Has he told you about Mandy yet?' she asked quietly.

'He won't speak about her at all. Or his marriage.'

'Typical. His father was like that. Would never speak of emotional matters or past hurts. So, do you really love my son, Rachel? Or is this just an affair of convenience?'

'I love him with all my heart,' Rachel confessed. 'But I daren't tell him that. He told me right at the start he didn't want my love. Just my companionship.'

'Oh, is that what prudes are calling sex these days?' Alice said with a dry laugh. 'Companionship.'

Rachel just smiled. 'I don't dare ask him about Mandy, either. Although I do know who she left him for. It was Carl Toombs. But I don't know why. I can only guess.'

'I see. Well, if he won't tell you what happened then I will,' Alice pronounced firmly. 'That cruel bitch.

There is no other word for her! She told my son that the reason she was leaving him for another man was because he was no longer physically attractive to her. Just because he'd put on a few pounds. At that time he was a dealer, working crippling hours. And slaving away on his own private projects with every spare minute, just to give her the best of everything. When he combined a sedentary job with take-away food and no energy to exercise then of course Justin put on some weight. But he was far from fat. Still, that's what she called him the day she dumped him. Fat and flabby. And boring to boot. She also complained about their sex life, but what time did he have for fun and games when he was beating himself to death making himself rich enough for her? Not that Justin could ever have been rich enough for her, not compared to Carl Toombs. She wanted to justify her appalling behaviour and to do that she sacrificed my son's self-esteem. It was wicked what she did to him that day. Wicked.'

'Poor Justin,' Rachel murmured.

'He was shattered afterwards for a long, long time. His only refuge was in work and exercise. God knows the hell he's been through as a man, emotionally and mentally. I can't tell you how happy I am that he's finally met a decent girl like you, a girl who can truly appreciate the fine man he is. You *do* really love him, don't you?'

'Alice, I'm crazy about him. As for Mandy, she had to be stupid not to appreciate what she had.'

'That's the strange thing. I honestly thought she did. She seemed to love Justin when she married him. And she always said she'd have a baby as soon as they were financially secure. Frankly, when she did what she did I was almost as shocked as Justin. She didn't seem that sort of girl. Of course, she *is* the sort men always made a play for.'

'She's really that beautiful?' Rachel asked, her heart twisting with jealousy.

'I have to admit she's stunning to look at. And she has a captivating manner as well. A real charmer, no doubt about that. I'm not surprised that the likes of Carl Toombs went after her. What did surprise me was that he succeeded in getting her. I honestly thought she loved my son. Obviously, she had us both fooled. Maybe she was always a little gold-digger at heart. Though, to give her some credit, she didn't take a cent from Justin when she left him. Guilty conscience, probably. Though I dare say she was already getting enough money out of her wealthy lover. Mistresses of men like that don't want for anything. Still, if she thought he was going to leave his wife and marry her then she's been sorely mistaken.

'But Justin will marry you,' Alice added, and Rachel's heart jumped.

'Why do you say that?'

'Because he'd be crazy not to. And my son is not crazy. You wait and see. I suppose you haven't told him you love him.'

'No way. Why? Do you think I should?'

'Not yet. Men like to think love and marriage are their idea entirely. It's a male-ego thing. And, speaking of male ego, I think we should rejoin said male ego before it begins to feel neglected.'

Both women were chuckling away when they entered the family room, only to be shushed into silence by said male ego watching male stuff. They looked at each other and pulled appropriate faces, then withdrew to the kitchen to make afternoon tea and exchange the exasperated view that they didn't know why women bothered falling in love with any man in the first place!

CHAPTER SEVENTEEN

RACHEL insisted Justin drop her off home after the luncheon at his mother's. Without his coming in.

'I have washing to do,' she told him. 'And a host of other little jobs to organise myself for the coming week. I'm sure you do, too,' she added firmly when he looked as though he was going to argue.

He sighed, then went.

The following morning Rachel was so glad she'd taken that stand. Glad she was alone and travelling on the train to work. Very glad she'd got a seat and she could read the front-page story in the daily newspaper privately.

TOOMBS FLEES AUSTRALIA, the headlines screamed.

TYCOON IN INVESTMENT SCANDAL.

The details were a bit sketchy, but it seemed Carl Toombs had finally done what many people had forecast for him. He'd gone bust, and taken a lot of creditors and investors with him. The journalist writing the article implied it was only his company that had gone belly-up. On a personal basis, Toombs himself was probably still as rich as Croesus. Being a conscienceless but clever crook, he would have siphoned money off into Swiss bank accounts, or other anonymous offshore establishments, before doing a flit at the weekend, minus his family.

There were photos of his wife and children at the gate of his harbourside mansion, plus the classic comment from the wife saying she knew nothing about her husband's business dealings, and had no idea where he was. She claimed to be as devastated as his employees and business colleagues, who'd all been left high and dry without their entitlements etc etc etc.

Did that include his PA-cum-mistress? Rachel wondered. Or had she vanished with the disgraced tycoon?

Only time would tell, she supposed. But how would Justin react to this news? Rachel couldn't even guess. This was one area where she still didn't have all the answers, despite what Alice had told her the previous day. The subject of Mandy was *verboten* with Justin.

Rachel arrived at work in a state of nervous anticipation over Justin's mood. No use hoping he wouldn't have seen the headlines and read the story. He worked out every morning with people who lived and breathed such news. It would be the main topic of conversation in AWI's gym this morning. It would be the main topic for discussion in just about every office and household in Sydney that day. But not hers. She didn't dare bring the matter up.

Or did she? It wouldn't be normal not to mention it. Oh, she didn't know what to do for the best!

Justin was already in his office when she arrived, with his door firmly shut. She dumped the paper on top of her desk in full view, then set about making his usual mug of coffee, determined to act naturally. When it was ready she tapped briefly on the door then breezed right in, as was her habit these days.

Justin was sitting at his desk with his nose buried in the morning paper.

'So what do you think of Carl Toombs going broke like that?' she remarked casually as she put his coffee down. 'I was reading about it on the train on the way in. The papers are full of little else.'

When he glanced up at her, he didn't look too distressed. Just a bit distracted.

Rachel's agitation lessened slightly.

'Couldn't have happened to a nicer bloke,' came his caustic comment.

'I guess he's not really broke, though,' Rachel remarked. 'People like that never are.'

'Maybe not, but the media will hound him, wherever he goes. He won't have a happy life.'

'I pity the people who worked for him,' Rachel went on, and watched his eyes.

They definitely grew harder. And colder.

'People who work for men like Toombs are tarred with the same brush. If you lie down with dogs, don't complain when you get up with fleas.'

Rachel was shocked by the icy bitterness in his voice. Shocked and dismayed. He wasn't over Mandy at all. Not one little bit.

Her phone ringing gave her a good excuse to flee his office before she said something she would later regret. She was quite glad to close the door that separated them.

It was Alice, who'd seen the news about Toombs on a morning television programme.

'There was no mention of Mandy,' she said.

'No,' Rachel agreed.

'She always did keep a very low profile. How's Justin?'

'Hard to say.' Rachel didn't want to get into the habit of gossiping about Justin to his mother. 'Would you like me to put you through to him?'

'Lord, no. No, I was just wondering. I also wanted to say again how lovely you looked yesterday, Rachel.'

'Thank you, Alice. And let me say that was one fantastic spread you put on. You're sure you weren't trying to fatten me up?' she joked just as the door from the corridor opened and the most striking woman Rachel had ever seen walked in. She looked like something you saw in the pages of the glossies. Long blonde hair. Even longer legs. Enormous blue eyes. Pouting mouth. A body straight out of an X-rated magazine.

'Er—Alice,' Rachel went on, trying not to sound as sick as she was suddenly feeling. 'I…I have to go. Someone's just come in…'

Not just *some*one, of course. *The* one. The cruel bitch. The cruel but incredibly beautiful bitch.

'Can I help you?' Rachel asked frostily as hatred warred with fear. It was no wonder Justin hadn't got over her. Who could ever compare with this golden goddess? She was the stuff men's dreams were made of.

Admittedly, she was wearing a tad too much make-up for day wear, especially around her eyes, and she was dressed rather provocatively, if expensively. Her camel suit had to be made of the finest leather—since it didn't wrinkle—but it was skin-tight, with a short, short skirt and a vest top with cut-in arm-holes and a deep V-neckline. Her gold jewellery looked real, though, again, there was a bit too much of it for Rachel's taste. Several chain necklaces, one of which was lost in her impressive cleavage. Dangling earrings. A couple of bracelets on each wrist. Even an anklet, which drew Rachel's gaze down to the matching camel-coloured shoes, along with their five-inch heels.

She looked like a very expensive mistress. Or an equally expensive call-girl.

'I was told this was Justin McCarthy's office,' she said in a voice which would be an instant drawcard on one of those sex phone lines. Low and husky and chock-full of erotic promise. 'Is that right?'

'Yes. And you are...?'

'I'm Mandy McCarthy, Justin's ex-wife,' she informed Rachel without a hint of hesitation. 'And you must be Justin's new PA,' she added with a strange little smile.

Rachel stiffened. 'That's right.'

'I see,' she said. 'Yes, I see. Is Justin in here?' she added, going straight over to Justin's door and winding her long bronze-tipped fingers around the knob.

Rachel was on her feet in a flash. 'You can't just walk in there.'

'You're wrong, sweetie,' the blonde countered, her smile turning wry. 'I can. And I'm going to. Please don't make a scene. I need to speak to Justin alone and I don't have much time.'

'If you say anything to hurt him,' Rachel ground out through clenched teeth, 'anything at all...I'll kill you.'

She laughed. 'You know, I do believe you would. Lucky Justin.' And then she turned the knob and went right in.

Rachel sank back down into her chair, ashen-faced and shaking.

Justin couldn't have been more shocked when the door opened and Mandy came in.

'What the—?' he muttered, automatically rising to his feet.

'Sorry to drop in like this, Justin,' she purred, shutting the door behind her. 'I don't think your girlfriend outside is too happy about it, but that can't be helped. You can tell her after I've gone that I'm no threat to your relationship.'

'Relationship?' Justin repeated, his head reeling.

'Don't bother denying it. Charlotte told me all about you two.'

It took Justin a couple of seconds to recall who Charlotte was.

'I have no intention of denying it,' he said coolly enough, pleased that he'd managed to find some composure.

'She looks very nice,' Mandy remarked and started to sashay across the room towards his desk. 'Much nicer than me.'

Justin couldn't take his eyes off her, the way she was walking, the way she looked. This wasn't the woman he remembered. Mandy had never dressed like this, or walked like that. Why, she looked like a tart! An expensive tart, admittedly. But still a tart.

'I won't take up too much of your time,' she went on in a voice he didn't recognise either. It was all raspy and breathy. 'I have to leave for the airport shortly. I'm joining Carl overseas. Don't ask me where and don't look so surprised. You must have read the paper this morning, and you must have guessed I'd go with him. Mind if I sit down? These high heels are hell. But Carl likes me to wear them. He says they're a turn-on.'

She pulled up a chair and sat down, her skirt so tight she had difficulty crossing her legs. When she did, he had a better view than a gynaecologist. Thankfully, she was wearing panties, though he didn't look long enough to check what type.

Justin sank back down into his chair, stunned. She was misinterpreting his surprise but it didn't matter now. What mattered was that he wasn't feeling what he always thought he'd feel if he crossed Mandy's path again. There was no pain. No hurt. Hell, he couldn't even dredge up any hate! When he looked at this…stranger…sitting across from him, she bore no resemblance to the woman he'd loved. She'd once been a truly beautiful person, both inside and out. Now she was exactly what she looked like: a woman for hire. Cheap, yet expensive. All he felt was confusion, and curiosity.

What did she see in Carl Toombs that she would do this to herself for him?

'Why, Mandy?' he asked. 'That's all I want to know. Why?'

'Why? I would have thought that was obvious, darling. I love the man. It's as simple as that.'

'I don't find that thought simple. One minute you were in love with me and then you were in love with him? What was it about Toombs that you fell in love with? From all accounts, he's an out-and-out bastard.'

She looked uncomfortable for a second. Then defiant. 'He's not all bad. You don't know him the way I do. Sure, he doesn't always play life by the rules, but he's the most exciting man I've ever known. I…I can't live without him, Justin. I'll go wherever he wants me to go; be whatever he wants me to be; do whatever he wants me to do.'

Justin was appalled. The woman was obsessed. But it wasn't a healthy obsession. It was dark, and dangerous, and self-destructive. The wonderful girl he'd loved, and married, was gone forever.

'What exactly are you doing here, Mandy?' he asked, feeling nothing but sadness for her. 'I don't understand…'

'I came here to apologise. In person. The things I said to you the day I left you. I didn't mean them. Any of them. I was just trying to make you hate me as much as I hated myself that day. You'd done nothing wrong and, despite everything, I still cared for you very much. But I…I just *had* to be with Carl.' Tears suddenly welled up in her eyes but she dashed them away. 'Silly me. Crying over spilt milk. What's the point? I am what I am now and nothing will change that.'

'And what are you now?' he asked, still having difficulty taking in the change in her.

Her eyes locked onto his and they were nothing like the eyes he remembered. These eyes had seen too much. Done too much.

Her laugh made his skin crawl. 'I'd show you if I had time, and if your lady friend out there wouldn't have to go to jail for murder.'

'What are you talking about?'

'When I came in just now she told me if I said anything to hurt you again she'd kill me.'

'Rachel said that?'

'That surprises you?'

'Did you tell her who you are?'

'Yes. But she already knew. I could see it in her face. I had the feeling she knew quite a lot about me. *You* didn't tell her?'

'No.'

'Well, she knows everything,' Mandy insisted. 'Trust me on this.'

His mother, he realised with a groan. Yesterday. Or possibly earlier. He shook his head in amazement. 'She never said a word.'

'Women in love will do anything not to upset their man.'

Justin stared at her. Was she right? Did Rachel love him? Dear God, he hoped so.

'Did I tell you how fantastic you're looking, Justin?

How handsome? How sexy? I'm a fool. I know I'm a fool. But my fate is sealed, my darling. Just remember…I loved you once.' She uncrossed her legs and stood up abruptly. 'Marry your Rachel, Justin. Marry her and have children and be happy. I must go,' she added when her eyes filled again. 'I have a plane to catch.'

She was gone as quickly as she'd come, leaving Justin sitting there, staring after an empty doorway. When Rachel filled that doorway he blinked, then saw how worried she was looking.

'It's all right,' he said reassuringly. 'She's gone. For good.'

'But is she really gone for good, Justin?'

He rose, realising that was why Mandy had come. To set him free; free to love again. She'd taken time out from her not-so-good life to do a really good thing.

'Yes,' he said. 'Yes, she's really gone. For good.'

By the time he reached Rachel, she was crying. His heart turned over as he realised she had loved him all along. He drew her into his arms and held her close.

'We're going to get married, Rachel,' he whispered against her hair. 'We're going to work together, buy a home together and have children together. Oh, and one more thing. I love you, Rachel. More than I have ever loved before. Much, much more.'

Two months later, Carl Toombs' yacht was lost in a hurricane near the Bahamas. All on board perished.

Ten months later Justin and Rachel were married, with Rafe as best man and Isabel as matron of honour. Alice minded Isabel's newborn daughter during the ceremony and the baby didn't make a peep. Alice was duly voted by the wedding party as chief babysitter for all their future children and ordered never to sell her large home with its large back yard.

She didn't. And Alice's home was regularly filled with love and laughter for many years to come.

Barbara McMahon was born and raised in the American south but settled in California after spending a year flying around the world for an international airline. Settling down to raise a family and work for a computer firm, she began writing when her children started school. Now, feeling fortunate in being able to realise a long-held dream of quitting her 'day job' and writing full-time, she and her husband recently moved to the Sierra Nevada mountains of California, where she finds her desire to write is stronger than ever. Barbara loves to hear from readers. You can reach her at PO Box 977, Pioneer, CA 95666-0977, USA.

Watch out for Barbara McMahon's latest emotional read: WINNING BACK HIS WIFE On sale in October 2005, in Tender Romance™!

THE HUSBAND CAMPAIGN

by

Barbara McMahon

To Charles Mitchell, love from your western cousin.

To Kathy Stone: in honour of your new home state!

CHAPTER ONE

Let the man do the chasing—just don't run so fast he can't catch you.

—Megan Madacy's journal, Spring 1923

KERRY KINCAID TURNED onto the wide street and slowed for the long driveway. Ancient oaks lined the avenue, meeting overhead in a lush green canopy. Dappled sunlight spotted the asphalt and the scent of roses filled the air. She turned her car into the drive and headed straight to the back of the house.

Though she had visited Uncle Philip and Aunt Peggy every summer from the time she turned ten until her last year of college, she was surprised at the sense of homecoming that filled her. Her visits had only been for the long school breaks while her own parents, both anthropologists, used the months to go abroad to participate in archeological digs. She had been back for a few Christmas visits, but the unexpected welcome today warmed her.

The old house looked as familiar as ever, its dark green shutters and pristine white clapboard newly painted that spring, according to Aunt Peggy's most recent letter. The wide front porch still carried the comfortable old wicker rockers, though she thought the colorful cushions looked new. The yard needed work, the grass to be cut, the flower beds weeded. They'd been neglected since her aunt and uncle's departure on their longed-for cruise a couple of weeks ago. Her cousin obviously put off the yard care as long as possible. It seemed nothing had changed.

Kerry stopped the car near the small back porch. She leaned back in her seat, exhausted. Hoping she had enough energy to make it into the house, she idly contemplated the flagstone walkway. The grass growing between the flat stones needed trimming. Maybe in a couple of days she'd have enough energy to get out the mower and take care of the yard. It would be a small return for staying in the house while her aunt and uncle were gone. But in the meantime, she felt as if she could close her eyes and sleep for a week right where she was.

The key word was energy. And inclination. She sighed. She didn't expect to find either sitting in the car.

Movement to her right caught her attention. Slowly she turned her head. Her aunt's next-door neighbor, Jake Mitchell, strode across the yard, heading in her direction. Tall and well-built, he was barefoot, snug cutoff jeans his only attire. It was obvious from the wet black Trans Am and the water running from the hose lying near the car what he'd been doing. His dark hair looked tousled. The cool mocking gray of his eyes was not yet visible. But she knew what to expect. Her heart lurched, then raced as she stared through the windshield at the approaching man. As a teenager, she'd had a huge crush on Jake.

And he'd never once looked her way.

Taking a deep breath of resignation, she withdrew the key and grabbed her overnight case. Time enough later to unpack the car and dream over long-ago days. The things in the small bag would tide her over until morning. After a solid night's sleep, she'd have the energy she needed for the task of unpacking. Or so she hoped.

Climbing out of the car, she stretched and once again wondered why people rarely used the front door to her aunt's house. It had to do with parking, she supposed. Though visitors were fond enough of sitting on the front porch once they arrived, almost everyone used the back door. Including family.

''Kerry?'' Jake asked as he drew close. For a moment his gaze ran from the top of her head to her feet. Then the familiar, mocking smile tilted up the corners of his mouth. ''Kerry Kincaid.''

Kerry's heart pumped hard against her chest, her hands grew damp and every nerve ending tingled. Just from his look. She swallowed hard and nodded. Had nothing changed in the years since she'd last seen him? The old, remembered feelings swept through her, tingling and magical. For one second she wished that he'd whisk her into his arms and kiss her like there was no tomorrow. Of course she'd wished that every summer while she was growing up. Wishes that never came true.

''Well, well, little Kerry Elizabeth Kincaid, all grown up. And you did it so well,'' he drawled, folding his arms across that wide expanse of chest and leaning against the hood of her car. His gaze made a leisurely trek over the feminine curves and valleys of her body. From the glint that appeared, Kerry knew he approved.

Anger flared at his arrogant perusal, his mocking tone. She was in no mood to deal with this. Ignoring the tantalizing expanse of bronze chest, she glared at him, holding her own. All grown up and not about to make a fool of herself over this man ever again.

''Well, well, John Charles Mitchell, still obnoxious as ever,'' she returned, refusing to be intimidated. She'd dueled with champs these last few years. She was no longer the shy teenager with a monstrous crush. She could hold her own these days—time her cocky neighbor realized that. Start as you mean to go on, her aunt had always said.

A glint of appreciation lit his dark eyes as they met hers. Slowly he nodded. "I try to please."

And she bet he pleased any woman who gained his attention. He was as gorgeous as ever. Thirty-four years old and he still looked good enough to eat. She'd known him over half her life. Had once tried everything she knew to entice him to see her as an available, interested female when she'd been younger. And failed miserably. The differences in their ages had worked against her. And that bad experience he'd had in college, combined with the example of his own mother, had made him extremely wary around women. Fine for casual dates, Jake was a perpetual playboy. Good for as long as he was interested, but commitment had become an anathema to him. Love 'em and leave 'em had been his motto when she'd last seen him and she suspected nothing had changed.

It wasn't fair, she thought, as her gaze wandered over him. Shouldn't he start looking a bit worn around the edges instead of drop-dead gorgeous? He was approaching middle age, after all. Yet his shoulders and muscular chest gleamed in the late afternoon sun, tanned and sleek. Muscles moved when he uncrossed his arms and she noticed he looked as fit as a teenager. His long legs were spread as he leaned arrogantly against her car. Just looking at him made her knees weak.

She sighed, too tired to even muster up a flirtatious smile for the man. What was the point? She recognized lost causes when she saw them—at least recently, she acknowledged. He'd ignored her most of her life. It was past time she gave up any hopes of a relationship between them. He was Jake, forever unattainable. And she was tired. Very, very tired.

"Here for a visit?" he asked.

"Yes."

"You must need it, you look like hell."

"Gee, thanks, Jake. I'm always a sucker for honey words. Careful, you'll turn my head."

"I deal in facts."

"Ha, as long as they suit whatever client you're defending. Otherwise, you change them to suit your needs." Kerry swayed a bit. She had to get inside.

"Whatever works. And I don't change the facts, though I have been known to suggest a different way to look at them." He shrugged and tilted his head to better study her.

"What works for me right now is bed. See you around." Turning, she started for the house.

"Staying long?" Jake called after her.

She shrugged and kept walking. She was too tired to banter with him today. Too tired after the long drive to do anything but find a bed and crash. Maybe if she slept a week she'd feel better.

The air inside the old house felt fresh and cool. Smiling at the welcome that seemed to seep into her with every step, Kerry wandered through the lower floor to the wide stairs leading to the second story. It was seven o'clock on a late spring evening. Too tired to even think, she quickly climbed the stairs, entered the room that had always been hers, stripped off her clothes and climbed into bed—grateful to find someone had made it fresh for her arrival. Probably Aunt Peggy, or maybe her cousin Sally. She was too tired to even consider who might have been more likely.

Job burnout. She'd always scoffed at the concept before. But the reality proved all too true—and frightening. If she had half a brain, she would have seen the writing on the wall. But she'd been too busy trying to prove to the world that she was invincible. And it had caught up with her. Big time.

Tomorrow she'd begin to make plans for the future. But not tonight. The trip had been long, boring and endless. She craved oblivion as never before. Even the thought of seeing Jake again couldn't keep her awake.

In only seconds, she fell sound asleep.

''Good morning, sleepyhead.'' A familiar voice woke Kerry the next morning. Opening one eye a slit, she frowned at her cousin standing in the doorway. Sally had always been cheery in the morning. A trait Kerry did not share.

''Go away.'' She pulled the pillow over her head and tried to block out the soft rustling as Sally moved into the room. She heard the soft clink of china. Even beneath the pillow she could smell the rich aroma of freshly brewed coffee.

Slowly she eased the pillow back a couple of inches and peered out.

''I may forgive you if that's coffee,'' she grumbled.

Sally sat on the edge of the bed with a bounce and grinned at her cousin. ''You look like something the cat dragged in. When did you arrive? I expected you to call me. If I hadn't stopped by last night I still wouldn't know you were here.''

''Last night I was too tired to do anything but sleep. Isn't it awfully early for you to be visiting?'' Kerry gave up thoughts of going back to sleep and pushed herself up against the headboard. She reached for the delicate china cup. Her aunt had a flair for the romantic and all her china was delicate and fragile.

''I waited until ten,'' Sally said virtuously.

"It's after ten?" Kerry hadn't slept that late since college days. She shook her head to clear the cobwebs and then sipped the hot brew. "Ummm, all's forgiven. This is delicious."

Sally smiled smugly.

Kerry looked at her cousin and tried to hate her. Sally was beautiful, always had been and always would be. Her dark glossy hair glowed with health. While Kerry's own mousy hair gained golden highlights in the sun, it now hung in waves around her shoulders in a plain dull brown. She hadn't spent any time in the sun for months.

Where Sally looked great without a speck of makeup, if Kerry didn't wear mascara on her light eyelashes, they were lost. She did think her own dark chocolate-brown eyes were striking, where Sally's eyes were a nondescript hazel.

"Are you all right?" Sally asked, tilting her head as she studied her cousin.

"Just taking inventory. Why are you so darn beautiful and I got stuck with average looks?"

Sally laughed. It was an old familiar complaint. "Kerry, you're pretty, you just don't take time to make the most of what you've got. Take your eyes, for instance, they're your best feature. A bit of the right makeup and they'd be the focus of your entire face."

"Yes, I know. Old story. Maybe I'll play around with makeup this trip. We can do dress-ups. So why are you here? Don't you have a job?"

"Of course I have a job. I'm just taking today off. When I stopped last night, Jake said he'd seen you come in but hadn't seen any sign of life since. I came upstairs looking for you, but you were fast asleep. Tough drive down?"

"It's a long way from New York City to West Bend, North Carolina."

"You didn't have to drive it all in a day. If you'd taken your time, it would have been easier."

"I wanted to get home," Kerry said softly, sipping her coffee.

"I guess. How are you doing, really? I know it couldn't have been easy to give up your job."

"I didn't precisely give it up. When the company was sold, it became a matter of time until most of us lost our jobs. Restructuring is the official term these days."

"But you worked so hard."

"Right. Dumb move on my part. I should have seen no matter what I did, the new company had its own agenda. So the long hours and all the stress didn't pay in the end. I'm so tired now I can hardly think. Having more time on my hands than I know what to do with, I decided to take up your mom's offer to visit for a while. Regroup until I decide my next move. I'm due some down time. The new company was generous in their severance money, so I'm not in dire straits. After I rest up, I'll plan for the future. Maybe I'll get a job in Charlotte. Or go back to New York. I have a lot of friends there."

Kerry wasn't sure what she would do for the future. And right now, it was too much effort to even begin to decide. She felt lonely, adrift as never before.

"You have friends here. And family," Sally reminded her gently.

"There is that," Kerry acknowledged. She'd been so excited when she first moved to New York after college. Now the thought of living closer to home—or the only place she considered home—held a huge appeal. Was it backlash, or was she due for a change?

"Oh, speaking of family, guess what I found! Wait a

minute.'' Sally jumped up and rushed from the room. Ruefully, Kerry reached for a napkin to mop up the spilled coffee. Another trait Sally had, unbounded energy. Kerry thought she envied her cousin for that right now more than her looks. She hated the lethargy that seemed to invade every cell. When would she bounce back?

Kerry finished the coffee and snuggled down in the covers. She'd always had enough energy to suit her until recently. She'd recoup, it would just take some time. The thought of doing nothing all day except maybe dabbling at gardening or just lying in the sun, sounded like heaven. And it felt good to be home.

Her parents were in the Aegean this summer. And for the last two years had taught at a university in California. Prior to that they'd done stints at numerous colleges and universities across the country. She wondered how the only child of nomads could so strongly yearn for a permanent home and roots. Often she felt closer to her mother's sister than her own parents.

''Look what I found when Mom and I cleaned out the attic a couple of months ago. It's hilarious.'' Sally held out a leather-bound journal. ''I haven't read that much, but what I did was funny.''

Kerry took the book and brushed her fingers across the cover. The rich leather felt soft and supple, though it looked old.

''What is it?''

''Great-grandmother Megan's diary. She started it the day she turned eighteen. The journal was a birthday gift from her father. And Mom said she wrote in it up to the birth of her first baby, great-uncle Lloyd. You have to read it. She has a recipe for getting the right man for a perfect marriage.''

''A *recipe* for getting a man?''

"Yes, ingredients she calls them for how to entice a man, how to get his interest and hold it. It's so funny and old-fashioned. You can read it while you rest up. I bet it cheers you up. Then I'll read it. Do you remember her?"

"Vaguely. She died when I was ten. The year I first started coming here for summer vacation. Wasn't she old?"

"To us at ten she sure seemed to be, but I think she was only in her mid-seventies when she died. This book is almost an antique."

"How much did you read?" Kerry asked, turning to the first page, fascinated. Her great-grandmother Megan had written this, a bit of family history that she had never expected to see. Megan had beautiful handwriting, clear and perfectly formed. Kerry began to read the first paragraph.

"Read it when you're alone. I'm here to visit," Sally took it from her cousin. "I only read the first few pages. Mom said she got first dibs. I think she finished it before they left. What do you want to do today? I thought we could go to the country club for lunch. They have a wonderful salad bar during the week. Maybe lie by the pool for a while. I want to do lots of fun things on my day off." She slipped the book onto the table beside the bed.

"Sounds fine with me," Kerry said, glad to have someone else take charge for a change. She'd been living on her own for so long, it was nice to be cosseted.

"I think I'm in love," Sally said abruptly.

"Again?" Kerry said, unsurprised. Her cousin was in love with someone new every time she saw her. And it usually lasted a month or two and then she'd move on. Did she fear commitment? Maybe there was something in the water. Jake Mitchell never committed to a woman. West Bend, North Carolina appeared on the outside to be the perfect rendition of a friendly southern town. Yet her cousin was twenty-nine, same age as Kerry, and she had not found the right man yet. Of course, Kerry thought ruefully, neither had she. But she had a reason. Not that she would ever tell anyone that Jake had spoiled her for other men. She used him as the measure for everyone she dated. So far, no one else had come close.

"Who's the lucky man this time?" Kerry asked pushing back the sheet to get up. She crossed to her carryall and began looking in it for something to wear until she unloaded the car.

"He's a friend of Jake's, actually. Moved here on Jake's recommendation. His name is Greg Bennet, and he's the newest vet in town."

"Vet? An army vet?"

"Veterinarian."

Kerry paused and turned to stare at her cousin. "Veterinarian? Sally, you don't even like animals."

"That's what he does. *I* don't have to do anything with animals. But I'm really interested in him as a man. He's fun to be with and doesn't talk shop."

"How old?"

"He knew Jake in college, so he's about the same age."

"Never married?"

Sally shook her head. "What does that have to do with anything? You and I have never been married either."

"But we're still in our twenties."

"Right, for a few more months," Sally said dryly.

"The point is that we're still young, Jake's thirty-four."

"And that's old? It's only five years older than we are."

"We both know Jake has no interest in getting married." She paused a moment, remembering his scathing laughter when she'd shyly shared girlish dreams with him one summer. The humiliation had run deep at the time. "We both know why Jake's in his mid-thirties and still unmarried. But what's kept this Greg from forming some lasting commitment before now?"

"Good grief, Kerry, how should I know? Maybe he was waiting for me. Just because a man isn't married by a certain age doesn't mean he won't ever marry. Not every man is as cynical as Jake. Besides, who knows, maybe one day the right woman will come along and find a way to get around even Jake's defenses."

Kerry looked out the window. At one time she had fervently wished she would be that woman. But she'd grown up over the last few years. And the events of the past few months firmly showed her the error of tilting against windmills! She'd learned to stop beating her head against an immovable barrier. Practical would become her new watchword.

She looked at Sally and smiled. "I'm happy for you, Sally. When can I meet him?"

Mollified, Sally bounced up. "This weekend for sure. I'll have you both over for dinner or we can go out or something. Hurry and get dressed, there's lots to do today. I have to make the most of my time. I'm not normally a lady of leisure like you, remember?"

It was late afternoon by the time Sally dropped Kerry at home. Lunch at the country club had been pleasant. Kerry spoke with a couple of friends from the past who wanted to know how long she'd be visiting, and they made plans to get together. Sally had then dragged her to the new mall, to show off the stores, and urged Kerry to get a few new things.

Shopping with her cousin could wear anyone out, Kerry thought as she waved at the departing car, though Sally's intent had been to cheer her up with new clothes. Smiling, she headed for the house. It had worked. The two sundresses she'd bought were totally unlike the severe business suits she'd worn for the last seven years. She loved New York, but it hadn't taken a day to fall back into the slower rhythm of West Bend. Was she a chameleon that changed colors to suit her background, only in her case changing lifestyles to suit her locale? She liked the slower pace. It suited her own state of mind right now.

"Kerry?" Jake called.

She turned. What was it about Jake Mitchell that threw her into such turmoil? She had met handsome men in New York, successful, dynamic. Yet none of them had set her nerves on end, dampened her palms and interfered with her breathing.

Jake looked as if he'd just come from his office. The light gray suit was formal, nothing like the cutoffs of yesterday. His white shirt and silver tie emphasized the deepness of his tan. It was just early June and he already had a tan. She felt anemic next to him. A few days by the pool would change that.

"Hi, Jake," she said calmly, belying the involuntary butterflies dancing in her stomach. It wouldn't hurt to look, she argued, as her eyes feasted on the man. His tie was loosened and his shirt unbuttoned at the top. She liked him better in cutoffs, she thought irreverently, though the style of his suit showed off his broad shoulders, his tall lean frame. His gray eyes seemed to peer right into the heart of her and she dropped her gaze lest some lingering foolishness showed.

"You ran off pretty quick last night," he said when he reached her.

"I was tired. It was a long drive." She didn't have to answer to him. She'd long ago given up on the man, so she saw no point in wasting time. Frankly, she didn't have the energy yet to join in some verbal sparring and come out ahead—or even hold her own.

He reached out and gently traced the skin beneath her eyes with a fingertip. "You look a bit better today, but still tired. Tough few months?"

"I've had better." Even when his hand slid into his pocket, she felt the lingering impression of his touch. Swallowing hard, she reminded herself she was not interested in the man.

Not, not, not, she chanted inside, wishing she could believe it. There was no point in submitting herself to dreams that something would come of his neighborly greeting. He and his brother and father had lived next door to her aunt and uncle for years. When his father retired to Florida, Jake had bought the home and continued to live in it. Her Aunt Peggy kept her fully informed of the doings in West Bend.

Except for his years at college and law school, the house next door had been Jake's home all his life. He had the roots she'd longed for.

But it wasn't roots that caused her awareness of the man. It was his own presence, his dark good looks, his eyes that seemed to see down into her soul. His humor had enchanted her as a younger woman, his arrogance and self-assurance appeared so glamorous to someone who had felt shy, uncertain and out of place for much of her childhood.

When she'd been younger, Kerry had flirted for all she was worth in an effort to make him interested. First she'd been too young. He'd treated her casually, like a younger sister. Then when she'd grown up, Jake had changed and become cynical and bitter and took no pains to hide the fact from her or anyone else.

''Finally tired of New York?'' he asked, his gaze moving across her face. He'd seen the shadows beneath her eyes—did he also see the weight she'd lost?

''Tired, in any event. I'm here on vacation. Maybe I'll see you around.'' She smiled politely and turned back to the house. She'd taken a dozen steps when he spoke again.

''If you need anything, call me.''

She turned around and began walking backwards. ''Thanks, Jake, but Sally's nearby. And it's not as if I don't know my way around.''

He stood with his hands in the pocket of his trousers, his gaze steady. Again she noticed how his starched white shirt contrasted with the deep bronze of his tan. How much time had he spent outdoors this spring? A successful attorney would be too busy to have a lot of time to spend idly in the sun. She wondered how his practice fared. She knew he was formidable in the courtroom. When he'd first started, she'd attended a court session to see him in action. The intervening years had honed his skills, she was sure. Though even in the early days, he'd been dynamic.

''You haven't been here for a while. Things change,'' he called.

''I've made a few visits—I was here two Christmases ago,'' she said, glancing over her shoulder. The front porch stood only six feet away.

''And before that it was a couple of years, I believe.'' He took a step toward her, as if to close the distance between them.

She smiled involuntarily. He sounded as if he were cross-examining a witness. How accurate did she have to get?

"That's right. I really have to go, Jake. These packages are getting heavy. See you." She turned and ran lightly up the front steps and into the house.

Jake watched Kerry skip up the steps to the porch. For an instant he stared after her. Something was wrong. He couldn't put his finger on it, but it nagged at him.

Suddenly, he realized what it was, what had changed. Kerry made no attempt to flirt with him. All the years he'd known her, she'd flirted for all she was worth. As a teenager, she'd hung around and had done all she could to test her new-found femininity on him. Even while she'd been in college she'd tried to get his attention. He hadn't seen her in years. Where had he been Christmas two years ago?

And what had caused the change? Her smiles seemed polite, yet her manner had been decidedly un-Kerry-like. Distant, disinterested. Had she finally gotten over her crush on him? Her persistence had been embarrassing when he'd been younger. Then amusing during his college days. Finally annoying. He'd told her so, if he remembered correctly. Obviously he had convinced her.

He'd had no time for starry-eyed teenagers bent on a grand love affair. He didn't plan to repeat the mistakes of his father. His mother hadn't stuck around, leaving instead for the glamor and excitement of New Orleans. And after Selena, he'd begun to view all women with a jaundiced eye. Maybe his father had been right, women couldn't be trusted. A man was better off on his own.

Still, for years nothing had diminished Kerry's determination. Until now.

Not that he *wanted* her to have a crush on him, or flirt with him every time they met. There was no future in it for either of them. But oddly he felt something was missing with her lack of interest. Had he gotten so used to her devotion he now expected it?

What had she been doing these past years? Peggy Porter had mentioned at one point that Kerry worked in an advertising firm as a project manager or something. He wondered if she enjoyed living in New York—she looked exhausted.

He turned toward his house, anxious to change out of the hot clothing he'd worn to work. How long did Kerry plan to visit? Not the entire summer as when she was a child, he felt sure. But long enough for him to see her a couple of times? Hear about life in New York? She would be his neighbor, might as well do the right thing.

Jake walked back to his place, curious about his temporary neighbor. Maybe it was nothing more than Kerry had finally grown up. Maybe now their relationship would evolve into a comfortable neighborly friendship like he enjoyed with her cousin Sally.

Jake snagged his briefcase from the front seat of his car and headed inside to change. It was hot for early June. The humidity level rose steadily each day and he knew the summer would arrive in full scorching force before long. In the past he would have known it was summer by Kerry's arrival.

He didn't remember much about the summers he'd been in college. Of course falling for Selena had taken his mind off everything else. To find out she'd lied about everything, had used him for her own means had cut deep. That discovery caused his vow that entanglements with women were thereafter forbidden. Casual dates set his limit.

But sometimes in the dark of midnight he wondered if he really wanted to spend his entire life alone. Would he ever get lonely enough that he'd chance a more permanent relationship? Find a woman he could tolerate enough to have children with? He thought he might like to have some kids. He wondered if his brother ever thought about getting married. Nieces or nephews might satisfy these odd thoughts about children.

After changing into comfortable chino slacks and a cotton polo shirt, Jake went back downstairs. His house was built similarly to the one next door; both were two stories tall, with high ceilings and large rooms. He'd made few changes since his father moved south. The comfortable and sturdy furniture had been there as long as he remembered, acquired for comfort rather than for esthetic beauty. Solid upholstered furniture his father had chosen when his wife had run away and never returned. There was nothing in the house to show his mother had ever lived there. For a moment Jake tried to picture some of the furnishings that had been around when he'd been very small. Only a hard, cherrywood chair came to mind.

Jake didn't remember much about his mother. His brother, Boyd did, but he was three years older than Jake, had been ten when their mother left.

Mrs. Mulfrethy came once a week to vacuum and dust. The rest of the time he was on his own. Which was the way he liked it.

He pulled a beer from the refrigerator and looked out the window. He could see into the Porters' backyard. It was empty. Was Kerry cooking dinner? Had she made plans for the weekend? He'd further satisfy his curiosity by spending a little time with her. Dinner at the barbecue place on Route 23 would offer her down home food she probably hadn't had in New York. And the atmosphere was casual. Nothing she could read into dinner together. Though she didn't seem to be reading anything in his direction.

Giving in to instincts, Jake reached for the phone. Kerry answered on the second ring.

"Hi, Kerry. Thought we could get dinner together on Saturday," he said easily, leaning against the counter in the kitchen. He knew there was a danger she'd immediately assume he was interested. But he could deal with that.

"Sorry, Jake. I'm already busy. Thanks anyway."

Startled, he realized he'd expected her to leap at the opportunity. Another indication of the change in her attitude and maybe his. Was that a trace of disappointment he felt?

"No problem. How about Friday?"

"Tomorrow?"

"Yes."

"Nope, sorry, already going out to dinner. Maybe some other time. Oops, I have to go, the timer just went off. 'Bye."

He looked at the phone before he replaced it. "A bit cocky in our old age, aren't we, Jake?" he said aloud. "Thinking she'd jump at the chance to go out with you." If he needed further proof that she no longer had that damn crush, he'd just received it.

Suddenly, his interest rose. One of the facets of becoming a successful lawyer was questioning things until he understood every aspect. Kerry's behavior was totally at odds with what he had come to expect from her. Intrigued, he wanted to know why. And find out a bit more about what she was doing with her life.

Perseverance was another trait of a successful attorney. He'd try again. She could not have already booked every night of her entire visit. She'd just arrived—how many evenings had she already committed? Tomorrow he'd call again, and nail down a day.

The clock on the mantel chimed nine when Kerry went to bed. Still feeling tired and a bit listless, she wanted an early night. Her day with Sally had done a lot to raise her spirits and she could feel some of her enthusiasm return when she looked at the journal still resting on the bedside table.

Slipping beneath the covers, she reached for the book, opening it with a sense of adventure that had been long missing. In only seconds she became totally engrossed in the scenes unfolding between the pages. Her great-grandmother had painted a very detailed picture of her life, of her parents and brothers and sisters. The descriptions were enthralling and Kerry felt as if she were meeting each of these ancestors in person.

Then the tone changed. Megan had written:

> Turning eighteen is a milestone. Sometime soon I will have to find a husband and settle down to the life for which I was raised. Patricia Blaine has already become engaged and she is but seventeen. I know my future husband is out there, but it may be up to me to find him. I've asked my mother and aunts about this, wanting to do the best I can for myself. And they've given advice, some contradictory, some old-fashioned. But from everything I've heard, I have decided to devise a recipe for finding the perfect mate for a perfect marriage.

"Well, Great-grandma Megan, I hope it's a good recipe. I could use one myself. If you think eighteen is old, what would you have thought about twenty-nine and unwed? And with no man even on the horizon,'' Kerry muttered as she turned the page.

> The first thing to always remember is that a man likes to do the chasing—just make sure not to run so fast he can't catch you. An occasional glance in his direction would be acceptable, I believe, but in this wild and open time demure and shy are strong lures. I would never be so bold as to brazenly speak first to a man, or show by my demeanor that I was interested in him. He needs to be the hunter, so Aunt Thomasina said. Though most of the men around here no longer hunt, it must be a trait from the Colonial days when hunting was so necessary for survival. So I'll be the quiet prey and let the man chase after me. Showing casual interest should work. I wonder if Frederick has noticed me. I could walk past him at church on Sunday and make sure I do not acknowledge him until he notices me. Would it work?

Kerry skimmed the next few pages until she came to the entry for Sunday. Avidly caught up in the story of her grandmother's plotting, she was anxious to see the result of the first of her recipe ingredients. She'd never known her great-grandfather and couldn't remember his name. And she'd only met Great-grandma Megan once long ago. Madacy had obviously been her maiden name but what had her married surname been? Her mother's grandmother, Kerry wasn't sure she'd ever heard her great-grandmother's full name. Did her recipe succeed or fail with Frederick?

* * *

Frederick spoke to me after church. I didn't tarry, told him I had to get home to help Mother with the Sunday dinner. I wasn't rude, I would never display such unmannered behavior, but I kept walking and seemed distracted. It was all I could do to refrain from laughing. He followed me all the way to the walkway of our house. It was the first time he'd paid any attention to me. Maybe Aunt Thomasina was right. I need to let him chase me. The key is to make sure I don't move faster than he does.

Kerry laughed softly. How different things were today. If her great-grandmother thought the Twenties were wild, she'd have a conniption in today's society.

Then a sudden thought sparked. Jake had come after her when she'd made no effort to seek him out. For a moment Kerry stared off into space, replaying that afternoon's encounter in her mind. She'd been tired and wanted to put down her packages. She had definitely not been in the mood to linger and chat. Even when he continued talking to her, she'd been walking away. The first time she'd ever done that with Jake.

And for the first time since she'd known him, he'd pursued. Even calling later to invite her out. She'd said no. That should have ended things, but now she wondered.

She picked up the journal and reread the passage. Was there a grain of truth in one of Megan's ingredients for finding a perfect mate? Maybe she'd see what happened if she played hard to get.

She'd read more of the journal. It would give her something to do—she had nothing else planned over the next few weeks.

For a moment she wished she could see into the future. Would following Megan's advice cause a change in the way Jake saw her? She smiled, switched off the light and lay in the dark, planning how to play hard to get with a man who normally acted as if she didn't exist. Tonight had shown a definite sign he'd noticed her. Would remaining aloof have any effect on how he viewed her in the future?

What could it hurt? she wondered just before sleep claimed her. Tomorrow she'd put the plan into action and observe the results. It would be a campaign of a kind, similar to her ad campaigns. Nothing was decided with one layout, there were several needed to ascertain if the overall plan had a chance of success. Now how could she test this premise?

CHAPTER TWO

Don't accept an invitation at the last minute. Make sure he thinks you are busy and have to make an extra effort to spend time with him.

—Megan Madacy's journal, Spring 1923

WHEN KERRY AWOKE the next morning, she felt refreshed for the first time in months. Smiling as she dressed, she glanced at the journal resting on the bedside table. How silly she'd been last night. As if following Megan's recipe would insure a happy marriage with the man of her dreams. She must have been more fatigued than she suspected. To think ignoring Jake would make him interested in her. Ha! She'd been ignoring him for years while she lived in New York. She hadn't seen any signs he even noticed she was gone.

When Kerry went down to prepare breakfast, it was already late morning. She couldn't believe how much sleep her body craved. A direct result of all the long hours she'd put in over the last months, she knew. But for the first time in weeks, she felt rested and ready for anything. Maybe she'd tackle the yard.

During the day Kerry mowed, trimmed and weeded. Wearing skimpy shorts and a halter top, she added some color to her skin as well while doing the yard work. Shortly before noon she pulled on a light yellow cotton shirt with short sleeves to protect her shoulders. She didn't want to burn. But it felt good to be doing physical labor in the hot sun. Her mind wandered, skipping on topics, drifting in and out of daydreams.

By midafternoon, she finished. The lawn looked as if a gardener had taken pains with it. The grass was evenly mowed, edges trimmed. The flower beds had been weeded and deadheaded and now the colorful blossoms flourished. Satisfied with a job well done, she made a pitcher of lemonade and took it into the backyard, pouring herself a large glass. Gratefully, she sank onto a recliner beneath one of the huge old oak trees. The shade felt good. She had yet to shower and get ready to go with Susan and Greg to dinner at the Fibbing Fisherman Café, a local restaurant. But she had time to spare and deserved the break—*needed* a break after all the work she'd done. It was a good kind of tired, however. Not like what she'd experienced in New York.

When Jake's sleek Trans Am pulled into his driveway two minutes later, Kerry went still—suddenly remembering the journal entries and advice written by Great-grandma Megan. Sipping her cool lemonade, she wondered if she dare try to ignore the man. He had not pursued anyone that she knew of since he'd been in college. Would her acting distant pique his interest? More likely it would make him happy to be left alone.

He climbed out of the car, briefcase in hand. Taking work home on the weekend's not worth it, she thought cynically. She'd done that for months and her reward had been the loss of her job. Looking away from Jake, she frowned, wishing she'd known before what she'd learned over the last year. She would have enjoyed life more and left the work to those who were now in charge of the company.

"If you are going to be there for a few minutes, I'll

change and join you,'' Jake called when he spotted Kerry.

She looked at him, her heart skipping a beat. His dark hair looked as if he'd run his fingers through it. The business suit fit as if it had been made exclusively for him and the fine tailoring emphasized his height and enhanced his air of confidence and success. Even at the end of the day, he looked as fresh and sharp as early morning. She wondered if he'd been in court today. If so, she bet every female witness lost her train of thought just looking at him.

Kerry nodded once, then lay back, studying the puffy clouds drifting by, trying to remember all Megan had written in her journal. She felt flutters of interest. Try as she might, there was no denying she'd once been attracted to Jake Mitchell and probably always would have lingering feelings for him. Saying she wanted nothing further to do with him was a lie. But she would not let herself get caught up in some impossible fantasy that they would fall in love and live happily ever after. She knew better than that.

But it couldn't hurt to see how far his new interest would progress. Not that she believed her own lack of response sparked his. He probably felt an obligation to watch out for his neighbors' guest while they were away.

Jake crossed the yard ten minutes later, his eyes fixed on the woman lying in the recliner. He'd changed into shorts and a cotton T-shirt. If she planned to sit out in the hot afternoon sun, he wanted to dress as cool as decency allowed. Approaching Kerry, his gaze traced over her. Her bare legs were bent at the knees, the shorts falling back almost to the crease where her thighs joined her hips. Her skin looked supple and silky, her legs curvy and sleek. The shirt she wore appeared grass-stained.

Obviously she'd been working in the yard. A glance at the smoothly cut grass and pile of weeds near the shed provided further evidence.

Her hair was tousled and a hint of pink highlighted her cheeks. She'd matured, yet her expression still displayed a certain innocence that belied the experiences she must have gained living in Manhattan. With color in her cheeks, she looked downright pretty. He'd never noticed how much before.

When she heard him, she turned and smiled. Jake felt it to his toes. He never hesitated in his stride, but the shock of that flicker of physical awareness surprised him. Had he been too long without a woman? Or was there something different about Kerry?

"I made lemonade if you want some," she said casually. "But you need to get your own glass from the kitchen."

"Or I can share yours," Jake said easily, pulling the second lounger close to hers and sitting on the edge. When her eyes widened at his comment, he smiled. He still didn't know what was going on, but he intended to find out.

"You've had a busy day," he said, boldly reaching out to take her glass. His fingers touched hers. She yanked back, then tried casually to brush her hair away from her cheek, as if not sure what to do with her hand.

Maybe she wasn't as sophisticated as he suspected. Pouring cold lemonade into the glass, he drank. "Good—it's not too sweet. You make it from scratch?"

"Yes." She looked at him, her gaze wary. "So, it's been a long time. How have you been?"

He almost laughed. She sounded like a properly brought up little Southern girl.

"As ever. You, Kerry?"

"Fine."

"Sally said you plan to stay for a while," he said, refilling the glass and holding it out to her.

"A few weeks, anyway."

When she took the glass, she made sure she didn't touch him. Interesting. How far could he push her, he wondered, a hint of mischief rising. She'd bedeviled him as a teenager. Maybe it was time to return the favor.

"Then?" he asked.

"I don't know. I'm considering my options." She took a sip of the cold beverage as if stalling. He'd interviewed enough witnesses to know a stall when he saw it.

"Thought you went to New York to spread your wings and set the world on fire." His gaze trailed down her, noticing the softly feminine form hidden beneath the yellow top, her slim waist, her long legs that beckoned for his touch. Was her skin warm from the sun, would it feel as silky beneath his fingers as it looked?

"I did. But I didn't realize that I could get my wings singed."

"Meaning the job isn't all it's cracked up to be?" he asked, his gaze sharp.

"There isn't a job at all anymore. There was a takeover."

"Tough break."

"Are you still the up-and-coming hotshot lawyer in Charlotte?" she asked.

"I have my practice there."

"Ever cautious. You sound like a lawyer. I bet you do extraordinarily well at it."

"I keep plugging away. What are you doing for dinner tonight?" he asked abruptly.

"Going out like I said."

"With whom?" It came out more sharply than he intended.

"Not that it's any of your business, but Sally."

He relaxed marginally. She'd turned down his invitation in favor of dinner with her cousin. He could understand that. After all, they had been close as girls and Kerry had been away for a while. They probably had a lot of catching up to do. "And tomorrow?"

"What is this, an interrogation? I'm not a witness for anything."

"Just curious. You arrived on Wednesday evening. I didn't know you could make so many arrangements that quickly."

"There're probably one or two things about me you don't know," she murmured. "We never were what you'd call close friends, were we? And we haven't seen each other for years."

"Tomorrow night?" he persisted.

"Don't you ever give up? I have a date with Carl Penning. We ran into each other at the country club yesterday and he invited me out to talk over old times."

Jake frowned and settled back on the chair, one knee raised. He rested a forearm on it as he studied the trees growing in the back of the Porters' yard. Carl Penning was closer in age to Kerry. They'd played tennis a lot, as he recalled, when she'd come for the summers. He'd played with them one time, an arrogant college kid challenging the two young high-schoolers. They'd whipped the pants off him. Of course two to one had been high odds, ones he hadn't challenged again.

"How about Sunday afternoon?" Jake asked. "We could play some tennis."

"Maybe."

He looked over at her lazily. Her eyes were closed.

She balanced the full glass on her stomach, her hands on either side of it. Studying her, he liked what he saw. She wore her brown hair long enough to brush her shoulders. One summer it had been down to her waist. The next year she'd cut it short. He liked this length.

When her eyes flicked open they stared into his, the warm chocolate color soft and mysterious. Her lashes were gold-tipped. Jake wondered how long it would be before she tried one of her flirtatious blinks he remembered from when she was younger.

She didn't blink. And her wide, innocent gaze had him thinking thoughts best left for the dark of night. She was the crazy girl who had driven him wild several summers with her pestering and flirtation. He'd be the crazy one this time if he gave in to the lascivious thoughts that had begun to build.

"If not tennis, we could drive down by the river, go swimming or something. End up at the country club. They have a nice buffet during the weekend," he said. He wanted a commitment from her to spend some time with him. The thought surprised him. Normally he didn't push. If a woman said no, he figured it was her loss.

Kerry stared at him for another moment, then looked away, shrugging slightly. "I'll check with Sally, but I think I can fit in an afternoon. I'll let you know if it doesn't work out."

Jake smiled slowly. It took more perseverance than he'd expected, but he knew she'd say yes eventually.

"Maybe next weekend?" she asked.

"What?" The smile left his face. She was stalling for another week?

"I have plans for this Sunday, but would love to see the river if the following Sunday would work for you."

"What do you have going on this Sunday?"

She smiled, flashing amusement in her dark eyes. ''Are you acting *in loco parentis* for Aunt Peggy this summer? You sound just like she used to when I was fourteen and thought I was all grown up.''

He shook his head, his eyes narrowing. ''Just curiosity.''

''You need to watch that, Jake. Tell me about your law practice. Still doing courtroom cases?''

He nodded. ''Come by one day. I'm scheduled for court all week.''

''I went to see you once, years ago.''

''I remember. You and Sally snuck in the back, and giggled the entire time.''

''We did not. Giggle, I mean. I thought you were—'' She grinned ruefully and shrugged. ''I thought you were as good as Perry Mason.'' She checked her watch and sat up, sliding her long legs over the edge of her chair, between the two. Jake lowered his own feet to the ground, his knee almost brushing against hers.

''Going somewhere?'' he asked.

''I have to get ready for tonight,'' she said, her eyes watching him warily. He made no move to give her room. He was so close he could feel the heat from her body, could smell the sweet scent that emanated from her skin mingle with that of the fresh cut grass. Rising languidly, he reached down a hand to pull her up, his palm absorbing the feel of her softer one.

Jake stood several inches taller than Kerry, not so much it would give him a backache to kiss her. Where had that random thought come from? He did his share of dating, but for the most part had to know a woman pretty well before having any interest of that nature.

''Skip dinner with Sally. Have it with me,'' he said, to his own surprise.

"I can't do that. I said I'd go to meet Greg."

"And that's important?" He didn't like the spark of jealousy that flared. "Greg's just another guy."

"Ummm." She took a breath and glanced to the side, to see if there were room to pass, probably. "Well, I'll have to see, won't I? Sally especially wants me to meet him."

"You could invite me to join you." He slid his hand up her arm, his fingertips caressing her silky skin. Was she this soft all over? His fingers brushed against the cuff of her sleeve, slid beneath the cotton.

"It's not my dinner invitation," she said, her voice breathless. Jake felt a certain satisfaction that this odd attraction didn't appear to be all on his side.

"If you're planning to visit for a few weeks, you'll have plenty of time to meet Greg. Have dinner with me," he coaxed.

She swayed, biting down on her lower lip. Jake tracked the action, suddenly wanting to be the one to gently bite that soft flesh, then soothe any sting. His gaze rose to lock with hers.

"I can't," she said.

He grasped her other arm with his hand and drew her closer still.

"You can do anything you want, Kerry." Slowly his thumbs traced random patterns against her skin. Her eyes glazed slightly. Her breasts rose and fell swiftly, as her breath caught then released. A few more minutes and she'd capitulate. He knew how to read the signs and she was broadcasting her indecision so clearly a first-year law student could pick up the signals.

Leaning forward, Jake slowly moved his hands from her arms to her shoulders, then to the delicate column of her neck. Tilting her head back, his thumbs brushed against her jaw. He wanted to kiss her. He wanted to feel the warmth beneath his fingers flare into heat, to taste the tempting lips that seemed to be waiting for his touch. He wanted—

"Are you trying to lead the witness?" she asked breathlessly.

Jake smiled, liking the sound of her voice. Would it sound this way if he took her to bed? Bemused, breathless? Or would she grow wild and wanton, flaring into passion and sharing her delight?

"That might be unethical," he murmured. A scant inch from those tantalizing lips, he covered the distance in an instant. For a moment he felt her surprise, then she relaxed and leaned into him.

And poured the rest of the ice-cold lemonade down his leg.

"Damn!" He jerked back, tried to avoid the cold sticky liquid. The edge of the recliner caught him behind his knees and he fell in a sprawl half on, half off, the lounger.

"Oh, I'm so sorry. I forgot I had the glass in my hand. Are you all right?" Kerry set the glass down on the table and stepped closer. "I don't have any napkins out here. I can run inside and get something." Trying to hide her amusement, she watched him. Kerry wasn't sure dumping lemonade on a man was considered hard-to-get, but she'd soon find out. Was that diary bewitching her?

"Don't bother." He rose, slicking some of the lemonade from his leg. His shorts were sopping wet on the left side. His skin felt sticky.

Kerry stared at Jake, trying to force some sincerity into her voice, "I'm sorry, it was an accident." A bubble of impishness rose. She tried to keep from smiling and giving herself away. Did he think just because she had a crush on him years ago, she still did?

''I'm sure it was. If I thought for a moment it had been deliberate, I'd dump the rest of the pitcher on you,'' he said, looking with disgust at the wet shorts. When he glanced up at her face, his own expression changed.

''You can make it up by having dinner with me tonight.''

She frowned, all thoughts of laughing gone. ''Good grief, don't you ever give up? No way. I told Sally I'd go out with her and I'm sticking to that. Honestly, Jake, if you and I made plans would you want me to back out?''

''Sally's your cousin, she wouldn't care.''

''Doesn't matter, I'm not changing my mind.'' Kerry drew herself up to her full five feet six inches. There was a principle here, and she was sticking to it—diary or not.

He nodded in acceptance. Unexpectedly his hand shot out and gripped her neck, gently pulling her up against the length of his hard body. His mouth lost its tentativeness, his kiss this time plundered. Hot and demanding, his lips crushed against hers, his tongue teasing her lips. She opened in response and he deepened the kiss, tasting her, skimming across her teeth, brushing against her tongue. His mouth moved against hers. For endless moments, time seemed to stand still, and the earth spun.

Feelings exploded in Kerry. Surprise was instantly swamped by the hot surge of desire that coursed through her. She wanted more, but before she could formulate any kind of thought, he pulled back.

''Maybe you won't break your other dates, but at least you can think about me during them,'' Jake said. He brushed his lips once more across hers then turned and walked across the grass toward his house.

Stunned, Kerry stood and stared after him. In all the years she'd known him, he'd never kissed her before. She'd tried it once and he'd firmly put her in her place. He'd laughed at her, teased her before. But never kissed her.

And what a kiss.

The first attempt had been gentle, an exploration of a kind. But the second had been frankly and blatantly sexual. His mouth had been demanding and exciting and may have spoiled her for anyone else. She ran her tongue over her lips, tasting him. It had been too quick. And she didn't like his reasons for kissing her. Narrowing her eyes, she glared after him.

''Arrogant creature! The last thing I need is any involvement with someone who has no use for women beyond a few casual dates,'' she chastised herself as she gathered the empty glass and the pitcher. How typically conceited of the man, to expect her to think of him while out with someone else. And now she probably would.

Heading for the house, she tried to convince herself that the attraction she felt for Jake was purely physical. It had nothing to do with love or future or even mutual respect. She remembered his scathing comments from years ago. They'd been burned into her mind. He had no use for fatuous teenagers, or women in general. He'd made that clear at the time.

Yet something seemed to have changed. She wasn't sure what. Why had he come on to her? Usually he ran as fast as he could in the other direction. He'd really pushed her for a date. And hadn't taken no very gracefully. She wasn't sure she knew what he was up to, but for a brief moment it had been gratifying. And, darn it, he was probably right—she *would* think about him tonight.

While taking her shower, Kerry wondered if there was any truth to the steps her great-grandmother had listed in her journal. It seemed preposterous on the surface, but she couldn't deny Jake had paid attention to her for the first time when she had made up her mind to stay away from him. Even the lemonade had not dampened his enthusiasm. She grimaced at the awful pun and shut off the water. She'd have to give the idea some serious thought.

Dinner proved to be a lively affair. Greg was funny and entertaining and seemed delighted to include Kerry on his date with Sally. At tall as Jake, Greg was a bit stockier, and had sandy-colored hair. His sports coat fit nicely, but he didn't exude the same elegance and arrogance that Jake did. He also didn't seem to pay any special attention toward her cousin, while Sally all but devoured him with her eyes. Kerry wondered if Sally's feelings were reciprocated. And if so, how long before Sally grew tired of Greg and moved on to another man?

Kerry had worn one of her new sundresses and liked the softly feminine feeling it gave her. She laughed at Greg's stories, and shared smiles with her cousin when they recounted some of their wilder escapades as teenagers.

When Sally excused herself after dinner to use the ladies' room, Greg turned to Kerry with a teasing smile. "I've heard about you before, you know," he said.

"You have?"

"From Jake Mitchell."

"Oh." Color flushed her cheeks as mention of Jake brought memory of their last encounter—and his kiss. She swallowed hard. She refused to give in to that particular memory. "Jake talked to you about me?"

"It was while we were in college."

''Oh. Well, don't believe everything you heard back then,'' she said, laughing. She could imagine what Jake had to say a decade ago.

''He'd come back from holidays or summer vacation and complain about this bratty kid who hung around and wouldn't leave him alone.''

''Ouch. I had such a crush on him when I was younger.'' She was over that, she assured herself. It had been a normal teenage crush, that's all.

''So he said.'' Greg chuckled. ''I sometimes wondered if he didn't secretly like it, though, for all his complaining. You were certainly steadfast. I knew him for the last three years at college and he talked about you a lot.''

''I bet.'' Kerry took a long drink of her iced tea, then looked at Greg in consideration. Here was a man who had known Jake in college. ''Did you know the girl Jake fell for?''

Greg's expression grew serious as he nodded slowly. ''Selena Canfield.''

Kerry hadn't known her name, Selena. Pretty. ''What was she like? What happened between them?''

''Maybe you should ask Jake.''

''Maybe I should, but you know he won't tell anyone a thing. Was he really in love with her?''

Greg shrugged. ''He thought so at the time.''

''And she didn't love him?''

''She pretended for a while. But it was an elaborate hoax to get back at the man she'd once been engaged to. I think Jake thought he'd found the pot at the end of the rainbow, only it turned out to be fool's gold. As soon as her former fiancé showed up, she dumped Jake in a public and humiliating manner. Almost viciously, I always thought. And for no reason, except I guess to prove to her fiancé that she really was through with Jake.''

Kerry's heart ached for the younger man Jake had been. It had probably taken a lot of faith for him to open up to a woman after seeing his mother desert her family. To have that woman trample on his feelings would have been crushing. No wonder he was so cynical about the whole female gender. She sighed, wishing things had been easier for the man. Would it have made a difference to how he saw her? Probably not. But her heart ached for the lonely boy she'd known.

"Kerry, did you give away all my deep dark secrets while I was gone?" Sally asked gaily, rejoining them. She smiled brightly at Greg.

"I didn't know you had any to give away," Kerry said observing her cousin's flirtation with the handsome veterinarian. Greg didn't seem particularly bowled over to be at the receiving end.

"What were you talking about?" Sally persisted.

"Jake, actually," Kerry replied.

"Jake Mitchell? What about him?"

"Nothing much. You said Greg knew him in college. We were just chatting."

"Jake mentioned Kerry a time or two," Greg added.

"I bet he did more than mention her," Sally said shrewdly, narrowing her gaze at Kerry. "She was forever following him around, pestering him to death, wanting to make him her boyfriend."

Kerry felt the heat steal into her cheeks. "Thanks, cousin, I defend you and you throw me to the wolves."

"Well, it was true. I never could see what you saw in him. He was so much older than you and didn't seem to care a bit about girls. Until he fell for that one at college. Must not have amounted to much, he dumped her and never hooked up with anyone else on a long term basis. And not for lack of women trying. I've had more friends ask to be introduced to him at various functions around here over the last five years than I can count.''

''So did you introduce them?'' Kerry asked. It was hard to remember her own disinterest in the man when her cousin brought up such a tantalizing piece of information.

''Sure, for all the good it does anyone. Sometimes he takes a woman out for a couple of dates, then never calls again. Other times, he never even invited them out for a first date. A lost cause.''

''Did you know his mother?'' Greg asked, glancing at Sally then Kerry.

''No, she left when I was around two. And that was years before Kerry started coming to stay the summers. I've heard my mother talk about it, though. She said it hit Adam, Jake's father, really hard. As well as the two little boys. They ended up getting a double dose. First they lost their mother, then Adam became lonely and bitter. Never made an effort to find another wife. So Boyd and Jake constantly heard how awful their mother was with no balancing to soften the recriminations. No wonder Jake can't trust a woman enough to fall in love.''

Kerry met Greg's gaze, knowing he was thinking about Selena—as she herself was.

''I've got room for dessert,'' Sally said brightly. ''How about you, Greg?''

It was after ten when Greg and Sally dropped Kerry at the house. She invited them in for coffee, but Sally declined. Kerry smiled. She knew Sally had had enough of family, she wanted Greg to herself for a little while before the night ended.

Waiting by the door while the car drove away, Kerry caught a glimpse of movement coming from Jake's backyard. Was he outside? Waiting to see when she came home? Unlikely. There was no reason for him to take any interest in her life.

Turning quickly, she let herself into the dark house just in case. She was not up to another confrontation with her sexy neighbor tonight. She needed distance and some perspective before she was ready to see him again. Time to decide how she would handle the memory of that hot kiss they'd shared. And time to come up with a way to guard her wayward heart. She knew playing with Jake would be dangerous. After losing her job, and her enthusiasm for her career, she dare not risk her emotional state as well.

Taking the journal when she got into bed, she settled against the pillows. This was more fun than worrying about how to deal with a man. Or her own turbulent emotions.

> Don't accept an invitation at the last minute. Make sure he thinks you are busy and have to make an extra effort to spend time with him. This is from Aunt Caroline. But it does go with Aunt Thomasina's advice of being unavailable. Pretend you have other plans, even if it is only washing your hair. And if you truly have another date, let him know others find you appealing as well. Men like to pursue women who are also pursued by others.

Gazing off into space, Kerry nodded. It made sense. But it was not earth-shattering news. Still, hadn't Jake pushed for a date once she'd refused? And especially after she'd told him she was seeing Carl. Interesting. Was there more to this recipe business than she first thought?

She could pretend she was too busy to see him—if he

asked again. And make it seem as if she were doing him a favor to squeeze him in.

Laughing softly at a situation that would never arise, she began to read again.

CHAPTER THREE

> A woman should always be perfectly groomed, and avoid any hint of appearing like a tomboy.
>
> —Megan Madacy's journal, Spring 1923

KERRY REREAD THE WORDS, frowning a little. She was tired, probably should have been asleep hours ago, but was too fascinated to give up even a few moments with her great-grandmother's journal. Megan was writing about her mother's admonitions to dress appropriately to her age and gender rather than trying out the new trousers that were the rage.

> Mama is shocked with the girls in town wearing the trousers everywhere. She said if the good Lord had wanted women to wear pants he would never have invented dresses. I think trousers look chic, but Mama won't hear of me wearing them. I have to do something to compete for Frederick's attention. I think I'll see about making a couple of new dresses. Lacy, frilly, ultra-feminine. If I can't be on the leading edge of fashion, maybe I'll become known for my femininity. Maybe it will make Frederick feel more masculine.

Kerry chuckled and lay the book on the bedside table. She wanted to know if Megan's ultra-femininity succeeded in making Frederick feel more masculine. She hoped the answer would be in subsequent pages. But it would have to wait for another time. The words were blurring before her eyes.

Snuggling down against the pillows, she flicked off the light. How different things were in the early part of the century when people found trousers for women shocking. Kerry smiled again. She wore pants all the time, at work and at play. Sometimes she went weeks without wearing a skirt or dress. Wouldn't Megan's mama be totally shocked!

But just before sleep claimed her, Kerry wondered if wearing feminine clothes really had an impact on the males of the species.

"I'm going bonkers," Kerry said to herself the next morning. Sipping her coffee, she scanned the local paper for any sales. Somehow during the night she'd decided to try Megan's idea about dressing ultra-femininely. Today she planned to look for some more dresses beyond the two she bought Wednesday, something feminine, yet comfortable. She was on vacation. A time to splurge. Though she had to watch her money since her source of income was temporarily interrupted, she had plenty in savings to tide her over. And a few more sundresses wouldn't cost a mint. Maybe she'd buy something this afternoon to wear when she went out with Carl.

Though it wasn't Carl she was thinking about, it was Jake. Damn that kiss!

"Practical!" she said firmly. "There is no future in that direction, no matter how much I once wished there were." She'd had a second lesson—working so hard to keep her position only to lose it—that trying for the impossible just didn't work. Folding the paper, she went upstairs to get dressed. It wouldn't hurt to consider what Jake might like. He was a man, after all. She could at least keep him in the back of her mind when choosing new clothes.

By the time Carl rang the doorbell that evening, Kerry had dithered back and forth a dozen times about her dress and her hair. She had called Sally to join her on yet another shopping expedition. When Sally heard what her cousin planned, she burst out laughing, then joined in with unbounded enthusiasm. Questioning her in detail about her intent, Sally commented that Kerry had obviously seen a lot more in that journal than Sally had when she'd glanced through it.

The result of the day: four more new dresses, new makeup and a new hairstyle.

Now Carl Penning was at the door and Kerry was not at all sure she'd done the right thing. Maybe she should have stuck with her regular clothes. Once she found a new job, these dresses would be relegated to the back of her closet, totally unsuitable for career work.

Still, she liked how she looked and felt in the dress. The scooped neck displayed her neck and shoulders nicely, and the light tan she'd acquired while doing yard work made her look fit and healthy. The fitted bodice revealed her slim figure. The flared skirt moved as she walked, in what she hoped was feminine allure. The soft pink went well with her coloring.

Her hair had been cut and layered and the natural wave brought out. Washed with a highlighting rinse, it sparkled and shone in the light. Framing her face, brushing her shoulders, it looked almost—sexy. Taking Sally's advice, she had splurged on makeup that enhanced her eyes. Satisfied she looked her best, she was pleased with the day's events.

"Hi, Carl," Kerry greeted him when she opened the

door. He was tall, with wide shoulders and a shock of blond hair. His cheerful grin, however, did nothing to raise her blood pressure. She smiled and stepped out, locking the door behind her. Why couldn't she be attracted to Carl? She'd known him since they were teenagers. Had enjoyed spending time with him during her summer visits, yet there had never been a spark of physical attraction between them. They were truly friends and nothing more.

Not that she'd found that spark with any of her dates in New York, either. The only man who once caused sparks was totally off limits. Time she got over Jake Mitchell and concentrated on finding something special with someone else.

"Carl, good to see you," Jake said, standing on the sidewalk beside Carl's car. He looked at Kerry as they walked down the flagstones, his eyes narrowing as his gaze scanned her from head to toe.

"Kerry," he said easily. The glitter in his eye gave away his emotions.

"Hi, Jake." She felt guilty, like a child caught with a cookie after being told not to have one. Swallowing hard, Kerry took a deep breath. She had *nothing* to feel guilty about. She was entitled to go out on dates. And she'd told Jake about tonight. Thinking about her grandmother's journal, she thought maybe it was a good thing Jake saw her leaving. Just because *he* had never wanted her didn't mean other men didn't. If only she didn't feel so awkward!

"How're things, Jake?" Carl reached out to shake hands.

"Can't complain. You?"

"Couldn't be better. Business is hopping. We'll be expanding soon and taking in some more help." Carl was in partnership with his father at the local hardware store. Jake had spent many hours there as a child. His father had loved hardware stores. Kerry wondered if Jake shared that trait with his dad.

"Going out?" Jake asked, his eyes now on Kerry.

The spark of attraction threatened to flare into something larger, but she smiled and stepped closer to Carl, nodding. As if he didn't know.

Carl opened the car door for her. "I ran into Kerry at lunch the other day. We're going to try that new place in town, Tarheel Tavern."

"Have fun," Jake said.

"Bye," Kerry said, conscious of his gaze on her all the while as she got into the car. She felt it as Carl pulled away. Once out of sight, Kerry sighed softly and turned to her date. She had to get over any lingering feelings for Jake Mitchell. Carl was a perfectly nice man and had been kind to invite her out. She would devote all of her attention to him during the evening.

When Kerry climbed into bed four hours later, she felt exhausted. Picking up the journal, she opened it, wondering if she could keep her eyes open. She'd read just two pages. The evening had seemed endless. Carl had told all about his business and what he'd been doing since she'd last spent the summer in West Bend. But he could have shortened the narrative by ninety percent, she thought.

The closeness she'd once felt as they played tennis and hung out at the country club seemed to have disappeared. Instead, the night had seemed endless.

The phone rang.

Instantly Kerry forgot her fatigue. Calls in the middle of the night usually meant trouble. She flung off the covers and ran for the hall phone. She hoped there wasn't something wrong with her parents. Maybe they forgot the time change and were calling to—

''Hello?'' she said breathlessly.

''Did you have a nice dinner?''

''Jake?'' Sagging with relief, she slowly sank down to the carpet, leaning against the wall. ''Do you know it's almost midnight?''

''Yes, you just got home. Seems like a long time for dinner. How much do you eat?''

''How do you know I just got home? Are you spying on me?''

''Of course not. I saw Carl's car, that's all.''

''You just happened to be looking out the window?'' she asked skeptically.

''I heard the car and being a conscientious neighbor, I checked.''

''Umm, neighborhood watch in West Bend.''

''Have fun?''

''Yes I did,'' she said defiantly. Even if she had not, she would never admit it.

''I liked your dress. I don't think I've ever seen you in one before.''

Kerry smiled at the compliment. She hadn't thought he'd notice, not when he had given a good impression of being more interested in talking to Carl than to her. ''Of course you've seen me in a dress before. I wear them to church.''

''The last time was years ago, and as I recall, it was not soft and feminine, but tailored and rather intimidating.''

''That was a long time ago.'' She couldn't imagine anything or anyone intimidating Jake, especially not a woman. But she was surprised to be remembered.

"So your wardrobe is chock-full of frilly dresses? You surprise me, Kerry."

She opened her mouth to tell him she'd just bought the dress, then snapped it shut. Slowly an idea glimmered. Jake didn't know her. It had been years since she'd followed him around like a puppy. She'd grown up and moved away. That made her a stranger to him, for all their shared youth.

"I like feminine dresses," she said slowly. She was glad she'd read that passage in Megan's book. She'd felt deliciously feminine all evening.

"Oh, I'm not complaining, honey. Not a bit. You looked good in it."

Honey? She caught her breath. He'd never called her honey before.

"Change your mind about going out with me tomorrow?" he asked.

Make sure he thinks you are busy and making an extra effort to spend time with him, had been her great-grandmother's advice. But Kerry *wanted* to spend the day with Jake. She was taking careful care of herself to recover from burnout. And part of that was indulging herself in things she wanted. Sacrifices were fine in their place, but she'd sacrificed enough for now.

"I'll have to see," she hedged.

"About what?"

"I have other things to do."

"Like?"

"I'm not on the witness stand, Jake. Don't interrogate me."

He chuckled. "I'll back off if you say yes to tomorrow. We can go down by the river, then have dinner at the country club. There's dancing on the terrace, and they have a Sunday buffet that's well worth going for."

''Ummm. Okay, you've convinced me. If I can change my plans, I'll go.''

''It's about time you said yes. I'd hate to see you on a witness stand. You'd put everything back weeks.''

''Just because I had things to do—''

''Nothing as important as spending the afternoon with me.''

''Ha!'' She wrinkled her nose and stuck her tongue out at the phone. Still as arrogant as ever, she thought, warmed by the fact he hadn't changed as much as she might have thought.

''Get to bed. You've been up late two nights. I thought you were tired from New York.''

''What are you, my watchdog? I can stay up as late as I want. And just how do you know I was up late last night?''

''I saw your light when I went to bed. I imagined you all tucked up safely in bed. And I have to tell you I think your dress today radically changed my concept of you.''

''Oh?'' Was that good?

''I figured you as a no-nonsense kind of woman. One who wore jeans and tailored suits. And a cotton T-shirt to bed. Now I suspect there is an entirely different side to you, Kerry. What do you wear to bed, silk and satin? Lace and ruffles? Is your bed piled high with fancy pillows and frilly sheets?''

She glanced down at the serviceable cotton T-shirt she usually slept in. How long since she had bought feminine and frilly sleepwear? She remembered feeling so glamorous in the long diaphanous gowns she'd worn when she'd been a teen. Daydreams had filled her mind, and she'd spent hours finding just the perfect gown for her allowance.

''Kerry?''

"I think discussing my sleeping attire is a bit personal, don't you Jake? After all we hardly know each other," she stalled, wishing she had on some lacy confection that would have men drooling if they ever saw it. Wishing she had the kind of body that caused men to drool.

Sighing softly, she acknowledged wishing never got her anything. Look at her wishes for Jake. Her wishes for her job.

"Hardly know each other? How can you say that? You've plagued me for years, trailing after me everywhere I went. Have you forgotten your protestation of undying love?" he asked.

She closed her eyes in embarrassment. "It's totally unnecessary for you to remind me of my childish infatuation," she said slowly. "I was a kid, who had a foolish crush on you. Times change. I have to go now. Goodbye." Kerry hung up the phone and leaned her head against the wall. She would not remember that last awful scene when she'd told Jake she loved him, would always love him. He'd been mad as a bee-stung dog in those days, at her, at the world. He'd laughed harshly and told her to leave him the hell alone and take her stupid childish infatuation away. He had better things to do than put up with some goofy teenager who didn't know the meaning of the word, much less the emotion. And forever was a long time. She would forget him before she was twenty.

That had been eleven years ago. Kerry thought she'd forgotten how awful she'd felt, but at his words the old sensations flooded. She had been so hurt at his laughter, vowing eternal revenge. Instead, she'd grown up and moved on in her life. She didn't need him to remind her now.

The phone rang.

Glaring at it, she ignored it and rose. Going into the

bedroom, she switched off the light and climbed into bed. She'd read more of the journal tomorrow. Tonight she was going to sleep and forget all about Jake Mitchell and the attraction she'd once felt for him. Wasn't *practical* her new mantra? How practical would it be to continue to see him, to try out her grandmother's recipe? The man was a hopeless case and she'd do well to remember that. She didn't need any more grief. Finding a new job, deciding where to live, she had enough on her plate.

The silence that echoed in the house when the phone stopped ringing was a welcome relief. But it was a long time before Kerry slept.

"Dammit." Jake slammed down the receiver. He couldn't believe she hung up on him and then wouldn't answer the phone! Pacing to the window, he looked over to the house next door. The light in her room was out. He had half a mind to storm over there and pound on her door until she let him in. He had intended to tease her about her crush on him, not make her mad.

He sighed and rubbed the back of his neck. He shouldn't have brought it up. Especially since nothing since he'd seen her earlier this week indicated she felt the same anymore.

And that was part of the problem. If he were honest with himself, as he always tried to be, he'd admit he missed her devotion, her wide-eyed worship. Tomorrow he'd make sure she stuck to her promise to spend the afternoon with him. If she could arrange to see Carl after being in town only three days, she could damn well make time to see him!

At least she and Carl had not been long in saying goodnight. Though they were late enough if they had gone just for dinner. Had there been more? He didn't think

Kerry was the type to do more with some guy on a first date, but then what did he know? He hadn't seen her in years. And even then it had been brief glimpses as she came and went at the Porters' place. She was all grown up now, and a woman on her own. Eleven years had passed since she'd tried to kiss him, make him believe she loved him.

Was he still trying to hold on to that? She'd moved on. She dated other men, kissed them, maybe more.

His gut tightened at the thought of Kerry and Carl kissing. He remembered the taste of her when he'd kissed her in the yard. He didn't want another man touching her like that.

And why not?

Not liking the trend of his thoughts, Jake headed for the shower. Kerry was her own person. She could do what she wanted with her life. But tomorrow he'd make sure she spent the day with him! That would banish all images of her with Carl Penning.

And if she wanted kisses, Jake would see she got all she could handle!

''How did the date with Carl go?'' Sally asked as Kerry slipped into her car when she stopped by to pick Kerry up for church the next morning.

''Fine. We had fun. We might play some tennis next week.'' Kerry tried to put some enthusiasm in her voice. The evening had not been special by any means, but it had been pleasant enough. It sure beat sitting home by herself.

''Carl's always loved tennis. I remember you two were evenly matched at one time.''

''That was ages ago and I haven't played since I moved to New York. I'm sure I'm as rusty as can be.''

"Maybe it's like riding a bike, you never forget. I like that dress."

"Do you think it's all right for church? Not too casual?" Kerry asked.

The dress was cool and comfortable. The light blue top was elasticized, hugging her curves like a second skin. The bodice could have stayed in place without the thin straps over her shoulders. The cream colored skirt with scattered blue flowers moved with her as she walked, the fullness caressing her bare legs, soft cotton against silky skin. Sitting in the car, it covered her knees and pooled around her like a cloud.

"I think it looks lovely. I like the blue sandals with it."

"And I like the comfort. No panty hose, no tight waist. It's just what I wanted."

"So do you feel ultra-feminine now? What else did you read in Megan's journal last night?"

"I didn't read last night—I got home late. Carl took me to that ice cream parlor near the new mall for dessert, and we talked forever." Kerry left it at that. No sense in telling Sally about Jake's call. It wasn't important.

When Sally parked in the lot by the huge red brick First Baptist Church, Kerry looked around. She recognized many of the people standing in groups, chatting before the service began.

"There's Greg," Sally said quietly, reaching for her purse. "Oh, interesting, he's talking with Jake. It's been a while since Jake's come to church. I wonder why today?" Sally glanced speculatively at Kerry as she shut the car door.

Kerry's heart sped up, despite her efforts to appear cool and collected. Just what she needed, to run into Jake after hanging up on him last night. She should have mentioned it to Sally. If Jake said anything, her cousin would wonder instantly why she hadn't said something.

Reluctantly she followed Sally toward the two men, both dressed in suits. The sun glinted on Jake's hair, its rich darkness almost blue black beneath the hot rays. Next to Jake, Greg didn't look quite as big as he had at dinner the other night. Both men turned when Sally called out a greeting.

"Good morning, Kerry." Jake's voice was low, almost intimate when she joined the small group. His eyes danced in amusement. "Sleep well?"

"Hi Jake, Greg." Kerry ignored the question and tried to walk by.

Jake's hand shot out and grasped her arm, effectively stopping her. Slowly he drew her beside him.

"We still on for this afternoon?" he asked.

"What are you doing this afternoon?" Sally asked, looking charming in a yellow sundress with a white short sleeve jacket. Her eyes darted suspiciously between Jake and Kerry.

"We're going down to the river, then dinner at the country club." Kerry shrugged, trying to appear casual.

"Sounds like fun. You didn't mention that in the car." Sally turned to her cousin, her eyes narrowed slightly.

Kerry shrugged, conscious of Jake's touch. His fingers seemed to burn into her skin, the tingles rushing through her making it next to impossible to think, much less come up with a coherent reason to give her cousin. She pulled against his hold, but Jake only tightened his grip.

"Nothing's definite. I have to see if I can rearrange things," Kerry muttered.

"You said yes on the phone last night," Jake reminded her softly.

"After your last crack, I don't think—"

"We should be going in," Sally interrupted.

"Good idea." Jake slid his hand down Kerry's arm and clasped her fingers with his.

"I don't need you to hold my hand," she snapped, tugging free. Kerry resented his taking charge. She was aware of the covert glances given them, especially from some of the women who probably had tried to capture Jake's attention and failed.

Eleven years ago, seven, even five, Kerry would have been thrilled with the attention Jake paid. But now she knew it meant nothing. She would not let herself be caught up in dreams and schemes again. Life threw hard lessons, sometimes, but it was up to her to learn from them.

No more dreaming? A voice inside questioned. What about trying the ingredients to Megan's recipe for a happy marriage partner? Kerry quelled the voice. Trying one or two suggestions didn't mean she was scheming to capture Jake's undying love and devotion. It was merely a practice run for when she found a man with whom she wanted to build a future. If it worked with cynical Jake, it would work with the man of her dreams.

"I'll take Kerry home," Jake said to Sally at the end of the service. "Save you the trip."

"Thanks, I'd appreciate that."

Kerry frowned at Sally. What was she, unwanted freight? She could have driven herself to church this morning. Sally had volunteered to pick her up.

"Don't do anything I wouldn't do," Sally said gaily as she turned back to Greg.

"She's going to smother him, if she's not careful," Jake said as he turned Kerry toward his black car and started walking.

''She likes him,'' Kerry said in defense.

''And sometimes I think he likes her. But she comes on too strong. And we both know Sally has no staying power. She'll burn out soon and flit along to the next man.''

''Maybe this time it's for real,'' Kerry said just for the sake of arguing. She agreed with Jake, but had no intentions of telling him so.

''Yeah, and maybe pigs fly.'' Jake reached out to open the door for Kerry.

She slid into the car, and tried to muster some argument against Jake's allegations. She came up with none. Sally had a track record of falling in and out of love as often as some people changed their hairstyle.

Yet she couldn't let it alone. When he got into the car, she turned to him.

''You view her through cynical eyes. Sally's a wonderful woman, and will make someone a good wife.''

''How long do you think she would last the course? She can't even stay engaged for longer than six months.''

''Just because your mother left your father doesn't mean every woman walks out of a marriage.''

''Enough do.'' His tone cooled.

''I suppose you see a lot of that in your work.''

''No, I'm not into family law. But I have colleagues who discuss it.''

''Oh, and fathers don't leave?'' she asked.

''They do. Marriage as a whole is outdated and overrated.''

''What? I can't believe you said that! It's a wonderful institution. We need marriages to keep our society strong.''

He looked at her. ''If it's so great, why aren't you married?''

She closed her mouth and turned to look out the windshield. There was no way she would tell him how her foolish childish infatuation had influenced her. No man had ever measured up to her ideal since Jake. Wouldn't he roar with laughter if he knew?

"I'm busy getting a career started," she said after a moment.

"Then you plan to get hitched?" He started the car and pulled out on to the street, turning for home.

"Maybe. If I find the right man."

"And how do you *find* the right man?"

"Find isn't the word. Connect with, maybe." She frowned. It was a good question. She certainly had not connected with anyone in New York. Were her standards too high? Or had she just been spoiled by the man beside her?

"Fall in love." Sarcasm laced his tone.

"Cynic," she murmured.

"Idealist."

"I'd rather be idealistic than cynical."

"I prefer to think of myself as realistic," Jake said smoothly.

"Not every marriage ends in divorce. Look at my parents, or my aunt and uncle."

"Lucky. And it isn't over yet. There's still time."

"You're impossible."

He pulled into his driveway and turned off the engine. "I'll just be a few minutes. Are you going to change?"

"Do you think I need to?"

"You look fine just the way you are." One finger traced the soft skin on her shoulder.

Kerry shrugged away from his touch, a moment of panic threatening. She was out of her mind to think she could spend the afternoon with him and not find herself in deep trouble. His lightest touch about drove her crazy. And he'd mentioned dancing at the country club that night. Could she stand to be held in his arms, swaying her body with his to soft sultry music? Could she do that and not give away her heart?

"I'll be right back."

Trying to calm her nerves, she recalled the passages from Megan's journal. Had she attended the same church where Megan had flirted with Frederick? She'd have to ask her cousin, or wait for Aunt Peggy to get back. Had Megan practiced her ideas before Frederick, or was he the original test case? Kerry wondered if she ought to do that, practice before going in for the real thing. She could practice on Jake. She knew he would never seriously entertain the notion of marriage. She could try the different suggestions from the journal and see what worked and what didn't, then be ready to seriously attract her perfect mate when she was ready to settle down.

Speaking of which, she needed to get busy looking for another job. The three days' rest had already buoyed her spirits. The listlessness and lethargy were fading. In fact, she brimmed with ideas and energy. Unfortunately they all seemed centered around Jake.

Maybe she'd seriously consider looking for a position in Charlotte. It would be nice to be near Aunt Peggy and Sally. And while New York had been exciting, it was a long way from the only home she really loved. The apartments and houses she and her parents had shared were gone. They had even put their furnishings in storage before this last assignment. Uncertain of where they would go when it was complete, they didn't want the expense of a house that would be vacant for several months.

Jake came out of the house wearing the same white shirt he'd worn to church, but paired with chinos. A dark blazer was slung over one shoulder. He tossed it into the backseat when he opened his door and slid behind the wheel.

"I thought we'd stop at the Dairy Freeze for a burger and then head for the river. You haven't seen the new interpretive center, have you?"

"No, but Aunt Peggy wrote me about it. Has it changed things a lot?"

"No. It's upstream from the swimming area. Theoretically the natural wildlife finds a haven there. There are boardwalks lining both sides of the river with signs telling you what flora and fauna is nearby. We can always go swimming if you want."

"I didn't bring a suit."

"Guess that answers that. Ready?"

Kerry nodded. She would remember all she'd read in the journal and apply everything to today's outing. Practice as well as practical, two new watchwords.

Kerry enjoyed the afternoon. But she wasn't sure Jake did. Lunch had been quick, then they'd driven to the river. Half the families in town had the same idea. It was crowded. The boardwalk thundered with the sound of children running back and forth. The benches spaced every few hundred yards were occupied by the older visitors, and even the secluded areas were filled with teenagers laughing and listing to loud music.

Jake took Kerry's hand when they left the car, and wandered along the raised boardwalk. From time to time they had to walk single file because of others, but even then Jake kept firm contact, shifting his hold from her hand to her shoulders. Kerry gave up protesting and set out to enjoy the afternoon. Conversation was of necessity sporadic. But she didn't mind. She enjoyed seeing what the local town council had done to improve the riverfront area.

In the late afternoon Jake took her to the swimming beach. Young children in bright life jackets played in the shallows, while older boys and girls used the two ropes suspended from overhanging branches to swing wide and drop into the deeper part of the river. Parents lounged in chairs at the river's edge.

Instantly memories of long-ago summers surfaced. Kerry and Sally and their friends had spent many wonderful hours playing at the river. She wished she'd brought her suit to see if she could recapture some of the memories. Another day, maybe.

"We could have gone swimming," he said as they watched the children frolic in the lazily meandering water.

"Was it this crowded when we used to swim here?"

"Sometimes. Only we were the ones in the water, so it didn't seem to matter. We should have gone somewhere else today."

Let the man do the chasing—just don't run so fast he can't catch you.

Kerry leaned a bit closer to him and her hand drifted to his shoulder. She could feel the heat beneath his shirt. "I can't think why. I've enjoyed seeing all the changes, remembering back when I was a kid. I've had a great afternoon."

He tightened his hand and drew her even closer. "If there weren't a hundred people within eyesight, I'd take up where we left off the other afternoon."

She blinked, heat spreading throughout, washing up into her cheeks, moving swiftly all the way to her fingertips. Swallowing hard, Kerry held his gaze, slowly licking her lower lip.

Jake groaned. ''Are you doing that deliberately to provoke me? That sexy dress is driving me crazy with the way it fits like a second skin on top and then flares out to sway and swish as you walk. Quite a change from shorts and a T-shirt. Your hair begs for my fingers to test its softness.'' Even as he spoke he gently rubbed several strands.

Kerry caught her breath. The dark gleam in his eyes clearly announced his interest. Or was she reading him all wrong? How much was real, and how much wishful thinking after reading Megan's journal?

CHAPTER FOUR

Encourage a man to talk about his work and his future.

—Megan Madacy's journal, Spring 1923

THE AFTERNOON SPED BY and as soon as the sun began to sink, Jake drove them to the country club. Because West Bend was so small, there were few restaurants in town—the city of Charlotte was close enough when a couple wanted a night out. Most of the locals belonged to the country club, so it was always well patronized.

This night was no exception. It was crowded. The Sunday buffet proved to be a popular item. Kerry and Jake were seated at a table on the terrace, near the open area where dancing would commence later. The late afternoon sun was blocked from the terrace by the elegant brick building. Umbrellas still stood spread over tables, their usefulness diminished as evening approached.

The tennis courts were empty, but the high night lights that had been installed a few years ago offered die-hard enthusiasts a few more hours of play after the day ended. While no one was taking advantage this evening, the cooler hours after sunset made it a popular place.

"So, tell me what important plans did you finally change to come out with me today," Jake said after they had been seated and handed menus.

"Writing a resumé," Kerry said, reaching for a roll and then offering the basket to Jake. He stared at her, ignoring the bread.

"Writing a resumé? You almost gave up spending a day with me to write a resumé?"

Kerry looked at him innocently, almost laughing at his incredulity. "I do have to look for another job, you know. I don't have unlimited funds. The sooner I get started, the sooner I'll find something."

"I thought you might stay for the summer, or a good portion of it at least," Jake said, taking a roll from the basket and tearing it in two.

"I'm not a child any more. I have to work," she said reasonably, wondering if he wanted her to stay for the summer. Or was he merely being polite?

"You can always write your resumé when I'm at work, spend time with me when I'm home," he said.

She laughed softly. "You sound like a petulant little kid. I'll write it when I want. You're lucky I decided I could wait another day. Besides, nice as this is, we won't make a habit of it."

"I'm supposed to be impressed with my luck? We spent the morning with your cousin and Greg in church, the afternoon surrounded by half the town of West Bend and now the other half is here for dinner."

"Aren't you glad not to have that puppy-lovestruck girl dogging your every footstep?" she asked lightly, buttering a piece of warm roll. What had she read most recently in the diary? Something about asking about his work. That should be easy. Most men liked to impress women with their accomplishments.

"Instead of dogging my footsteps, she's doing her best to avoid me or annoy me," he grumbled, laying down the menu. "Decided what you want yet?"

Kerry looked up, her eyes bright with amusement. "Think I'm avoiding you?"

"You can't suggest you're the same girl who once thought she was in love with me?"

"No, of course not. But you took a risk asking me out, don't you think? What if I still had that crush?"

"No risk. Since you've arrived you've shown me you couldn't care less. It challenges a man, you know."

Megan had been right. Chalk one up for great-grandmothers!

"So are you now going to try to make me fall for you just to meet some challenge?" she asked sassily. And if he did? How would she feel about that? This had started as a lark, see if any of the advice from the diary actually worked. She didn't believe for an instant that Jake would really fall for her. Or that she wanted him to, now. She'd grown up. Both had moved beyond the stages of their lives when she'd known him before.

And she was still uncertain what she wanted to do next. Would she stay in North Carolina, or return to New York? What she ought to do was fly to Greece and spend some weeks with her parents and look for a new job in the fall.

"No, the last thing I want is some woman thinking she's falling in love with me. Or what she imagines is love. That's nothing but a trap for unwary men." Jake's tone took a hard edge.

"So why ask me out? Actually almost demand I go out with you?"

"For old times' sake?"

Kerry leveled him a look. "And?"

"And to get some questions answered. I haven't seen you in a long time. I wanted to discover what you're like now, Kerry. Maybe we could share a few fun dates together before you move on."

"Safe and practical," she murmured, oddly disappointed. Yet why should she feel disappointed? He proposed almost the exact terms she would have.

He nodded.

Murmuring her new watchword beneath her breath, she wryly shook her head. She didn't feel very practical sitting opposite Jake listening to him propose they date casually. Her heart had flipped at his words, now it pounded in her chest. Her hands grew damp and she put them in her lap. The familiar tingle resonated on her skin. For one moment she almost blurted out an acceptance. Then the words of her great-grandmother echoed in her mind.

It was one thing to practice her new guidelines with Jake, but she knew nothing would come of a relationship between them. He as much admitted it himself not two seconds ago. Did she still want to practice those long-ago words of wisdom?

"Thanks, I think, but I'll pass."

"Saving your time for Mr. Right?" he asked lightly.

"Just not interested. Oh, look, is that Mr. and Mrs. Gramlin?" Kerry indicated an elderly couple being shown to a table near theirs.

"Yes."

"Aunt Peggy wrote me last month about their anniversary celebration." She smiled triumphantly at Jake. "They have been married fifty years. See, there are marriages that last."

"So far."

Kerry laughed aloud. "You're so cynical. That must make you one of the best lawyers around. Tell me more about your practice."

Jake looked at her for a moment—assessment in his gaze. "What do you want to know?"

"Everything. How you like it, what gives you the

greatest pleasure, what you dislike about practicing law. What cases have been unusual. Do you have a partner?''

He hesitated a moment as if not sure he knew what she expected. Then slowly he began to speak.

Kerry became instantly fascinated. Jake had a flair for captivating her interest and holding it as he spoke of the difficulties of building a private practice, of the frustrations with all the rules and guidelines that seemed to protect the alleged criminals more than the actual victims.

He spoke of struggling alone for the first few years and then joining another firm in which he was now partner. Discussing the differences between a solo act and a team effort, his voice shimmered with enthusiasm. She took delight in his quiet confidence and pride in his successes.

The music began as they were eating dinner and by the time Kerry finished, several couples were circling the area on the terrace set aside for dancing. Time flew by as she listened to Jake quietly discuss some of his unusual cases.

''Are you bored yet?'' he asked.

''Never. It's fascinating! If I find some free time this week, I might stop in and watch you in action. You said you were in court every day, right?''

''Right. So you'd slip in like you did years ago?''

''I hope I'm a bit more adult now. I promise not to giggle.''

He nodded, watching her thoughtfully.

''You've let me talk on forever. Your turn.''

''Me?''

''Tell me about Kerry.''

Idly she traced the rim of her glass, her eyes watching her fingertip. What could she tell him?

''I think I should defer that question until later. I'm at

a crossroads now. What I defined myself as a month ago has all changed. Once I've decided what I want to do with my future, I'll probably change things again.'' She looked up, catching her breath at the understanding in his dark gaze. Flustered, she glanced around, watching the couples dancing to the soft music.

''It must have been hard to lose your job. Your aunt said you loved it.''

''It was hard. I don't want to talk about it now.'' She fixed her gaze on a couple and wished for a moment she felt as carefree as the woman appeared. Carefree and happy.

''Looks like fun,'' she said, sipping the last of her iced tea.

''If you want to wait for dessert, we could dance.''

''Sure.''

The song was slow, the lights dimmed, the air warm and sultry. Slowly Jake drew her close, encircling her with both arms, pulling her against the hard muscles of his chest. He linked his hands at the small of her back and started moving with the music. Kerry put her arms around his neck and rested her forehead against his cheek. The scent of his aftershave filled her, sexy and disturbing. She felt feminine and young and almost starry-eyed once again. How many times as a teenager had she fantasized about dancing with Jake, about his arms around her, her body pressed against his?

Now that those long-ago dreams had become reality, it was too late. She knew he was not the man for her. It was past time to put away childish wishes and focus on her future. Maybe Jake had the right idea, spend some time together until she moved on. Knowing she could not fall for him again would safeguard her heart.

And there were still more of Megan's ingredients to

test. Kerry sighed softly and tried to ignore the clamoring to snuggle closer, tried to ignore the tingling sensations that danced across her skin at Jake's touch.

Slowly they swayed, not talking, simply enjoying the melody and the evening. The song ended and another began. Jake didn't miss a beat. They drifted around the dance floor as if they'd been partners forever. Kerry knew she'd never forget this night. A few magical hours out of time. She felt a bit sad. She would have given anything to have him dance with her like this eleven years ago. Now, they were two strangers sharing an evening.

When the small combo took a break, Kerry excused herself to visit the rest room. While she drew a comb through her hair, she studied herself in the mirror. Her eyes were bright and sparkling with hidden emotion, the flush on her cheeks did not come entirely from being in the sun that afternoon. The dress was perfect. All in all, not a bad turnout. And one Jake seemed to appreciate. Was it the novelty of having her not fawning over him that made him more interested? The feminine dress?

Five minutes later she rejoined Jake.

"Dessert?" he asked.

"No, just coffee. It's a beautiful night, isn't it."

"A bit warm."

"Umm." She nodded and looked around the terrace. Waving at a friend, she noticed the area was as crowded as ever. The buffet wasn't the only attraction. It seemed the people from West Bend liked to dance as well.

When the music resumed, Jake rose. "Dance?"

"Maybe another one or two. I need to get home before too long," Kerry said.

"Right, you need to get to sleep if you're going to be writing a resumé tomorrow."

"Don't you have to go to work?"

"Yes, but I can get by on a few hours less sleep one night."

"Lucky you. Even with court tomorrow?"

"I'll manage. If you do come into Charlotte one day, I'll take you to lunch."

"Umm, I'll see," she murmured.

Once on the dance floor, Kerry gave way to impulse and snuggled closer. It was probably a once-in-a-lifetime chance. Not wanting to miss a second of it, she could feel her heart pounding and hoped Jake did not. If nothing else, she wanted to portray a cool sophisticated woman.

Boldly, she threaded her fingers through the thick hair on the back of his head. Jake pulled her even closer, until she felt the hard muscles of his thighs. Her skirt caught and released against his pants as they swayed and moved to the music.

"It's hot," Jake murmured in the crush of the crowd. The breeze from earlier had died down. Even on the patio, the night air felt sultry and warm. She could smell the scent of jasmine.

Matching the tempo of the melody, she gave herself up to move with the music. When Jake's hand drifted up and down across her back, she almost melted against him.

For a second she let herself consider whether she thought she could entice the man. If Megan's recipe really worked, could she make Jake fall in love with her?

No, his shell was too hard. His defenses firmly in place. The most she could expect was some indication that her great-grandmother's advice had some merit. Practice made perfect. Once she was assured of her direction, she'd look for a man she could love, and that would love her in return.

She wanted to share her life with someone. Make a

family, set down roots and start traditions. She'd had her fling in the big city, had her shot at a career. No reason she couldn't scale back a bit to make room in her life for that family.

Jake moved his hand across Kerry's back, surprised at the physical awareness that flared with the woman in his arms. For a moment he almost forgot this was the pest of his younger years. The unexpected desire that erupted surprised him. Normally immune to women, he wondered why he felt differently about Kerry.

She had spent several minutes telling him she didn't plan to remain in West Bend forever, didn't know what she was going to do in the future. She'd probably return to New York and he'd not see her again for another few years. But while she was here, he could spend some time with her. Learn what made her tick these days. Find out just why she fascinated him.

From the first moment he'd seen her pulling into the Porters' driveway, he'd been interested. It had been a long time, and maybe he had missed her adoration. He could feel her skirt encircle his trousers, fall free as they turned and swayed. He was growing more and more intrigued with this woman. She remained a mystery, refusing to talk much about herself and instead asking him what he was doing. He wanted to know her better—intimately. His head snapped up. It was time to call a halt to thoughts like that. His future was mapped out and it did not include getting involved with anyone—especially Kerry.

When the music ended, Jake dropped his arms and guided her from the dance floor. "Get your purse, we're leaving."

"So soon?" Kerry's tone mocked. Narrowing his eyes,

he looked at her. Not for an instant did he believe that innocent expression.

"What game are you playing now, Kerry?"

"No game. If you want to leave, we'll leave." She made a big production of taking another sip of her water, of reaching for her purse. He glanced at her long bare legs. Did they go on forever? That sassy skirt played havoc with his senses when she walked. It swished and swayed around her, displaying, concealing. Driving him up the wall. Her skin had been velvet soft beneath his fingers. He liked touching her. Wanted to—

"I'll get your purse." He reached around her and snatched it up from the floor, handing it to her. If he didn't get her out of there soon, he wouldn't be responsible for his own actions. Or reactions. And he didn't like the feeling. He'd been in charge of his own hormones for a long time now. What was going on?

Kerry remained silent on the ride home, wondering why Jake had cut the evening short. They had been close tonight, she knew it. Closer than ever in their lives. Talking like two friends, rather than adversaries. Yet he'd slammed that door closed and was now the silent distant man she remembered. Had she done something to make him think she was chasing him? Thinking back, Kerry remembered nothing.

Sighing gently at the vagaries of the male species, she relaxed in her seat. At least there was no heartache attached to this. She'd bid him good-night and that would be the end. Unless Jake changed his attitude, she doubted she'd go out with him again. He was too unpredictable. Maybe she could practice her newfound advice on someone else. Carl had invited her out again. And Peter Jordan.

Jake pulled into his driveway and stopped the engine.

"I'll walk you over," he said.

"No need. I can see myself home, it's just next door."

"I took you out, I'll walk you home," he said grimly.

Kerry looked at him in the dark, wishing he'd left the lights on. Even the dim glow from the dashboard would have helped gauge his expression, his mood. "We are just neighbors who went out for dinner. No big deal. I can dash across the grass and be home in a couple of seconds."

The overhead light seemed bright when he thrust open his door. "I'll walk over with you." It was the kind of voice no one argued with.

Kerry shrugged. A few more minutes and the evening would be finished. She had mixed emotions about the success of her venture. But Jake was not an ordinary man. She shouldn't dismiss Megan's advice just because it didn't work with him.

When he opened her door, she slid out, and quickly moved toward her aunt's house. Jake matched her step for step until they reached the porch. She withdrew her keys and he took them from her to unlock the big door. Before handing them back, he closed his fist around the keys, reaching out to cup her face with his other hand.

"A kiss good-night?" he asked softly.

"I hardly think this constitutes a date, Jake. Just neighbors going out for dinner," she said primly. Her heart raced. Would he really kiss her? Her mind, mouth, entire body remembered the kiss in the yard. She had no lemonade tonight, nothing to stop him if he really wanted to kiss her. Nothing to stop him and every inch of her yearning for that kiss.

"Then a neighborly kiss," he said, lowering his head and covering her mouth with his.

Kerry knew she was in trouble the moment he touched

her. Senses spinning out of control, she responded. It was unlike the kiss she'd attempted so many summers ago. Jake was in charge, deepening the kiss, thrilling her to her toes. She encircled his neck with her arms when his came around her. Vaguely in the back of her mind she registered the dropping of her keys as his hands pressed against her back, holding her tightly against that strong, masculine body.

Then gradually sanity surfaced. Kerry pushed against his shoulders. When he released her, she spun around and entered the dark house. Closing the door, she leaned against it, trying to get her breathing under control. She'd spent the entire day telling herself not to get involved with Jake, to try the different steps Megan had listed, but keep her heart whole. One kiss threatened her entire equilibrium.

The knock sounded impatient.

"What?" she asked, knowing it was Jake. She couldn't face him. She wanted to fly up to her room, climb into bed and pull the covers over her head. Maybe she should return to New York tomorrow, before she had a chance to see him. Before wild impetuous dreams took root.

"Your keys."

Flinging open the door, she held out her hand. Jake dropped them in, peering in as if trying to see her in the dark.

"You okay?"

"Of course. Thank you for dinner. Goodbye." Kerry shut the door carefully, though she longed to slam it. Turning, she almost ran to her room. She snatched up her sleep shirt and headed for the bathroom. In only moments she was ready for bed. Now if she could only sleep. Her heart raced, her mouth still felt the press of Jake's. And her thoughts spun round and round.

Opening her window wider for any hint of air that stirred, she stared at Jake's house. There were lights on downstairs. He was still up. Resentfully she wondered if he even gave a second thought to that devastating kiss. He about turned her world topsy-turvy, and probably didn't even feel a speck of anything. Just another casual date to him. Probably satisfied whatever curiosity he had. No need to invite her out a second time. She'd just be another in a long line of women he took out once and never called again.

She turned away, and tried to forget.

Jake took a sip of the whisky and waited while it burned down to his stomach. Normally not a drinking man, tonight had him wound tighter than a watch spring. It was Kerry's fault. She'd changed—and he didn't like the unsettled feelings that her change wrought. He prided himself on his ability to read witnesses, to anticipate the moves of the prosecution, and to gauge the mood of a jury. But with Kerry, he was at a total loss.

Or was it just ego that couldn't let go of the idea she was playing some kind of game? That she still wanted him and was trying a new tactic to get his attention. For years she'd thrown herself at him. It seemed out of character for her to virtually ignore him since she'd arrived.

Yet that kiss proved she wasn't indifferent to him. He looked out the window at her place. It was dark except for her bedroom. She was still awake. Remembering their kiss? He took another swallow. She'd tasted as sweet as hot honey. Her body had fit against his perfectly, as if they had been created for each other. Her scent had filled him, feeding the burning desire to a hot flame. He wanted her. And hadn't a clue what he was going to do about that.

He shook his head and poured another inch of amber liquid into his glass. No one person was created especially for another. And those fool enough to delude themselves that they had some special bond soon discovered the truth in an ugly fight that left both parties bitter and resentful.

His father had made sure both his sons learned that lesson well.

But there was something about Kerry that had Jake intrigued. Trying to reconstruct the day, he realized he'd dominated the conversation. She'd asked questions about his work, about his life in West Bend, and given very little away about herself. Damn, he wanted to know more about what she'd been doing, how she liked her job, the men she had dated. About her plans for the future.

Turning, he dialed the familiar number. The phone rang several times before she answered.

"Kerry, it's me, Jake."

"Yes?" Her wary tone made him smile.

"I didn't get you out of bed, did I?"

"Did you call just to ask dumb questions?" she replied with some asperity. "I have gone to bed, but I wasn't asleep yet. Do not call back in ten minutes just to ask if I had fallen asleep."

"Don't hang up. I wanted to talk."

"We talked all day."

"I did. You are a very good listener. But I realize I learned very little about you, what you've been doing for the last few years. How you liked New York, what you did in your job, who you've been seeing."

The silence stretched out for several moments. She

cleared her throat. A sign of nervousness, Jake thought. Interesting. Why would Kerry be nervous?

"It's late, Jake. I want to go to bed. Couldn't we have this conversation another time?"

"You name when." He'd pin her down before hanging up.

"I don't know, I'll call you."

"Not good enough, Kerry. We make a date now."

"A date?" The wary tone in her voice startled him. Didn't she want to see him again?

"A date. Lunch Tuesday," he said. He was not going to be put off by some vague promise. She could commit and he'd hold her to it.

"Tuesday's not good. I'm busy," she said quickly, almost too quickly.

"Thursday, then." Jake refused to get into a discussion of what constituted busy. If she said she was writing her resumé again, he'd throw the phone against the wall and storm over to talk to her tonight.

"Okay, lunch Thursday."

"Come to my office and I'll give you the nickel tour."

"Fine. Good night." She hung up.

Slowly Jake replaced the receiver, wondering what was going on in Kerry's mind. Maybe by Thursday, he'd find out.

Thursday lunch, she thought, climbing back into bed. She should have made an excuse. That kiss showed her more than anything she was in danger of falling under his spell again if she weren't extremely careful. And she knew nothing lay in that direction but heartache.

Reaching for the old diary, Kerry flipped through to the pages she'd skimmed that morning.

Mama said I should make sure I have plenty of questions to ask about his work, and the other areas of his life. Men enjoy talking about themselves, and by doing so give us a good idea of what it would be like to be paired with them forever. If he bores me on a date, he would certainly bore me throughout a marriage. I can't imagine Frederick boring me ever. Just the sound of his voice seems to fill me with a exuberant happiness that I have never experienced before.

Kerry closed her eyes, remembering Jake's voice. It was as smooth as Tennessee whisky and as intoxicating. His inflection carried a touch of Southern accent, but the deep richness was uniquely his own. Megan had loved Frederick's voice, Kerry thought she loved Jake's. He could probably read her the *Law Review* and she'd find it fascinating because he was reading it. What would it be like to hear that voice beside her in the dark? To reach out and touch him in the night and know he was near?

And if today was any indication, Jake filled her with an exuberant happiness.

Breathless, she placed the journal on the table and flicked off the light. The darkness offered a safe haven for dreams. And Kerry knew she'd dream about Jake. What she needed to do was forget the impossible and concentrate on making plans for her future.

But for a few moments, she weakly gave into the daydreams of a shared life with the man next door. Imagining the kisses they'd share, the midnight hours they would fill with love and laughter. Time enough to be practical in the morning!

CHAPTER FIVE

Do the unexpected. Don't let a man become complacent. Keep him guessing.

—Megan Madacy's journal, Spring 1923

KERRY AWOKE EARLY the next morning and for the first time in ages began to feel more like her usual self. Her energy level was approaching normal. Coming to North Carolina had been the best thing for what ailed her, she thought whimsically as she lay in bed and listened to the birds chirping and trilling. It would probably be hot again today, but she didn't care. Her dresses were cool and comfortable. And she'd done all the yard work she needed to do for a few days.

Donning one of the new sundresses, Kerry lightly applied makeup and brushed her hair. She made her bed, darting a quick glance at the house next door. All was silent. Jake's car was gone. He had to work today and had obviously already left for Charlotte.

The memory of his kiss jumped into her mind and Kerry took a deep breath, trying to calm her instantly-ragged nerves. It was too late for regrets and might-have-beens. She knew that. This was simply an interlude in her life. Once she decided what to do next, she could throw all her energies into that and forget the sexy neighbor who had one time filled her dreams.

Today, however, she had nothing pressing and planned to take one step at a time.

Fixing a light breakfast, she read the local paper, jotted

notes of things she wanted to be sure to include in her resumé, and savored the delicious hazelnut coffee her aunt loved so much. If she had still been in New York, by this hour she would have already attended two meetings, placed a dozen phone calls and be scrambling to get everything accomplished in a hectic day. For a moment she remembered. It had been exhilarating, exciting. But there was no urgency to her days now.

Kerry took her second cup of coffee, and the old journal, and went to sit on one of the wicker rockers on the front porch. Across the street the Bandeleys were leaving together. She waved. They had lived there since long before she started making her annual summer visits. Friends of her aunt and uncle's, they had had no children. Idly Kerry wondered if she was destined to remain single, or would she one day find a man to whom she'd be able to apply Great-grandma Megan's ingredients. Would they be blessed with children? The lack hadn't been detrimental to the Bandeley's marriage. They still appeared very much in love.

Another example she could hold up for Jake. She smiled wickedly. He didn't seem to like her models of marital bliss.

In fact, when she thought about it, his parents were the only ones in the neighborhood who had split. In this case, his family was the anomaly, not the rule. Had he ever thought of that, she wondered.

Sipping the delicious coffee, she turned to Megan's journal.

Aunt Dottie came to tea today. She asked me how I was faring and I told her about Frederick. She laughed and exchanged glances with Mama, then told me to always remember to keep a man guessing. To keep a mystical aura that will have him wondering what I'm thinking. Do the unexpected, she told me. Don't let a man become complacent. Keep him guessing. Try something outrageous and see how he takes it. Life is long: if your husband can't be open to new ideas, you'll be unhappy.

Mama laughed and nodded. Sage advice, she said. I use it with your father.

Turning eighteen is a wondrous time, at last the other women consider me an adult and are sharing their worldly wisdom. Tonight, I'll try that with Frederick. He is coming to escort me to the church social. What can I do that he would find unexpected?

A few minutes later Kerry gazed across the lawn, a smile on her face. Megan was a gem. She wished she could have known her. For an idle moment she wondered what she could do that Jake would find unexpected. Maybe ignoring him was enough. That was certainly unexpected given her past infatuation. Though she thought Megan would consider that remained as a hard-to-get ingredient. Was there truly any correlation between her behavior and the fact Jake seemed more interested this visit than ever before? Or was it just coincidence?

Time would prove it, one way or the other. And time was something she had in abundance. The few days she'd spent in West Bend had already begun to heal. She didn't miss her job as much as she thought she would. She did miss some of her fellow workers, but most of them had been let go as well and were either already working for another firm, or still searching for a new position.

Which was what she should be doing. First, however, she had to decide where to look. New York was exciting, energizing, dynamic. But a bit lonely—even with good friends. Here she had family and longtime friends. Charlotte was a fast-growing metropolitan area with jobs that would offer the same kind of challenge as the one she'd loved so much. And if she were closer to home, wouldn't that be an added fillip?

Her decision made, Kerry spent the rest of the morning working on her resumé. In the afternoon she went to the country club to swim and lie in the sun. Time enough to be ambitious when she was fully recovered from burnout. This was a well-earned vacation and she planned to take full advantage of every moment.

Whiling away the afternoon let her spin ways she could appear totally unexpected to Jake Mitchell. What would surprise that jaded cynic? Nothing obvious or trite. She needed to come up with something totally different from his usual routine. Remaining a mystery wouldn't work. He knew too much about her. Her aunt, she was sure, kept him apprised of major events. Her parents had visited a couple of years ago and mentioned they'd talked to Jake.

No, mysterious wouldn't work. But doing the unexpected might. But what?

Just before she slipped into a light nap, the perfect escapade occurred to her. Smiling, she knew it would surprise him as nothing had in ages. If she could only pull it off!

Kerry fixed a light meal for supper, eating it before the television. She'd spent a little too much time in the sun and her glowing skin was tender to the touch. By tomorrow her skin would begin to tan, but tonight she felt like a lobster. Considering an early evening, she surfed through the different channels on the TV. Nothing caught her attention, held her interest. Maybe she should read more of Megan's journal. It was so much fun. But she hated to read straight through because then she'd be finished. Even though her curiosity hummed, she liked savoring each section. Maybe one more example wouldn't hurt. Washing her dishes, she retrieved the journal and sat in one of the wicker rockers.

The evening breeze cooled the air, carrying with it the soft fragrance of roses and star jasmine. The scents were a tangible reminder she was truly home. Until she smelled it, she hadn't realized how much she'd missed it in New York.

Jake's car was not in the driveway. Was he working late? Or did he have a hot date tonight? Kerry frowned, not liking the idea. Not that she expected him to date her, but for some reason he seemed a loner. Yet she knew he had not been sitting around for years while she moved on in life. Even though Selena had turned him off relationships, he was a virile, healthy male, not likely to remain at home alone.

Thinking about Jake dating sophisticated, sexy women made Kerry restless. She fixed a glass of iced tea and sipped it. Watching his driveway was not the way she wanted to spend her evening, she thought in disgust when she realized what she was doing. Going inside, she firmly shut the door. She had better things to do than watch for her next-door neighbor. What he did with his evenings didn't affect her!

Yet she couldn't help but notice the time when she heard his car two hours later. It was after nine. Too early to end a date. Maybe he had just worked late. Her restlessness faded.

Jake pulled into his driveway and stopped, glad to be home. He was bone weary. Court cases always took a lot of energy and today's session had not gone well. Even after working in this profession for years, it amazed him that clients would lie. Why couldn't they understand their best interests were always served when they told their attorney the truth in everything? He hated to be blind-sided in court as he had been today.

As a result, instead of leaving the office at a reasonable hour, he'd had to call in the investigating team, and together they'd worked to find a solution to the unexpected turn of events. Normally he didn't mind working late. But tonight he'd wanted to get home earlier.

He climbed out of the car and glanced at the house next door. The downstairs lights were on. Kerry was still up. For a split second he hesitated. What he'd really like to do was walk over there and see her. Find out what she'd done that day, and maybe share a bit of his own frustrations.

Heading for his front door, he shook off the urge. Give that woman an inch and she'd take a mile. He dare not show any interest lest she take it for more than he intended and resume her schoolgirl crush. Or would she? The last few days had been a totally new experience with Kerry. All evidence indicated she was no longer interested in any kind of relationship.

Perversely, he wished she wanted to spend time with him. Opening the door, he noticed how empty the house seemed, how quiet. Maybe he'd see if she'd like to come keep him company while he ate. It would be worth having someone around to take his mind off the day's events. A man could spend too much time alone.

He reached for the phone.

When she answered, Jake was startled at the jolt of awareness that crashed through him. Her voice was feminine and sweet, without the familiar Southern drawl so many women he knew had. She had very little accent from any location—an obvious result of her moving so often as a child. Had she liked moving all the time? Funny, he'd never asked her that.

"Kerry, it's Jake."

"What's up?"

"What are you doing?"

"Getting ready for bed, why?"

Instantly the image of her in a frilly sexy gown flashed before his eyes. Her arms would be bare, the neckline scooped to show her creamy shoulders and the top swells of her breasts. It would drift around her legs like her dress had the other night, soft and feminine and utterly alluring.

Alluring? Kerry? He was losing it.

"Isn't it a bit early?" He loosened his tie, shrugged off his suit jacket and tossed on the back of the sofa.

"I'm on vacation, I can do what I want, when I want!"

"Still, it's early. Come over."

The silence lasted longer than he expected.

"Come over?"

"I just got home and could use some company."

"Take it from an expert, Jake, working all hours doesn't pay off. I used to do that, but it's more important to have outside activities. Something to fall back on if something happens."

He smiled. Was she lecturing him?

"What's going to happen?"

"I don't know, you could lose your job."

"I'm a partner in the firm, I won't lose my job. There is always a need for lawyers."

"I guess."

He leaned against the wall, staring through the window toward her house. Where was she? Was she already dressed for bed?

"What did you do today?" he asked. If she wasn't

coming over, he'd talk on the phone. He wasn't ready to hang up and face the rest of the evening alone.

"Did you call me up just to interrogate me about my day?"

"I called you to invite you over. You're the one getting ready for bed. Wearing that slinky nightie?"

Her voice dropped to a deep, sultry drawl, "Jake, honey, I can't believe you'd ask me what I'm wearing. Why, what if I told you I had nothing on at all? It's been hot all day and I'm so uncomfortable, I just couldn't bear the thought of covering myself with hot clothes. I like the feel of the cool air against my bare skin. I like the freedom of movement without the restrictions of cloth."

Stunned, he could envision that with no trouble. Except for the trouble he had breathing—the trouble he had even thinking.

Her soft laughter floated across the phone wire. "Gotcha," she said softly and hung up.

Torn between frustration and amusement, Jake hung up. Kerry surprised him. He'd never expected anything like that from her. He had to admit he'd thought she'd jump at the chance to come over. Though he should have known better. Nothing she'd done since she'd been back had been in character as he remembered. It wasn't a game; she'd changed since the last time he'd seen her. Now he was curious—what other aspects had she kept hidden from him all these years? He had half a mind to go over there and demand she open the door, just to verify she was teasing—that she actually had clothes on.

He punched in the number again.

"Hello?"

"Kerry, you could get in a lot of trouble leading people on."

She laughed. The sound warmed him to his toes. What was there about her that caught his attention this visit?

"Didn't expect that, huh?"

"Not at all. Do you lie in bed at night and think up things like that?"

"Almost—today I thought it up by the pool."

"Any more tricks up your sleeve?"

"Why, Jake, didn't you hear me? I'm not wearing sleeves, I'm—"

"You're playing with fire. If you keep that up I'll have to come over to check to see exactly what you are wearing. Or you can come over here."

"Thank you for the invitation, but I really am getting ready to go to bed soon. Why are you so late coming home?"

"Had some work to catch up on tonight and no, it couldn't wait. I'm due in court tomorrow at nine and had to get all the facts straight before then. Did you go to bed this early in New York?"

"Of course not. But maybe if I had I wouldn't be so tired now."

"Tell me something about living in the Big Apple."

"Why?"

"You cross-examined me to the *n*th degree at dinner last night, don't you think turnabout is fair play?"

"I'd hardly call it cross-examining you. I just asked a couple of questions."

"And now I'm asking some. Tell me about New York."

She hesitated at first, but soon began to offer brief sketches of her apartment, her job and a few friends. She was strangely quiet on the topic of boyfriends. And for some reason, Jake didn't want to ask. Another time she could regale him with her romantic conquests. Tonight, he liked listening to her, trying to understand the hectic and exciting lifestyle she'd enjoyed for the last few years. A world of difference from West Bend. But not too distant from Charlotte's pace.

When he recognized some of the product brands she'd worked with at the marketing firm, he was startled. He hadn't realized her job had been so important—so national in scope. Obviously he needed to reassess his thinking.

"So there you have it in a nutshell. I saw the Bandeleys today."

He'd been coasting, listening to her talk, and trying to remember all the nuances of her expression as he imagined her face while she entertained him on the phone. "What do they have to do with New York?"

"Nothing, I'm changing the subject. They are a happy couple, wouldn't you say?"

"As far as I know."

"Umm. Another happily married couple. And they're not young. They seemed old when I first came to visit."

"The point to this being?"

"No point, just another couple who have had a long happy marriage. You should consider that, counselor. Good night, Jake. I'm really going to bed now."

He bid her good-night and hung up, surprised to see it was almost eleven. Debating whether to eat anything or just go to bed himself, he wondered why she'd brought up the neighbors. Did she still think of him in a romantic manner? She had done nothing overt this visit. No throwing herself at him, no flirting. Unless her kisses could count. Or rather her responses to his kisses. Yet she kept bringing up happily married couples. What was her game? The old defenses rose.

If she thought to convince him to change his mind, to

give marriage a try—and with her—she didn't know him at all. He'd made up his mind years ago and nothing had happened in the intervening years to change it. Nothing would.

Kerry turned off the lights and opened her window wide. The breeze still blew from the west, cooling her room, feeling soft and balmy against her skin. She grinned, remembering her daring conversation with Jake. Had that caught him by surprise? She wished she could have seen his face. "Is that what you meant, Megan?" she asked softly into the night. One incident, however, wouldn't be enough. She needed to keep him off guard.

And her idea from that afternoon still seemed strong. She'd try to surprise the man again. And maybe again.

She was having fun, she realized. Feeling young and carefree, she could do whatever she wanted—as long as she knew it was just for fun. There was no permanent future with Jake, but to tease him and practice her new feminine wiles was proving to be quite a lark. Who knew how far she could take this? She couldn't wait to see.

Once in bed, she reached for the journal. What had Great-grandma Megan come up with to keep Frederick on his toes?

Kerry planned her unexpected event with the precision of a general going into a major battle. Working for years as a project supervisor and then a manager stood her in good stead. While she tried to anticipate all the different contingencies, she didn't worry about it. What happened happened. She hoped she could pull it off, it would be fun and show Jake Mitchell not to take her or any woman for granted in the future. But if it didn't work, she'd shrug and go on.

But she hoped it did.

Thursday morning she dressed in another of her new dresses. This one was of soft yellow, with small daisies scattered throughout the material. The bodice clung to her figure, the thin straps giving the illusion of holding up the dress. Her slight case of sunburn had mellowed into a golden tan. Brushing her sun-streaked hair until it gleamed, she was pleased that the new cut required little care. Curls danced against her head as she hurried downstairs. The long scarf she'd draped around her neck trailed behind her.

Operation Unexpected was about to begin.

She had not spoken with Jake since their phone conversation of the other evening. Last night she had taken the phone off the hook. Playing hard-to-get required a lot of forward planning. Megan had not had it that bad. Of course people moved more slowly in those days. Kerry couldn't help but wonder if Jake had tried calling last night. And if so, what had he thought when the line was continually busy?

She drove to Charlotte and found a parking place close to Jake's office building. A sign, she thought, pleased with the proximity. Gathering her purse, Kerry checked one last time that everything was in place. Taking a deep breath, she headed inside the high-rise building.

Studying the other women as she waited in the busy lobby for the elevator, she was pleased to note none looked as carefree and adventuresome as she felt. Their somber suits or elegant business attire seemed a world away from what she planned for today. Yet just a few short weeks ago she would have matched their attire and scoffed at anyone dressed as casually as she was. Covert glances didn't bother her at all. Excitement bubbled up inside. She couldn't wait to see Jake's reaction. Couldn't wait to see him.

The law firm occupied the entire eighth floor. The elevator opened directly into the reception area.

The young receptionist smiled a friendly greeting. Kerry told her she was to meet Jake and the woman had obviously been briefed because she nodded immediately.

"He's expecting you, but he's been held up in court. They should be recessing soon."

"Not a problem. Actually, I came early for a reason. I need your help." Leaning closer, glancing around to make sure no one was within hearing distance, she shared her plans with the young woman. Delighted to hear the laughter that greeted her, Kerry nodded, "So I can count on your help?"

"Absolutely! I wouldn't miss this for anything. Though I have to warn you, he will likely explode. Most of the partners have an inflated sense of their own worth."

Kerry waved a hand dismissingly. "I can handle Jake Mitchell. We've known each other for years."

Pointing out his office, the receptionist smiled broadly. "Good luck. I might just try something like this myself—if it works."

Kerry headed for Jake's office, hoping it did work. It was as unexpected as she could come up with on short notice. Wondering what she could devise given enough time, Kerry mentally rehearsed every step in her plan.

Keeping an eye on the elevator from the slightly ajar door, she waited impatiently. Now that she was here, she wanted Jake to show up. Did this delay in court mean his lunch time would be shortened? Should she change her plans? Delay them for a better day?

The elevator door slid open and Jake and two others

stepped out. He spoke to them and then turned to head for his office, barely acknowledging the receptionist's greeting. Kerry gave thanks he didn't seem to notice the brimming amusement in the woman's eyes.

Moving behind the door, Kerry waited, slowly pulling away her scarf.

Jake entered.

Kerry threw the scarf around his eyes, and fastened it snugly.

''What the hell?'' His hands immediately yanked on the scarf.

''Hold it, mister,'' she said trying to disguise her voice. Afraid the laughter that threatened would give it all away, she took a deep breath. ''This is an official kidnapping.''

He hesitated, then dropped his hands and turned around, making no further attempt to remove the covering from his face.

''Official kidnapping?''

''Uh-huh. Don't make me get rough.'' Kerry tried to keep her voice low, wondering if Jake was fooled for a single second. He was so tall, and looked good enough to eat in his lightweight suit and the pristine white shirt with the silver-and-red tie.

Slowly one side of his mouth raised in a half smile. ''Rough? I'm fascinated.''

''Good.'' She reached around him to tighten the scarf so it wouldn't slip. When she pressed against him, his arms came around and before she could move he held her pinned tightly against his chest.

''This is an interesting development,'' he murmured softly.

''Unexpected would you say?'' she asked, conscious of his strength, the long hard body held against hers.

"I've never been kidnapped before, officially or unofficially," he murmured.

"There's always a first time," she replied, knowing she should push away but captivated by the sensations that filled her, that set every nerve ending tingling.

Then to Kerry's surprise, he kissed her.

"Is that the ransom?" he asked a moment later.

She could scarcely think, much less make sense of his statement.

"What?"

"Is my release dependent upon a kiss?"

"No. What time do you have to be back in court?"

"At two."

She pushed against him and stepped back as soon as he released her. Slapping his hands when he raised them to remove the scarf, she took one in hers, startled when he laced his fingers through hers.

"Behave and you'll be back in plenty of time," she said, remembering at the last moment to disguise her voice.

"And if not?" Amusement danced in his tone.

"Just come quietly." She opened the door and led him out. The receptionist covered her mouth to muffle her laughter as her eyes watched Kerry lead Jake to the elevator. Kerry looked around. There were not many people around, but those that were stopped and watched them, wide smiles on their faces.

Fortunately there were only two businessmen in the elevator when they got on. Both looked stunned at the tall man wearing a suit blindfolded by a yellow scarf. One studied Kerry, looking almost wistful. But no one said a word when she raised her finger to her lips. Kerry gripped Jake's hand tightly. She hoped he wouldn't be mad. If he were, he could have removed the scarf by now. Maybe he would go along with this.

"Come on," she urged when the reached the ground floor. Trying to avoid all the stares and laughter, Kerry led her captive through the bustling crowd in the lobby and out to the sidewalk. Thank goodness she had been able to park close by. The few moments it took to get Jake into the car seemed endless. Flushed with embarrassment and triumph, she ran to the driver's side. In seconds they were away.

"Is it in order for me to inquire where we are going?" he asked relaxing in the seat.

"You'll see."

"Then at some point I do get to remove the scarf?"

"I'll do that."

"You forgot to disguise your voice," he commented dryly.

"Did you know it was me?"

"From the first."

Well, at least he wasn't kissing just anyone. If he'd known it was her, he'd meant to kiss her. Kerry licked her lips, tasting Jake again. Excitement still bubbled.

"How?"

"Next time, don't wear honeysuckle perfume. It's unique to you."

Kerry ignored him as she found her way to the park she had in mind. It was large, with a children's play area at one end and several acres of grassy meadow. Parking, she lifted the picnic basket and blanket from the back and went to let Jake out. When he stood, she wrapped his hand around the handle.

"You can carry this." Taking his free hand, she led the way to a stretch of level grass.

"Okay, you can take off the scarf," she said.

"I thought you would do that," he replied.

Eyeing him uncertainly, she reached up to loosen the material. He didn't move and when the scarf came away, he blinked once and gazed down at her.

"I thought we could have a picnic," she said, gesturing around the park, watching him warily, trying to gauge how he felt by the gleam in his eye.

"A simple invitation would have been too much, I suppose."

She shrugged, amusement dancing now that she knew he wasn't angry. "Isn't this more exciting?"

Jake stared at her for a long moment, then slowly nodded. "I've never been kidnapped before. Do you make a habit of it?"

Relieved, Kerry began to shake out the blanket. "No, my first venture. But if it turns out well, I might try again."

Jake placed the basket on the edge of the blanket and took off his suit jacket. Unfastening his cuffs, he rolled the sleeves back before sitting.

Kerry sank to her knees, her dress billowing around her. Reaching for the basket, she quickly unpacked.

Her aunt loved romantic things and the picnic basket was no exception. China plates, silver utensils and delicate wineglasses soon were in place. She removed the food containers and opened them all. Glancing around to make sure everything was as she wanted, she looked at Jake.

"This is your idea of a picnic?" he asked, looking at the elegant setting.

Kerry nodded, hoping he'd like it.

"You're full of surprises, Kerry Kincaid."

"And is that good?"

"Today, it's very good," he said.

CHAPTER SIX

Study the man and understand him. He will not change. The woman who thinks she can change a man is forever doomed to failure.

—Megan Madacy's journal, Spring 1923

JAKE STUDIED HER smiling face. For a moment he let go and just went with the moment. No one had ever kidnapped him. He was startled she'd even think of doing such a thing. Yet, wasn't that part of Kerry's past—doing outrageous things. Like the time she tried to get him to kiss her. She'd declared her love for him and he'd turned away.

Had that been the end of her infatuation? Was that the reason she kept her distance this visit? He had been angry at the world at that time, still hurting over Selena. He'd wanted to ruthlessly end Kerry's devotion—had he hurt her deeply that day? For a moment a pang of regret hit. He had not been kind to the young girl who had followed him so faithfully. He pushed thoughts of the past away. Today was a fresh day. They had a few hours to share and he would not let the past intrude.

And this unexpected picnic was a great idea. Suddenly he had a thought.

"How many people saw us come out of the building?" he asked, wondering why he hadn't objected. Was it the novelty? Or had he just been unable to upset her plan?

She grinned and heaped fresh potato salad on his plate. Using tongs, she grasped a piece of fried chicken and daintily set it on the china. "Lots. Will your reputation forever be tarnished?"

He could feel her high spirits as he shook his head. "I'm in hopes the blindfold covered my face so no one knew."

"Everyone at your work knew," she said gleefully. "And if it works out, your receptionist is going to try it with her boyfriend." Suddenly she looked stricken.

Was it the word boyfriend? Jake wondered if Kerry still harbored feelings for him. None had been evident since she'd returned. But maybe she was better at hiding how she felt these days.

"The rolls may still be warm," she said quickly. "I baked them just before I left and wrapped them well." She offered the covered basket. "When was the last time you went on a picnic?" she asked.

Jake paused in eating to try to remember. "It's been a long time. And I've never been on one as elaborate as this." His father had not been a man to indulge in tomfooleries such as a picnic. It was all he could do to get through the days after his wife left. He hadn't spent time in doing many things with his boys.

"Sally and I love picnics. We used to go on them all the time as kids. Remember that section in the stretch of woods just beyond the river? We found a clearing there when we were twelve. It was our favorite spot to eat and then lie on our backs and watch clouds drift by. It was partially shaded by the trees, so was cool even in the heat of summer. Wine? I know you have to work this afternoon, but one small glass can't hurt, right?"

"Are you coming to court today?"

"Yes. I want to see Perry Mason in action." Her smile made him catch his breath. Her eyes sparkled and Jake almost forgot about eating. He'd like to lean closer and—

Slamming down on the thought, he nodded, sipped the wine and watched her as she ate her own lunch. What was going on, he wondered cynically. She'd done her best to ignore him ever since she'd arrived. Ignore him or drive him crazy. Now this. A romantic picnic for two. Did it mean anything, or was she just filling her days until she found a new job?

"Any luck in the job hunting?" he asked.

"I've got a dynamite resumé ready to go. But I'm not in a huge hurry to find something. Maybe in a week or two. In the meantime, I want to enjoy myself." She took a sip of wine and glanced around the park. "I never did this in New York," she said thoughtfully. "I think I'm going to make a major lifestyle change and opt for a slower pace of life. Why shouldn't I enjoy things as I go along?"

"I thought you liked your life in New York."

"I did, it was great. But now that things have changed, I have to consider whether I want to go back to something like that. I really threw myself into my job. Then in a single day it was gone."

Jake nodded, knowing he'd feel totally adrift if he couldn't practice law. It was logical and orderly, yet challenging—and afforded him the opportunity to make a difference in people's lives. Finding new ways to influence decisions was exhilarating.

Kerry talked about nonessentials as they ate. When finished, she packed up the picnic basket and looked expectantly at him. "Did you enjoy this?" she asked almost diffidently.

Jake nodded, surprised to realize how much he had enjoyed their novel adventure. Maybe he was getting too set in routine.

And maybe he was getting too close to Kerry when he realized how good he felt to see her smile.

''Time to head back,'' he said abruptly, standing and rolling down his sleeves. He had work to do and no time to spend getting close to this woman, or any woman.

She rose and began to fold the blanket, her manner subdued. He hadn't meant to ruin the mood, just needed to get back on track. A brief interlude, now time to go back to reality.

''I appreciate your making lunch,'' he said. Damn, he sounded formal and polite. Couldn't he at least put enough enthusiasm in his voice to bring that sparkle back in her eyes?

''Good, I didn't want you to be mad.'' Kerry turned to head for the car. Jake shrugged into his suit jacket and followed. Her skirt swayed as she walked, brushing against her long legs, mesmerizing in its tempo. She looked pretty, he realized. Prettier than he remembered. And sexier. Her legs were long and tanned. Her feet arched daintily in her sandals. And her hair was so shiny and glossy, it appeared to capture the sunlight.

Rubbing his fingers across his eyes, Jake picked up his pace. He was not one to give in to foolish, romantic descriptions. Her hair was clean. Her legs lightly tanned. He'd seen a hundred women look as good.

Only for a moment, he couldn't remember a single other one.

He joined her before she reached the car and took the picnic basket. ''I have to stop by the office before returning to court. Let me have the keys, I'll drive.''

Kerry hand the keys over, feeling generally satisfied. The picnic had gone well. And she almost hugged herself with the delight in Jake's comment that she proved to be unexpected. She wished Great-grandma Megan was still alive, she would have loved to share the event with her. Maybe she'd call Sally tonight to tell her about the picnic. Or stop by and see her. Since her cousin hadn't read the journal, Kerry could entertain her with some of Megan's stories.

What further things could she do to prove unexpected, she wondered as they entered the courtroom a short time later. Jake indicated several rows of chairs where she could have a seat, then moved down the center aisle to the defendant's table. Ignoring the rows he'd indicated, she moved across the aisle so she had a better view of the man while he worked.

He was impressive. Calm and logical in his presentations, his questions to witnesses were hard-hitting and insightful. A curious blend of cynicism and compassion kept every eye on him while he was examining the witnesses.

Kerry enjoyed the afternoon, fascinated to see this side of Jake. She remembered the day she and Sally had come to watch him. She'd been too young then to fully appreciate the talent of the man. And he'd just been a beginner. Today she basked in his performance. If she ever needed an attorney, she'd pick Jake in a heartbeat.

As the afternoon drew to a close, Kerry reluctantly slipped from the courtroom. Another unexpected turn, she hoped as she wandered through the cool hallways down to the first level of the old courthouse. She knew Jake expected her to be there when he was finished. And a few years ago she would have been. But she hoped she had grown beyond foolish infatuations in the intervening years. Even if she still had that crush on the man, she would not be so blatant in her attempts to capture his interest.

Their relationship was solely that of neighbors.

Kerry swung by Sally's apartment. Finding her cousin at a loose end, they ordered in pizza and rented a movie. While they ate, Kerry shared her lunch escapade, embellishing it where she could to make it sound even more fantastic.

Sally laughed when Kerry got to the part about blindfolding Jake with a yellow chiffon scarf. "I can't believe you'd even try such a thing! And I can't believe that he let you do it!"

Kerry grinned in remembrance. "It was surprising. Maybe he needs some fun in his life. For a moment I thought he'd snatch it off, but then he left it." And kissed her silly, but she didn't need to tell her cousin everything. Some things were just too private, too special to be shared.

"And you got that idea from Megan's journal?" Sally asked when Kerry finished her tale.

"No, just the idea of doing the unexpected. But I figured the last thing a staid respectable attorney did was get kidnapped."

Chuckling, Sally tilted her head. "So is he falling for you?"

Kerry looked at her cousin warily. "No way. I don't want him to." The niggling voice that whispered *liar* was ignored. She'd learned her lesson. No more tilting against windmills.

"Then why are you doing this?"

"For fun, mostly. I really worked hard these last years. And I almost feel betrayed—where's my reward for all that hard work? I was fired."

"Let go, downsized—it's different from being fired," Sally said.

"Doesn't feel any different. I'll be thirty soon. Time to live a bit, don't you think? Anyway this is fun. And if it looks like it's working, I can try it out on some man I might want to develop a permanent relationship with.''

''What if Jake falls for you?''

''Get real, Sally. He's sworn off women for life. You told me how hard it is to get him to even go out with someone. Do you really think he's going to fall for me? Especially when he's done his best to push me away all our lives?''

''Doesn't seem to be pushing you away now.''

Memories of recent kisses flashed into Kerry's mind. They meant nothing. Nothing beyond a momentary impulse.

''Leopards don't change their spots,'' Kerry murmured. Hadn't she just read that before falling to sleep last night? She'd have to reread that passage in Megan's diary again. In fact, when Sally finished the journal after her, she might reread it, to make sure she hadn't missed anything.

''So what are you going to do next?'' Sally asked.

''About Jake? Nothing. You want to come to dinner on Saturday? I could cook some jambalaya. You always like that.''

''I love that. I'm so glad your parents moved all around so you have a wide selection of cooking treats. Can I invite Greg?''

Kerry shrugged. ''If you want.''

''Then you'll have to invite someone so we'll be even,'' Sally said slyly.

''I'll ask Carl.''

Sally wrinkled her nose. ''No. Invite Jake. He and Greg are good friends.''

''I guess.'' For some reason she was reluctant to include Jake in her dinner plans. Was she taking the hard-to-get stance too seriously? Suddenly she didn't want him to think for an instant she was chasing him. She'd been so embarrassed as a teenager when he'd rounded on her and blasted her for her clinging ways. There was no future in a relationship with her sexy next-door neighbor. Maybe she should repeat that litany a hundred times a day until she completely believed it.

When Kerry slowed for the turn into her driveway later that night, she saw Jake's car parked in his. Lights shone from his house, but she didn't pause. Driving to the back, she stopped and quietly entered her aunt's home. She thought dinner with Sally would be the thing to do, but now she had mixed emotions. Maybe she should have stayed after court and seen what Jake might have suggested. Dinner in Charlotte? Or would he have had work to do and merely thanked her again for lunch?

She got ready for bed, donning her comfortable sleep T-shirt. Maybe tomorrow she'd go shopping for some really sexy nightgown. Though what would be the point, except to feel luxuriously daring when she went to bed—alone.

She reached for the journal, but it was not on the night stand. Hurriedly she went downstairs and hunted for it. Where had she left it? There, in the kitchen on the table. Was she getting absent-minded? No, she remembered now. She had brought it down to read at breakfast and been sidetracked by the local paper.

Snuggled beneath the sheet, she turned to the page she'd skimmed before falling asleep last night.

> A leopard won't change his spots. By the time a man is grown, he is set in his ways. And all the blandishments a woman tries won't change a thing. Aunt Dottie told me that this afternoon after she had taken a short nap. We were sitting in the backyard snapping beans.

I love Dottie, she is a wealth of information that she freely gives. Much more so than Mama. Study the man and understand him, she said. He will not change. The woman who thinks she can change a man is forever doomed to failure. So I must make sure I can live with the man the way he is.

Frederick is a bit somber sometimes. I think he needs something in his life to make him laugh more. But I do like him. He is kind to others, listens to me, even when I try to get him to talk about himself, and is generous in his compliments. He said he found the dress I wore to the church social elegant and refined! I would not want to change him. Just make him like me a little. Is he the man for me? To marry and spend the rest of my life with? I could do that. Would I be enough for him?

Kerry closed the book. Jake certainly wouldn't change at this late date. The man was thirty-four years old. Firmly established in his career and his life. He had everything just the way he wanted, Kerry thought. No need for changes. When he wanted companionship, he asked a woman out. When he wanted solitude, he just went home.

He'd spoken the truth all those years ago. There was no future together. She had to admit deep down inside that she had hoped following Megan's old-fashioned advice would cause a change of heart in the man. She secretly still yearned for more from him. For a spark of affection or closeness that would bind them together.

Foolish thoughts, Kerry decided, switching off the light. She had no more chance of that happening than of flying to the moon. Time to end the fun and move to more serious ventures. She could begin with sending out her resumé, and start to date other men. Maybe she would invite Carl to dinner Saturday instead of Jake. Greg could handle it, and she wasn't sure she wanted to spend more time with a man who really didn't want to be with her.

But it wouldn't be easy. Years ago she'd been in love with Jake. He set a standard that proved hard to match. Yet somewhere in the world there had to be a man for her. Her perfect soul mate. She just had to find him.

Jake watched as the light in Kerry's room was extinguished. He sat in a chair in the yard, a beer forgotten in his hand. She'd come home an hour ago. Never even glanced in his direction. He almost called to her, but hesitated—too long. She'd slipped inside.

Staring at the dark house, he wondered where she'd gone after disappearing from the courtroom. He didn't even know when she'd left. One moment he'd seen her from the corner of his eye, the next time he noticed, she was no longer there.

Had she grown bored? Litigation was a time-consuming, sometimes tedious task. He knew everyone didn't find the same fascination with the subject as he did. But he had wanted to hear her views of the afternoon. See how it compared to her visit with Sally years before.

He admitted he wanted to see that rapt attention she'd shown Sunday night when he'd talked about his job. She'd acted as if it were the most fascinating topic under the sun. Grimacing briefly, Jake wondered how she did that. Had she added acting to her skills? Or had she genuinely been interested?

Expecting her to fawn over him at the close of the day, he'd been surprised to find her gone. Another unexpected view of the woman he was beginning to think he didn't know at all. Lunch had been unexpected. Her conversation lately was different. Either she flirted just like she would with anyone or she hung on his every word. Heady feeling for a man who spent most of his evenings alone.

His life suited him. He would not open himself up to the fallacy of love. But sometimes he did get lonely. Did Kerry ever get lonely?

He rose and headed for her house. She'd proved she had unexpected impulses today with that picnic. He'd taken a bit of razzing when he returned to the office. But he wasn't mad. It had been surprisingly fun. Maybe frivolity was something he'd been missing for a while.

Knocking on the back door, he waited impatiently. She couldn't be asleep, she'd just turned off the light a few moments ago. Knocking again, he wondered if he was going to have to break into the house to see her.

The back porch light came on and Kerry opened the door a crack and peeked out.

"Good heavens. Jake! What's wrong?" She opened the door and looked at him, then beyond to the dark yard.

Jake stared at her. Unless she'd changed in an instant, she didn't wear sexy nightgowns to bed. Yet the soft cotton T-shirt that draped her suddenly seemed as exotic as any lace and satin creation ever could. Her breasts were firm and high, and clearly delineated beneath the shirt. Its hem reached her thighs, baring her long legs. Jake's gaze traveled down the length of her and then slowly rose until he stared into her wide puzzled eyes.

"Jake?"

"Sometimes others can do the unexpected," he murmured. Reaching out, he caught her wrist and gently pulled until she stepped forward. "Come on." He had no idea where he was going, just that he wanted to be with this provocative woman. He wanted to hear how she liked his performance in court, tell her what he thought would happen when the case went to the jury, spend some of the magic of the midnight hour with her.

She resisted, but he kept walking until she half skipped to catch up. ''Wait a minute. I'm not even dressed. We can't go anywhere. Jake!''

''Relax, Kerry. We're just going to my backyard. I missed you after court.''

''Wait a minute.'' She dug in her heels and stopped. He stopped and looked at her, wishing there was more light. The faint illumination from her porch light didn't reach this far. The starlight was too faint. Yet he could see her. Her hair looked tousled, and her eyes were shining in the faint moonlight.

''Is there a problem with doing the unexpected?'' he asked silkily.

''Do you do things like this often?'' she asked.

''Never have done it before.''

''A leopard can't change its spots,'' she murmured.

''Meaning?'' He leaned closer, breathing in the sweet fragrance she always wore. He wanted to do more than stand in the cool grass and argue about leopards.

''Meaning what are you up to?''

''I find I have a penchant for kidnapping. Maybe it's addictive.''

''It's too late for a picnic.''

''But not too late for dessert. Mrs. Mulfrethy made apple pie today. We can heat it up and top it with ice cream.''

''It's after eleven.'' Did her tone waver just a bit?

''Ah, too late for a swinging New Yorker like yourself?''

''Out of character for a staid attorney?''

''Ouch, is that how you see me?'' He pulled her closer.

No man wanted to be thought of as staid. Unless maybe he was a hundred and three and couldn't move. He wrapped his arms around her and kissed her long and deep. She made no struggle for freedom and Jake took it for acquiescence. Teasing her lips, when she parted them, he plunged in to taste her sweetness.

To Kerry the world seemed to spin around. Jake's touch ignited a blazing hot fire deep within. Her knees grew weak and desire rose wild and free. She loved the feel of him against her, loved the sensations that crowded, far too many to decipher. She didn't want the kiss to end—ever. Eternity could come and go and she'd be satisfied to remain right here in Jake's arms.

For an instant the thought bubbled up that he'd been reading Megan's diary as well. He certainly was acting in an unexpected manner. But she was too consumed with the passion that rose between them to question it. Time enough for that when she could think coherently!

Finally he ended the kiss, trailing soft kisses against her cheek, along her jaw, tilting her head back to kiss her neck, pausing on the rapid pulse point at the base of her throat.

He moved to her ear and whispered, "Wait right here. I'll get the dessert and we'll have it on the patio."

She nodded, speech beyond her. When he let her go with another quick kiss, she swayed for a moment, then sank to her knees in the cool grass. Pressing her fingers against her cheeks, she could feel the heat. What had Megan written? Something about understanding the man? Kerry now knew she hadn't a clue to who Jake was, or what he was thinking.

Suddenly the game was on again and she was unsure of any of the rules. The only thing she was certain of was she'd never been kissed like that before. Even if she could stumble to her house, she wouldn't have moved an inch. She wanted to see what happened next.

Growing cold in the grass, she rose and stepped onto his flagstone patio. The stones were warm beneath her feet, still retaining the heat from the sun. She sat on one of the lounge chairs, drew her knees up to her chest and covered her legs with her loose shirt. It was a balmy, warm night. The lights from various houses in the neighborhood cast a soft glow. The moon was low on the horizon, almost full. Providing enough light to see by, now that her eyes had adjusted.

She remembered other Southern summer nights. A long time ago, when she'd first started coming, she and Sally and the Simmons boys had rousing games of hide and seek long after dark, roaming all over the neighborhood, playing with all the other teenagers who lived nearby. As she'd grown, she and Sally spent time sharing confidences and dreams beneath the oak tree near the back of the yard—long after her aunt and uncle had retired for the evening.

"Apple pie à la mode."

Kerry reached up for the plate and fork. She straightened her legs, letting the T-shirt pool around her. Taking a bite, she smiled as the taste of apples, sugar and cinnamon exploded on her tongue.

"Ummm, delicious," she said, taking another bite. "Mrs. Mulfrethy still makes the best pie I've ever eaten."

Jake sat in the chair beside her. For several moments they were silent as they savored the tasty dessert.

"Penny for your thoughts," he said, setting his empty plate on the flagstone.

"I was thinking about being a kid here, about all the fun we had after dark. You were too old to play hide and seek with us, but it was great. And then Uncle Philip used to barbeque. It was easier than heating up the kitchen, Aunt Peggy always said. Now I wonder if it was just easier for her having him prepare dinner. But to me, it was magical. My folks get enough of meals outside on their digs that they don't find it appealing when they're home.''

''Philip never seemed to mind cooking. They still barbeque several times a week in the summer. Some of the world's best chefs are men.''

''Theirs is a good marriage, a blending of two lives that complement each other. And permit each other to do the things they like. My folks are a bit like that. Of course they both are consumed with archeology and anthropology, so that strengthens their tie.''

''You're doing it again,'' he said looking up at the stars scattered across the dark sky.

''What?''

''Bringing up long-lasting marriages.''

''Oh.'' Kerry hadn't meant to be obvious. Should she say something about his parents being the exception? To what end?

''Maybe I want you to consider that marriage isn't such an antiquated institution. When I was thinking about it the other day, your parents are the only ones I know who separated. My friends still have their parents together, my folks and aunt and uncle...''

''So they are the exceptions.''

''Or maybe your mom and dad were, did you ever think of that?'' When he remained silent for several minutes, Kerry could have bitten her tongue. Better just to keep quiet than try to change his mind.

''Why do you do that?'' he asked.

''Do what? Bring up uncomfortable topics?''

"No, go silent sometimes. The Kerry I remember was a real chatterbox."

"The Kerry you remember was also very young. I'm grown up now, Jake."

"With different life experiences. What was living in New York really like?"

"I told you the other evening."

"Not much, seems to me I've dominated most of our conversations. You told me about your job on the phone and about some friends you have there. But nothing about men. Do you date a lot?"

Her pie finished, Kerry set her plate on the flagstone and lay back in the recliner, conscious of her scanty attire, of the fact she wore nothing beneath the T-shirt except her panties. Yet it was dark. She could scarcely make out Jake's silhouette against the night sky. He would not be able to see anything. And it was fun to talk with him, share a bit of her past few years. How odd that he zeroed in on her romantic past. Not that she planned to tell him about it—or the lack of it. She turned the subject.

"I really liked seeing you in court today," she said. "You looked formidable, yet came across that you were on the side of the witnesses. I expect you are really very good at what you do."

"It comes from years of experience, practice and some failures. But nothing comes without its price."

"And what price did you pay?" she asked.

Jake thought about it for a few moments, then shifted on his chair, sitting up. "Being single-minded in one's career doesn't leave a lot of time for other pursuits."

"Light on the social life?" she guessed, remembering how when she was in the throes of a big campaign she ruthlessly focused all her attention on the project to the detriment of her own social life. In fact her entire stay in New York led to little in the way of activities that didn't complement her job.

"It certainly takes a backseat. You changed the subject—tell me about your social life."

"Not much to tell. I've got to go, Jake. It's really late and I'm starting to get cold."

He rose and held out his hand to assist her. Kerry hesitated, then put hers into his. When his warm fingers covered hers, she caught her breath, her heart rate increasing again. Why did she have this reaction every time the man touched her? For goodness sakes, it was just Jake Mitchell.

"Next time I kidnap you, I'll do the blindfold bit," he murmured, drawing her close, putting his arms around her.

Kerry braced her arms against his chest, but couldn't resist the fluttering sensations that washed through her as he drew her tighter and tighter against his own hard body. And truth to be told, she didn't want to resist. Slowly she raised her face, and met his kiss.

Eons later, or was it only moments, he released her. "Midnight madness," he murmured.

CHAPTER SEVEN

The way to a man's heart is through his stomach.
—Megan Madacy's journal, Summer 1923

MIDNIGHT MADNESS. Kerry nodded. It was as good a name as any for what had just happened. She turned and walked swiftly toward her aunt's home, thoughts and emotions and feelings all churning inside until she thought she'd go crazy. She was *not* going to fall for Jake Mitchell again.

But it was hard to convince herself when her body still tingled from being held by him, when she could still taste him on her lips. Maybe he'd changed. Maybe leopards *did* change their spots. No, she shook her head to dispel the notion. By his age, he was firmly set in his ways. It would take a miracle to change the man. And she was fresh out of miracles.

The dew was forming on the grass. Her feet were getting cold. And she couldn't believe she wore nothing but her nightshirt. Her aunt would be scandalized. Even her very liberated mother would probably raise an eyebrow at her attire.

"Good night, Kerry," he said when they reached the porch steps.

"Good night." She dashed up the steps, pausing at the door. Looking at him over her shoulder, she impulsively blurted out an invitation.

"I'm making jambalaya on Saturday. Sally and Greg are coming for dinner. Want to join us?" She held her breath. If he said no, she'd invite Carl. But before the thought could even make itself known, he accepted.

"What time?"

"Sixish." Committed, she entered the house and closed the door firmly behind her before she could do something foolish like turn around and fling herself into his arms. Proudly she resisted peeking through the window to watch as he walked back home. It would never do to show such an interest. Though what he thought of her after the way she responded to his kisses was beyond her. He had to know she would never turn him down.

And yet, maybe that was exactly what she needed to do. Instead, she'd invited him for Saturday.

Shivering slightly in the night air, she hurried up to bed. But sleep was the farthest thing from her mind. Her blood hummed through her veins. Her skin tingled and her heart rate was still out of control. Switching off the light, she tried to fall asleep, but it proved impossible. All she could do was remember his kiss, relive the touch of his skin against hers, his mouth moving, his tongue stroking, his hands molding her body to his.

Sitting up, she flicked the light back on and reached for Great-grandma Megan's journal. If she couldn't sleep for thinking about Jake, time she took her mind off him.

> Mama seems to have an old saying or old wives' tale for every event in life. Today she and I were preparing supper when she looked at me and winked. The way to a man's heart is through his stomach, she said. Daddy loves red-eyed gravy and so we were fixing one of his favorite meals that included gravy over rice. A happily fed man is content, and easy to be around, she added. So am I to cook for Frederick? I don't see when I can. Except for maybe the box social that is usually

held the Fourth of July. But that is months away. How can I show him what a good cook I am before then? I love getting all this advice from other women, but hate to let everyone know of my interest in Frederick. What if he never returns my regard?

I think Mama suspects, however. She did say maybe I should think about preparing a Sunday dinner soon. We could invite the pastor and his wife. And maybe Frederick. She didn't say anything more, and it is a good idea. But I've never known her to include anyone else when we have the pastor and his wife for Sunday dinner. I already know Frederick loves fried chicken. Cousin Biddy says I make the best fried chicken in the family. Wonder if Frederick will like it.

Kerry reread the passages she'd read that morning. Well, chalk up another one for Megan, she thought. Now if Jake liked her jambalaya—suddenly aware of where her thoughts were leading, Kerry tossed the journal aside and settled down to go to sleep. She'd think of how hard she'd worked in New York, of where she wanted to find another job, of what she'd wear on Saturday night.

Kerry went shopping Friday morning for the ingredients for her jambalaya. She spent the afternoon cleaning the house, though she planned for dinner to be served on the patio. Still, it was nice to mindlessly do tasks at her own pace. She had quickly bounced back from her feeling of listlessness after working so hard all winter and spring. In fact, she was beginning to get a little restless.

Monday, she'd seriously begin to look for that job. And maybe check out apartments in the Charlotte area. If she found something soon, she'd have to make a quick trip to New York to pack and arrange to ship her furniture and belongings south. Maybe Sally would take a few days off and come with her. They could take in a Broadway show and she could show off New York to her cousin before heading back.

Saturday dawned hot and humid. Kerry prepared the jambalaya early, wanting it to simmer all day to blend the flavors. She planned to serve a fresh mixed green salad and hot cornbread with pineapple upside-down cake for dessert—her aunt's recipe. It had been a favorite of Jake's. She remembered him stopping by when she was younger and eating huge pieces of her aunt's cake.

Hearing a lawn mower, Kerry glanced out the window sometime later. Jake was cutting his lawn. Fascinated by the man he'd become, she watched for several long moments. He wore only those ragged cutoffs and tatty old tennis shoes. The sun gleamed on his skin—his shoulders and chest muscular and solid looking. The dark tan was still surprising so early in the summer, yet if he did all his yard work without a shirt, that explained it.

Oblivious to everything but the task at hand, he never glanced her way. Gratefully, Kerry watched until he moved to the front yard. Sighing softly, she returned to her cooking. If she didn't watch herself that crush she had once had so badly would resurface and she'd be in a pickle. She should have invited Carl tonight. Or not listened to Sally and kept her guest list to her cousin and Greg. The three of them had enjoyed dinner last week. They didn't need a fourth.

Too late now to change everything. But she would keep it casual. Three old friends and Greg.

Kerry was debating whether to slip out to the country club for a quick dip in the pool that afternoon when the phone rang. She would like to swim a little, but knew the pool would be crowded with families and children.

Still, it would be nice to cool off and work on her tan a bit more. Her days of being a lady of leisure were fast waning.

"Hello?"

"Kerry?" a familiar voice croaked.

"Sally? What's wrong? You sound terrible."

"I feel even worse! I have the most awful cold. I can't believe I got one now! I'm so miserable. I can't come to dinner tonight. I called Greg and told him already."

"But you have to come. I have a ton of food. And I already invited Jake!"

"Even if I could crawl out of bed, I wouldn't want to infect everyone. You and Jake have dinner. Freeze what you don't eat and we can have it next week when I'm feeling better. If I ever feel better."

"Colds don't last that long, you'll be fine in a couple of days." Kerry's heart sank. She had been counting on her cousin and Greg to be there. Would Jake believe they'd been invited when they didn't show up? He'd probably think it was just a ploy by Kerry to have him over.

"Maybe, but right now I feel terrible. I'd much rather it be cool and raining outside than have this cold when the weather is so beautiful," Sally complained.

"Drink a lot of fluids—"

Sally laughed, then coughed. "Now you sound like Mom. I'll take care of myself. Have fun tonight, sorry I'll miss it. But I wouldn't even be able to taste anything feeling like this."

Tonight? There was no way she was going to entertain Jake alone. Kerry hung up and looked out the window. No sign of Jake. The lawn mower had stopped long ago. Was he inside? Should she call him and cancel? It was one thing to have him over when there were others.

Something else again if it were just the two of them. Going to the phone, she quickly dialed.

After four rings the answering machine responded.

"Hi Jake, it's Kerry. Sally is sick, so can't make dinner tonight. I guess we'd better cancel. I have a ton of food, though, so I can make you a plate if you like?" She frowned. If she were going to feed the man, why not have him eat at her place. "Or you can still come over if you want, but Greg and Sally won't be here. It'll just be you and me."

Obviously.

She felt like an idiot. Would he think she was coming on to him?

"Or you can take it home."

Now she sounded like a take-out place.

"Call me," she ended and hung up before she said anything else stupid.

Looking out the front window, Kerry saw Jake's car was gone. He'd get her message when he returned.

By five-thirty, she had not heard from him. Nor was his car in the driveway. Where was he, she wondered. And should she expect him at six or not?

The blue dress she wore was short and sassy. The sandals barely shod her feet and she'd splurged and painted her toenails a pale pink. The color looked nice against her newly acquired tan.

Entering the kitchen, she made the cornbread batter, poured it into the pan and set it near the stove. Quickly tossing a salad, she placed it in the refrigerator. She had to eat, even if Jake didn't show up. And if he did show, once he learned that Sally and Greg weren't here, he might wish to take a plate home and not bother making small talk while they ate. Pacing the kitchen, she kept looking out the window. Where was Jake? Had he received her message?

When six o'clock came with no Jake, Kerry knew he wasn't coming. He'd probably called his phone for messages from wherever he'd gone that day. She'd pop the cornbread into the oven and eat when it was done. She wasn't really disappointed. It might have proved awkward to entertain him after last night's kisses.

Sighing softly, she checked on the cornbread. She'd be eating early. She had planned to have a glass or two of wine on the patio before cooking the bread and serving the meal. But that's when she expected guests. Now she was on her own.

Retrieving Megan's diary, Kerry sat at the kitchen table reading it while the cornbread baked. The fragrance filled the room and her mouth watered. She didn't mind eating early, she was hungry.

The knock on the back door startled her. Jake stood on the small porch, dressed in casual slacks and a pullover knit shirt in deep green.

''Sorry I'm late. I got held up.''

''I didn't expect you,'' she said noting how handsome he looked. Suddenly she remembered how great he had looked earlier when cutting the lawn. There was no getting around the fact he was a fine figure of a man, as Megan would have said.

He looked at her quizzically. ''You said sixish. I know it's fifteen after, but surely that's close enough. Are you going to let me in?''

Flustered, she nodded and stepped back.

''Smells good,'' he said, looking around. ''Where are Sally and Greg?''

''I left a message on your answering machine. Sally's

sick, so she canceled for them both. I called this morning, tried to reach you.''

''I didn't even stop to check the machine. Sorry to hear she's sick. Is it bad?''

''Just a summer cold, though she feels miserable. But since it's just the two of us now, I thought maybe you'd rather not.''

''I think we can muddle through a meal together, don't you?'' he said. Slowly he let his gaze skim across her shoulders, down the length of her body, stopping when he saw the polish on her toes. His mouth quirked up.

''Sure. Want a glass of wine?'' Kerry turned away before her knees gave way. The look he gave her was hot enough to melt iron. ''I had planned to sit outside and have dinner around seven, but I've already put in the cornbread. It'll be ready in a few more minutes.''

''That's fine with me. I missed lunch. Had an appointment.''

So that's why he was late—he couldn't tear himself away from a date. Why had he even agreed to come to dinner? Or had he invited the other woman out after Kerry's last minute invitation so late Thursday night? She almost groaned aloud. She had not followed her great-grandmother's tenet about not being so readily available. She should not have invited him. Not that it mattered. And the twinge she felt had *nothing* to do with him seeing other women. He could see every woman in North Carolina if he wanted to!

Oh, no? her subconscious challenged.

''You could have called and canceled tonight,'' she said, relieved her voice sounded normal. Pasting a bright smile on her face, she turned to hand him a glass of wine.

Jake was leafing through the journal.

''Oh no, don't read that!'' She hurried across the wide

kitchen and thrust the wine glass at him, reaching to snatch away the journal at the same time. The last thing she wanted was for him to realize what she'd been doing since she arrived. He'd instantly suspect she was trying to lure him into some commitment trap. Given their history, he'd never believe she was just passing the time until the real Mr. Right appeared on the horizon.

He frowned, took the glass and looked at the leather-bound journal.

"A diary of some kind?" he asked.

She nodded. "Sally and Aunt Peggy found it when cleaning out the attic this spring. From our great-grandmother. Mine and Sally's I mean. It was from Aunt Peggy's and Mom's grandmother. Their mother's mother." She knew she was babbling, but couldn't stop.

"From when she was a child?"

"Not exactly. Actually it was from the day she turned eighteen. Back in those days that was considered all grown up. She writes about the family and about court—ah, I mean cotillions and things like that." Turning away, she placed the journal on top of the refrigerator and peeked into the oven. The cornbread was a golden brown.

"Dinner's ready," she said. "Want to eat outside?"

Settled on the patio a few minutes later, Kerry was pleased to see Jake enjoy the meal. She, on the other hand, could scarcely eat. She pushed some of the meat around, took a small bite of jambalaya. Nervous, she picked at her salad.

"Something wrong?" Jake asked watching her.

"No." She smiled brightly, not quite meeting his eyes. Reaching for her wineglass, she took a sip, wishing now that she'd served iced tea. "Did you have a nice afternoon?"

Kerry closed her eyes in disgust. The last thing she

wanted to hear was about Jake's date that day. How could she have said that? Bravely studying her plate she hoped Jake thought she was making small talk. Not that she really cared how he spent his time. Or with whom.

"Nice? Wasn't that kind of appointment," he said, buttering a thick wedge of cornbread.

"What kind?"

"The kind where you have fun."

Kerry frowned. "What kind did you have, then?"

"A business appointment, what did you think? A meeting with a private investigator for the case I'm working on." His eyes gleamed. "Did you think I left a hot date with another woman to join you for dinner?"

"I'd never think that," she retorted, feeling the heat steal into her cheeks. She was glad mind reading wasn't his specialty. Or was it? The smug look on his face made her want to slap it off. He did think she was jealous. She'd have to prove to him that she couldn't care less.

"I saw you cut the grass this morning," she said, then remembered how she'd watched him from the window. Maybe this wasn't the topic she wanted brought up. "I would have thought you'd hire a gardener."

"I had one a few years ago, when Dad first sold me the house. But one day the man couldn't make it, so I did the work—and found I liked it. Having to do it as a teenager seemed a chore. Now that the place is mine, I feel differently about it. And mowing gives me time to think. There is a surprising sense of satisfaction when I'm all done."

"I like gardening for the same reason. I hope I can have a balcony or something in my new apartment so I can grow flowers. I had a window box in New York, but that's all. Some day I'd like a huge old house where I could garden to my heart's content."

''New apartment?''

Trust him to pick up on that.

''Umm.'' She met his gaze, wondering what his thoughts were. ''I'm going to see if I can obtain a job in Charlotte. Then I'd need a place to stay.''

Jake studied her thoughtfully. ''What's wrong with staying here in West Bend? I commute. It's not that far.''

She shrugged. ''I think I'd like Charlotte. It's got more going for it than West Bend.''

''Too quiet here for you?''

Toying with her wineglass, Kerry tried to find the words to explain what she was feeling. She didn't want to get into an argument with the man, but she had her own needs to consider.

''Actually, I think West Bend is a wonderful place to live. To raise a family.'' She met his eyes. ''But until I do get married and get ready to start that family, I would rather be where there is more action.'' And away from temptation in the form of a tall, sexy, dark-haired man.

''So you can pick up some guy?'' His voice was tight.

''Pick up? I don't think so. But meet, date. Not everyone is like you, Jake. I do want to find a mate, build a life together, share things with someone special.''

''Marriage only gives the illusion of longevity. Depend on yourself, Kerry. You'll be less likely to be hurt that way.''

''Cynic,'' she murmured.

''Realist, I believe. Where you are like Pollyanna, always seeing the best.''

''Nothing wrong with that. There are a lot of people who have very wonderful marriages. Do you think I should cultivate cynicism like you?''

''No.'' The clipped tone virtually ended the discussion.

Sipping from her wineglass, Kerry was puzzled. She'd

almost think Jake cared about her dating, except the notion was too outlandish.

The silence stretched out for a long time. Finally, Jake laid down his fork.

"The meal was delicious, Kerry," he said formally.

"Thanks. I have pineapple upside-down cake for dessert, want any?"

"Your aunt's recipe?"

"What other one would I use? I know you like this one."

"Ah, did you bake this cake for me?"

Flustered, Kerry stacked their plates and rose, heading toward the kitchen. She glanced over her shoulder and shook her head. "Sally and I like it, too. And I thought Greg would as well."

Jake rose and followed her into the kitchen. "I'm glad you made it, whatever the reason."

Kerry had placed the cake in the oven to warm with the residual heat from baking the cornbread. She withdrew it and cut generous portions. "Ice cream on the side?" she asked, wishing he'd remained outside. He seemed to fill the kitchen, crowd her, though there was plenty of room. But he stepped closer and she almost panicked.

"Of course." Jake reached into the freezer and withdrew the carton of ice cream. "Shall I scoop it up?"

She nodded, moving away from the plates. He seemed to take up all the air. And she wasn't sure how her equilibrium would survive in such close proximity. But for a moment fantasy took possession of her mind. She could almost imagine being married to Jake, sharing tasks in the kitchen, preparing meals together, and discussing their day. Turning her head swiftly, she could almost hear the patter of little feet running toward them. Foolish thoughts. Hadn't Jake made it clear a hundred times he was not interested in the institution of marriage?

Settled on the patio a few minutes later, Kerry was pleased at the way Jake ate the cake. It tasted as good as any her aunt baked, and she was glad she'd prepared it. In fact, the entire evening was going better than she had hoped when Sally canceled.

Jake took the last bite of his cake and then leaned back in the chair. "Dinner was delicious, Kerry. You're a good cook."

"Thank you."

He watched her as she ate. Her ability surprised him. Somehow he still thought of Kerry as the obnoxious teenager who followed him around like he was some superhero. Logically he realized that she had grown up, moved beyond that. She had spent years in New York. Built a successful career. Just because it got sidetracked by the takeover didn't mean she wouldn't land on her feet. He was growing to know this new Kerry, and found himself intrigued by the different facets she revealed.

And the differences from his preconceived ideas. It was dangerous in his line of work to become fixed on any one idea. He needed to view things with openness, be aware of changes and clues that gave him insight into people. He didn't seem to be doing such a great job with Kerry.

Intrigued and perplexed was how he felt. He would not have expected this sophisticated woman across the table from him. He still looked for traces of that younger Kerry who had so adored him.

What kind of man did it make him that he now missed that adoration? He didn't deserve any of it. He had virtually ignored her existence for the last several years.

Now that her devotion was missing, he wanted it. At least some form of it.

He wasn't sure he liked her idea of moving to Charlotte. Granted, she'd lived farther away when in New York, but now that he'd seen her again, discovered they could spend time together without her throwing herself at him, he liked it. He felt comfortable around Kerry. They both knew the score, so there were no machinations trying to entrap him.

"You haven't mentioned Boyd. What's he up to these days?" she asked, referring to his brother.

"He lives in Los Angeles, works for an aerospace firm out there."

"Is he married?"

"No."

He heard her soft sigh. "That's too bad."

"Not necessarily." Jake could feel himself tighten at the trend of the conversation. Did she constantly bring up marriage? Or was it his own heightened awareness of the institution that made it seem a favorite topic of conversation?

"There are lots of happy marriages in the world, Jake. Why shouldn't Boyd have one? Or you for that matter?" Kerry said gently.

"There are many that are unhappy. What then? What if you have children and then can't stand the way your life turned out. It's unfair to dump that on children."

"It would be devastating. Is that how you felt when your mom left? Devastated?"

"We're not talking about me or my family."

"I think we are. It's colored your entire view of family life. That and the woman in college."

Jake stared at her. Leaning forward, his eyes caught

hers, held. "What do you know about a woman in college?" he asked, his tone deadly.

Kerry sat up and glared back. "Don't try to intimidate me, Mr. Hotshot Attorney. I knew you when you'd get all dirty practicing football and Mrs. Mulfrethy would yell at you to keep your muddy footprints off her clean kitchen floor. And I'm not some witness to be interrogated!"

"Kerry," his tone held a warning. What had she heard about Selena? And from whom?

She dropped her gaze, and traced a pattern on the edge of the table. "I heard that you fell in love and the woman dumped you."

Jake almost winced. He waited for the crashing pain of betrayal, the sharp edge of bitter unhappiness. Startled, Jake found there was none. Selena had mattered so much to an impressionable young man that he thought he'd suffer from her defection forever. Now he had trouble even remembering what she looked like. Had her hair been medium brown, or darker? What color were her eyes?

He had no trouble envisioning Kerry, even when they'd been apart for a long time. Her light brown hair had golden highlights that drew the eye. Her dark brown eyes changed with her emotions. Suddenly Jake wondered what they would look like when she was making love. Would they glow with inner fire?

He had not paid attention to her eyes when he'd kissed her. He'd been too absorbed in the feelings that exploded every time his mouth melded with hers. Too caught up in the feel of her tantalizing woman's body pressed against his, too captivated by the sweet taste of her. Too enthralled with the sound of her soft reactions to his kisses. Next time he'd look into her eyes and see what happened.

Next time?

''It's none of your business,'' he said.

''Maybe not, but it sure had an impact on your life. But not everyone is like your mother or Selena. You surely aren't expecting to live your life alone. Don't you sometimes wish there was a special someone to share momentous events with? I sure do. I had lots of friends in New York, but whenever I got a promotion, or a new project, I called home to share with those who genuinely love me. Who loves *you*, Jake?''

He drew in a sharp breath. She was cutting too close to the bone, now. ''I don't *need* anyone to love me, Kerry. That emotion is a myth, an illusion that people use to cover lust. It makes it sound so much better to sleep with someone if you're *in love*. But the fact is there's no such thing as a lasting love. You only have to look at my mother to see that. Even if she stopped caring for my father, what about her two sons?''

''I don't know. Do you have the full story behind that breakup? You were a little boy. And my aunt said your father changed after that. She knew them both, liked them both. Maybe she did try to see you and your dad wouldn't let her. Or maybe not. Whatever, it happened a long time ago. And why give her that much power if you don't like her? The power to keep you from finding someone who cares about you, who wants what's best for you—however you define that. Someone who would share her life with you. Let go of the past, Jake. Reach for the future.''

''Shouldn't we learn from our experiences?''

''I think love is a strong bond between people. I love my parents and they love me. They adore each other. My dad would walk through fire for my mom, and I want to find that kind of love for myself. I don't want to be alone all my life. I want a special person to share it with.'' She jumped up. ''But that's not you.''

Reaching for his plate, she leaned over a bit and glared at him.

''You're going to regret it when you are old and gray and can't work and there's no one around to remember the old days with you. Do you want to take some cake home with you?''

Jake almost laughed at her abrupt change. Almost, but not quite. He wanted to be angry at her tirade, but there was a glimmer of truth in her words.

''If you can spare a piece,'' he replied evenly.

''I certainly can. If it's around I'll eat it and I don't need the extra calories.''

He watched her sweep into the kitchen. For a moment he wanted to follow her, but reconsidered. He'd stated his position. She'd stated hers. Stalemate. Neither believed the other's stance appropriate. He just hoped she didn't end up in a marriage that made her miserable. Or walk away from her children in ten years.

The thought of Kerry getting married nagged at him. Frowning, he tried to put the thought out of his mind. But he could envision her walking down the aisle at the Baptist church and escorted by her father wearing some extravagant, beautiful white wedding gown. Pledging herself to some faceless man.

Clenching his fists, Jake wondered if the man would be good to her. No matter what, Kerry had been part of his childhood, and he didn't want any harm to come to her.

Rising, he started toward the house when she came out, carefully carrying a covered plate.

''Here it is. Don't eat it all at once.'' Her smile was

friendly. Her eyes clear. There was no subterfuge with this woman.

"It's a wonderful cake. I'll enjoy every bite," he said taking the plate.

"Sorry Sally and Greg didn't make it. Maybe another time." She backed up a step.

With a hint of mischief, Jake stepped forward. Kerry moved back another pace. Reaching out with his free hand, he caught the nape of her neck and gently pulled her closer.

"I have to get the dishes done," she said breathlessly.

"They can wait. Is this good-night?"

She fidgeted beneath his gaze. Was she nervous? Of him? Not likely after blasting him a few minutes ago.

When she looked up, her eyes were uncertain. Remembering what he wanted to know, he kissed her. Her lips parted and she responded perfectly. Pulling back a bit, Jake stared into her warm eyes, burning with inner fire.

He wanted her. Stunned at the revelation, he couldn't think. The schoolgirl from his younger years had metamorphosed into a beautiful, compelling woman. One he wanted to know in every way possible. When had this happened? What had Kerry done to change? Or had he been the one to change?

Her hair skimmed across the back of his fingers. He could feel the warmth of her body as she stood so close, yet not quite touching. He wanted more. More than mere kisses. He wanted all of her.

CHAPTER EIGHT

Make home a calm and serene place so a man can rest when he is there. Strive to fill his life with little things that show you care.

—Megan Madacy's journal, Summer 1923

"GOOD NIGHT, JAKE," Kerry said, slipping from beneath his hand. She was scarcely breathing. She had to get away before she made a total fool of herself over this man.

"Kerry, wait."

"I've got to go. 'Bye." She ran the short distance to the kitchen door and flew inside, letting the screen slam behind her. Taking a deep breath she wondered what she was doing. Arguing for the institution of marriage with a man who was dead set against it was an exercise in futility. And caring for such a man would be a dumb move. Really dumb. Hadn't she learned anything in life? Tilting at windmills got her nowhere. She'd done her utmost to stem the tide when the takeover came. It had accomplished nothing except wear her out.

As would caring for Jake.

Almost afraid Jake would follow her into the kitchen, she went to the sink and began to do the dishes. It didn't take long. Once done, she peered out into the darkened yard. He was gone. Thank goodness.

"A narrow escape. If he kept kissing me, I'd forget every lonely day since he so scathingly turned on me and fall back in love with the man," she whispered into the night. Horrified with the trend of her thoughts, she shook her head. No way was she going to fall in love with a man who wanted nothing to do with her.

Time she started looking for a new job. And a new place to live that was not right next door to Jake. Get herself so busy with other things she didn't have a minute to think about what might have been.

The phone rang.

"Hello?"

"Thanks again for dinner," the familiar, sexy voice said. Kerry shivered, and sank onto the chair. Maybe if she recorded his voice, she could play it over and over until she got so sick of hearing it, she would be immune to its attraction.

"I'm glad you enjoyed it. I don't get to cook often and I like to."

"You can cook for me anytime."

She smiled, thinking of Megan's advice. Would that breach the walls around his heart?

"I think Mrs. Mulfrethy would object. She'd think I was usurping her place."

"If you repeat what I'm about to say, I'll deny it all the way to the Supreme Court, but your cooking is much better than hers."

The warmth of his compliment washed through her. "Thanks, Jake. I'm glad you enjoyed it, but that's just based on one meal. You'd be better off staying with Mrs. Mulfrethy."

"Have dinner with me tomorrow night?"

She gripped the receiver. Two nights in a row? She almost said yes, then remembered Megan's words of wisdom. "Sorry, I'm busy."

"Doing what?" he asked quickly.

"You know, Jake, you need to watch that habit of

cross-examining everyone you come in contact with. As you said when I mentioned Selena, it's none of your business.''

''Monday night?''

Kerry suspected by the sound of his voice he wasn't used to being turned down. Perversity reared its head.

''Nope, sorry.'' She almost laughed, waiting anxiously to see if he'd counter.

''Tuesday?''

Biting her lower lip to keep from laughing, she remained silent wondering just how far he'd push? Did he really want to see her again, or was it a case of pushing until he got what he wanted?

''Wednesday then. In fact, I'll take you around to some of the apartment complexes in Charlotte Wednesday afternoon. I already know I won't be in court. We can get dinner afterward.''

''Why would you want to help me apartment hunt?'' she asked, surprised by the offer.

''Who better to advise you on the lease parameters than an attorney?''

Warily, Kerry agreed. ''Wednesday, then. About one?''

''Shall I pick you up?''

''No, I'll come into town. No sense you driving out here and then back.''

''Get home early Tuesday so you're not tired.''

''What are you, my new father?''

''No, Kerry, but if you're busy every night until Wednesday, I suspect you'll be exhausted.''

''I'll just sleep in late every morning,'' she said, almost laughing again. She had nothing planned for any evening, but she wouldn't tell Jake that. Let him think she was in high demand. Did it raise her worth in his eyes? She frowned. She wished to be wanted for herself, not because he thought she was some prize to be won.

Taking the journal upstairs after Jake hung up, Kerry planned to read until she fell asleep. The dinner had turned out unexpectedly well. In a way, she wished Sally and Greg had been able to attend. She would have learned more about her neighbor if he and Greg had exchanged reminiscences. Then her thoughts veered toward Wednesday.

She couldn't imagine Jake arranging to take time from work to help her do anything eleven years ago. Couldn't imagine him kissing her, either. She'd tried that once, with disastrous results. But there was nothing wrong with his kisses now. They were simply wonderful.

"Forget it, he's not for you," she admonished herself firmly.

But as she stared at the list of ingredients her great-grandmother had written down in her youthful exuberance, Kerry shivered, wondering if they alone were responsible for the change in the way Jake acted.

"You should have published them, if they really work," Kerry murmured, slowly turning the pages already read.

Did they work with everyone? She needed to meet a man she felt she could connect with and try them again to prove their worth. Maybe the move to Charlotte was the best thing. She'd have a new circle of friends and find the opportunity to meet nice eligible men.

Not that Jake wasn't nice. She almost cringed. Somehow the term sounded almost insipid when referring to him. Dangerous, intriguing, sexy—all more powerful terms to describe the man.

And eligible would never apply. Not unless he made a major change.

* * *

Kerry purposefully avoided Jake during the first part of the week. She made sure she was inside before he arrived home each evening—not sitting on the front porch until long after dark, when he couldn't see her.

Tuesday evening, she went to Sally's. Her cousin was feeling much better, and they cooked on a small grill on Sally's balcony. Sitting at the tiny table to eat, Kerry mentioned Jake planned to take her apartment hunting. Sally frowned.

"Why?"

"Said he'd look over the leases for me," Kerry said, trying for a nonchalant attitude. Sipping her iced tea, she gazed over the grass of the apartment complex in which Sally lived, avoiding her cousin's gaze lest she guess Kerry truly didn't feel that nonchalance.

"He seems a lot more attentive than he used to. In fact, it's almost a complete turnaround, don't you think?" Sally considered her cousin for a moment. "Watch yourself, I wouldn't trust him for a minute."

"He's my next-door neighbor, nothing more," Kerry said, hoping her cousin couldn't detect the lie in her voice. Jake was growing more important to her every time they met. She had thought herself immune to his charm, to the attraction that she'd used to feel for him. She'd been convinced his scathing denouncement years ago had cured her of any feelings.

She'd been wrong. Each minute they spent together only brought a bit more uncertainty. And flared the attraction that had never really died.

If she didn't want to lose her heart to the man, she'd better start looking elsewhere for companionship!

"Just be careful. You know he has no interest in a long-term commitment."

"I know. If I get an apartment, I'll be away from temptation."

"Aha, so you feel there *is* temptation with Jake?"

"Have you ever looked at the man? He's a walking testament to masculine perfection." She closed her eyes briefly, seeing his tall, lean body, his wide shoulders, remembering the defined muscles when he mowed his lawn. She sighed softly.

Sally laughed. "Kerry, you have it bad. I personally think Greg is a walking testament to masculine perfection, and I'm crazy about the man. I thought you got over your crush on Jake years ago."

"I did. I know better than to fall for Jake. Let's change the subject. I have something else I wanted to ask you. Did Megan marry Frederick?"

"What?"

"The journal tells me how she's enticing the man by doing all these different tactics—like being unavailable, cooking his favorite meals. I've only read some of the journal and so far it's taken place over several months. Did she and Frederick marry?"

"I don't know."

"You don't know? I thought you said you'd skimmed through the journal."

"I skimmed through it here and there, read the first few pages and the last few pages. It covered several years altogether. I didn't think I needed to read it closely. And Mom really wanted to read it."

"What was Megan's last name?"

Sally sighed, "I don't know that either. She died when we were young. I always called her Great-grandma Megan."

"Me, too. You'd think someone would have mentioned her last name. Or our great-grandfather's name."

"She was our mothers' grandmother. Her daughter was their mother. I don't know if I ever heard her last name. And he died before we were born. I guess there just wasn't any need to mention him by the time we came along. We can ask Mom."

"By the time they get back I'll be through the journal."

"Well, read ahead and find out."

Kerry shook her head. "I don't think I want to do that. But I sure hope she married her Frederick. She seems so in love with him. And she's doing her best to follow all the advice her mother and aunts are giving her. Some of it seems to work. How could we know so little about our family?"

"Ask your mother. I expect with her interest in anthropology, she also knows everything there is to know about the family."

"Maybe, I haven't been all that interested before. But after reading Megan's diary, I feel as if I know her. And for all the decades that separate us, she's a young woman on the threshold of the rest of her life—which is how I look at myself."

"A bit older than she was," Sally murmured.

"Yes, but just as interested in her recipe as any of her friends might be."

"What do you mean?"

"I'm doing the same thing, and—" Kerry stopped as an idea hit her.

She looked at Sally with consideration. It would be perfect.

"Sally, if I give you some pointers, would you try them and then tell me the results?"

"What is this, some kind of experiment?"

"Sort of."

Kerry explained her idea—for Sally to try Great-grandma Megan's advice on Greg to see if she noticed any change in the man and their relationship. Wringing a reluctant agreement from her cousin, Kerry soon left for home. She'd have to write down all the different *ingredients* and give them to Sally. Once her cousin tried them with Greg, Kerry would have a better feeling about if they really worked.

Were they sound ideas, or was it just serendipity that it seemed to be working with Jake. Not that he had done or said anything to lead her to believe he was looking for a long-term relationship. But the times they'd been together were well worth the small effort she had made.

She liked wearing flowing dresses, delighted in their picnic, enjoyed cooking. Was it all that simple? Do what you like without artificial posturing and see what happens?

When the receptionist announced Kerry's arrival on Wednesday afternoon, Jake felt a sense of relief—he'd been worried she wouldn't show. He hadn't seen her since their dinner on Saturday night. And been surprised to find over the last few days that he missed her.

"Hello, Jake." Kerry breezed into his office with a bright smile on her face. He felt the impact like a kick. She looked beautiful, and so happy it almost hurt to look at her.

The dress she wore emphasized her slender curves. The pale peach color was perfect with the deepening tan on her shoulders and arms. He wished he could spend time with her when she was in the sun. He'd like to see her long legs gleaming with oil, observe how her swimsuit covered that slender body, yet revealed the soft curves and valley of the woman.

"No kidnapping today?" He'd better think of other things before he embarrassed them both, he thought as he rose and crossed his office to greet her. It seemed natural to kiss her. His hands covered her arms, and he drew her closer. It was briefer than he wanted, but permitted him to set the tone of the afternoon.

She blinked and shook her head, tilting it to one side as she smiled at him. "Not today. Be on your guard, you never know when the kidnapper might strike again."

Feeling ten feet tall at the rising color in her cheeks, a clear reaction to his kiss, Jake reached for his suit jacket and shrugged it on, all the time watching her. Was it his imagination or did his office suddenly seem brighter? He glanced over his shoulder at the window. The sun had been shining all day. It made no sense that it was brighter now.

"Did you eat?"

"Yes. Did you?"

"I grabbed a sandwich. I have a list of places on the West side that are in good neighborhoods. You didn't mention your price range, but these are moderate," Jake said, handing her a computer printout from the corner of the desk.

"I didn't expect all this," she said, scanning the list. "I brought the paper. I read all the ads this morning and circled a couple that looked appealing."

"Maybe we can find something today," he said, ushering her out. But only if it was perfect. It wouldn't hurt her to remain in West Bend a bit longer. Long enough for him to get her out of his system, at least.

The first apartment had already been rented. But the second looked promising to Kerry. She followed the manager through a winding walkway lined on both sides with neatly trimmed shrubbery. The grassy area was small, but neatly cut. Flowers dotted the landscape providing colorful spots of color against the deep green expanse.

"Two bedroom, but the price is real competitive," the manager said as she opened the door and stood aside for Kerry and Jake to enter. "You two take your time. I'll wait here." Smiling, the woman turned to look over the grounds.

Kerry walked around the living room. It seemed small after her aunt's spacious house, but was larger than her apartment in New York. There was a small patio area beyond sliding glass doors. She walked over, wondering if she could put planter boxes there. It was in the shade now, but maybe it received morning sun.

"It's a bit small," Jake said.

She turned around. "Not for an apartment. My place in New York is smaller than this and I was lucky to get it. You're spoiled, living in that big old house."

He raised an eyebrow but remained silent.

Kerry walked down the short hall to the first bedroom. It was tiny, with a window high in the opposite wall. Moving to the next room, she knew it was the master bedroom. It was a bit larger and had an adjacent bath. Like the first bedroom, it only had a single window high in the wall. The room was rather dim, but it didn't matter if all she planned to do in it was sleep.

"Let's check the kitchen," she said, turning. She almost bumped into Jake. He studied the room for a minute, then looked at her.

"I don't like it," he said. "It's dark and small. You wouldn't like it here."

"I like the living room. If the kitchen is adequate, it would be a possibility. But I would want to see the others first."

By the time the afternoon drew to a close, Kerry was no closer to finding a place than she had been that morning, and about ready to scream in frustration. Jake had criticized every place they'd seen. Either the apartment was too small, or did not provide enough security, or was in the path of too much traffic, too noisy, too old… His criticisms never ceased.

When they pulled away from the last building, Kerry glared at him. "This was a waste of time. You insulted that manager worse than the others."

"I insulted no one. If he can't stand to hear a few home truths about the neglect around the place, he shouldn't have let things fall apart. This is the worst of the bunch."

"I liked the first one we saw and that one on Rose Street."

"You wouldn't be happy in either," he stated.

"You'd be surprised what I can be happy in. I'd fix it up so it was perfect for me. And the price of that one on Rose Street is attractive."

"Probably hiding dry rot or a leaking roof, it was so cheap."

Kerry sighed, holding on to her temper by a thread. "You know, Jake, I don't think this was such a good idea."

"What?" he asked, maneuvering in the heavy rush-hour traffic.

"Your coming with me. You've never had to find an apartment. They are different from houses. I can't expect the same kind of amenities a house offers."

He frowned. "I had an apartment in college."

"Then think back, what was it like?"

"Small, noisy and crowded, just like half the ones we saw today. They won't do, Kerry."

She looked out of the window. It was a lost cause.

Next time she'd go apartment hunting alone. In fact, she might drive back to the one on Rose Street in the morning and see if she still liked it. Jake had no real say in her life. If she still wanted that apartment when she saw it again, she'd take it.

Kerry glanced at Jake. "At least your house now is totally different from your apartment. You have all those rooms and live there alone. It is large, quiet and empty."

He frowned. "It's home."

"Do you ever get lonely?"

"Do you?"

"I did when I first moved to New York. And even sometimes after I'd been there a while. But now that I'm back, I haven't been once. Sally is close enough we can see each other whenever we want. We talk on the phone almost every day. I've been seeing other friends. There's something special about being with people who have known me since I was a little girl that's missing with friends in New York. I'll miss them when I move, but I think coming to Charlotte will be the best thing for me."

Jake turned into the parking lot beside a large restaurant. "Italian all right with you?" he asked.

"Yes, sounds wonderful. I'm hungry."

They were soon seated in a quiet booth. Jake ordered a carafe of red wine, then waited for Kerry to decide what she wished to eat before placing their orders.

She smiled at him and raised her glass. "Thanks anyway for today."

"I don't think any of the apartments were any good for you."

"But that has to be my decision, right? You chose that huge house. What do you do in it, sleep in a different bedroom every night? You should have a large family to fill it up."

He shook his head. ''Never happen.''

''You never want children?''

''No.''

''You'd make a great father, I bet,'' she said.

Jake hesitated a moment, studying the wine the steward had poured into his glass. If he were honest, he'd admit to wishing for a son or daughter. ''The risk is too high,'' he said slowly.

''What risk?''

His gaze met hers. ''The risk of a failed marriage, of a woman deserting her children.''

''All life is a risk. Your wife could be killed. You could be killed by a runaway truck tomorrow. There are no guarantees,'' Kerry said softly, her heart aching for him. ''And why are you always looking on the worst-case scenario? What if she didn't leave? What if your marriage didn't fail, but ended up lasting for over fifty years?'' She wished he'd be willing to try. She would never leave him. If he married her, there would be no risk.

Appalled at the thought, she swiftly reached for her glass. She was not even in the running for Jake Mitchell!

''Maybe I need to find someone like you used to be. Someone who thinks I hung the moon.''

''If you ever do, don't turn on her and kill that adoration. It hurt,'' she said softly, remembering.

''I never meant to hurt you,'' Jake said.

''You meant to do whatever would discourage me.'' She shrugged. ''Water long under the bridge. Ah, garlic bread and salad. I love Italian food. This was a good choice.''

The conversation moved to different levels, strictly impersonally from Kerry's side. She had danced too close to the flames to feel comfortable discussing Jake's solitary state. He'd had a chance years ago and thrown it away. She was not in the running any more.

Jake knew the subject of children had been closed, but he couldn't discount the idea now that she'd brought it up. What would it be like to be a father? He knew he would not repeat the mistakes of his own father. But would he make others, equally wrong? Would he rear a child who didn't feel strongly about him? His father had essentially left the same time as his mother, only his body had remained to confuse his young sons.

If Jake ever had a child, he'd make sure that kid knew he or she was loved beyond belief every day of his life.

For a moment he glanced at Kerry, wondering what it would be like to have a child with her? His hair was dark. Would the child have black hair, or light hair like Kerry? Would his eyes be a warm chocolate brown?

Ruthlessly bringing his wayward thoughts under control, he listened to her chatter about the differences in apartments and wished she would stop talking about moving away. Her aunt and uncle would not be returning home for another two months. She should stay and house-sit. There'd be time enough after Peggy and Philip returned for Kerry to find a place of her own.

When they finished eating, Jake drove back to the office so Kerry could pick up her car. He followed her to West Bend.

Kerry parked in the back of the Porters' house. Shutting the car door, she waited. Should she just wave good-night? Or wait to see if he wanted to continue the evening. Slowly, she crossed the grass toward Jake. She didn't want the evening to end just yet.

"Come in for a nightcap?" he asked as she approached.

"I'd like that."

She had not been inside his house since they'd been teenagers. Curious to see what it looked like, she followed him through the back door.

The kitchen was tidy, though rather plain. He poured them each a small snifter of brandy and motioned to Kerry. "Go on through to the front. We can sit on the porch if you like."

The hallway leading from the back to front was plain. Kerry wondered if the entire house was this way, or if Jake had his stamp on certain rooms. A peek into the living room as they passed convinced her he didn't spend a lot of time decorating.

"Where are your pictures?" she asked, sitting on one of the chairs that lined the front of the house.

"I don't have many. Boyd doesn't send pictures. My Dad would never get before a camera."

For the first time since she'd known him, Kerry felt sorry for Jake Mitchell. The man who seemed so in charge of his life and destiny now seemed lonely and alone. Her heart ached to provide him all he needed. But she wisely kept her thoughts to herself. If he wanted something different, he'd go after it. Of that she had no doubts. But he'd missed a woman's touch growing up. Still did, it appeared.

"What are you going to do about an apartment?" he asked.

"Keep looking I guess."

"Saturday?"

"What?"

"I could go with you on Saturday."

"No, thanks. I think I'm better doing it on my own," she said with a teasing smile. "You intimidate the managers."

"Only that old lady who thought we were looking at it for ourselves."

"A natural mistake when two people look at a place together."

"Maybe. Stay here until your aunt returns."

"Why?"

"Why not?"

"Is that the lawyer's way of avoiding explaining?"

Jake reached out and lazily pulled her from her chair into his lap. Kerry went willingly, carefully setting her brandy snifter on the railing and leaning against his hard chest. He'd taken off his suit jacket, removed his tie and loosened the top buttons of his shirt. Wrapped in his arms, she could felt the heat radiating from his strong body.

"I want you, Kerry," Jake said before his mouth met hers. His lips were warm and firm as he moved to deepen the kiss.

Kerry answered his kiss with one of her own. If this had happened eleven years ago she'd have been in heaven. Now she was wiser. At least she hoped so.

But it still felt like heaven. His kiss shattered her composure and she reveled in the sensations that rushed through her. His hands moved against her arms, fingers threaded in her hair. Then he moved to cup one breast and Kerry's breath whooshed out in surprise. Heat exploded deep inside and she shifted slightly on his lap to give him better access. She was burning up, but could do nothing but respond with everything inside her to the delight of his embrace.

Sanity resurfaced and she pulled back. Danger loomed over her like the sword of Damocles. She had loved this man years ago and he'd spurned her. Was she crazy to allow herself to draw closer now?

Pushing herself away from Jake was the hardest thing she'd ever done, but she had to. "I have to go," she said, breathlessly.

"Don't go, Kerry. Stay with me."

"I can't."

She all but ran to the safe haven of her aunt's house. Jake's voice called her, but she didn't pause a step. Only after the kitchen door was firmly shut and locked behind her did Kerry draw a deep breath. It had happened. Despite all her efforts, all her good intentions, she'd fallen in love with Jake Mitchell.

"Oh, nooo," she wailed. She had thought herself immune to the man but she craved him like an addiction. She loved him just the way he was. Like Megan and her Frederick. Jake annoyed her sometimes, but she would never change a thing about him. If he'd only come to care for her. But she knew that was a foolish dream. One she'd thought she'd outgrown. Obviously not.

Too upset to even think, she grabbed the journal like a lifeline. She'd started jotting down the different ingredients to give to Sally. Quickly she reviewed the list, tucking the paper in the front of the journal. Tonight her emotions wouldn't allow her to think through the list. She'd read to see what Megan did next. The longing to skip ahead to see if Megan and Frederick had married was strong. But for some reason Kerry wanted to watch the relationship unfold as it had happened. She'd find out soon enough. For a moment, she fervently hoped that Megan had found all the happiness she wanted with Frederick.

Today is the last of the spring cleaning. We are doing the parlor. First we had to wash the curtains. They are so heavy when wet and wringing them out takes Mama and me working together. The boys dragged the rug to the line in the back and spent the afternoon beating the dirt from it. As I dust and rearrange the things on the marble table, I took special note of the different items. Daddy's pipe is always waiting for him. The derreotype is old and I carefully cleaned it, asking Mama where it came from. Her smile is secretive, her eyes distant. Your father and I bought that together long ago, she told me. She looked around the room and smiled. Most of the things here we bought together, she said.

It's a wonderful thing to make a home with another person, Mama told me. To find what is special to you both, and then keep it where you can touch it, enjoy it, remember the happy days when you obtained it. A home should be restful and serene. A safe place for everyone to return to at day's end. Especially for a man. He's been out in the world all day fighting to make a living that will suit him and his family. The last thing he needs when he returns home is chaos.

I wonder if Frederick and I will build a home together? Will we have furniture and decorative items that will hold special meaning for us? Make home a calm and serene place so a man can rest when he is there, Mama said. It is advice I must always remember. Strive to fill his life with little things that show you care. Mama and Daddy have the derreotype and the other things in the parlor and their bedroom. What will Frederick and I have?

Kerry closed the journal and dreamily gazed off into space. She could make Jake's house a real home. Fill it with color and pictures and paintings, with love and laughter and genuine caring. Show him he need not live like his father had, cut off from the special touches that make home a wonderful special place.

If she ever got the chance.

Which she wouldn't.

Sighing softly, Kerry closed the journal and tried to go to sleep. But the memory of Jake's lips on hers refused to fade. She wished she'd stayed for more.

CHAPTER NINE

A soft answer turns away wrath. You can catch more flies with honey than with vinegar.

—Megan Madacy's journal, Summer 1923

The parlor is spotless. And it gave me a good feeling when I entered to greet Frederick when he came over last night. Mama and Daddy sat with us for a while. Then they permitted us to sit on the porch alone. Frederick told me about his day and I told him what I had done. For a moment I felt like we were truly connected in a way strangely different from anyone else on earth.

Then he spoiled everything. He said he'd heard something about me that was displeasing. Without thinking, I flared up and before I could say spit, he was angry. He had the audacity to lecture me as if I were still a child. I turned eighteen months ago. I am a woman full grown and his saying I was childish was the last straw. I stood up and told him what I thought.

We were too loud. Mama rushed out on the porch to see what was going on. Frowning at me, she cordially bid Frederick good evening. Then she sat with me and asked what had happened. When I explained, still so furious I wanted to stamp my foot, she nodded and took my hands. Megan, she said, there will be many difficulties in life's road. But a soft word turns away wrath. Never forget that.

I tried to defend myself. His accusations were false.

She smiled and nodded, telling me she suspected as much. Another thing to always remember is you can catch more flies with honey than vinegar. Be your sweet self and he will come around.

Mothers can be trying at times. I wanted her to stand up for me, vilify his name. Instead, she gives me another old saying.

Yet, there is some merit in it I can see now that I've calmed down. Maybe I reacted too swiftly.

I shall bake him some cookies and take them round this afternoon. I'm sure Mama will say that is proper. And I will go as far as apologizing for my temper. But not for anything else. If he can't accept that, he's not the man for me.

KERRY JOTTED ANOTHER line or two on her list and closed her eyes. The sun felt good against her skin. The dark glasses sheltered her from the harsh glare. The warmth made her sleepy. She had to watch the time—Jake would be home soon and she didn't want to be in the yard sunbathing when he returned. Her discovery last night that she still loved the man continued to worry her. She dare not let him suspect.

For now the afternoon was perfect. She floated in that state between full sleep and awareness. She could hear the hum of bees in the patch of clover that grew near the back of the yard. The birds were silent—probably napping, she thought idly.

Had Megan and Frederick patched things up? Had Megan applied her mother's philosophy and been sweet to Frederick? Could Kerry be sweet to a man who made her angry? Probably not. She'd want to knock his head off. Yet people could be angry at each other and not end their relationship. Everyone got mad sometimes.

She wished again that she had known Megan. Wished they had grown up together and exchanged girlish confidences. Wished she could have discussed the different ingredients with her. Were they really the way to a man's heart? Or only the foolish imagination of a young woman at the beginning of the century?

Of course, she'd had Sally to exchange confidences with as a girl and that had been great. Her cousin was special. Which nudged her further. She still needed to finish her list to give to Sally. She was curious to find out if Megan's ingredients truly worked. She'd insist her cousin try them, just as Megan had listed them. In a minute she'd read some more of the journal and write any new points down. In a minute… Slowly Kerry drifted to sleep.

"I don't think Sleeping Beauty fell asleep in the sun," a familiar voice said softly in her ear. "She might have gotten a case of terminal sunburn."

Kerry awoke with a start. Opening her eyes, she looked into Jake's deep gaze.

"You'll get burned."

"It's late, the rays aren't so strong now," she said, her tongue scarcely able to form the words. Jake was here, just a few inches away. Her heart pounded. Would he kiss her again? Like last night's kiss? And if so could she keep any semblance of normality, or would he guess instantly that she had fallen in love again?

Again? Had she ever stopped? Had she just damped down her emotions until she thought she had recovered from lovesickness? He had been the standard against which she'd measured every man she'd dated. The others had all fallen short.

"You can still burn. What are you reading?"

''My great-grandmother's journal. I told you about it the other night,'' she said, gripping it tightly.

''Interesting?''

''Yes.'' Blinking in the bright sunshine, she tried to see him clearly. He was back-lighted from the sun, his face in shadow.

''Is it late, is that why you're home?'' she asked still a bit confused from her nap.

''I took off a little early. Want to have dinner together? I could throw some hamburgers on a grill.''

Kerry swallowed, remembering all the admonitions in the journal. But for once she did not give a thought to playing hard to get. Sometimes a woman needed to grasp an opportunity. ''Yes, I'd like that. I can bring a salad.''

''Come over when you're ready. I'm going in to change.''

Ten minutes later Kerry carried a large bowl through the backyard and knocked on his screen door.

''Come on in,'' Jake called.

Entering, she took a deep breath. She could do this and not let him suspect a thing. She'd been lecturing herself since his invitation. She'd be friendly, polite and follow Megan's advice to the letter. And memorize every moment spent with Jake.

''I'll fire up the grill in the back. When the coals are ready, we can cook these,'' Jake said, forming patties from ground meat.

Kerry nodded, letting her gaze follow the long length of his muscular legs showing beneath the shorts he wore. The white T-shirt outlined his muscular shoulders and back. Taking a deep breath, she repeated her vow to remain friendly, not lovestruck like the teenager she'd once been.

''I'll put this in the refrigerator,'' Kerry said crossing

to the large unit. Once done, she turned to walk back to stand beside Jake. How often had she longed for similar evenings so long ago? The two of them, together, preparing a meal?

''Can I help with anything else?''

''Don't think so. It's not a very elaborate meal.''

''I don't need elaborate.'' Leaning against the counter, Kerry watched as he worked. ''How was court?'' she asked.

''Went well. I think we'll do summations tomorrow and send it to the jury.''

''Will they work over the weekend?''

''No, probably begin their deliberations on Monday. It's not a sequestered jury.''

''And do you think you'll win?''

He smiled grimly. ''Yes, but it's been a tough case. And I got blindsided at the onset by my client not telling me the full truth.''

''How did you know?''

Jake glanced at her as if to see if she really wanted him to continue. Seeing the interest on her face, he related as much as he could about the case without violating attorney-client privilege. Kerry listened attentively. Jake's work fascinated her. Jake fascinated her.

The sun was still warm when they moved to the grill. Kerry asked more question about the different cases Jake worked on and he answered them all. Soon the sizzling burgers were ready. Buns had been toasted and the salad brought out.

''I didn't bring any dressing, don't you have any?'' Kerry asked, peering into the refrigerator.

''No. I'll run next door and get it. Does Peggy keep it in the refrigerator door?''

"Yes, but I can go," she said. "I'm the one who forgot to bring any."

"No trouble. What do you want?"

"Ranch."

Kerry spread mustard on her bun, piled pickles on and then looked for the onions. Hesitating only a moment, she loaded them on the bun. She loved them. And if she kept her wits about her tonight, she wouldn't have to worry about her breath. She planned to stay out of arm's reach of Jake.

Where was the man? She looked out the window. Couldn't he find the dressing? She was sure she'd put it right in the tray in the door. Pushing open his screen door, she walked across to her aunt's house.

"Can't you find—" She stopped suddenly in the doorway, her heart freezing. Jake held the journal in one hand, the list for Sally in the other. She hadn't had a chance to give it to her cousin yet. She had just added the last bit, about the honey and vinegar.

His face appeared carved from stone.

"What is this?" His voice sounded cold as ice. His eyes flint hard.

Unable to move, Kerry stared at him, at a total loss for words. She had left the journal on the counter. Why had he picked it up? The list had been tucked inside, she was sure of it.

Why couldn't she have taken it back upstairs? Clearing her voice, she drew a deep breath. "My great-grandmother's journal," she said.

"And this?" He held the list by the corner as if it might contaminate him.

"Just a list," she said. Her heart raced. Panicked, she didn't know what to do. She wanted to snatch it from his hands, ball it up and throw it away. But she remained where she was, staring at him, unable to move an inch.

"'*Get him talking about himself.*' You did that one well. I hope you weren't too bored."

"I can explain," she tried, "It's for Sally."

"The list's for *Sally?*" Jake said incredulously. "For *you,* I'd say. *'The way to a man's heart is through his stomach—fix something really delicious that he likes—like cake.'* Another one you did well." Jake gave her no chance to speak.

Her heart sank. He was furious. And the cold control he held over that anger made it seem even stronger. She wanted to say something, but she couldn't. Fear slammed through her. Would he listen to her? Or would he jump to conclusions? Conclusions that would be all too close to the truth?

"'*Catch flies with honey?*' Is that supposed to be me? A fly?" He slammed the journal down on the table and advanced toward her, his eyes dark and dangerous.

"It's not what you think," she said, mesmerized by his anger. Would he give her a chance to explain? Attempt to understand?

"I think it is. I think you have practiced every one of the things on this damn list with me. *'Do the unexpected'*—like a kidnap picnic? *'Wear pretty dresses?'* You've done that to a fare-thee-well. *'Practice being feminine.'* Do you have to practice that, Kerry? I thought that came naturally. But then I thought everything about you lately was natural. I didn't realize it was a part of a big plan to capture my attention. What were you after? Marriage? After all these years, have you forgotten what I said last time? That I don't want you. I don't love you and I sure as hell don't plan to be a part of your stupid convoluted plans to land yourself a husband. Go back to

New York. Maybe things like this work with men back there, but they sure don't here!''

His anger seemed to shimmer in the air. Kerry held her ground; she knew Jake would never lose control no matter how irate he became. Frantically she sought the words that would quench his fury.

Crumbling the page into a tight ball, he threw it on the floor and stormed out.

''I guess this means dinner is off,'' Kerry said softly, still staring straight ahead. The pain began in her heart and spread until she was almost shaking. Tears filled her eyes, but she blinked quickly to dispel them. It was no more than she deserved. And no more than she expected. He had never had a use for her. Nothing had really changed. Except for a few weeks, she'd let herself believe there might be a chance for her. He'd been attentive, loving, romantic.

And it all meant nothing.

Slowly, she reached out for the journal and carried it upstairs. Her appetite gone, she didn't want dinner. She didn't want anything except oblivion to the pain that gripped her. She couldn't even read about Megan and Frederick. Was it coincidence or prophesy that told of Megan's and Frederick's fight right before her fight with Jake? Had the entire sequence of events been tied somehow to the past, like an endless loop that played over and over with each generation?

She didn't care. Falling into bed, she gazed dry-eyed at the ceiling, clutching the journal to her breast. Truth be told, she'd been happier than ever these last few weeks. Without a job, unsure what she would do with her future, it hadn't mattered. She'd been so caught up in Jake the rest had faded to insignificance.

More fool her.

She had known intellectually as soon as she'd seen him when she arrived that nothing had changed. But her heart refused to believe it. Maybe now it would.

Jake stormed across the yard. Glancing at the table set for two it was all he could do to refrain from tipping it over and sending the food and utensils sliding off onto the grass. He yanked open the screen door and stepped inside. Her scent still lingered in the air. He drew a deep breath, imprinting it forever.

"Damn!"

He'd thought things were different this time. He was supposed to be the clever hotshot attorney. Yet he'd fallen for her routine like a raw law clerk. She'd been much more sophisticated in her pursuit this time. Of course she'd had years to perfect her technique. It seemed so smooth.

Clenching his hands into hard fists, Jake paced the kitchen remembering that blasted list and how Kerry had played him like a first-class idiot. She'd been so attentive when he spoke about work. He'd thought she had been genuinely interested; he'd actually reveled in sharing his thoughts about the cases with her. Had been proud of her interest.

And it was all a farce!

He leaned on the sink and looked out the window, across to her house. He wanted to go back and yell at her, to rant and rave about the shameful way she'd deliberately enticed him. Flaunting her long legs in those dresses, making him want her like he hadn't wanted anyone in years. Rail at her for the shameful way she captivated his interest, and his heart, when it had been nothing but a challenge to her. A game.

His heart?

"No, never that," he said firmly. Pushing away, he went to the cabinet and found the whisky. Pouring himself a glass, he went through to his study, on the opposite side of the house from Kerry's. He would not even glance her way accidentally. Not tonight, not ever again!

Nursing his drink, Jake gazed out the window, his mind churning with raw fury—and hot memories.

Friday morning Kerry rose early. She'd spent a miserable night. Nightmares had plagued her. She'd been running after Jake and every time he disappeared. "No need to be an expert to know what that means," she grumbled as she stood beneath the hot shower. "How can a woman be so stupid? I wonder if it's genetic?"

Drawing one of her new dresses from the closet, she hesitated a long moment. Then defiantly put it on. She liked wearing the dresses. Once she had a new job, she might have to resume her suits but she could please herself until then.

She ate a hasty breakfast, toast and tea. Then tackled her resumé. Writing letters to a dozen firms, she proofed everything and then went to mail them. By next week she should be hearing something. And in the meantime, she'd continue to look for a place to live. The sooner she moved away from Jake's proximity, the better for her sanity.

After driving to the apartment complex on Rose Street later that day, she was disappointed to discover the apartment had been rented. It was the one she'd liked the best. "But, it wasn't good enough for Jake. I should have acted on my own impulses," she said to herself as she got back into her car.

The rest of the afternoon she spent looking at apartments. The one on Coldridge was almost as nice as the first one she'd liked. But it was nearer the train tracks and might prove to be noisy. Telling the manager she'd be in touch, she headed for West Bend.

On impulse she checked her watch, then drove to Sally's.

"Hey," Sally greeted her when she rang the bell.

"Doing anything tonight?" Kerry asked as she entered her cousin's apartment. For a moment she gazed around. Maybe she should see about an apartment in this complex. It wasn't that far to Charlotte, and she'd be close to Sally.

"Nope, what's up? You look like you lost your best friend."

It was unexpected. Kerry would have sworn she would never do such a thing, but at her cousin's words, she burst into tears.

Startled, Sally crossed over to her and hugged her tightly. "Oh, Kerry, what's wrong?"

Rubbing her eyes, trying desperately to stem the tears, Kerry sniffed and shook her head. "Delayed reaction, I guess."

"To losing your job?" Sally patted her shoulder, looking into her tear-drenched eyes.

"I guess." She looked for a tissue, saw a napkin on the table and used that. Taking a shaky breath she tried to smile at her cousin, but it was more than she could do. "I blew it big-time."

"Your job?"

Kerry shook her head. "Jake."

"Jake?" Sally sat on the arm of the sofa and looked puzzled. "I don't get it."

Kerry drew a deep breath and sank on the sofa. Opening her purse, she withdrew the crumbled sheet and held it out for Sally.

"Remember I told you about Megan's advice?"

Sally nodded and reached for the paper.

"I wrote down the different suggestions to show you. I wanted you to try them to see if they really worked or if it had just been some kind of weird reaction that made Jake seem interested in me when I tried Megan's suggestions."

"And?" Sally scanned the list.

"Jake found the journal and the list and now he thinks I was just playing at getting him to be interested in me. Like I did when I was a teenager. He's furious."

Shrewdly Sally studied her cousin. "And that matters?"

Nodding her head, Kerry blotted her eyes again. "I love him, Sally. I did when I was a teenager, and I still do. I managed to build a life in New York. I was reasonably happy there. But no man ever appealed to me like Jake. And now I know why. He's the man I love. I guess I will always love him. What a depressing thought."

"Only if he doesn't love you back."

"He doesn't. He's always been up-front and honest about that—he has no use for women, except as a casual date from time to time, I guess. Why can't I get that hammered home in my brain?"

"Sometimes I think the brain and heart never talk to one another. Don't you think I could make better choices if I'd think things through?" her cousin said dryly. "I'm sorry, Kerry. I know you're hurt. But honey, I really think you should have had better sense. Jake won't ever change. And you can't live your whole life pining for a man who doesn't want you."

"I know."

Sally looked at the list again, her face slowly smiling. ''Tell me more about this list. I'm intrigued.''

Kerry explained the different points as Megan had written them down. She enjoyed telling Sally about the ins and outs of Megan's courting. ''I still think they got together, I can't believe you didn't read the diary in detail.''

''Never had the time. When you're finished, maybe I'll read it through.'' Thoughtfully Sally tapped her finger against the sheet. ''I've been trying to be a nineties woman. I call a man to ask him out. Isn't this a bit old-fashioned?''

''Maybe, but there's a lot of truth in her notes. If you ask a man out, and he goes, you've become the hunter. Men like to do the hunting bit. At least when he asks you out, you know he wants it.''

''It makes me feel like a squirrel.''

Kerry shook her head. ''Not really. It's more of doing what feels comfortable and seeing what happens. Try it. Just be yourself, but rein in some of your more aggressive tendencies. I tried each one. Some without even knowing that I was doing it.''

Sally nodded thoughtfully. ''Okay, Kerry. If you can do this, I can too!''

''It may not work, sure didn't with me. But I still think her suggestions are worthwhile. And I liked doing things this way. It felt natural and fun. Try wearing dresses for a while. I find I flirt just a bit more—even with the bag boy at the grocery store. I feel I move just a bit more femininely when I walk. It gives me a great feeling.''

''Shorts and pants are so convenient.''

''Dresses are fun, and feminine. Try it for a month and see what happens.''

''Are you going to?''

"What?" Kerry looked at her cousin.

"Are you going to continue with this?"

"I don't know, why?"

"I heard that you've had several calls from Carl and from Peter Jordan. You've put them off long enough, why not say yes next time?"

"Oh, Carl is so predictable. And Peter—"

"But if you're sincere about moving on, you have to forget about Jake and try spending time with others," Sally said gently.

"You're right." Kerry sighed. Life was difficult sometimes.

Kerry spent Friday night and all day Saturday with her cousin. When Sally was tempted to phone Greg, Kerry challenged her again to follow Megan's suggestions. When Sally hesitated, Kerry offered a pact—they'd both practice Megan's ingredients for one month and then take stock of where they were. And Kerry agreed to go out with whomever asked her to give herself a chance with someone besides Jake. But she would not take last-minute dates.

Late Saturday afternoon she returned home. Ignoring the house next door, she quickly drove to the back and hurried into her own house. She had the rest of the journal to finish. She wanted to know what happened with Megan and Frederick. Were there other suggestions her great-grandma could offer to help her?

The phone rang and her heart lifted.

"Hello?"

"Hi, Kerry, Carl here. I thought I'd see if you're free tomorrow." His voice was hesitant. For a moment Kerry almost refused to see him, then her common sense kicked in. She'd do better going out with Carl than brooding at home. And she and Sally had made a pact.

"I am, what did you have in mind, Carl?"

"That's great! I thought we could play some tennis at the country club in the afternoon and then maybe stay for dinner. They have a swell buffet."

For a moment the memory of another Sunday night at the country club flooded Kerry. She blinked. This was a chance to overwrite those memories with newer ones. Trying to put some enthusiasm in her voice, Kerry accepted.

As soon as she hung up, she wished she could call Carl back and cancel. How could she go out with another man when Jake held her heart?

Yet, if she didn't, she'd be condemning herself to many lonely hours. Jake had made it clear he was not interested. In fact, she'd be surprised if he didn't despise her after this. Taking the stairs two at a time, she hurried up to her room to fetch the journal. The sooner she finished the book, the sooner she'd know what happened to her great-grandmother. If she hadn't been pacing herself while reading it, and dreaming about what could never be, she would have finished days ago.

Her date with Carl was pleasant, Kerry thought when she went to bed Sunday night. Nothing earth-shattering, but it had been fun to play tennis again. And she'd been reacquainted with several other citizens of West Bend. It had certainly been better than staying home alone all day.

Monday she received a call from a company which had just received her resumé. And a call from Carl inviting her out on Wednesday night. Then Peter Jordan called. He'd been one of the men to stop by their table Sunday night and he wanted to know if she were free on

Friday evening. Kerry said yes to the interview, to Carl and to Peter. Maybe she couldn't have the man of her dreams, but it wouldn't hurt to show him just because he didn't want her, others didn't feel the same way.

Kerry's interview was Tuesday morning. Kerry loved the prospects of the job. It sounded exciting and offered more potential than she expected. She met several different people during her interview—from the man who would be her immediate boss to the president of the firm. When they offered to take her to lunch, she was sure she'd have the position if she wanted.

The offer came later that afternoon. Thrilled at finding something so soon after losing her job in New York, she quickly accepted. Agreeing to start in two weeks, she planned to use the intervening days in finding a place to stay and returning to New York to pack and move.

She longed to share her good news with Jake, but prudently avoided him. She had not seen him since he'd stormed out of the kitchen Thursday night. And she would do her level best to avoid him until she moved—or maybe even beyond. Rubbing her chest, over her heart, she tried to ease the ache that seemed a permanent affliction. No use crying over spilt milk, as her great-grandma Megan had written.

She and Sally celebrated her new job Tuesday night. Carl was delighted with her news and insisted on champagne at their dinner on Wednesday. By the time she had dinner with Peter, she'd located the perfect apartment and put down a deposit.

Her flight was due to leave early Saturday morning. She planned to spend several days in New York, wind up her affairs there, and arrange for movers to come for her furniture. When she returned to North Carolina, she'd move straight into her new place. Sally would understand why she couldn't stay in Aunt Peggy's house. And if the yard needed more work soon, she'd do it during a business day, when Jake was sure to be at his office.

It was late when Peter brought her home Friday. They had gone dancing in Charlotte and Kerry tried to make the evening as enjoyable for her date as she could. He was an interesting man, charming and funny. She enjoyed herself. And she knew he was interested in her when he tried to press for another date. She explained she would be tied up for a couple of weeks, and he promised to call her as soon as she got her phone in her new apartment.

Slowly Kerry packed her clothes. She planned to drive to Sally's in the morning and have her cousin take her to the airport. Since she didn't plan to return to her aunt's house, she made sure she had all her things. Inevitably she was drawn to the window that overlooked Jake's house. For a long moment she stared at it, her heart aching with loss. She'd been so happy for several weeks. Smiling sadly she remembered every hour spent together. She would miss him. Miss what they might have had. But it was time to move on. The whole world was waiting for her and she couldn't stay in the one spot she longed to.

She had practice in this. Eleven years ago she'd had to move on. Now she knew she could succeed. Life might not be as wonderful alone, but there were joys to be found along the way. And maybe another man some day.

"Goodbye, my love," she said softly, pressing her hand against the glass as if she could reach across the yards and touch his home. Touch him.

CHAPTER TEN

Then abide faith, hope and love, these three. But the greatest of these is love. We learned this in church, and now I've learned it in my heart.

—Megan Madacy's journal, Summer 1923

JAKE LEANED AGAINST the porch railing and watched as Peter walked Kerry up to her door. He'd glance at his watch, but didn't want to make any move that might draw their attention. He knew it was late. He'd been sitting out here for hours. When he'd seen Peter pick her up, he'd been curious. She'd been out three times since last Friday night. He wondered if she were practicing her feminine wiles on all the men in West Bend as she had with him.

Anger roiled inside. He wanted to purge the sensations that wouldn't turn loose, but not at the cost of seeing her again. She'd proved as shallow as Selena. Each out for her own gain. Never mind how the man felt.

For a long moment he tried to recapture the anguish he'd felt when Selena had thrown him over. There was nothing. Except a certain nostalgia for the young man who had thought himself in love for the first time. Looking back now, he should have spotted the inconsistencies. She had never declared her undying love, he'd projected his own feelings onto her. He'd wanted her and had been out to prove something. What, all these years later, he wasn't sure.

His anger tightened toward Kerry. She had deliberately sought him out this visit. Planned her campaign like a general. He'd thought she'd changed, but she'd just become more crafty.

Really? An insidious voice inside whispered. *Really?* Who called her to ask her out? Pushing until she agreed? Had she even asked him for anything? Only the one night when she said Sally and Greg were also coming to dinner. Other than that, he'd done all the asking. Done all the pursuing.

He tightened his fists. What was Peter doing? If he was kissing her, Jake had half a mind to wander across the lawn and stop it. A quick sock on his jaw should do nicely to put the man in his place and assuage some of Jake's anger.

Almost growling with disgust, he shifted his eyes away from the house next door and tried to erase the images that danced before him—of Kerry with her arms around Peter. Her soft body pressed against the other man's. Kerry's sweet mouth moving against Peter's. Jake tried to hold on to his anger, build the wall higher around his heart. Dammit, he was not going to have anything further to do with her!

His gaze focused on the Bandeleys' house. He'd seen the elderly couple just that morning. Mr. Bandeley had mowed their front lawn. Mrs. Bandeley had come out right afterwards with a large glass of lemonade. They had talked softly and laughed. Jake had looked away when Mr. Bandeley had leaned over to kiss his wife of forty-two years.

His gaze moving, he looked at the Foresters' home. They'd been married a long time, lived on the street their entire marriage. All their children were grown. He'd heard a few weeks ago that their eldest son and his wife were expecting a baby.

Peggy and Philip would love for Sally to marry and

give them a grandchild. He was sure Kerry's parents would love it as well.

He wondered for a moment if his father ever thought about grandchildren.

Peter walked down the sidewalk to his car. Jake watched, his eyes narrowed. Took the man long enough to tell her good-night, he fumed. Not that he cared what Kerry did, or with whom. But Jake didn't move from that spot on the porch until the house next door was completely dark. In the morning, he'd return her salad bowl from the ill-fated dinner they never ate. See if she wanted to apologize. See how she looked. See—

He rose and shook his head in disgust, letting his gaze travel along the length of the street. Every family there except his had remained a family unit. Each husband and wife still greeted each other with affection, caring, and love. Grown children came back to visit, laughing and hugging their parents upon arrival.

Kerry had been right about one thing. His family had been the exception on this street. And he didn't know the entire story—only the part a young seven-year-old felt when he never saw his mother again. When his father had changed to the embittered man he was still. What had gone wrong? Could it have been avoided? Wasn't love enough?

Kerry hugged her cousin goodbye and smiled. "Thanks again for the lift. I'll see you in a week or so." Sun streamed in the high airport windows, dazzling in the early morning sky. The concourse was not crowded except around the departure gate.

Sally nodded, yawning. "I wouldn't get up this early on a Saturday for just anyone," she said with a mock grumble.

"I appreciate it. Take care of yourself. And remember our pledge!"

"As if you'd let me forget. Where's the journal?"

"I left it by my bed. I still have some left to read. But I knew you'd have more time to read it this week than I will. Take it if you want. I'll finish it when I get back. Oops, I've got to go, that's the last call. Bye."

Soon airborne, Kerry relaxed against her seatback. She had a million things to do in New York. Some favorite places she wanted to see one last time, friends she had to tell goodbye, and her apartment to pack. When she returned to North Carolina, it would not be to the arms of a tall, dark, gorgeous man, but to a new job, a new apartment and a new start in life.

She wished she could have finished the journal, but she had not. The last passage she read stayed with her, though, as the plane flew north.

> My grandmother Witherspoon came today for Sunday dinner. She is a real tartar. I've been afraid of her most of my life. But today she asked to speak to me alone. I thought for sure I'd done something wrong, but she just wanted to congratulate me on reaching eighteen. She gave me a lovely lace handkerchief that she said she'd made as a young girl. Then she looked at me sternly with those dark eyes that seem to see everything and said, remember what the Good Book says, Megan: Now abide faith hope and love, these three, but the greatest of these is love. Faith that all you need to know in life your parents have taught you. Remember those lessons, girl.
>
> Hope for the future. It will be what you make of it. There will be hard times, too, but don't give up on hope. And love, child. I hope your life will be enriched

with all the love your heart can hold. Now tell me about this Frederick I hear so much about!

I almost cried, she was so sweet. I'll never be afraid of her again.

I told her about the fight we had, and how I had gone with cookies to talk with him. How when I explained what had truly happened he was so quick to apologize and ask my forgiveness. Of course I did not tell her of his kiss. That is just between us. But I know I love him and told him so. He loves me and will be speaking to Papa this week.

Kerry wished telling Jake she loved him would convince him that they should be together. She had faith in herself, however. In knowing she had done all she could to show the man she truly cared. While she had practiced some of the suggestions laid down by her great-grandmother, none had been artificial. Just a slower, old-fashioned courtship. Wryly she wondered if she could have explained that to Jake.

Her hope came for a brighter future. She had loved and not been loved in return. But that didn't change her feelings. She would go on and do her best to find another love to share in her life. She'd keep the faith and hope in a lasting love like the one that came to her great-grandparents, to her own parents, to most of the families she knew.

And for now, she had plenty to do to pack up and leave New York.

Jake frowned impatiently. Where was the woman? Her car had been gone when he rose this morning. It was now late afternoon and she still hadn't returned. He looked out the side window for the millionth time. Sally turned her car into the driveway and headed to the back.

Grabbing the bowl, he quickly crossed the backyards. Knocking on the door, he waited impatiently the few moments it took until Sally appeared.

''Hello, Jake.'' Her tone was cool. She didn't invite him inside.

''Sally. I'm returning a bowl. Where's Kerry?''

''New York by now,'' she said, opening the screen wide enough to reach for the empty bowl.

Jake went still. ''New York?'' For a moment he wondered if his heart had stopped beating.

Sally nodded, taking the bowl. ''Is this Mom's?''

''Yes. We had a salad—'' They'd never eaten the salad. He'd thrown it out the next day.

Sally nodded, placed the bowl on the counter. She waited. ''Was there something else?''

''I didn't know Kerry was returning to New York,'' he said slowly.

Sally shrugged. ''I'm sure she thought you wouldn't care one way or the other. I have to leave now.'' She glanced once around the kitchen, then stepped outside, closed the door and locked it. Jake didn't move. Heading down the steps toward her car, she glanced over her shoulder at him. She carried the worn leather journal in her hand.

''You've got what you wanted, haven't you Jake? No one and nothing to bother you? Or care about you? I can see you in another few years, as hard to deal with as your father. Don't worry about Kerry. She's young and pretty and has plenty going for her. She'll find a wonderful man who'll appreciate her for who she is and all the love she has to offer. I hope they have a dozen kids and are blissfully happy all their lives. The woman is a idiot who thinks she loves you. Goodbye, Jake.''

Sally slammed her car door and raced her engine before backing swiftly from the driveway.

Jake listened to the echo of her words. No one to care about you. How much had Kerry *really* cared? Hadn't she just been trying her tricks to get him to fall for her? Or had she loved him? She had followed him around as a teenager, tried to tell him years ago that she loved him, but he'd ruthlessly turned her away. He hadn't wanted some kid with a crush hanging around.

She'd come back. But if he were honest, and Jake was always honest, she had not pursued him. She'd all but ignored him until he asked to see her. Demanded to see her. Taken her dancing. Felt that sexy body press up against his. Kissed her until neither one of them could breathe.

The picnic had been fun. Discovering how she'd grown and matured had fascinated him. Listening to her talk about her job, about her friends in New York, had been enlightening. Looking for a place for her to live had been frustrating. She could stay at Peggy's, her aunt wouldn't mind.

He missed her.

He looked north, as if he could see all the way to New York. He'd been ruthless a second time. And driven her away again. This time forever?

Had he been too hasty in condemning her because of some stupid list? She said she could explain, but he'd never given her the opportunity. What kind of fact finder did that make him? Why had he set himself up as judge and jury?

Four years was too long to live in one apartment, Kerry decided as she hauled another bag of trash to the basement. People ought to move every year just to avoid accumulations of stuff that had no useful function. She was tired. This was the third trip today and she still had at least one more large bag of trash to haul down. Then she'd be finished sorting and could begin packing in earnest.

She stepped on the elevator and pushed the button for her floor. Tired as she felt, she had to keep going because the movers were due tomorrow and she had to make sure she didn't ship anything she no longer wanted. Money would be tight for a while and she couldn't afford the expense of recklessly shipping everything.

Stepping off the elevator, she reached into her pocket for her keys. The jeans she wore weren't very feminine, but necessary for cleaning and packing. Dresses would just be in the way. But she missed them and looked forward to wearing her sundresses again back in North Carolina.

''Kerry.''

She stopped and looked up. Rubbing her eyes, she sighed. She was more tired than she thought. Now she was imagining things. If she could get through the rest of the sorting soon, she could get an early night, catch up on her sleep and be ready to go again tomorrow.

''Not talking?''

''Jake?'' He wasn't a figment of her imagination? He was real?

''Last time I looked in the mirror,'' he said. He wore jeans and a pullover shirt. The casual attire showed off his broad shoulders, flat belly. She skimmed her gaze down his long legs. A small duffel bag lay at his feet.

''What are you doing here?'' Greedily Kerry looked at him, her heart thumping hard in her chest, her palms growing damp. She stepped closer until she felt the warmth from his body. Until she breathed in the scent of his aftershave. Her stomach dropped like a roller coaster and she just stared at him. The words of their last meeting echoed in her mind.

"I came to see you."

"In New York?"

"That's where you are. I went to your aunt's house on Saturday and Sally told me you had returned to New York."

"It's Tuesday," she said, trying to make sense of his being here.

"I had to make arrangements at the office yesterday. Are you going to invite me inside?"

Warily she watched him. "Why?"

"I want to talk to you."

The stubborn set to his jaw warned her what he had to say probably wasn't good.

"About what?" she asked suspiciously.

"Inside?"

"Okay." She stepped around him and unlocked her door. When she entered, she looked around at the shambles. She wished he'd seen the apartment when it had been tidy. It had been warm and welcoming and perfectly suited to her. Now it looked as if a hurricane had blown through.

She raked her fingers through her hair. She had not put on any makeup that morning, just pulled on her jeans and top and set to work. So much for appearing feminine and ladylike. She crossed into the small living room and turned to watch Jake.

He looked around the apartment and dropped his bag by the door. Shutting it, he leaned against it, his gaze moving to her.

''This is small. No wonder you thought the places in Charlotte were large.''

She shrugged. ''Real estate is at a premium in Manhattan. I was lucky to be able to afford this place without having a roommate. Did you come all this way to see my apartment?''

''No, I came to see you.''

His gray eyes gazed into hers. Even from across the width of the room, Kerry felt their impact. Swallowing hard she gestured to the sofa. ''Have a seat.'' Say what you have to say and get out. How many times could she say goodbye?

Jake lifted the stack of pictures leaning against the sofa and moved them out of the way. ''Housecleaning?''

Kerry shook her head and gingerly sat on the far edge of the sofa watching him cautiously. ''Packing up. I found a place and a job in Charlotte,'' she said.

''One we looked at?''

She shook her head.

He took a deep breath and looked around the room, then looked at her. Giving a halfhearted grin he tilted his head. ''I thought I had practiced enough I could do this easily.''

Frowning, Kerry stared at him. ''Do what?''

''Apologize first. I think I jumped to some conclusions the other night. But I've had a lot of time to think about things over the last week and I need to get everything squared away.''

He fell silent and Kerry waited. Was she supposed to say something at this point? ''Like what?'' she blurted out when she could stand the suspense no longer.

''When taking on a new client, or a new case, I make sure I know all the facts. I question, listen, analyze and get as complete a picture of the situation as I can. It never pays to jump to conclusions without knowing all the facts. But I did with you. And I think I owe it to both of us to remedy that.''

''Jake, you don't owe me anything. We had a few dates, shared some time together. You don't want to do that any more. End of discussion.''

''Maybe you're jumping to conclusions,'' he said. ''You look as if you're going to fall off the edge of the sofa.''

Moving to sit more fully on the cushions, Kerry couldn't relax—too aware of Jake's presence so close to her, of the scent of his aftershave which evoked deep memories of his kisses, the feel of his thick hair beneath her fingers, the sensations his lips brought when they brushed against hers, or nibbled against her neck, or her cheek.

He moved until his knee pushed against her leg, one hand stretching out along the back until his fingers could brush her shoulder.

Resisting the urge to jump up and put the room between them, Kerry took a deep breath. ''What conclusions am I jumping to?'' she asked, trying to concentrate on the conversation. At a total loss as to why he really had come, she wished he'd get to the point before she did something really stupid like throw herself into his arms and beg he kiss her senseless.

''That I knew what I was saying.''

''Huh?'' Startled, Kerry stared at him.

''Tell me about the diary and the list I read at your aunt's that night.''

''There's not much to tell. Sally and Aunt Peggy found the journal when they cleaned out the attic last spring. It was written by my great-grandmother Megan when she turned eighteen. There is a lot of family information, she was a wonderful writer. And her handwriting's so clear it's easy to read.'' Kerry trailed off.

''And the list?''

Taking a deep breath, she looked at her fingers, twisting them in her lap. ''Megan was interested in a particular young man she knew and her aunts and mother were giving her hints on how to conduct herself as she and this young man got to know each other better. She called it her recipe to find the perfect husband. I told Sally and she wanted to know specifics about Megan's recipe, so I copied down what I could remember.'' Daring a glance at Jake, she knew she had his full attention.

''So were you trying them out on me?''

''Sort of. But it started by accident. And if you had stopped to think about it, the list is innocuous. Really common-sense suggestions. I guess for Megan they were new and wonderful, but I'm a lot older than Megan was when she wrote that journal, and I've heard most of these suggestions before. Only I guess we forget the old ways sometimes in striving to be on the forefront of things.''

''A recipe for a husband? You're looking for a husband and thought why not give old Jake Mitchell a try?''

His voice was low, even. Was he mad?

''Not exactly. Actually you were my practice guy.''

''Practice guy?'' It was his turn to look startled. ''What do you mean?''

''Well, if the suggestions worked with a hard case like you, they'd surely work with a different man if I found someone I wanted to marry.''

''And it didn't worry you to toy with a man's affections?''

She laughed. ''Jake—you've never let anyone toy with you since you were a kid. And as cynical as you are about relationships and women, I knew there was no worry about hurting you.'' Only herself when she was foolish enough to fall in love again.

''There you go jumping to conclusions again. You'd never make a good litigation attorney.''

''Well, darn.''

His hand slid down her arm and captured hers. Threading his fingers through hers, he rested their linked hands on his thigh. Kerry's heart rate exploded, raced. What was Jake doing?

''I'm glad you got a job in Charlotte,'' he said slowly, his thumb tracing random patterns on the back of her hand.

''You are? Why?''

''Makes it easier.''

''Makes what easier?''

''Courting.''

''Courting?'' Had she heard him correctly? Jake talking about courting? Her?

''As you said, we are always in such a rush we seem to forget the old-fashioned way of doing things. Maybe that's what we need here.''

''What we need here is some clarification of what you're talking about.'' And quickly, before she lost all sense of reason. His thumb was driving her crazy, her heart was about to pound out of her chest and the impulse to scoot over and lean against the man was so strong she marveled she could resist.

''For a week I had to watch you go out with every guy in West Bend.''

''Carl and Peter hardly comprise every guy in West Bend.''

''Doesn't matter, seemed like it at the time.''

''Oh?'' That raised interesting thoughts. Had Jake been jealous?

"And while waiting for you to come home each night, I had plenty of time to think. To think and consider the interesting ideas you raised. Maybe there was more to my family breakup than I knew. Maybe my father played as big a part in it as my mother. And then I discovered it no longer mattered. I'm not my father and you are certainly not my mother."

Kerry blinked. She was getting confused again. What did his parents have to do with courting? "Can you get to the courting part again?" she asked, her skin tingling from his touch, her internal temperature rising.

Jake smiled and raised their linked hands, kissing the back of hers. "I want to court you, Kerry." He turned her hand over and kissed the pulse in her wrist. "I want to marry you, Kerry." Releasing her hand, he placed a warm kiss in the palm. "I want you to live with me forever and never leave." Quizzically he looked at her.

The smile was tentative, and melted her heart. His eyes were warm with love yet hesitant as if he was still unsure. How could the man ever doubt it for an instant?

Tears gathered and slipped over her cheeks.

"Don't cry," he exclaimed, drawing her into his arms and hugging her tightly. "Don't cry, sweetheart. If you don't want to marry me, that's okay. No, it's not, but I'll learn to live with it. Kerry, don't be unhappy."

"Silly," she said against his neck, her arms creeping up to encircle him, hold him tightly against her as she closed her eyes and let the emotions flood through her. "I love you, Jake. I've loved you since I was fifteen years old. Through all the years, I've never stopped. I thought I could go on, but this summer sure made me question that. I love you so much!"

"Thank God. I love you, Kerry. I can't say I've loved you since you were fifteen, but it's been a long time.

Only I was too caught up in the idea all women were like my mother I couldn't bear to take the chance."

"And now you don't feel like that?"

"Not like I used to. What I feel for you is so strong, I'm willing to take a chance. It's better than living alone and imagining you with someone else, making love, having babies, and sharing your life. I want that all for myself. And if you think you've loved me all this time, I doubt you will up and leave any day."

"I'm never leaving!" she vowed, leaning back to gaze into his eyes. But only for a second before his mouth came down on hers with a searing kiss that immediately caused every other kiss to fade in comparison. This was Jake, the man she loved, the man who loved her! Kerry's heart was full to overflowing. Together they'd put down roots so deep nothing could ever tear them out. And with their love, they would find the happiness and delight in sharing their lives that others in her family had.

When the kiss ended, he looked into her eyes. "So how long do I have to court you before I can ask you to be my wife?"

"I don't mind a really short courtship," she said softly.

"How short?"

"If we count all the time we've already spent together, I'd say we've done it," she said daringly. Treasuring the look of love and devotion in his eyes, she wished she could capture the moment forever. But Kerry knew she'd never forget a single second of this day.

"I love you, Kerry Elizabeth Kincaid. Will you marry me?"

"I would be so honored to accept, John Charles Mitchell. Thank you for asking me!"

"Ever the proper old-fashioned girl," he said as he kissed her again.

* * *

They put through a call to Greece, sharing their happy news with Kerry's parents. Two brief calls—first to Florida and then to California informed Jake's father and brother. Kerry called Sally next, excited to share her happiness.

"Wow, I thought one of the tenets from Great-grandma Megan was a leopard couldn't change his spots—what changed Jake?" Sally asked after extending her best wishes to her cousin.

"Love, I guess," Kerry answered, glowing with that emotion herself.

"Well your timing is great, I have just the wedding present for you."

"What's that?"

"Mom called yesterday and I asked her about the journal and Great-grandma Megan. She told me Megan and Frederick had fifty-two happy years together before he died. And where to find a copy of their photograph from their fiftieth anniversary party. I'll have it enlarged and give to you so you and Jake will have something to live up to."

"It's nice to know how that story turned out. And to know mine will be the same."

"Sure, cousin?"

"As sure as love," Kerry said, reaching out to touch the man who would share her life. Maybe she should start her own journal. She could open with...*and the greatest of these is love.*

0905/01a

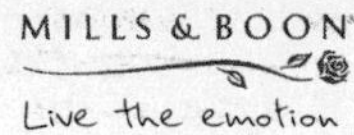

Modern romance™

THE BRAZILIAN'S BLACKMAILED BRIDE
by Michelle Reid

Anton Luis Scott-Lee is going to marry Cristina Marques. She rejected him years ago and his payback will be sweet: she will be at Luis's bidding – bought and paid for! But Luis will find that his bride can't or *won't* fulfil all of her wedding vows…

EXPECTING THE PLAYBOY'S HEIR *by Penny Jordan*

American billionaire Silas Carter has no plans for love – he wants a practical marriage. So he only proposes to beautiful Julia Fellowes as a ruse to get rid of her lecherous boss and to indulge in a hot affair – or that's what he lets her think!

THE TYCOON'S TROPHY WIFE *by Miranda Lee*

Reece knew Alanna would make the perfect trophy wife! Stunning and sophisticated, she wanted a marriage of convenience. But suddenly their life together was turned upside down when Reece discovered that his wife had a dark past…

WEDDING VOW OF REVENGE *by Lucy Monroe*

The instant Angelo Gordon sees model Tara Peters he wants her. But her innocent beauty isn't all he wants – he's out for revenge! Tara is not an easy conquest, and when she rejects him Angelo realises he must up the stakes and take the ultimate revenge – marriage!

Don't miss out!

On sale 7th October 2005

Available at most branches of WHSmith, Tesco, ASDA, Borders, Eason, Sainsbury's and most bookshops

Visit www.millsandboon.co.uk

On sale 2nd September 2005

Available at most branches of WHSmith, Tesco, ASDA, Martins, Borders, Eason, Sainsbury's and all good paperback bookshops.